The Doo Namdaron, Part Four.

Michael Porter

Copyright @ 2018 Michael Porter
All rights reserved.
ISBN: 9781790333905
ISBN-13: 9781790333905

DEDICATION

For all my children and grandchildren
Without whom some of my characters would be nameless.
I hope that you all enjoy the characters I have given you,
Though they in no way reflect who you are, or what you mean to me.
Even friends pop up here and there.

"No matter how evil may assail you.
Remember, there is still love in this world."

CHAPTER THIRTY EIGHT

"Gorgana or Gregor, whatever your name, why should you live?" demanded Namdarin, his voice low and hoarse.

"Gregor, please you have no idea how important it is that I am Gregor, I should live because I can help you in ways you cannot understand yet, nor probably believe. Please allow me to explain."

Namdarin moved the sword from the man's throat, but did not scabbard it, it stayed in his hand, the grip steady, not too tight but certainly prepared, Gregor was allowed to sit upon the grass, in such a place that a simple backhanded slash from the sword would take his head.

"Speak." muttered Namdarin.

"Thank you." nodded Gregor. "I think that I am now one of the rarest things on the planet, I am an ex-zandaar, hen's teeth are under every rock, four leaved clover behind every tree, but an ex-zandaar, now that is rare. I really have to make this quick because I don't have a lot of time, I joined the Zandaars because I wanted to learn their magic and there is no other way to do it, I was a priest, but only for the libraries, the books I craved, some of which I have brought with me." He opened his robe, slowly and showed the books that were stuffed into his underclothes and tied to the inside of his outer robe. "Recently I have come to see that my life is threatened by my very studies, there are those in the priesthood that would declare me heretic already, and there is only one penalty for heresy. This is not relevant. I know how they attack, I know how they work, I know how to defend against them, I know how to help you, but I am running out of time. I have taken a chance, thrown the dice of destiny, I need your help to stay alive. Will you help me?"

"No." said Namdarin.

"Hold." snapped Granger.

"Why did you have this sudden change of heart?" asked Granger.

"It was something simple, an accumulation of things, in Worandana's group was the best example of the hard line extreme Zandaar, he had no tolerance for anything other than the doctrine of the council of Zandaar, what they said was law, no matter what people thought or felt, the law is graved in stone and cannot be questioned. His name is Kirukana, he is a relatively new member of the group, he would almost certainly have laid charges of heresy against most of us by the time we got back to Zandaarkoon, these days charges are all it takes, to ruin a career, or pass a death sentence. The biggest problem is that more and more think like him, to get anywhere in the priesthood, even to stay alive you have to think like them, he is a deeply stupid person, but will go far. I went against his views more and more with each passing day, until I was shown another way, by two women, of all things. Women are forbidden to the priests of Zandaar. But in the last two days I have known two wonderful examples of womanhood, one showed me wonders with her body, and the other showed me wonders with her mind and her love. This is one of the things that has turned me against Zandaar, the god himself teaches nothing different between men and women, and that there is nothing evil about the relationships between the two, however the council sees things differently, now women are a second class of people, property to be owned and controlled, almost evil in their very existence. How can the people survive if half the population is evil?"

"It is not the people who are evil," said Namdarin. "It is their god."

"But it is the council that is making the edicts, not Zandaar."

"Zandaar is evil, he lives off people's lives, he eats life, you may not see it, you may not know it, but I have seen it."

"How have you seen it?"

"I travelled to Zandaarkoon in a dream and saw the people being drained of life, to feed their god."

"But that was only a dream, how can it be true?"

"A simple question for you, how long do people live in Zandaarkoon?"

"I don't know, until they die I suppose."

"But how long, in the country a hard working farming man, with a family to support, out in the fields every day from dawn until dusk can expect to live fifty to fifty-five years depending on sudden illness and accidents. In the cities, a merchant, fifty-five to sixty years, and less risk of accident, though more risk of illness or murder. How long do people live in Zandaarkoon?"

"I haven't actually looked at the figures but I don't think many live to be more the fifty-five."

"Simpler question, how old are the members of the council?"

"There is not one over fifty."

"How old do they look?"

"Old, like nearly dead sort of old."

"And these people are less than fifty years of age, living in a city, doing hard physical labour, wearing out knees and hips and backs with the loads they are carrying every day?

"Council members wouldn't know a day's work if it bit them on their arses."

"But still they age. I have seen what happens, the bells ring and all the people in the city start walking towards the central temple, Zandaar awaits them there, he takes their life from them, he feeds on them, so the ones that live closest to the temple will be drained more often, and those that live on the outskirts will be least effected. The council will be in the building when the bell rings and first to be drained. This I have seen."

"I have never looked at it in exactly this light before, but from what I have seen you may be right, but that doesn't really help me now does it? I still have to convince you that I should live, and then that you should help me. To be realistic I don't actually have anything to add, I can help you and will, the thought of Zandaar eating the people's lives is horrific, and though I haven't actually seen it, the evidence is there."

"I don't think you could ever see it, the people of Zandaar react to the bells, and don't remember anything afterwards. You are more closely controlled than any other people." said Granger.

"And that is why we cannot trust you." said Namdarin. "And why you must die."

"But I can break their control. I know I can. With some help."

"How can you break their control?"

"That is both easy and hard, they control a person they know as Gorgana, I intend to return to my original persona, I will be Gregor again. This man they cannot control and they cannot reach. Know this, they will know by now that I have changed sides, and they will consider me to be a heretic, they must try to kill me, there are many of them but they are tired, in a few hours, probably around dawn they will make an attempt to reach Gorgana and kill him. I must become Gregor again before they make that attempt or I will die."

"There is another matter to be considered." said Jangor. "What of Crathen?"

Namdarin's arm tensed on the sword, the tip twitched a little closer to Gorgana's neck.

"Now there is another thing." sighed Gorgana. "You will probably not believe this, but I have done you a service by removing him from this place, he is now where he can do you no real harm."

"How can that be?" said Jangor. "He was one of us, he meant us no harm."

"But," whispered Gorgana, "it was only a matter of time before he would have betrayed you all."

"Easy to attack someone who can't defend himself." snapped Jangor.

"This I know only too well." said Gorgana. "He was infatuated with the woman, this love was going to be used against you, he was going to be attacked mentally and turned into an ally in your own camp. A better chance came up, and another plan was attempted, so I decided rather than risk him still being here, I switched with him, taking him out of harm's way."

"I don't believe that for a single instant." snapped Jangor.

"I do." said Granger, softly.

"Explain." demanded Jangor.

"Fine. Namdarin please relax a little, if you twitch he will die." Namdarin nodded and moved the sword a little further away from the monk's throat. "Only last night whilst I was on watch Crathen had a long talk with me about how Jayanne loved him, and was only with Namdarin out a feeling of duty towards her village and the man who had saved her life. He was perhaps going to say something to her today, but never got the chance."

"You jest." said Jayanne.

"No. He was absolutely certain from the way you looked at him, and the way you avoided him, that you loved him."

"I barely noticed him, most of the time." she laughed. "He is deluded, and now I don't have the chance to tell him."

"Somehow I don't think that he would have believed you even if you told him. He is thoroughly convinced."

"How would you have turned him against us?" demanded Jangor.

"Simple." replied Gorgana. "We would have worked on his delusions, promised him the things he so clearly desired, and he would have worked for us, he would have told us of every move and plan before they were even decided. He would have slowed you down at every opportunity, we would have caught up in a matter of days. But all that cannot happen now, now all he can do is give Kevana information that is old, and clouded by his own delusions."

"So." said Jangor. "You say you have already done us a great favour, and now you want to do us more, by joining us. Is that correct?"

"Yes, effectively that is the truth, hard though it is to believe. My time is limited."

"Kern." said Jangor, pushing Namdarin out of the way and hauling Gorgana to his feet. "Take this man for a walk, if he runs kill him, we have things to talk about." Kern drew his sword and pushed Gorgana away from the camp, Namdarin was on the verge of following when Jangor took hold of his arm and guided him to a seat near the fire. Granger and Jayanne gathered around.

"What we need to decide right here and now is if we can trust this man in any way?" stated Jangor.

"No." said Namdarin.

"Perhaps we can." said Jayanne.

"Maybe." said Granger.

"That Is three to one against Namdarin. Granger your thoughts?"

"He has taken a great risk, thrown himself on our mercy, maybe he deserves a chance to change."

"Jayanne."

"He says that they were going to turn Crathen against us, and as far as I am concerned it wouldn't have taken much because he is already half way to their side, this goes in his favour." she replied.

"Namdarin?"

"He is Zandaar, and needs to die."

"I think that he seems to have changed sides but this could also be a plan of theirs to place a man inside our camp. Even if he is right and they would have had Crathen working for them. If we can turn him to our side then he could definitely be an asset, he knows their ways and their skills. If his friends try to kill him then that is a sure sign that he has turned, or is it? Perhaps even that could be an elaborate ruse to get us to accept him. This thinking makes my head hurt. I feel that he is genuine, he wants to get away from the Zandaars, he deserves a chance. Namdarin yours is the only dissenting voice, this man could be of great assistance to us, I know that you see only a black robe that must be killed, but inside that robe may be a man who wishes to change. What say you?"

"How can we ever be sure of him? The only time we can be sure is when his friends actually kill him, otherwise this is all a trick to get him in close." said Namdarin.

"If we kill him we may be throwing away a valuable resource."

"Or removing a terrible risk."

"We need to be sure before we make a decision that cannot be reversed."

"True."

"What can he really do for us?" asked Granger.

"He says he can teach us, and he adds numbers to our magical defences, I have no idea how strong his sword arm is, but sometimes numbers are all that counts." Jangor's reply was almost hesitant.

"He is still a Zandaar." muttered Namdarin.

"He deserves the chance to change. A convert is worth much more to us than another corpse."

"We have only his word for all of this." snapped Namdarin.

"I believe what he says about Crathen." said Granger. "The man was already deluded, and would never be persuaded otherwise. It wouldn't have taken me long to convince him that the only way to free Jayanne would be to slit your throat while you slept. I could have convinced him of that in a very short time, perhaps a day or two, with nothing more than the words he wanted to hear."

"I still don't believe we can ever trust him." growled Namdarin.

"Perhaps there is a way." Muttered Granger.

"What way?" Demanded Jangor.

"Perhaps the gods can make the choice."

"Nonsense." Said Namdarin.

"We can but try. Will you let me try?" Asked Granger, softly.

"How?"

"Do you trust that sword of yours?"

"Not entirely, somehow it does things I don't want it to, but so far it has always done what is best, though it does seem to have a thirst for lives, not so much as Jayanne's axe, but it certainly likes to kill."

"It feeds on the life of those it kills."

"Agreed." Nodded Namdarin.

"Fine. We get Gregor to swear an oath on the sword of Xeron, then see if the sword will kill him. If the sword won't kill him then we can trust him as much as we trust that sword, if it kills him then we can trust him all the way."

Namdarin liked this idea so much that a huge smile made his whole face light up with glee. "Great." He said. "Let's do it."

"Hang on." Said Jangor. "You are taking one hell of a chance on a man's life."

"I know." Said Granger. Namdarin laughed gently. "But look at the way his luck has been running today." Continued the old wizard. "If he fell in a barrel of shit he'd come out smelling of roses." Jangor smiled and nodded, then threw his head back and let forth a piercing whistle. Very soon Kern returned to the camp, with Gregor by his side.

"Any problems?" Asked Jangor.

"No. He talks too much. He asks too many questions. He's frightened."

"To be expected." Replied Jangor, then he turned to Granger. "You tell him."

"Tell him what?" Asked Gregor, more than a little shakily.

"We have a plan that could prove your worth to us."

"What plan?" Gregor's voice rose a pitch or two.

"Simple really."

"Just tell me." Snapped Gregor.

"You swear an oath to the god who's sword Namdarin is carrying."

"But that sword belongs to Zandaar."

"No, Zandaar wants it, but it belongs to Xeron. You swear to Xeron by the sword of Xeron, to serve Namdarin in his quest." Granger looked at Namdarin, who nodded.

"You would accept my word?" Asked Gregor.

"Of course, this is an oath that you will not be able to break."

"Shall we get on with this then." Said Gregor.

"Gregor." Said Granger. "Take the tip of the sword between the palms of your hands, be careful of the edges, it is very sharp, place the point of the sword over your heart. Then speak your oath, and make it a good one, as a god will be judging you."

"Give me the sword." Said Gregor. Namdarin raised the tip of the sword towards Gregor's chest, the monk took the sword between the palms of his hands, and moved it towards the centre of his chest.

"Gods." He exclaimed. "It's so cold." But he made no move to release it.

"Hold." Said Granger. Gregor looked at the old man, his eyes asking questions but his voice said nothing. Granger brought his staff down until it was just above Gregor's hands, he muttered something unintelligible and a soft yellow light bathed the tightly pressed hands. The light turned green on the man's hand, but blue on the sword.

"Better make this quick." Said Granger. "Before the sword drains his life away completely." Gregor's eyes opened really wide, then he looked round suddenly when Kern's heavy hands gently grasped his shoulders, it was obvious there was no way out. Gregor shivered briefly.

"I, Gregor, swear that I will do everything in my power to aid Namdarin in his quest, I swear by the sword of Xeron to the god Xeron that this oath will not be broken until the end of days." He head fell forwards and there was a moment of silence. "The sword is not cold anymore." He whispered, looking at Granger. Granger brought his staff over Gregor's hands and the yellow light appeared again, this time both the hands and the sword turned the light a soft green. Granger looked Gregor in the eyes and said "Don't move." Then he turned to Namdarin. "Time to test his oath." Namdarin smiled, Gregor felt Kern's hands stiffen on his shoulders, a moment of panic filled his mind, he felt the sword twitch, and saw Namdarin's shoulder muscles bunch as they tensed to drive the sword forwards, but the sword never moved. Namdarin threw his whole body behind the sword, but it wouldn't slide between Gregor's palms. Namdarin pulled the sword back in disgust, staring at it as if it were a traitor.

"How can this be?" He yelled holding the sword high above his head, as if to strike the monk down with a huge blow.

"It appears." Said Granger. "That both the sword and Xeron were pleased with Gregor's oath. Though I believe he may have gone a little further than he intended."

"What do you mean?" Demanded both Gregor and Namdarin simultaneously, each snapped a glance at the other before turning back to Granger, who looked at Gregor before speaking.

"Until the end of days, is what he said, not 'my days'." Granger turned to Namdarin. "Until the end of days. Does that remind you of something someone else swore?"

"The ends of eternity, I believe that is what I swore." Whispered Namdarin.

"Well." Said Granger, louder than was really necessary. "If this fight lasts that long it looks like there are going to be two of you standing side by side, or perhaps back to back." He laughed loudly as both sank slowly to the ground, the enormity of their oaths appeared to each to be doubled not shared. Granger turned to Jangor. "I think we are going to need a really big fire. These two need a little time to get their wits together, but we are going to need some rapid energy very soon." With only a few hand signals Jangor dispatched Mander, Andel and Stergin, to collect as much fire wood as they could find. Brank moved slowly to stand beside Kern.

"Are things always so exciting with this bunch?" He whispered.

"Sometimes we can go a whole day without something strange happening, no, that's not true, it's never a whole day." Laughed Kern.

"I think I am going to like it travelling with you." He paused briefly. "What's going to happen next?"

"Who knows? Today has been crazy enough, but it looks like the night is going to be even more so." At this point Jangor spoke up.

"Namdarin. We are going to need the horses, and soon." Namdarin nodded slowly, and climbed tiredly to his feet, he whistled for Arndrol, but the sound seemed to lack some of its usual penetration. Jangor merely looked at Namdarin, the look that said 'What was that?' Namdarin sucked in a huge breath and blew another note.

"That's better." Said Jangor. "You two." He said looking at Kern and Brank. "I want this camp packed and ready to ride, as soon as the horses get back. Once the magician has done what he needs, we are riding. Gregor." The monk looked up. "A moving target will be more difficult for them to reach, won't it?" The direct question seemed to shake Gregor from his lethargy, he climb stiffly to his feet.

"Definitely, I was the most skilled searcher they had, and it has always been hard to find something at extreme range if it is moving. You can't hide the sword from them anyway, even Kevana has found that a few times now. I am not sure about the staff though." He reached down to where the staff was still resting, untouched since he dropped it. Without thinking Namdarin moved rapidly, the sword swinging into place between Gregor and his staff, Granger's staff snapped round to point at the monk, a cracking charge building up inside it.

"Hold." Yelled Jangor. "I thought we had decided we were going to trust this man, well?"

"Sorry." Said Granger, immediately quenching the fire in his staff. Namdarin was slower to move back, but he did, though without any apology. Gregor nodded and reached for the staff again, tentatively he placed the flat of his hand against it, as if he was expecting it to hurt him in some way. When it didn't he picked it up in both hands and grounded one metal shod end, and leant against it, in much the same way that Granger habitually did.

"May I?" Asked Granger reaching for Gregor's staff.

The younger man tossed the staff across to Granger, who caught it quite easily in one hand. He inspected it quite closely before throwing it back.

"It is still carrying quite a charge." Said Granger.

"How can you tell?" Asked Gregor.

"I can feel it. Can't you?"

"I don't know, there might be something in there, but I don't really know what I am looking for."

"How did you use the staff to change places with Crathen?"

"I used it to direct power from the stone in the village, it was merely a conduit."

"So you don't actually store energy inside anything?"

"No, is such a thing possible, sorry, stupid question. How is it done?"

"It requires very little training, it is just the sort of thing that you should be good at, after all you use those special silver flames and lightning bolts as weapons?"

"How are they the same? The power is in the shape, it doesn't come from outside the pieces of silver."

"Who makes them?"

"There are specially trained monks that form the weapons."

"Describe the process for me."

"I have never seen it done, but I believe the liquid metal is poured into hard steel moulds and some words are spoken, there is chanting and incense I think."

"What happens to the metal?"

"It sets instantly and the mould becomes so cold that the silver almost rattles inside the steel. The mould is opened and the flame, or bolt, is removed. The mould has to be warmed before silver will flow properly through it again."

"You never even thought about this before, have you?"

"Not really, it just works, that is all that matters."

"Think now." Said Granger. Gregor reached into his robe and pulled out a small silver flame, he held it gently in his hand, staring intently at it. Then he looked up.

"It is still cold to the touch. There is a warning, one that is whispered when no high ranking priests are around, 'Watch out for the old ones, they hit harder than you would expect.' When this flame was formed, the liquid metal froze in an instant, and the mould likewise. Where did that heat go? It went inside, that is a lot of heat, and this small piece of metal is always cold, it is always pulling heat into itself, when it is used the heat inside is released, and strikes the target whatever it is."

"That is only partly true, much of the energy comes from the user, but some portion is from inside the weapon. You have never looked at it this way before. How did you make the link between the stone and the staff?"

"A woman of the village showed me, it took the power of blood to unlock the stone, but once the channel was open the power available was absolutely immense. I couldn't have used it all in years."

"You used your own blood?"

"Yes, but the cuts were shallow and healed by the power of the stone."

"How primitive. Can you remember the feeling as the channel opened?"

"I think so, I was sort of distracted by the blood and the pain."

"Well that is the feeling you have to make with your mind, a link between the staff and any source of power, say a nice roaring fire." Saying this he turned and placed one end of his staff in the fire, Gregor watched, amazed that the wooden staff didn't catch fire. Not only that, the fire itself changed, shifting colours down to the red, away from the hot yellow.

"How do you do that?" He asked.

"Place your hand on the staff, and feel the power flowing." Said Granger. Gregor did as he was asked, trying to feel the power was hard, but each time he felt it, it seemed to wriggle out of his grasp. After several such attempts he snatched his hand away in disgust.

"I just can't get it, it moves away every time I think I have it."

"This is the simplest of the magics we use."

"I'm just not thinking the right way."

"There may be something we can do about that." Said Granger. "Namdarin have you got the stones in your pack?" Namdarin nodded and collected the two biggest of the flashing stones.

"What are those?" Asked Gregor.

"Just some rocks from my old cave." Said Granger. "But they do have some strange properties, it is possible to communicate directly between minds."

"I never heard of anything like that. Though mind to mind contact over great distances is something that Zandaars use regularly, though that takes a great deal of training and some accurate knowledge of the person you wish to communicate with."

"These require no training only proximity and the wish to communicate. Are you willing to try?"

"Something new, of course I am."

"You are aware that this may send things you don't want me to know." Warned Granger. Gregor looked round at the expectant faces.

"You are saying that this may let out all my secrets, how can I refuse, this could be another test, if I take the test, and give you things you don't want to know, then you'll never trust me, if I don't take the test you never trust me. How does this thing work?"

"We don't exactly know, it can be a little like communicating without words, Namdarin used a sequence of pictures to talk to a being that didn't use language, or at least not one we understood as such. We have used it to talk to one another with out making sounds, I need to show you the feeling of opening the channel so the power can flow in a way that you need it to, so this will have to go a little deeper than words."

"Great, so what do I do?"

"As magicians you must use some techniques to focus your minds?"

"Of course."

"Fine, perform whatever rituals you use, focus your mind internally, and clear it as far as you can of extraneous thought, then place the crystal against your forehead, I shall do the same, and I will try to contact your mind directly. Understood?"

"No problem." Gregor sat cross legged with his staff across his lap, and reached out for a crystal. Granger handed him one crystal and kept the other for himself. Gregor held the crystal gingerly, as if he was afraid of it, he turned it over and over in his hand watching the colours flowing through it. "It's very pretty, and the colours seem to be perfectly matched in both crystals."

"They were originally one." Said Granger.

"I can see the place they were separated." Gregor ran his thumb along the sharp edge where the two had been joined. "Let us get on with this." He closed his eyes, and breathed slowly, first in then out, then even slower in and out, one hand rose slowly and placed the crystal against his forehead. Granger sat in front of him and went through a similar process, though he did take a few more breaths to reach the level of concentration that he required. Granger focused through the flashing rock, and reached for another conscious mind, he was completely surprised by the ease with which the contact was established, in an instant it felt like the two minds actually inhabited one brain, both men had to work hard to maintain their separate identities. Each pushed the other away and tried to create a wall to distance themselves.

'This is wonderful.' Thought Gregor, trying to think quietly, hoping the Granger would do the same.

'I have only done this the once but that was much harder, this is just too easy.'

'A certain amount of control is definitely required.' replied Gregor. 'What do I need to know right now, anything else we can try later?'

'You need to know how to charge your staff. It is quite easy, take hold of your staff, and make the connection between yourself and the staff.' Granger showed Gregor how this was achieved by putting the sensations and thoughts straight into the monks mind.

'OW.' thought Gregor. Causing Granger to shrink away in pain. 'Gently, try not to think too loud, it hurts.'

'Sorry.' replied Granger much quieter. 'Now. Once you have established your link to the staff, then you use the same sort of link to attach the staff to an energy source, I like fire, or at my cave the hot mud. By taking energy from the fire the staff puts energy into itself.'

'How much concentration does it take to maintain the link?'

'Once the link is properly made, it should look after itself.'

'How much energy can a staff hold?'

'Mine, with many years of practice, can carry quite a charge, yours, which has been redesigned to take an enormous transitory load, can probably carry more. Namdarin's sword and Jayanne's axe, they are weapons of the gods, I can't even imagine what they could carry, nor want to be there when they let it go.'

'Show me how to do it.' thought Gregor.

'Follow me while I start to charge my staff from the fire.' replied Granger. Slowly and carefully, so the younger man could feel the whole process, Granger opened the link between his own mind and his staff. Gregor felt the power in the staff and was surprised just how much was actually there. Once Granger was happy with his link to the staff, he extended the link to include the roaring fire, and let the heat flow into the staff. After a few moments he opened the channel wider so the energy could flow more quickly, happier with the conversion of heat to power in the staff, he gently broke the link between himself and the staff, and then the link between the two minds.

"Do you understand now?" asked Granger. Gregor looked slowly from man to staff to fire and back again, as if mulling the whole process over in his mind.

"I think so." he replied more than a little tentatively.

"Can you link with me and guide me?" asked Gregor.

Granger made no vocal reply but held the flashing crystal against his head, and waited for Gregor to make the link. Gregor tuned his mind to Granger's with the most delicate of touches, for some time Granger wasn't actually aware that the connection had been made.

'How do you do that?' thought Granger.

'Do what?'

'Make the link so gently that I didn't know it was even there. The problem is normally that the stones make the link so fast that it actually hurts.'

'You said to think quietly, so that is what I did.'

'I didn't even feel the connection until you sent an image of a woman.'

'Woman?'

'Yes. She was, or is, I get no real impression of which, impossibly tall, and beautiful in a strangely androgynous way, strange because her shape is exceptionally feminine.'

'That could be my mother, I haven't thought of her for many years, not since I joined the priesthood, I would be about fifteen when I last saw her.'

'That would be her. Now let us get on with the lesson.'

'Right.' thought Gregor, then followed the method that Granger had shown him, he made the link between his mind and his staff, it felt very different from when Granger did it, because Gregor's staff carried considerably less power. Gently he reached out to the fire, and made the second connection, making that connection stronger and stronger until he could actually feel the power flowing. Then he broke the connection between his mind and the staff.

'Is that right?' he thought.

'Should be, try opening up the channel, and increasing the flow, that way your staff will charge faster.'

Gregor nodded and linked to his staff again, this time he focused on the link to the fire, he made the pathway wider, brighter, hotter. Then broke the link again.

Granger pulled the crystal away from his head and severed the link between the two men.

"That looks fine." he said.

"How can you tell?" asked Gregor.

"Just look at the fire."

Gregor turned to the fire, and there was something strange about it, for some reason it seemed to burn a little dull, the colours of the flames were somehow subdued, and the sound was less than it should have been. "It looks cold somehow." he said.

"It is." laughed Granger, "But I wouldn't try putting my hand in it, it's not that cold. Between the two staffs we are probably taking a fifth of the available energy. Watch what happens now. Namdarin, Jayanne, start charging your weapons." Namdarin laid his sword with it's tip in the flames and stepped back, Jayanne put her axe near the fire. After a few moments of concentration they each nodded to Granger.

"That's strange." said Gregor. "The fire has become even colder, it looks like the flames are even burning slowly, you know? They are more red than normal and somehow they look just slow. Weird."

"That is true." said Granger. "If we were to increase the rate at which the weapons are charging then it is possible to take so much energy from the fire that it will actually go out."

Gregor thought for a moment before speaking slowly. "This could save many lives."

"How?" asked Granger.

"If you can stop a fire by taking the energy from it, then no one need to die in a fire ever again. We just kill the fire."

"And what are you going to do with all that energy? I mean this little fire will give us more than enough to fill my staff in a couple of hours, and we could still cook on the thing."

"My staff has been designed to handle a massive transfer of power, so this is the perfect tool for putting out fires, just channel the energy elsewhere."

"And start a fire somewhere new?"

"There must be some way to dispose of the power safely, perhaps dump it into a lake or river?"

"That would heat up the water, and probably kill off the fish or other life in the lake or river. Have you any concept of just how much power you are talking about?"

"None, but I am willing to learn."

"That at least is true. Let's hope that the lessons don't actually kill you."

"Anyway." said Gregor. "We are straying from the most pressing purpose, that of keeping me alive."

"Are you absolutely certain that is necessary?" muttered Namdarin.

"And exactly how do we do that?" Asked Granger.

"I don't really know."

"Well, how does the location spell work, what does it key to?"

"It sort of picks up the personality image of the person you want to communicate with, though if you want to talk to someone you don't know, then one sort of shouts out their name, and hopes that they hear it, a very unreliable process."

"But they know you very well."

"That is the problem. Even a shout will reach me, I will not be able to ignore them for very long."

"But you have a new name now."

"But I still remember the old one."

"Perhaps we can do something about that."

"What?"

"You need someone to help you, someone from your past that none of them know."

"Who and how?"

"How about your mother? That was a very strong image I got, perhaps you could use the memories of her and your life before the priesthood to block your colleagues from reaching you?"

"That might just work, they never knew her, and I don't think anyone has even heard her name mentioned."

"What about written records?"

"There may be some mention of her in the files at the master church, but it would be very difficult for people to access these from out here."

"Then perhaps you can use her to make a barrier they cannot even feel?"

"What do you mean?"

"If you create an aura around yourself that is more your mother than you then they will not even feel it, they are looking for you, so any search will simply pass by."

"Sounds like a good idea, how do we do that?"

"There's the rub, I have no idea."

"Then we still have no plan." snapped Gregor.

"You must have had a plan before you left?"

"Yes I did, but looking at it now it is more than a little weak, I was going to think of myself as Gregor, and try to get inside the persona, or perhaps build myself a new personality."

"A large part of the Gregor persona comes from your parents, perhaps we can reinforce your protection by using both parents?"

"I never knew my father, I think he was a member of the priesthood but I have no tangible evidence of him at all."

"Why do you think he was a priest?"

"Because mother seemed to think that the priesthood was the only career open to me, from my earliest memories that is all she had planned for me, of course as a teenager I rebelled and wanted to be a carpenter, but soon realised just how boring that would be and eventually joined up, as expected. Though the actually joining process seems, looking back, to have been far too easy. Some people had many tests and selection processes to go through, but I didn't, I simply turn up at a seminary and declared my intention to join and I was accepted, like they were waiting for me."

"Then we certainly can't use him as a defence. I suppose we better get started, Jangor wants to be moving as soon as possible."

"Well." said Jangor. "We are going nowhere until the horses get back. Namdarin find them please." Namdarin nodded, then his face attained the far away look. Which was rapidly replaced by a look of confusion.

"I can't feel them." He said, then he reached for his sword, and holding the hilt firmly in both hands he reached out for the herd mind again. After a moment or two he spoke. "They are a long way off, but they are coming, Arndrol is keeping them together, they were greatly afraid of Gregor's magic, and the wolf seems to be escorting them, which they don't like, I have told him to bring them as fast as they can. They will be here presently."

"How can he know that, and what did he do with the sword?" muttered Gregor.

"He can feel the herd mind of the horses, and he used the power stored in the sword to help increase his range." said Granger.

"You can do that?"

"Easy, I am utterly surprised that you don't"

"Storing power is not actually forbidden, but there are no hints that it is even possible, let alone achievable by men."

"We cannot afford too many more delays, we must be ready to move as soon as the horses get here, so let's get to this." said Jangor.

"Well." said Gregor. "What I would normally do at this point is get a circle of people to build up a powerful charge, so that I can use it in a single pulse to create the desired effect. However, I think that what I need is for the three of you to feed me some of the power in your weapons, so that I can reinforce the Gregor personality, and shield it with the images of my mother."

"Perhaps." said Namdarin, "But I think only two of us can give power in that fashion, Jayanne's axe does have a tendency to absorb rather than release."

Granger nodded, saying. "That is true, Jayanne carries it, but even she is unsure as to who actually controls it. Just the two of us it is."

"And." said Gregor. "It is far better not to deplete all the weapons of power that you are carrying."

"You think this a ruse, just to improve our odds should you turn against us?" snapped Jangor.

"It is the sort of thing that Worandana would do." said Gregor.

"Perhaps." said Jangor.

"How do we do this?" asked Namdarin.

"I suggest we feed power to the staff, then Gregor can control the way he uses it, he is used to that."

"I wouldn't say used to it, I've only done it once." whispered Gregor.

"Direct contact will give us the best control." said Granger, "Hold your staff in front of you and we will feed it." Gregor followed the instructions slowly, he braced his staff and spread his hands wide, Namdarin held the sword against it at one end, and Granger placed his own staff on it at the other.

"Are you ready?" asked Granger.

"I suppose so, not too much too fast please." said Gregor. Granger merely nodded to Namdarin, and the pair started the energy transfer, Gregor suddenly tensed as the power coursed through his body, he focussed it inwards, taking it into his mind and building intense images of his mother, he surrounded his very ego with these images, building a wall around his mind, something that could hold out the attacks of the Zandaars, filling his heart and mind with the love that he remembered from his childhood, the cool touch on a fevered brow, the gentle word that made everything seem to be all right. Each memory brought another, in a cascade that filled him to the very limit with all that was good about his mother, someone that he knew would give her life for him. The deeper the memories piled up around him, the stronger the wall became, and the more it began to hurt him, the pain of separation grew gradually stronger and stronger, this became the limiting factor for him, he could stand no more memories, they became too painful to add to. Suddenly he spun his staff away from the staff and the sword, breaking the link that was feeding him the power of all three. The sudden break made all three men stagger, each took a single shaky step backwards. Gregor slumped down upon one knee.

"Hells." he muttered. Then he looked up at the others in turn, first Namdarin, then Granger. Tears were streaming down his face, tears of both joy and sadness.

"Is it done?" asked Granger, his voice hoarse with the strain of exertion.

"As done as it can be." mumbled Gregor, coming slowly to his feet again.

"But will it be enough?" asked Jangor.

"I can only hope." said Gregor, "But I believe it should be enough."

"How will we know if it isn't?"

"I will most likely die, Worandana and Kevana will not look favourably on this sort of desertion."

"No loss to us then." said Namdarin.

"Enough." snapped Jangor. "Where are those horses, we need to be moving?"

"They will be here shortly." replied Namdarin.

"There is something else we need to consider." said Kern.

"What?" asked Jangor.

"Not all of Crathen's information is out of date, he knows we are going to find the elven kings tomb."

"And he knows what direction it is. Damn!" said Jangor.

"Why would you brave the undead elven king?" asked Gregor.

"He has something we need." said Granger.

"It must be something of the utmost value to face that."

"We have been told by a god that we need it to complete our mission to destroy Zandaar."

"I have studied something of the old elven magics." said Gregor. "The only thing they have of any power is their mind stone, but I thought that passed into history many years ago."

"That is indeed what we seek."

"From what I remember that stone gets its power directly from the elven peoples, they would have to give it over willingly for its power to be of any use to you."

"Well that is some new information for us." said Granger. "We'll have to come up with some form of plan by the time we get to their city."

"Even getting to the city is going to be difficult, they tend not to welcome strangers, or so I read."

"No surprise really, considering how many wars have been inflicted on them."

"Many by the Zandaars, so they may be persuaded to help end this threat once and for all." Gregor stopped, his brow furrowed with intense concentration.

"Something else we should know?" asked Granger.

"There is something, but I cannot remember what it is. This is very strange, my memory is usually very reliable. It is something about 'once and for all'. But I just can't get it."

"Perhaps it is 'once and until the end of days'." laughed Mander. The others joined in.

"Maybe." laughed Gregor, "but not quite. I feel there is something else, but I can't reach it, it worries me."

"You're just a worrier." said Stergin. Looking round to the sound of horses. Arndrol was leading the small herd towards the camp, trailing a little way behind was a large wolf.

"Kern." said Jangor. "Take Branks saddle off that pony and put it on the bay mare, she'll be a good horse for him to learn on."

"That's way too much horse for me." said Brank.

"She is only a couple of spans taller, and even tempered, she won't be happy lugging your weight around but she will manage. Kern make sure all his other gear goes on the pack animals, a sword and a Brank is enough for any horse."

It took very little time for the horses to be loaded and the fire extinguished, Kern helped Brank onto his new horse, much to the big man's disapproval.

"Kern." shouted Jangor. "East and set a reasonable pace, we have a lot of distance to cover. Mander, Andel, make sure there is no one following us."

"If the sky stays clear then we should be able to make good speed, but if the clouds cover the moons and the stars we will have to slow down." replied Kern, loudly. Jangor merely nodded.

"You don't honestly expect there to be anyone following already do you?" asked Granger.

"No, but no reason to be lax about these things."

Jangor took off after Kern, leaving the others to catch up as they could. Kern set his horse to a good trot, with Jangor matching him, stride for stride. Namdarin and Jayanne fell in behind them , with Granger next, the two newest recruits, Brank and Gregor next, with Stergin behind them bringing the baggage train, and finally Mander and Andel, bringing up the rear. The wolf kept up with the horsemen with no real difficulty, it's steady run was more than enough to match the pace of the horses, in fact it was patrolling around them, it would appear for moment or two pacing along with them then vanish into some copse or gully to reappear in a completely new location, behind, in front, to the other side. Occasionally game would be spooked from its hiding places, to take to the wing, or run across the path of the horses. One such occasion a bird came from Namdarin's right, its short wings clattering together as it came through the brush, Namdarin snatched his bow from its holder by his left knee and an arrow from its quiver, only to find that the bow wasn't strung.

"Damn." he muttered, Jayanne laughed softly and reached for her head with the right hand and her pocket with the left.

"Damn." she whispered, her sling was in her pack, and she had no idea at all where the pouch of stones was. They looked at each other and laughed aloud, as the bird flew over their heads. Suddenly there was a loud crack, which caused hands to leap to sword hilts, and everyone to turn towards Granger who was just lowering his staff back into its usual position across his knees.

"What's the problem?" asked Granger.

"Was that you?" said Namdarin.

"Yes."

"What did you do?"

"Well I thought you two were hungry so I took down that bird."

Everyone looked along the path the bird had taken, and sure enough there is was on the ground, unmoving, just smoking a little. The wolf appeared from behind a bush and had a quick sniff at the corpse, but shied away, there was something it didn't like there.

"I have never seen anything like that." laughed Gregor, easing his horse alongside Granger's. "Even the prepared magic that the Zandaars use takes some time to focus and release, you seemed to just raise your staff and instantly shoot a blast of fire at a moving target, a fast moving target."

"I've never done that sort of thing before." said Granger. "Everyone else's weapons are ready in the blink of an eye, except when a bow isn't strung, or someone has left their sling somewhere, so I just gave it a try."

Mander was beside the fallen bird, reaching down out of his saddle, and picked it up by a clump of charred tail feathers.

"Presumably someone planned to eat this. Normally one would remove the feathers before cooking and the innards, I feel that Granger's culinary skills leave a little to be desired, even the wolf wouldn't eat this." With a simple flick of the wrist he discarded the smoking mass into the brush, eventually something would eat it. As Mander walked his horse back to the others the wolf appeared out of the brush and followed, at a distance but he was certainly following Mander.

"Let's get moving." shouted Jangor. "We need to get some distance between us and that town, and those Zandaars will be looking for us very soon. Kern move out, and pick the damned pace up." Kern did just that, trot then canter, depending on the ground conditions at the time, this was a pace that puts a lot of strain on the riders, but also some strain on the mounts. A few hours of this would begin to hurt the riders, but the horses would still have something left if the need came upon them. Kern knew that Brank would be the one who would fail first, his almost complete lack of skill would put serious load on muscles he never uses. Kern understood Jangor's need for speed, and did all that was feasible to make it happen. Even the wolf was having a little difficulty keeping up, it was not ranging as far out from the group, more and more it was within view, gradually it settled down to match their pace, running a couple of horse lengths off to the right, a steady ground eating gallop, tail streaming in the wind.

Kern looked at the wolf and laughed aloud, the wolf replied with a simple yap, he had no spare breath to howl, running in the deepening night didn't bother the wolf, though the horses weren't at all used to this, their pace began to drop in line with the rapidly failing light. A break appeared in the thin clouds and twin moons shone through giving the open grassland an eerie appearance, there were no real colours to be seen, only shades of grey, and black, pools of the darkest ink gathered under the trees, the whole aspect of a simple copse changed in the bright moonlight, the thunder of hooves and the jingle of gear filled the night around them. Kern's night vision was excellent, even so the wolf was taking over slowly as guide, it pulled out in front of Kern and picked a path that was easier for the horses than the path the man could see.

High in a blasted tree sat a huge owl, a fine example of the largest breed in the whole country. It had already feasted on a fat ground squirrel, bloody shreds of flesh clung to it talons, the thunder of horses attracted it's attention, long before they came into view the owl was watching for them to come over the crest into the valley where it had taken its most recent meal, first it saw the flash of yellow in the eyes of the wolf, then the dark tide of rippling shapes as they poured like a running river into the valley, dark with one patch of light, a single grey blotch in the pitch of the night, the river flowed across the valley floor, moving around the clumps of brush, without a pause it flowed across the sliver of silver that was the stream, the black shattered the reflected moonlight in the stream, though it swiftly reformed after the passing. The owl shuffled its feet and ruffled its feathers as if mildly disturbed by the passing of a dark tide. It waited patiently for the valley to settle down again, the noise of the passing had caused such a disturbance that all the potential prey in the valley was now fully alert, the owl fell forwards from the branch spreading his huge wide wings, the soft feathers making no sound as he drifted away from the distressed valley, looking for an easier hunting ground, the slow beating of his wings moved him quickly away, over the ridge and into a more open valley to the south.

As the night was half way done, the riders came through a large open area, smooth and flat, slowly rising to the edge of a huge forest, this forest stretched from horizon to horizon, an unending darkness, deep and forbidding. The wolf slowed as it approached the eaves, looking back, uncertain that the man actually wanted to enter.

"Halt." shouted Jangor. "Cold camp. The horses need rest, we move out before dawn." He slid from his saddle, just out of the reach of the branches of a tree, he dropped his bed roll on the ground then dropped his saddle next to it. The others followed suit, an almost wordless camp was established in short order, the horses were unloaded and left to run free, which they did, though not far from the people. Kern sat on his blankets, the wolf almost with in arms reach staring at him, its yellow eyes flashing in the light of the moons. Kern poured a bowl of water from his canteen, and placed it on the ground between them. The wolf stepped forwards and drank deeply its huge red tongue lapping water noisily, while the man drank straight from the bottle.

Brank lay face down on his blanket moaning gently. "Damned horses, why can't they ever be comfortable?"

"Think how the horse feels with you on its back." laughed Mander.

"Get some sleep." said Andel. "Jangor means it when he says before dawn."

"How can I sleep with this pain in my backside?" mumbled Brank.

"Just do it, because tomorrow will be more of the same." Andel waited for a reply, but none came, only a muffled snoring, he smiled and settled into his own blanket.

Jangor looked at Kern, and whispered. "I'll take the next watch." The answer was a simple nod. As Jangor closed his eyes he saw the wolf settle down with its head on Kerns leg and close its eyes.

Namdarin had great difficulty getting to sleep, the presence of Gregor in their camp was bothering him, the man in black was oblivious to Namdarin's discomfort, the fatigue of the ride had taken its toll, even the closeness of Jayanne's sleeping form did nothing to calm Namdarin. 'I don't care what the rest of them think, I don't trust him, I will never trust him, no matter what the sword of Xeron thinks of him.' He laid is palm against the hilt of the sword, a soft and gentle warmth flowed into him, but this did little to help the hatred in his heart. He breathed as slowly as could, trying to relax, even if sleep evaded him entirely the relaxation would help, slowly he focused his mind, on the more pleasurable memories of his past, he thought of the times he went hunting with his father, creeping slowly through the woods above his home, tracking down a lone stag, following it more by the coughing sounds it made to attract females, than its actual tracks. His bow clenched in his fist, awaiting that moment when the quarry would present itself, or vanish into the darkness, leaving them with the long walk home, empty handed. The images of broadleaf trees were nothing like the darkness of the trees he could see from the corner of his eye. The happy times of his youth, did help him to relax a little, but not enough to make him fall asleep. He turned his head away from the trees, and looked out over the others at the gradually sinking moons, the starlight only blocked by the occasional wisp of high cloud. Slowly the slowly changing light of the stars eased his mind into a state that was not exactly sleep, but something akin, a deep relaxation, his breathing slowed until it was almost impossible to see, the merest hint of mist leaving his nostrils was the only indication that he was even alive, though his eyes were open, he saw nothing from around himself. His mind wandered high above the camp, turning south it sped once more towards Zandaarkoon, drawn by some force he didn't understand. As soon as it dawned on his consciousness that his destination was the city of the god, he turned away, then was suddenly without a destination, drifting almlessly, he turned back to the camp, and rushed upon the scene, less than what seemed to be a single heartbeat and he was looking down on his friends sleeping. The thought came to his mind, 'Zandaars, where are they?' He turned back to the direction they had come from. His mind moved at incredible speed, the terrain blurred into nothing below, he paused briefly over their most recent campsite before heading towards the village with the lightening stone. His mind was getting used to this strange mode of travel, and stopped in an instant exactly over the centre of the stone. Across the green he could see the camp of the priests, drifting slowly he approached, he saw a large man sitting a short distance away from the central fire, obviously on watch, Namdarin entered a tent, drifting though the cloth of the wall. Inside were two priests sleeping, one coughed but didn't wake, Namdarin moved on, this was not who he was looking for. The third tent actually contained the target he was after. Crathen was alone, not restrained, fast asleep, and dreaming. Generating the necessary focus, Namdarin invaded the man's dream. This was a soft and warm place, full of simple colours and simple forms, a man, a woman, entwined in an intimate embrace, writhing slowly as if to music that only they could hear. They moved together accompanied by their own moans and groans of pleasure. The man was obviously Crathen's vision of himself, the woman was barely recognisable as Jayanne, the skin was too pale and smooth, the breasts too full, the hips too curved, the legs too smooth without the muscle definition that Jayanne has, the hair too red and tidy without the loose strands that are part of the attraction of the original. Namdarin changed his presence in the dream to be just another pink cushion, part of the furniture of Crathen's dream. Gradually he took control of the Jayanne figure, changing its movements to be more active, less passive, more demanding, insistent, aggressive even. The arms developed muscle, the legs the same, the arms closed around Crathen's neck, the legs grasped his hips, the body thrusting even harder upon his manhood. Namdarin changed the hair into a nest writhing red vipers, the snakes hissed and Crathen opened his eyes, suddenly aware that something had changed, he stared sharply into the green eyes that flashed into black as he watched. Now he starts to struggle, but to no avail, the arms will not release, nor the legs. He tries desperately to pull his face away from the snakes as they hiss and spit droplets of burning venom into his face. Now Namdarin shows himself. Crathen screams, a wordless howl of anguish.

"She is mine, you will never have her." Said Namdarin, he made one more small change to the Jayanne simulacrum, he gave the centre of her womanhood a set of teeth like a shark, these snapped shut with an audible crack, severing a very important part of Crathen. Blood pumped from the joining of the bodies spraying liberally around the scene, turning cushions from pink to red. The dream dissolved, as Crathen woke, the scream continued for some time, his grasp on his manhood could not be removed without serious force. The whole camp was roused and half the village, before the priests managed to calm him with a well-aimed slap. Namdarin waited for a while until he felt that the oldest of the priests was searching for something, and that the something was him. He formed a picture of the camp in his mind and travelled back there in the space between two heartbeats. In another his essence returned to his body. He drew a huge breath, his body felt as if it hadn't breathed for a while, once the dizziness had faded he rolled away from Jayanne and lay on his back, shaking with silent laughter. Jayanne turned to him.

"Are you all right?"

"Better than that, so much better than that."

"Why?"

Namdarin told her of his recent travels. Soon she was laughing but not silently. This attracted Jangor's attention. He had avoided listening to whispered conversation between the two, but her loud laughter brought him over.

"What's going on?" He asked.

"Namdarin has invaded Crathen's dream." She answered. "He woke up screaming, terrified that his manhood was gone, screaming like a child."

"Their camp is awake?" He snapped at Namdarin.

"Yes."

"Fool." Jangor stood, staring hard towards the east. Then he looked back at the two of them lying on the ground. "We cannot risk that forest without light, and those bastards are awake, and probably know that one of us was there."

"I don't care, it was worth it to give that bastard a fright that might just have killed him. And it will give the other bastards something to think about." Namdarin jumped to his feet. Jayanne came to her feet in a smooth languid motion that captivated the attention of both men, it was something to do with her total lack of clothing and the fact that at some point during the manoeuvre her right hand had found the strap for her axe and wriggled into the loop, or perhaps the axe had found her wrist. Her right hand rested casually on her hip with the axe swinging slowly to and fro. Jangor turned away, scanned the horizon looking for the first light of the pre-dawn, the merest lightening in the east was just becoming visible. He snapped a look over his shoulder at Jayanne, then shouted.

"Mander." A figure sat up in the near darkness. "Cold breakfast for everyone, move. Andel pack the camp, get the horses loaded, someone kick Brank, we have to move, some idiot woke up the damned Zandaars." The camp started to move, Stergin kicked Brank, who groaned mightily before rolling to his feet.

"It's still dark." he muttered.

"Yes, but we need to be moving." said Stergin, softly.

"I need more sleep, and something that is not that damned saddle underneath me."

"What is the rush?" asked Gregor, of no one in particular.

"We need to be on the road." repeated Stergin.

"Why?"

"Someone has been stirring up your ex-friends." he nodded in the general direction of Namdarin ,who was still standing with Jangor and Jayanne. Gregor looked towards the group.

"Ye gods, she's naked, should I say something?"

"She's not naked."

"Yes she is."

"See the axe." said Stergin, without a single glance.

"Yes."

"She is fully clothed, ready to meet any one, or any danger. Question her at your own risk. That axe will take your head in a heartbeat."

"I'll find out what has happened." he walked over the Jangor and the others.

"Why the urgency?" he asked, trying to avoid staring at Jayanne.

"Namdarin has informed your old colleagues that he is a little upset with Crathen."

"How did you do that?"

"I turned his dream against him, he woke up screaming, not what I actually wanted, dead would have been better."

"You can't enter a dream from this far away, you need to be close."

"You need to be close, I, on the other hand, do not."

"They are days away, and you invaded his dream and took it away from him?"

"This is going to sound strange but I was actually in the tent with him, just my body was here."

"That can't be."

"Believe what you want, or what you have been told, I don't care." Namdarin turned away and started wrapping up his bed roll. Gregor turned to Jayanne. "Can he really do that?"

"If he says he did it then it is so. If you doubt his word, then you could put yourself in danger" her voice was cold and hard, and the axe no longer hung by its strap, it slapped into her palm.

Gregor looked down, at the axe, not the rest of her naked body, only the axe.

"I am sorry to doubt him." he said looking again into the green eyes. "But all my training says this cannot be done from this distance." he stepped back, only half a pace, but a step away.

She turned away her red hair lashed his face, and he looked down as she moved away watching her backside as she walked to her bedroll. He turned away, and walked slowly back to the other group.

The predawn light started to turn the sky silver in the east, and birds in the forest started singing their morning greetings. Gregor turned to the forest, the brightening sky and the joyful songs did nothing to alleviate the darkness of the trees, the gloom seemed to seep into his mind through his eyes.

"Granger." he called softly. The old wizard walked over.

"Can you feel anything from that forest?"

Granger stood for a moment focusing his mind on the darkness beneath the trees, he closed his eyes to help the concentration, but still he could sense nothing out of the normal for a forest full of life.

"Nothing unusual, just the everyday coming and goings of the average residents of such a place, rodents, birds, small amphibians, nothing more."

"I sense something larger, a lot larger, very strange, and I don't know what else. Just something."

"Could be your own nervousness, it has been a rough couple of days for you, complete life change, not the sort of thing a mind can get used to quickly."

"Mine has to, if any vestige of my old life is visible to them, they'll find me, and kill me."

"That might be an interesting battle of wills."

"Interesting when your life is not in the balance."

"I have already beaten one of them in face to face combat, and that was actually surprisingly easy. His lightning bolt did carry a great deal of power, but not too much for me."

"I have heard of that battle, he was a soldier, not a magician. The magician is far more proficient, and when the two of them get together, a formidable force indeed."

"What aid can the others lend in a battle?"

"They have power and strength, with their training they can generate a charge that can burn a man to the bone in a moment. They proved this when the bird god destroyed the ring, the back lash from the power charge fried Helvana, if they organise properly, they can cause some serious damage."

"We'll just have to make sure they don't get organised. How organised do they have to be to generate all this power?"

"They have to form a circle. Normally this will involve standing in a circle and touching each other, but this is not actually essential, nearness is important and coordination vital, but they could do it without it being obvious, well the clerics could but the soldiers need physical contact, and the circle to ensure they do things right, if a person is in one of these circles and the energy pulse comes from the wrong side or at a time when one is not expecting it, it can hurt or even kill if the charge is big enough."

"So, we need to break any circles and keep them distracted, not too hard a task."

"Harder than you may think, once the circle forms it automatically defends itself, reflecting or absorbing incoming energies, it can take an enormous amount of energy to break one. If it comes to actual face to face combat then the clerics will form a circle, and the soldiers attack with physical weapons."

"It will still take them time to build a charge, we have it instantly to hand." Granger slapped his staff, which generated a small blue light from each end.

"They can build a decent charge in only a few heartbeats, don't underestimate them."

"I hope that it doesn't ever come to that."

"I wish that it could be so, but somehow I feel that this quest will certainly come to a physical confrontation, if not with those that follow us, then with a god. Not something that I look forward to."

"I have been giving this some thought, in the darkness of the night, I don't think that I will be there when this all comes to its conclusion. I don't think that most of us will be there."

"You are willing to die for this cause?"

"Not as such, but I really can't see me surviving."

"What of the others?"

"Namdarin will be there at the end, Jayanne must be there, Jangor probably will be there, you, I am unsure as yet. But the rest of us are all expendable."

"Jayanne must?"

"Definitely, at the final confrontation Namdarin is almost certainly going to be carrying enough power to destroy the world, without Jayanne, that is what he will do. He doesn't see it, or know it, but it is true."

"Are you a seer?"

"Not in any way that you mean, but despite many years in isolation I understand the forces that drive people, and these are the most driven people I have ever met."

"Is that what convinced you to join them?"

"It is certainly one of the factors."

"Mount up!" shouted Jangor. Brank merely sat upon the ground groaning. Stergin poked him with a foot and offered a hand to help him up. This only solicited more groans.

"Brank." said Jangor, loudly. "Choices are simple, arse or belly. Sit in the saddle or tied across. Choose now."

"You are an evil man."

"Yes, I know but it is for your own good, now mount up!"

Brank accepted Stergin's proffered hand and heaved himself to his feet, staggered over to the horse and allowed Stergin to help him into the saddle. More groans, and soft curses, as the horse stamped it's hooves at the load it was expected to carry.

"Kern." shouted Jangor. "You take point, heading east through this forest."

"It's still too dark to travel amongst the trees."

"We need to be moving before the priests get themselves organised. Ideas anyone."

"I can light the way." Said Granger. "But not enough to give any real guidance."

"That will do for now. Once it gets light Kern will be able to navigate by the sunlight. Everyone else keep bunched up tight until the light improves. Move out."

Granger moved up until he was alongside Kern, in a few moments a small blue flame sprang from the tip of his raised staff, casting an eerie glow that lit the boles of the trees as they all turned towards the darkness. Picked out in the blue light the trees were clearly visible, but somehow they appeared a little unreal, almost like a painted image on a wall, to Stergin and Mander who brought up the rear of the column it looked like their friends walked into a picture that was hanging on a wall. The forest seemed to swallow the whole party. Stergin turned to Mander. "Creepy." he whispered, as he kicked his horse to keep it moving towards the trees. "Weird." was the muttered reply. Stergin's mount was almost nipping the flanks of the last of the pack horses when he passed between the trunks of the first trees.

The darkness in the forest was almost complete, Granger's small light did little to light their way, more it gave to entire party a target to hold on to, it lit the branches above them and the trees around them, but precious little else. In the depths of the forest the wolf became even more of a ghost, it's grey coat reflected almost none of Grangers blue light, only it's eyes flared brilliant green as it turned to look back at Kern and Granger, never too far away, always just inside the cast of the light. Gradually the ground beneath their feet started to climb, a gentle slope that slowly tilted down to their right, a small stream crossed their path, racing down the hill, presumably towards a larger watercourse.

"We need to be going east." said Jangor.

"In this light," answered Kern, "we are heading as close to east as I can tell. Once the sun comes up we will have a better idea."

"The sun should already be up."

"Agreed, if you have any idea where it is, then give me a hint, in these trees I can't be sure."

"Just keep moving, we'll sort it out soon enough." Jangor lapsed into silence, though he didn't stop worrying. The steady uphill travel could have been guiding them almost anywhere, but it felt like they were going east. As they walked the horses the lower branches of the trees moved upwards out of the range of Granger's staff, and the trunks of the trees grew further apart, though the light didn't increase to any appreciable amount. The litter strewn floor gradually hardened until dark soil was visible in patches. The wolf stopped, standing perfectly still, it looked back at Kern and let out a tiny whine. All the horses stopped and Kern dismounted, he walked very slowly towards the wolf, he knelt beside the animal and ruffled the fur of his mane. The wolf relaxed a little, but still showed no intention of moving. It was standing on the edge of a wide path, hard beaten ground that several horses could ride along side by side, this path was going in almost exactly the direction they had been travelling. Kern looked carefully both ways along the path, listened for what appeared to be minutes to the others, then he stood.

"We have a road, well used, and heading sort of east. Follow it or not?"

"We have no idea how far we have to go to get to the elves city, so we must follow it, it could save us days." said Jangor, looking around for assent from the others. There was no specific dissent, so Jangor assumed agreement. "Follow the road, and pick up the pace." As Kern was returning to his horse Brank groaned quite loudly.

"If we meet a fast moving group of horsemen on this road we will not be able to hide from them." said Kern.

"We are heading to their only known city, we have to meet them sooner or later."

"I am not sure I really want to." replied Kern. "They are not known for their hospitality."

"They have something we need. Move out." again Brank groaned, but Kern did as he was told, and walked his horse onto the elvish road, the wolf stayed close by his side, turning east Kern kicked his horse into a trot, with the wolf pacing alongside, Granger's light was of no use here, the height of the canopy and the separation of the trees let enough of the morning light onto the roadway, as the sun climbed it would only get brighter. Granger fell back down the company and dropped in beside Gregor.

"Will you be able to feel if the Zandaars are looking for you?"

"I don't actually know, but I should be able to feel something, once they find the sword, then they will know that I am nearby, it would be so much easier to hide from them if we weren't carrying the sword."

"Somehow I don't see Namdarin giving up his most powerful weapon, do you?"

"No, and if he did, I'd probably leave this group as soon as I could."

"Why?"

"Without the sword he doesn't have a chance to survive this quest."

"Sorry, but I don't believe that survival has even crossed his mind, he is certain he is going to die, successful or not, he will die."

"We'll just have to do what we can to change his thinking, a man who believes he will die will generally find a way to make it happen."

"I agree. Let's work on this and see if we can find a way for us all to survive."

"You have already stated that some if not all will die in this endeavour."

"It is fairly certain that some will not survive, after all, we are at war with a god, and one that you used to serve. I believe there is an old saying that fits your situation quite well, it's something about griddle and fire." Gregor paused for a moment then threw his head back in laughter.

"In so many ways you are far too right." he answered once the laughter had subsided. "Jumped off the griddle and into the fire, sums up my situation accurately."

"Perhaps you should have taken your chances on the griddle."

"No. With every day that passed it became more obvious to me that I was going to fall foul of some rule or other."

"You think your chances have improved? After all, your old friends are going to try to kill you as soon as the chance presents itself."

"True, but I think my chances of survival have increased. They will have to get up close and personal, that will be hard for them. I don't think are going to catch up with us in a few days, I believe it's going to be weeks."

"What makes you think that? You have admitted that they can feel the sword where ever it goes, they'll be following as fast as they can."

"That is true, but we are entering the demesne of the Elves, and that is not going to be easy for them. There is no shortage of bad blood between Zandaar and the Elves. If it comes to a confrontation Kevana will be fighting every step of the way, so he'll either have to find some way to appease the Elves, or avoid contact with them, which is going to slow them down, or go all the way around their woods. That is a journey of some weeks."

"How did you know we were heading for elvish territory?"

"I didn't, but I did hope for a few days to find some way to hide the sword from Worandana. Now I think we can wait a while, it'll drive Kevana crazy to know we are so close but so far away."

"Will you be able to tell how far away they are?"

"Perhaps, the intensity of the search can give a clue to distance, but there are a lot of factors, but it is possible to get some form of gauge for the distance."

CHAPTER THIRTY NINE

The camp settled down to sleep, the village did the same, in a very short time there was nothing moving in the whole village, at least nothing larger than a hunting cat, Alverana sat a distance from the fire, keeping watch, though none was needed. Briefly he wondered about waking someone to replace him, but decided that he could do with the time alone. Focusing his thoughts inwards, leaving only the smallest part of his consciousness on guard he descended into his mind. This was his preferred method for relaxation, he usually returned from these internal explorations as refreshed as a whole night's sleep. Drifting slowly downwards he let things just happen around him, letting pure randomness be his guide, gradually the scene formed around him, a somewhat stylised vision of the village where he actually was, though many things had actually changed, the whole scale of the place was changed, everything was much closer together, the green was only a few paces across the tavern was just strides away, his dream self-climbed to his feet and walked past the lightening stone, which scattered light from deep inside itself, lights that appeared to move around chasing this shadow, and then another, as if they were looking for something, or perhaps were just pursuing shadows because that was what they do. Crossing the veranda Alverana entered the tavern, to find a huge airily open room, it had walls but felt like an open plain, the floor was even covered in grass, but only when he wasn't actually looking straight at it, as he looked down it was a stone flagged floor, covered with a scattering of straw. Moving to the bar he called for a drink, and while the beer was being poured, foaming from a jug into a large tankard, he felt more than saw the rabbit approach from behind. He picked up his drink and turned slowly towards the rabbit, not wishing to surprise it, knowing that this could make it vanish and be replaced by something more mundane, the rabbit was wearing a colourful jacket, all greens and reds, with brilliant blue pants.

"Good evening." said Alverana.

"It is neither evening, nor good." snapped the rabbit, reaching up with both hands and pulling down his left ear, he slowly smoothed the fur out and released it, the ear sprang back into the upright position and twitched as if scanning the room before focusing on the man. Alverana merely raised his eyebrows knowing that the rabbit would be unable to resist telling him of all its problems. The rabbit stepped up to the bar, and slapped both hands down on the bar top and then waved one at the ill-defined barman, a full tankard appeared in its hand, as he took a deep draught from the tankard his upper lip obtained the white moustache of a beer drinker. Alverana struggled not the laugh aloud as a colourful forearm brushed away the white foam.

"Is something funny?" asked the rabbit.

"Nothing of any import." said Alverana, smiling, with one hand he rubbed his nose. Unable to resist the rabbit mimicked the action and removed the last of the foam from its nose. Alverana nodded.

"Thank you." mumbled the rabbit feeling the wetness in his hand. "You wouldn't believe the day I've had."

"Do tell."

"Damned badgers."

"You have a problem with badgers?"

"Yes, they move into an area and it turns into a nightmare."

"How do you mean?"

"The whole neighbourhood goes downhill. They just steal others homes, and take all the best places for themselves."

"What are you going to do about it then?"

"I don't know, perhaps we could hire someone to get rid of them. You look like a strong man, you looking for a job?"

"Not at the moment, I am sort of busy, plenty going on for me."

"What are you doing?"

"Chasing a thief, he stole a sword."

"But you have a sword." The rabbit points at the one on Alverana's hip.

"No, this is a special sword, a very special sword."

"I know nothing of swords, but I know farming, and badgers are no good for farms."

"I've always found badgers to be industrious, and intelligent."

"What are you, some badger lover, what do they need all those stripes for anyway? Why can't they be a simple colour like real people?"

"Badgers are simply badgers, why should they be anything else?"

"Because they should, they should be just like the rest of us."

"If they were, then they would be rabbits."

"And what is wrong with that? Do you have something against rabbits?"

"I have nothing against rabbits or badgers, but sometimes I have problems with thcm both."

"How can you have problems with both?"

"Simple, I can get caught in the middle like I am now." Alverana thought that this was far more silly than usual, his dream excursions, as he thought of them, did tend to be strange but this was just too much. There was also something strange about this rabbit.

"How can you be in the middle? There is only me here, not a badger to be seen, I am glad to say."

Alverana focused closely on the rabbit, but nothing out of the ordinary came to the fore, he swept the bar with his gaze, intent on anything that was out of place, everywhere his eyes rested for more than an instant the real world around the camp became visible below the dream, not exactly through it, but somehow alongside the vision of the bar. Not wishing to break the dream Alverana relaxed a little, hoping that this would show him what his brain knew was wrong, but his semi-conscious mind couldn't fathom. He turned his back to the counter, and perched upon the tall stool that was suddenly just where he needed it to be. The rabbit crashed his tankard to the bar and waved for a refill. Alverana focussed on the misty area behind the bar, but the barman refused to come into view, he remained indistinct, blurred and grey. Turning back to the room he scanned the rafters, which behaved just like every other aspect of the dreamscape, they showed the real world behind them, many stars were visible in the almost cloudless sky, a slightly distorting column of energy or heat rose from the lightening stone, causing the stars in that area to twinkle more than the others. A small dark cloud passed through this patch on sky quite quickly, then did something very unusual, it paused for a time less than a single heartbeat, then continued across the sky falling behind the trees. Alverana considered the actions of the cloud, was the pause an illusion, or did it actually happen? With only a moment's hesitation the dreamscape burst like a soap bubble, he scanned the camp, looking for the cloud, whatever it was. Nothing showed itself, but then the camp was dark lit only by the embers of the small fire. He closed his eyes, and used the sight of his mind, the fire shone more brightly, the grass took on a soft light, more grey than green. The tents showed as dark patches against the background light of the village. Still nothing to see, then a tenuous dark cloud slipped out of one tent and into another, the tent where the prisoner was currently sleeping. Alverana felt no loyalty to Crathen so he chose not to intervene, but merely stood watch, to be sure this darkness didn't attack any of his friends. After a short time he decided to see what was going on in the tent, without moving physically he separated his mind and tried to invade Crathen's tent. The tent was easy, but getting into Crathen's dream was much harder than he had expected it to be. As he forced his way in through the boundaries of Crathen's mind his concentration was shattered by Crathen's scream.

Kevana was the first to force his way into Crathen's tent, the man's continuous scream, and tightly clenched fists told him all he needed to know. He stepped up close and slapped Crathen hard with an open hand, the shock of the blow stopped the scream, but did nothing for the rigidity of his body, and no force at all would move his hands.

"What has happened?" demanded Worandana.

"Obviously someone tore his dream apart." snapped Kevana.

"Who?"

"You?"

"Not me, you?"

"No. Who then?"

"One of the thieves?"

"They have this sort of skill?"

"One of them, or one of us, these are the only possibilities."

"If it is one of them he may still be around. You search for him."

"Kevana." said Briana.

"What?"

"Alverana, he seems to be ill." Kevana turned and saw that Alverana was lying in the ground, he rushed over, and placed a hand on the younger man's chest. He felt the slow rise and fall, and the very slow thump of a gentle heartbeat.

"He's alive. Worandana check him out." Worandana shifted his focus, it took him only moments to report.

"His mind is almost completely absent, like he has gone to invade someone's dream." Everyone turned to look at Crathen. Kevana stamped over to where Crathen was lying on the grass, drew his sword, and placed it against the recumbent man's chest.

"Was Alverana in your dream?" Crathen tried to move away from the sword point.

"Was Alverana in your dream?" yelled Kevana. finally eliciting a response.

"No. No, it was Namdarin."

"You're certain?"

"Very." whispered Crathen.

"So where has Alverana gone?"

"I don't know, he was not there."

"Worandana. Where can he be? Is he still here somewhere, just lost?"

"May be, but how to find him?"

"We can do it. We have to."

"Any idea how?"

"We perform a simple summoning, then he should be able to find his way back."

"How do you want to do that?"

"We who knew him best will call him, the rest of you just channel power into our call." He sat on the ground beside Alverana's head and motioned for the other soldiers to form a circle. "We knew him, so we must bring him back, he is lost somewhere nearby, think of him and call his name, shout it loud and strong, I know you are still tired from last night's exertions, but our friend is lost and needs us. Ready?" All answered with a single nod.

"Worandana, once we have the call set up, you feed your power to me, I'll find him. Understood?"

"Yes. Get started, time could be very important." Kevana lowered his head for a few moments, then raised it, swept the circle with his gaze, then started the silent call to his old friend. 'Alverana'. The thought rang from his mind, projected outwards, joined by the similar, but not identical calls of the others. Worandana started the charge of energy moving around the outer circle, building with every pass, with no soldiers in this circle the cycle rate was much higher, the power build up, much more intense.

'Alverana.' The thought shouted, louder, stronger, but still as silent. Each caller putting everything that Alverana meant to them into this voiceless shout.

'Alverana.' The thought screamed silently in the predawn light, horses flinched, spooked by something they couldn't hear, dogs cowered threatened by something they couldn't smell, cattle rattled the gates of their pens, desperate to get out, but for no reason they knew. Kevana threw back his head, Worandana directed the cycling power at his friend, a charge so heavy that it was almost tangible.

'Alverana.' The thought howled, such a shockwave of thought that the whole village, even the very grass beneath them flinched, the trees shook, and sparks jumped from the lightning stone. A tenuous contact was made, which quickly strengthened into something more solid, a warm feeling filled the callers, their friend had answered.

"Alverana." whispered Kevana. 'Come back to us, come back to yourself.' With a sudden rush they all felt the presence of Alverana suffuse them then moved on into his own form. He found his way back into his own mind, returning to consciousness with a rush, and a scream. His voice shattered the rings that surrounded him, their energy no longer required was dissipated harmlessly, the lightening stone settled into is usual acquiescent state, no sparks, nor lights showed from within its structure. Alverana ran out of breath, only to refill his lungs and scream again. Kevana reached forwards and grasped his friend's shoulders, showing such care as none had witnessed before.

"Be calm. My friend." he said. Alverana turned slowly to look back over his shoulder, and let the scream go, it petered out into silence.

"You're fine." said Kevana. "Aren't you?" Alverana looked over his extremities, as if checking on their actual existence.

"I seem to be all here at least." was his shaky reply.

"What happened to you?"

"I was tuned to the other plane, just day dreaming, as I do sometimes. And then I saw a dark presence drift through the camp, I wasn't sure it was actually there, for a while, but when it moved into the prisoner's tent I saw it for sure. I followed it in, perhaps I should have taken my body with me." He laughed a little uncertainly. "The prisoner was dreaming but I could no longer see the darkness, so I tried to enter his dream, the dream boundary was very hard to break through, it took some real effort, and not the sort of thing I am used to. I found a sort of weakness in the barrier, and started to wriggle through it, then all of a sudden the whole thing just exploded, and I got scattered along with the rest of his dream, it was dreadful to feel myself being spread out, I go to be spread so thin that I couldn't actually think, at least not in any meaningful way. I think I was fading away, until you called me. That was just the best feeling in my life, thank you all."

"So, it wasn't Crathen that tried to kill you?"

"He can't have even known that I was there."

"He can live a while longer then."

"What are we going to do now then?" demanded Worandana. "It is almost dawn, and we have a traitor to kill, or so you vowed yesterday."

"Damn." snapped Kevana. "We are too tired now, at least I am, that bastard will have to wait. At least until I have had some breakfast. Someone get to the cooking." He slumped to the ground, fatigue lined his face. "Sometimes I just feel so old."

"Sometimes?" laughed Petrovna. The scowls only made him laugh harder as he walked over to the fire to start the cooking.

Kevana and Alverana stayed seated resting, recuperating, relaxing. They said nothing, just looked around, somehow Kevana was more tired than he could ever remember. His thoughts turned inwards. 'How can I be so tired? I've never put so much of myself into any action. Why is this man so important to me? I don't understand how this can be.' He turned to look at Alverana, questioning his own feelings.

"Hey." Their heads snapped round towards the shout. Anya was walking towards them, she was crossing the green, walking with a smooth and steady stride, hand in hand with a man. As the pair passed the lightning stone she reached out with one hand, barely touching the stone, sparks leaped to her finger tips, green light poured into her hand, and she laughed aloud.

"How are you?" asked Kevana as the two came close.

"I am great." said Anya, she stood with her chin up, he eyes sparkling, and her hair shining in the light of the rising sun.

"Who is this with you?"

"He is my husband. Porto. He is all better now." Her eyes challenged them to gainsay this statement. Kevana looked carefully at the old man with her, for he was certainly old, but there was a presence about him, a feeling of heat upon the face as Kevana looked deep into his old eyes. Kevana closed his eyes and felt the heat on his face, then the flood of green light filled his mind.

"Woman. What have you done?"

"What do you think?" She laughed aloud. "By the time I had sealed the stone after your stupidity, I was so full of power that I had to do something with it, and I did."

"How long will this last?" asked Kevana.

"You think I actually care? Every moment is more than I can hope for. Every heartbeat is filled with joy."

"He is carrying so much power, he is dangerous."

"I can deal with that, can you?"

"I don't know. Did I see the stone flash as you passed?"

"Yes, it seems like I now have a permanent link to its heart. I can tap its power whenever I want."

"How much power does it have left?"

"More than I can spend in a life time."

"Are you sure about that? Could be that your lifetime is now considerably longer than you realise."

"We shall probably live a little longer than most, but I am certain we will die, and together."

"Can you give us some of your strength, we are dreadfully tired?"

"What would you use it for?"

"You know well what we need to do."

"I'll not help you kill a man, and will actively defend that one."

"We could force you."

"You think so? I doubt it. You want to risk losing some more men. I want to thank your leader. Where is he?"

"He is not my leader."

"Well elder then."

"Oh. He is that." laughed Kevana. "He is resting, the stress of last night and again this morning. That tent over there." He pointed at one of the tents near the fire. Anya nodded her thanks then lead her partner over to the tent.

"Worandana." she called, then waited for an answer.

"I need a word." she continued, another pause, followed by the sounds of movement from within. A grey-haired head poked through the doorway of the tent.

"What do you want?" he demanded, looking up at her.

"To thank you and to introduce my real husband to you."

Worandana took a second look at her companion, then a third. He crawled out of the tent and allowed her to help him to his feet, the warmth of her hand surprised him.

"This cannot be him." said Worandana.

"But it is." she laughed leaning towards her man and kissing him soundly, a kiss that was enthusiastically returned.

"How?"

"I was carrying so much energy last night, after shutting down your mistake. I just decided that I would cure him or kill us both. Turns out we survived."

"So you did, and you still carry quite a charge. How do you feel?" he asked of the man.

"Better than I can remember, but then my memory seems to have some large gaps in it."

"That may be a good thing, but it could be short lived."

"I understand, Anya has explained everything to me, how sick I was, and how she cured me. If this only lasts long enough for me to thank her, then that is just fine by me." he hugged his wife to him, and smiled.

"Anya, how could the power of the stone do this?"

"I think it likes me. I seem to have a sort of permanent connection to the thing now. I can feel it, it is still more than a little unsettled, but I think this will dissipate when you leave."

"There have been developments this morning, one of our enemies attacked us. One of us was nearly killed, not as a direct consequence, but indirectly he was placed in extreme danger."

"But you are all alive."

"Yes, but very tired, the act of retrieving our friend has exhausted us all."

"You cause too much disturbance in our village, it would be best if you left." Anya frowned, and gripped her husband even tighter.

"We will leave as soon as we can, have no fear."

Her glanced turned to the lightening stone, Worandana's eyes followed hers.

"We will not chance that again." Worandana answered the unasked question. "It is far too dangerous for us, but you could always lend us some of your strength."

"I'll not do that, I know what you intend, and I'll not help you there, about the stone, in that you are right, the stone is quite disturbed by your presence."

"We have an idea where we are heading, I believe our enemies are heading for the ancient elven kingdoms."

"South then east is your path, into the great forest. That is where the elves are, if they still live. It has been many a year since we heard anything of them."

"They are a secretive people, so it could be that they are keeping to themselves. We can only hope they are still alive, they might slow down our enemies a little."

"You should set off soon, the quicker you get moving the more chance you have of catching up."

"I know that you want us to leave, but you could be a little subtle about it."

"That was subtle." she laughed.

"We will be leaving just as soon as we can."

"Good." She turned away and walked slowly arm in arm with the husband back across the green towards her house.

"She's a witch and a whore." muttered Kirukana.

"From the hunger in your eyes you'd give her every last penny you had, just for a chance to prove how much of a man you really are." laughed Petrovana. Kirukana snatched his eyes away, and glared at Petrovana, who only laughed the louder.

"Petrovana." snapped Kevana. "Food. We will rest on the road; the traitor will be dealt with at sunset. Anyone with enough strength left to search for him?"

"I think I can manage that." said Worandana. "I probably knew him the best anyway."

"Yes." muttered Kirukana. "You two are so much alike."

"And what do you mean by that?" demanded Worandana. Kirukana looked up, fear filled his eyes, he had obviously not intended this comment to be heard. He glanced swiftly around the group hoping for some ally, finding none that would meet his gaze in a friendly fashion, he knew he had made a fundamental mistake.

"Just, just, er."

"Yes."

"You two are the same, you concentrate on the learning, you both know things that are actually banned, you should not learn these things."

"Who are you to decide what knowledge cannot be learned?"

"It's not me, it's the council that decide these things."

"Stupid old men, who fear for their own safety." snapped Worandana.

"Why do you say that?" muttered Kirukana.

"Because it is true. They fear any power they do not control themselves. They fear any learning they have not mastered, and they master little."

"But they are the rulers of the faithful."

"Only as long as they maintain their power over the people."

"Do you intend heresy?"

"If I did, we would not be here. I would be in the council chambers right now, an elected member, changing things from the inside. I work for the glory of Zandaar, not for the aggrandisement of petty fools."

"You call the council fools?"

"Yes. For such they are. You think otherwise?"

"Of course, these are the leaders of our church, duly elected, they disseminate the desires of our god."

"They seem to have some problems differentiating between their desires and those of Zandaar."

"You think that you know the whims of our god?"

"Better than any of your councillors do."

"My councillors?"

"Yes, definitely, though more accurate to say that you are theirs."

"What do you mean by that?"

"Simply that you are their creature, not mine."

"Is he going to be a problem?" demanded Kevana, pushing Kirukana to one side and facing Worandana.

"If he does become a problem, then he is mine to deal with. I didn't want him, when he was forced upon me, so if he gets to be too much of a pain, then he'll have some form of accident." The two leaders turned to Kirukana, waiting for the younger man to understand the situation he was in.

"You wouldn't do that." he muttered, staring at the ground. "Would you?"

"Actually." replied Worandana coldly. "I would. And without hesitation. You have learned much from the teachers of the council, but now it is time to learn of the real world. What do you know of the sword? The one that we are chasing?"

"It is Zandaars sword and he wants it back."

"What else?" yelled Worandana.

"What do you want?"

"You know something else, it is written all over you face, what do you know?"

"I have heard whispers."

"What have you heard?"

"Zandaar wants the sword, wants it real bad, but the council want it for themselves."

"The council?"

"Well, some of them."

"Some?"

"There are two factions on the council, one wants the sword, the other wants to give it to Zandaar."

"Why?"

"I don't want to say."

"Petrovana." whispered Kevana. "This man doesn't want to tell us things we want to know."

Petrovana came forwards slowly pulling his knife from his belt, the scrape of the blade as it cleared the metal edges of the sheath told every one that this knife is always sharp. The long blade glinted in the morning sunlight. "Which bits of this man do you not need?" asked Petrovana, looking straight into the eyes of Kirukana.

"So long as he can talk, that is all I need." said Kevana.

"Great." said Petrovana, moving closer and holding his knife so the sunlight reflected into Kirukana's eyes.

"You can't do this." muttered Kirukana.

"Riding accident." said Kevana. "He fell from his horse."

"A sad loss to the church." said Worandana.

"If I tell you what you want to know then you have no reason to keep me alive." said Kirukana.

"Sharp, all of a sudden, isn't he?" said Petrovana, coldly.

"You'll just have to prove yourself worthy of living." said Kevana.

"How can I do that?"

"Start by talking."

"There is an old tale, one that says Zandaar's reign will be ended by a man with a sword, a very special sword, one that used to belong to a god. The two factions of the council each want the sword, one so they can use it to control Zandaar, and the second to appease him, hoping to completely destroy the first faction."

"Which holds sway at the moment?"

"Neither, each vies for supporters, but they have a hard time getting such. Nothing is spoken openly, everything is whispers and innuendo."

"Which faction do you support?" Demanded Worandana. Kirukana glanced from man to man hoping for some clue as to the right answer to this question, each of the leaders faces were completely blank, and more disconcertingly Petrovana was paring slivers from his fingernails with his knife.

"I support neither." Kevana snapped his fingers, and while the sound was still echoing in Kirukana's ears he felt the cold touch of steel to his throat, the hard edge of the knife dragged on the stubble on his neck.

"Truth?" snapped Worandana.

"Truth." muttered Kirukana. "Each faction wanted its own man in this party, they knew your two parties would come together. More than their own man they wanted the other faction not to have a man here, so in the end a neutral was chosen, me."

"How can you be working for the council and not with one faction or the other?"

"It is not easy, I don't think that either is wholly right, so I refuse to choose."

"You choose very easily for other ideas of theirs, but not this one, why?"

"Some are simple, the matter of the sword is not. Some ancient texts say that the sword is dangerous, some say that it will save the world. It is very difficult to make any choice."

"What about the more modern texts?"

"Some of those are so recent that the authors are still alive, their writing is clouded by their own desires."

"And the older texts are not?"

Kirukana frowned, deep in thought, the threat of death seemed far from his mind at the moment. "The older writings are more likely to be true."

"So I have found." said Worandana. "Equally they can be complete fabrications."

"Straying a little, aren't we?" asked Kevana.

"Indeed." said Worandana turning back to Kirukana. "How did the council know we would be together?"

"One faction has a great seer, it was foretold that you would join forces to pursue the sword."

"So they knew that someone other than us would find it first?" snapped Kevana.

"Yes, but they knew you wouldn't give up, and that you would need some help, so they sent the second force to meet you and made sure that I would be in that force."

"This seer," asked Worandana. "Who is it? And which faction controls him?" Worandana smiled to himself. An expression that was not lost on Kirukana.

"You know very well, that the seer is called Mauraid."

"The blind seer from the islands in the southern sea."

"Yes." Kirukana stared at the ground.

"The blind woman who lives alone on a smoking mountain far to the south of Zandaarkoon?"

"Yes."

"Your council that believes women to be evil, puts absolute trust in the words of a mad woman?"

"Yes, but they say she has the soul of a man, that is why she sees the future and is so tormented by the life she leads."

"I have heard this sort of garbage before, they find a justification, a rationalisation that makes anything they want appear to be reasonable, even though it cannot actually be proven. Such duplicity and they control everything."

"You think they are wrong?"

"No, I think they lie to further their own beliefs, and people like you follow blindly."

"I don't follow blindly, I question everything."

"You question nothing." laughed Worandana. "You follow the wild ramblings of a mad woman, simply because she agrees with whatever the council had decided. Who collected her words?"

"Two council members went to her island, they talked to her at length. They recorded her words and reported to the council."

"Don't you realise that the mere act of observing seers like her changes the way they speak, they read people and tell them the things they want to hear. No doubt after the councillors returned her words were then interpreted for the common man to understand?"

"As you say her ramblings were far too obscure for anyone to understand. The learned members of the council deliberated for days over the meanings."

"You mean they worked for days to make their interpretations seem reasonable to other people."

Kirukana thought for a while about this before finally nodding slowly.

"They said that a group of clerics lead by a man of dubious loyalty would join with the team of soldiers sent to collect the sword, so they decided this would be me and mine, and they added you to my team so that you could report the true extent of my heresy, and that of Kevana?"

"That is indeed their intention, though it has been known for many years that the sword would not be simple to collect, not just it's guardian, but the fact that it would get loose in the world, for a while at least. The council knew they could do little about this but hope to recover the sword before any serious damage is done."

"He has been reporting on us." snapped Kevana, reaching for his sword.

"Almost certainly." said Worandana as he laid a hand gently on Kevana's sword arm. "And he's been telling them things that will not make us look good in their eyes."

"What is your intention?" snarled Kevana.

"My initial thought is to simple take his head, but then I feel that head could be of use to us."

"How? He tells our every move."

"There has to be some way to use that to our advantage."

"We can't trust him ever. He will always report to them, we cannot stop that, nor can he lie to them, he doesn't have the sort of mind that can do that, if he did they wouldn't have assigned him here."

"No one can lie with their mind." said Kirukana.

"Generally, that statement is true." said Worandana, "However there are exceptions, some people can make themselves believe anything they want, and that belief is transmitted with their thoughts."

"I have never heard of such a thing."

"And that means it can't be true?"

"Well the teachings say that a mind can never lie."

"And that means it can't be true?"

"I have never heard of a mind that can lie."

"See Kevana, even a well-trained dog like this one can be taught to think, all it takes is the right incentive."

"You hope to teach him to be one of us, not just some tool of the council?" demanded Kevana.

"It would be the best way for him to learn, but it has to be his decision. Well Kirukana?"

"You want me to change everything I believe in?"

"No. All I want is for you to think about the reasons behind the things you have been taught. Much of the current teachings are about control of firstly, knowledge, and secondly, the people."

"You actually believe that?"

"How can I believe anything else? What you have told us today has only reinforced my belief. The council want to control the whole world, but first they have to control our god, one sect are looking for favours, the other will use the sword as a threat, they will control Zandaar and thereby the world."

"Is there something wrong with our god ruling the whole world?"

"In itself, no. But the council want control for themselves, not for Zandaar."

"They are the representatives of Zandaar."

"They may have been such in the past, but now they are only looking after their own interests."

"Surely Zandaar has the overriding control, he must know what they are doing, and he will guide them in the direction he wants them to go?"

"Where does Zandaar get his information?"

"He is all seeing, he knows everything."

"If that was true then why set a guard over the sword? He had no idea when it would be liberated from its prison, he had to use human guards, but he knew that he had to have this sword, he went to extraordinary lengths to ensure it would be delivered straight to him, and still he failed."

"It wasn't Zandaar that failed, it was Kevana." Kirukana looked round suddenly, realising the true extent of his words, expecting to see swords raised to take his life.

"Your mouth is almost certain to get you killed someday." whispered Kevana. "But not by my hand today, your death is Worandana's responsibility."

"Kevana did everything a man could, and more, men died trying to retrieve that sword. And more most certainly will. You may even be one of them. Now I have a serious question for you, did you see any of the unedited pronouncements of Mauraid?"

"No I didn't, but what do you know of the ramblings of a mad woman?"

"A mad woman who has been known to be stunningly accurate."

"You would believe her?"

"Not without supporting evidence, her insights can be helpful."

"Sorry only the council saw the unedited materials."

"We'll just have to labour on with what we know, and get that sword when the chance presents itself."

"It's more than just the sword now." Said Kevana,

"Yes, there is Gorgana to see to." Muttered Worandana.

"Another example of your failures." Said Kirukana.

"You really should think before you speak." snapped Worandana reaching for his sword. Kirukana made no motion at all, Kevana slammed the sword back into it's scabbard and turned away.

"We need to be after those thieves as soon as we can, we have to be out of this village before mid-morning, so everyone who is not cooking, get to work." Kevana's voice was so loud that Anya turned around from the other side of the green and paused for a moment before she moved out of their view.

The monks set to work, tents collapsed, and horses were loaded, a hasty meal was eaten and then they mounted their somewhat skittish horses and trooped slowly out of the village, out the southern gate, and onto the sparsely travelled road, more used to the hooves of cattle than the steel of horseshoes. There was little conversation, they had little to say, Alverana rode alongside Kevana, he was slumped in his saddle, nothing like his usual self at all, Kevana was worried that his friend may have suffered some permanent damage from the scattering of his mind.

"How are you feeling?" he asked. Alverana turned slowly towards the older man.

"I feel a little thin, is the only way to describe it, like butter spread over too much bread. I think I'm going to need some time to get everything back together again. That was one hell of a shock you know."

"I cannot imagine how that must have felt. How can I help you?"

"I think I just need some time to meditate, I need to find my way back to who I am, it should be easy enough, I just need to get the focus back."

"Once we are away from these people, then we'll have a rest, after sundown, I think. We have to make some attempt to kill Gorgana tonight, so rest as much as you can today, the others can take care of the scouting for a day or two, about time they did some of that."

"It's not like it's going to be difficult, after all we know where they are going." Alverana turned away and looked down at the horn of his saddle, almost as if he was asleep, rocking slowly to the motions of the horse. Kevana really wanted to be moving at more than a walk but knew that the slow pace would improve their recuperation, and by the evening they would be much more like their normal energy levels, it would be a long and hard search, which would hopefully end in Gorgana's death. Despite the slow rocking of the horse underneath him, Alverana retreated into a meditative trance, returning as he usually did to his forest stronghold, that warm green woodland, that was his ultimate sanctuary. From the dappled sunlight he gained both energy and surety, he needed to be certain that he was still himself, still whole and alive. Searching through the grove he found everything to be in its place, and he took heart from this, while his grove remained his strength would be renewed.

"We need to pick up the pace." said Worandana, to Kevana, staring pointedly at Alverana's slumped form.

"Not until he is feeling better, then we can push on, he needs to rest."

"He can rest when the rest of us do."

"No. We are going to need him tonight, before we make camp. He brings a lot of power to our circle, and he is probably the best searcher here, now that Gorgana is gone."

"Apostana is a good searcher."

"He is more like a soldier than a scholar, but he doesn't make any real effort to show himself."

"He has power, and a very quick mind, he knows much that even I don't understand, and has proved himself to be a good searcher in the past."

"At what range? We are all working at our limits here, for all we know the thieves have been riding all night."

"No, it was just before dawn when Namdarin attacked Crathen. He cannot have done that from the back of a horse. They must have been resting then at least. Range is very important, we need to be closer to them than we are, and we are losing ground with every passing moment."

"Alverana needs to recover, then we can move faster, but not until. Tonight, we can test out Apostana as searcher, see if he can find Gorgana, it should be easier as we know roughly which direction they have gone."

"But only if the information we have can be trusted. Do you trust this Crathen?"

"Not entirely, he thinks he is telling us the truth, and they trusted him before he came to us, so he can be trusted, but very soon his information is going to be out of date. Then he is of no use to us."

"His connection to the woman, can still be of use to us, we could even train him to be one of us."

"What are the chances of him having the talent, even in its weakest forms?"

"Same as the rest of us."

"Most of us come from families with priests already in them. This talent of ours runs in families as you well know."

"Maybe he has some latent talent that we can use, you may have noticed, we are running out of men here."

"How could I not? Most of them were mine to start with. You have only lost one."

"No. One dead, one traitor, that's two."

"Sorry I forgot about Helvana."

"He may have been a pain but was one of us."

"Every group has its pains. Even mine."

"Yours seems to work so well though."

"All I need are fighters, they need a firm hand, you need people with brains, capable of learning such mysteries, mine can't do that, but they will die for the cause, given a physical foe they are second to none."

"We have a long way to go before we have a physical foe, they are a long way off yet. You think your men could deal with the thieves, given the difference in numbers?"

"I am certain, or they will die trying."

"Crathen." shouted Worandana. "Come here." Crathen dropped back from his place in the column and fell in beside Worandana.

"What can you tell me about our enemies?" Demanded Worandana, looking up at Crathen, who sat much higher in his saddle than did the elderly monk, the grassy peaks of the valley behind his head.

"Not much more than I already have, Namdarin is in charge, most of the time. He is intent on your destruction, all of you, and your god. He has sworn such. The soldiers are along for the loot, perhaps, their motives aren't actually all that clear. Jayanne owes her life and the liberation of her village to Namdarin, he killed the Zandaar priest that had taken over the village. Granger I think feels that this is his last chance to do something meaningful with his life. The new man, Brank, I have no idea about."

"What power does this Namdarin have?"

"He has the sword and a bow, that I think used to belong to one of the old gods, I don't think he has any magic as such, other than the fact that he seems to come back from the dead."

"No one can come back from the dead." laughed Kevana.

"He can, the others have told of it. The Zandaar from the village killed him in a dream, and they took his body out of the village, into the wilderness. Within the day he returned."

"How can that be?"

"Don't ask me, the way Jayanne tells the tale, they dropped his body off in the forest and moved many miles away, after dawn they released his horse and sometime later he rode into their camp, ate and went back to the village to kill the priest."

"What about Jayanne?"

"Her axe is dangerous, it seems to have the power to heal and kill, either that or it merely thirsts for blood, I have seen it absorb spilled blood from a wound, and I am told that when it cuts, it always comes out of the wound clean, it's a little strange."

"Sounds like some form of magical blade to me." said Petrovana.

"Heresy!" snapped Kirukana. "All power comes from Zandaar!"

"Kirukana." said Worandana, very quietly. "Do be quiet. Even you should understand by now that dogma can only take a person so far in this world." He turned back to Crathen. "Carry on, any other weapons of note?"

"Jayanne carries a bow, but it appears to be normal, quite powerful, but nothing special. The soldiers carry simple weapons, swords, knives, they don't have bows, they each have some armour, but nothing major, just chain mail with some plate."

"What about magical abilities?" Worandana glared at Kirukana daring him to say anything. The younger man simply turned away.

"Granger carries a staff that seems to be very powerful, he uses some form of magic to charge it. The same is true for the sword and axe, they carry a reservoir of energy. Though I have not seen them discharge this power, Granger's staff throws bolts of energy that can kill. Namdarin talks to horses and Kern has an affinity for all animals."

"This is ridiculous." said Kirukana. "These things are clearly impossible. Magical power cannot be stored, it must be live and in motion. Talks to horses! Gibberish!"

"Kirukana." snapped Worandana. "Just because something is outside your experience doesn't mean it is impossible."

"Power cannot be stored. This is one of the basic rules of our faith."

"Explain the lightning stone. It has stored power for hundreds of years, and though it has given up much in the last few days, it will continue to recharge itself at every opportunity. If what Anya tells us is true, we didn't make any real impression in its reserves, despite the huge amount of energy we used."

"What can a mere woman know about magic?"

"Kirukana. Be silent. You are simply going over the same dogma, time and again, you wont see that anything beyond your extensive knowledge can exist. You are a fool, and rapidly becoming tiresome."

"By far the most powerful weapon they have is Gorgana." said Kevana.

"And he carries that modified staff." agreed Worandana. "We are going to have some real opposition when we catch up with them.

"Perhaps we should pick up some help along the way?" asked Petrovana.

"We can't. We're alone. Our own people will be hunting us by now, we have been absent far too long, and suffered too many loses."

"We need some help." said Briana. "The powers just keep stacking up with our enemies, even if we catch them they're going to be too strong for us."

"Nonsense." said Kevana. "They may have some power, but they lack our training, we will catch them and destroy them. Though I do feel a change of tactics coming on. I had planned on taking these thieves and skinning them alive over a slow fire. Now I think we should call down the black fire on them, from a distance. The sword will survive that, won't it?" he turned to Worandana.

"Most metals survive the black fire." said Worandana. "The really soft ones, can soften and flow a little, but even lead tends to hold some of its shape under the effects of black fire. So the sword should do fine."

"Then we can take the sword of Zandaar home and be heroes." said Petrovana.

"It's not the sword of Zandaar, it belongs to Xeron." said Crathen.

"Lies." shouted Kirukana. "The sword is Zandaars, stolen by some heretics."

"Fool." stormed Worandana. "Can you learn nothing? Don't you realise that you cannot even hear what people are saying if you are spouting your own dogma incessantly? Be quiet, and learn something for a change." He turned to Crathen. "How do you know this?"

"Namdarin says he has spoken to Xeron in a dream, or an hallucination, which ever. Xeron told him about the sword, and his oath, and his quest."

"That is interesting." Worandana glanced at Kevana, then nodded towards Kirukana, just as the monk was taking in a deep breath, Kevana's knife pressed lightly against his throat, and strangled murmur was all that issued from his mouth, a flashing and angry stare which had no effect, the movement of the horses made his situation even more dangerous. "I thought the old gods had long ago left this plane." he continued.

"They had, but they seemed to think that Zandaar was going with them."

"Why would Zandaar have left, he has so many followers?"

"That may be the problem, he has too many followers, but the rest of the old gods decided that it was time for humans to move on, it's time for the younger gods to take over." Kirukana gurgled in protest, but got no further, Kevana simply pressed the knife harder against his skin, a thin red line showed the limit of Kirukana's resistance.

"It could even be that the presence of Xeron's sword in the plane is holding the old god here, and presumably Zandaar as well." Worandana paused for a moment, holding up a hand to prevent any interruptions. Kevana relaxed his knife hand for a moment, distracted by the thoughts rushing around in his head.

"This is heresy." said Kirukana, before Kevana's knife strangled his voice again. Kirukana looked surprised when Kevana pulled the knife away from his throat, he was even more surprised when the heavy hilt smashed into his solar plexus, driving all the air from his body, this surprise was short lived, as Kirukana slumped forwards in his saddle the hilt connected with his head, and he passed out, which was for the best really as the fall from the horse would have been very painful. Worandana scowled as he pulled his horse to a stop.

"Sorry." said Kevana. "He's such a pompous ass, he really needs to learn when to shut the hell up."

"Agreed. Apostana, you wait here with him, give him a few minutes then wake him up and get him back on his horse, catch us up when you can." Worandana laid his heels to his horse's side and walked on, Kevana fell in alongside his old friend.

"What do you think?" asked Worandana.

"With this sword, Zandaar may be able to banish the other gods entirely."

"Alternatively, they could banish him by using this man as their tool."

"Yet another, the council could take control of the sword, and use it as they see fit, they could banish Zandaar and take all his power onto themselves."

"Yet another." replied Kevana. "One faction hands over the sword, and gets the other faction killed off as a display of gratitude, they then become completely dominant and take control of the whole nation."

"I have a seriously heretical suggestion."

"Go on."

"We take the sword and destroy it. Our enemy is intent on destroying Zandaar with the sword, even if we take the sword from him, and I believe he will not survive, the sword still exists for someone to take up and kill Zandaar. Even if we give it to Zandaar he may lose control of it and have it turned against him by a 'friend'."

"Our god wants us to bring him the sword and you are going to deliberately disobey?"

"I only suggest and alternative course of action, we now know more about that damned sword than any of us ever has. Zandaars secrecy was, I believe, specifically to stop us learning about the sword and even considering any action other than running straight to Zandaarkoon, waving the thing aloft."

"Is it possible that this is the only tool in the world that can kill a god?"

"It's possible, it could also be that this is the easiest tool to kill our god. Another tool could be made to perform the same task, but it may take more effort, whereas the sword of Xeron is ready made for the job."

"Then why are they going to the elves, what are they after?"

"Crathen." called Worandana. "What are they going to the elves for?"

"I have no idea, I wasn't really listening when it was discussed. Something from a dead elvish king, or maybe not dead."

"A trinket from a dead or not dead king?" said Kevana, Crathen simply nodded and raised his eyebrows. Worandana shook his head slowly. "Either way," said Kevana, "We are going to stop them. I am going to take that sword from his dead hand."

"Then we can make the decisions." agreed Worandana, lapsing into silence and glancing back to see black robed shapes catching them up.

"Do you believe that Kirukana is ever going to learn?" asked Kevana, following his friends glance.

"Who can tell. He has been able to learn many things and managed to walk the tightrope between the two factions, he should be able to learn more. The problem is convincing him to think."

"Perhaps this is how he has managed to stay alive within the council, they don't believe he can think, and so can be no threat to either faction."

"Or perhaps, his enthusiasm for dogma will keep us from finding out what is really happening?"

"Circles are so much a part of the way we work we have started to think in them." laughed Kevana.

"Possibly." Worandana chuckled. "But our circles always have a point, and generally an end." Kevana looked away for a moment, scanning the horizon, for nothing in particular.

"Worandana." he spoke softly, looking back into the old man's eyes. "Is it possible to create the perfect circle?"

"There have been many attempts, some more successful than the others, there are just so many factors that affect the performance of a power circle, the number of participants, the skill levels of them, cycle rate, and all it takes is one mistake or one person to miss time the pass off and the whole thing just falls apart, sometimes fatally, we can generate a lot of energy, but always at a risk."

"Here's a strange thought," said Kevana, "that stone has a huge reserve of energy, just waiting to be tapped, why can't we create something similar?"

Worandana looked quickly around, checking to see how close some members of the group were.

"Don't even think that too loudly." he whispered. "Though not actually prohibited, even thinking it can get you a nice warm bonfire."

"What do you mean?"

"I have known a few who have looked into researching energy storage, and everyone has died, some just disappeared, some committed some act of heresy, some died in accidents, but all died."

"Why?"

"I'm not sure, but I have a theory, one that I am never going to test, or even think about too much."

"What theory?"

Worandana looked around again, before speaking very quietly.

"Zandaar is afraid that we may be able to accumulate enough energy to kill him."

"Surely not?"

"It's a theory, that is all."

"Have you any evidence?"

"Dead researchers not enough?"

"Perhaps we should try something, after all the thieves have some source of stored power, I have come up against that staff of Granger's and it beat me in a heartbeat."

"We have no experience as to how this could work, and no information. We have been specifically denied this knowledge for a reason, whatever it is. The risks are too great."

"When we meet them, you can take on Granger and his staff, let's see how you fare. Here's another question, how is it that Granger is labelled 'Charlatan'? Everyone knows this to be true, but where did this 'knowledge' come from?"

"Granger's presence has been known for many years, and he has been designated charlatan for as long, I haven't wasted any time researching him, nor I believe has anyone else, perhaps this is the plan, maybe the council made this decree some years ago, to stop our people challenging Granger. Can you imagine the attraction of taking on a powerful magician and beating him? Many up and coming clerics would be rushing into the mountains to try out their power against this heretic. However, if he is a charlatan, where is the incentive?"

"But why make this declaration?"

"Perhaps some young fools did take him on and died in the attempt. Maybe they were followed by some older fools, who met the same fate. Eventually the council would have to act to cut the losses, his home was naturally defended, and obviously he is quite powerful."

"How can he be powerful?"

"Did you see the power the three of them expended to bring down that cave exit? The blue flash from Granger's staff was brighter than the sun. That was a lot of power to let loose in one hit. Somehow, I don't think it was the first time he had hit something that hard. Imaging that blast when you are trying to climb that damned scree."

"So, charlatan he isn't, power he has, how can we beat him? We are few, and forgive me for stating the obvious, every time we come up against these people we end up so tired that we can barely walk. When Gorgana switched, there was energy flying around, just everywhere, but we were wiped out. When Alverana got scattered, we recovered him, but again wiped out. We need some sort of strategy."

"I agree. How can we fight these people?"

"We will have to reduce their numbers from afar, if we can kill some of their major members, Granger, Gorgana and this Namdarin, that Crathen speaks of, then we stand some form of chance of getting close enough to kill the rest and take the sword."

"I know that it is hard to believe, but what if Crathen speaks the truth and Namdarin cannot die?"

"If he is the last one left alive, then I am fairly sure we can kill him for at least enough time to take the sword. It seems like he stays dead for at least a little while, perhaps even hours."

"Feels like a plan of sorts, so who's first?" asked Worandana.

"Gorgana, of course, a lesson must be taught, and by Zandaar he will learn."

"I presume we are going to try for another sundown." smiled Worandana.

"Or sunrise." laughed Kevana. "Fabrana!" he yelled. "Pick up the pace, we need to do some catching up." Fabrana waved then kicked his horse into a fast trot, the rest of the column following suit, Alverana's horse was pulled along somewhat reluctantly with the flow. Turning slightly east of south they travelled through the open scrub at a reasonable pace, the movement of the horses and the noise of their gear made conversation impossible, so the priests thoughts turned inwards.

Kevana's thoughts turned his friend Alverana. 'How would I have been if Alverana had died? That would have been a hell of a problem, I can't really imagine my life without him in it. We have been together so many years, and through so much, we just keep on surviving, no matter what the world sends against us, we always win through in the end, but this latest mission has taken such a toll, and cost us so much, to lose Alverana is completely unimaginable.' Kevana looked across at his friend slumped in his saddle, he reached over and placed a hand on his friend's shoulder, Alverana slowly looked up.

"How are you doing?"

"I'm not sure." answered Alverana, "I still feel more than a little strange, like some of me has gone missing, but I can't find any gaps in my memories or anything like that, I just feel very odd."

"You've always been odd." laughed Kevana.

"Must be, to hang around with you weirdos."

"But you're going to be all right?"

"I think so, just a little difficult to get any focus right now."

"We have to catch up with those thieves and Gorgana, so focus on that, should give you something to think about, something better that dwelling on what might have been."

"How do you know what I was thinking about?"

"Because I was thinking the same things. Losing you would have been just one step too far."

"Losing me was what I was struggling with, but you came for me, and we will be fine."

"I'm just happy I found you before I ran out of power."

"Would you have given up?"

"No. I would have brought you back or died."

"I'm not sure that is a good thing."

"Why?"

"That sort of determination should only be for Zandaar, to give up your life for anyone else is regarded as heresy by some." Alverana glanced in the direction of Kirukana.

"I have come to see that what they think is of no importance to me. None at all."

Alverana reached across his body and rested a hand on Kevana's.

"Rest assured, that had the situation been reversed, I would have done the same." The look that passed between the two said far more than any words.

"Rest my friend, it's not yet midday and we will be making an attempt on the traitor around sundown, I really need your strength behind me when we start that search."

"Just keep us moving in the right direction, we should be fairly close anyway if Namdarin managed to invade Crathen's dream."

"Somehow, I cannot believe we are that close, I feel that we are so much further away than we could ever reach into someone's dream. This Namdarin character doesn't seem to understand the rules of dream invasion."

"How can he, if no-one has explained them to him?" laughed Alverana.

"What are you saying? No one has told him of the limitations, so he just exceeds them anyway?"

"Basically, would you attempt what he did this morning when he must be some days ride away?"

"Of course not, I know it to be impossible."

"He doesn't have that knowledge, so it's not impossible just difficult, obviously not too difficult."

"Didn't you say you saw a shadow moving around the camp before this happened?"

"Yes, and?"

"Perhaps he wasn't that far away, if he had travelled in the other plane, and was actually in camp, but not physically, then his essence was here, though his actual body was elsewhere. Would that count as being nearby?"

"This is starting to make my head hurt." said Alverana. "Ask one of the damned clerics."

"I'll do just that. You rest we have about half a day before we go hunting for Gorgana."

Alverana simply nodded as Kevana dropped back down the line to were Worandana was next to Kirukana.

"Worandana." he said, "Is it possible to travel on the other plane a great distance, then invade someone's dreams?"

"I have never heard of such a thing." said Worandana.

"Impossible." said Kirukana, "all the teachings say that physical proximity is very important when taking over a dreamer."

"There you go again." said Worandana. "Just because the teachings say, it must be true, do you have any evidence, personal evidence?"

"Well, no, not really, I've never been very good with dreams."

"That's because you lack the necessary imagination, it is impossible to take over someone's dreams if you cannot at least match their imagination."

"Why do you ask?"

"Because Alverana says he saw a shape on the other plane that went into Crathen's tent, this was most likely Namdarin, if what we are told is true. So from a projection he invaded Crathen's dream, is this likely?"

"Kirukana," said Worandana, "if you say impossible I will slap you. Given the information we have that is the most likely explanation. Though it does go against things we have been taught."

"Fine." said Kevana. "How can we use this new knowledge to our advantage?"

"Any new knowledge has to be approved by the council." said Kirukana.

"Write them a long letter, detailing all that you have learned, and once they deny permission to use this new technique, we'll have to stop using it." snapped Worandana. Then he turned to Kevana. "Any of your people skilled with planar projections?"

"Swords, that's were their skills lie."

"I had two, Helvana was good, and travelled far, though more than a little unfocused, Gorgana, he was learning. I have tried, but I am told that my self is too rooted in the here and now to be able to travel on the other plane. Apostana, he's a good man, but not in the required fashion. How about Alverana? If he's sees into the other plane, then he should be able to travel there?"

"We nearly lost him already today, I don't want to risk his life again."

"The risks can be controlled to some extent, we can hold onto enough power to bring him back again, if he can do it, then he most likely our best bet."

"After this morning he may not be able to see the other plane, let alone travel there."

"Again, that's up to him."

"What could he do if he could travel to where ever they are?"

"Even travelling there would be difficult. Though there is some correlation between the other plane and reality, it's not always easy to see how the two fit together. How people appear doesn't always match who you think they are."

"So how did Namdarin find us?"

"The lightning stone, it must have really prominent presence on the other plane, it is, after all, a very powerful artefact. He probably tracked it."

"But how is that done? I have had no real training but have no clues as to how this is performed."

"I have an idea, but you're not going to like it."

"Pray tell."

Worandana looked hard at Kirukana before proceeding.

"Most of our magic is very simple, even the chants, herbs, and images, are mainly to focus the mind of the user. Do you understand?"

"Of course, get on with it."

"Our magic relies on the belief of the user, you believe the silver flame will be fire when it reaches the target your mind has specified, and that is what happens. Do you agree?"

"Of course, get to the point old man."

"If you believe it can't happen, then it won't."

"So you have said, I don't see the point though."

"Kirukana has, haven't you?"

"Yes, old man, and your words are heresy."

"Careful how you spread those charges around, you may get caught yourself."

"I don't understand." said Kevana.

"Think about it." said Worandana. "What is the simplest way to limit the effectiveness of our magic."

"To believe it cannot work."

"Or?"

"To promote the belief that it cannot work. Teach that something cannot happen, and it can't."

"You get there in the end."

"Are you suggesting that the council are restricting our abilities by training us to believe things cannot be done?"

"Either the council or someone else."

"There is only one other." whispered Kevana.

"Heresy." mumbled Kirukana.

"But why?"

"Perhaps they want to keep certain powers unto themselves, or himself."

"Again, why?"

"I can think of only one reason, fear."

"Heresy." said Kirukana.

"Kirukana, think for a change and play a different tune."

"So." said Kevana. "What could it be that we aren't supposed to believe can be done and why?"

"It looks like planar travel is one of them, as Namdarin has proved it can be done and he affected a person at extreme range, something we are told cannot happen."

"I keep asking the same question, I'm beginning to feel a little stupid, why?"

"You're the strategist, you tell me."

"The council members are very close to our god, in daily communion with him, they must have a large presence on the other plane, and should be easy to find, if their dreams can be breached from the other plane, they could be killed from anywhere, if dreams can only be breached by someone local they have less area to protect for people who mean them harm.

"An interesting hypothesis. Care to test it?"

"How?"

"Travel to Zandaarkoon, find a member of the council, have a chat in his dream. Simple really."

"You can't do that." said Kirukana, "You can't just invade their minds. They are important people."

"Kevana could report his findings about the sword, who's sword it really is, he could tell about who currently has it, and where they are going. All this information could be important to these important people."

"No, you can't."

"Why?"

"Because I haven't been in direct contact in weeks and haven't been able to contact any locals to relay my messages since we left Mount Indran."

"I see." Worandana laughed. "Kevana would make you look useless, I think your life expectancy is most likely linked to your usefulness."

"I have been told to keep them informed, failure is punishable by death."

"And still you took the assignment?"

"Yes, the possibilities for advancement seemed really good at the time."

"And now?" asked Kevana.

"I begin to feel that I have been set up to fail. I don't believe that I will even be able to meet the requirements that they have set, at least not to their satisfaction, they can simple decide that I have not given them enough information, so any failure is mine, not theirs."

"But failure is death?"

"Yes."

"You may be right about being set up." Kevana laughed. "Once they had whatever information you could provide, you become expendable, or is that immediately expendable, you've been expendable since the day you took the assignment. Seems to me that dealing with these councillors is a dangerous business."

"Yes." Kirukana's head fell forwards, the realisation that he had been duped by the people he believed in shook his world to it's very foundations.

"Go and talk to Alverana." said Worandana. "Leave us for a while."

Kevana pushed his horse forwards up the line, and settled in alongside Alverana.

"How are you feeling now?"

"A little more together, it's really hard to put it into words, but I think I'm better."

"When you saw Namdarin on the other plane, what did he look like?"

"Just a black shapeless shadow, no human form, and somewhat transparent. We are only believing it was Namdarin because of what Crathen has said. It could have been a coincidence, just a passing shadow."

"Are these things common on that plane?"

"No things are common there, everything is jumbled and mixed up, hey, I was talking to a rabbit in a waistcoat that didn't like badgers, so don't ever think about common."

"Worandana thinks he may have used the lightning stone as a target to aid his travelling, could that be right?"

"It certainly scatters a lot of light on the plane, so it is possible."

"Could someone use the sword to track them?"

"Possibly, I've not seen it there, but it is a magical artefact, so it should be usable, there is a better one though."

"What?"

"The staff that used to belong to Worandana, though modified quite extensively, we have all worked with it, and I don't believe Gorgana would leave it behind, after all he didn't leave it here."

"Could it be classed as magical?"

"I would think so, it carried a huge charge for a short time, so perhaps it still has something left."

"Could you track it?"

"Why me?"

"To be honest, other plane work is beyond most of us, it appears the only ones good at it were Helvana and one other."

"Gorgana?"

"Yes."

"I really don't want to even look into the other realm, let alone walk there right now."

"I understand, we will maintain a constant watch and be holding enough power to pull you back if need be. Please my friend. Our numbers keep dwindling and the power of our searches falls, we need accurate information with the minimum expenditure of our reserves."

"But you are willing to risk my mind?"

"Only if you believe you will survive."

"According to the teachings belief is everything."

"We've just had that discussion with Kirukana, he really didn't like the outcome."

"How so?"

"He's just worked out the council may have set him up to fail, and so die, he's likely to be carrying information they won't want public."

"That must have been a fun conversation."

"Actually, he had very little to say."

"Now, that does surprise me." Alverana laughed. "Let me rest a while and I'll try later to first look in to the other plane, then maybe travel to where they are."

"Right, we will be watching over you, you know that."

Alverana nodded slowly, then pulled his hood forwards over his face, lowering his head he left the horse to find its own way, and settled into his own thoughts. Not quite the sunny place they usually are, a much darker and colder existence inside. The problem of the morning caused some serious effects to his inner peace, there was a level of fear in the background of everything going on. Alverana focused on the fear, tracking it slowly through the paths of his brain, hunting out in all the dark corners where it was hiding, by shining the light of reason on it, he was able to gather it all together. 'Fear is the little death that leads to total obliteration, I will face my fear, I will let it pass over me and through me, and when it is gone I will know its name and it will have no power over me.' Gradually the light returned to his thoughts, and inner peace was restored, though the scattering of the morning was still a fact that couldn't be denied, fear of it would not affect Alverana in any major way, a little wariness is perfectly acceptable.

Returning to his centre of inner peace Alverana slowly opened the inner eye, to see into the other plane. A small shudder of apprehension shook him as the bright and confusing colours impinged on his mind. Many miles behind him the lightning stone was casting beams of light into the sky, and all around the somewhat distorted world. Somehow, it's light seemed quieter than it had been, like it was settling down, now that they had left. 'Why didn't I see those beams this morning, there was only a glow from the stone?' Looking forwards again, he noticed that all the members of his group were a little agitated, perhaps frightened, except one that was behind him. This one was dark, his shape barely human, roiling and twisting, blue and dark violet, colours boiling to the surface, to be subsumed by the deepest black. This person was having a seriously hard time dealing with whatever was going on inside his mind. Perhaps Worandana should be told. Later maybe. The horses were still horse shaped, but seemed to be working hard, the pace set was hard on them, but they were relatively happy, they had people around them, and this made them feel so much better, the predators stayed away and the fire was warm and comforting, though only a moment away from conflagration, the control the humans had over all their enemies made them happy to serve. Survival being the strongest instinct, they knew that the foals would be born and protected, and that is all that is important for them. The harshness of the life, the fatalities caused by the service, these things weren't important, the herd lives on, and grows, in numbers and strength, the herd is what counts, local and extended. Alverana snapped back to the real world. 'Extended?' What did this thought from the horses mean?

"Kevana." said Alverana, raising his head and turning towards his friend. "What does a horse mean when he says extended herd?"

"Horses talk?"

"No, but they think, and you would be surprised how much they think."

"What have you been drinking?"

"No. I've been looking into the other plane, and I have information, Kirukana, is struggling with something, his colours are all confused, the horses are working hard but happy, because the herd is doing well, some of this makes sense but some doesn't."

"Kirukana does have some serious decisions to make about his life, we are hoping he'll sort it out and end up on our side, I don't think he as yet understands, it's our side or dead, but then the other side has him dead as well. As to horses and herd, I have no idea at all. Perhaps you should ask them."

"Who, in their right mind would talk to horses?"

"What, pray tell, is right mind? Consider everything that has happened recently? Nothing makes any sense at all."

"Agreed. I'll just ask the horses, shall I?"

"At this point I have no issues with you talking to horses."

"Fine, I'll ask them."

Alverana pulled his hood forwards again and relaxed into the mental state necessary to reach into the other plane. Reaching out with his mind he focussed on the horse underneath him, the soft red and orange colours showed him that the horse was relatively happy, once contact was established he attempted to communicate with the horse, it was a struggle to make any sense as to what the horse was really feeling, let alone thinking, but the impressions came in more as blurry pictures than anything else. Happy horses rolling on green pastures, and foals kicking their heels in the air. Reaching through the horse he felt the rest of the horses in their party, the colours and sensations flooded his brain, it took him many minutes to sort them out, each horse has its own image of itself and its place in the herd, each has its own colour, He followed the horses down the line to the one that was at the front, this one was calm and clear what it should be doing, leading the local herd, at this time he was alpha male, but that could easily change as the humans were actually in charge, lead seemed to change for no reason that the horse could ever hope to understand, so he didn't try, he was just happy to be there leading for the moment. Alverana reached further for the 'extended' herd, and to his surprise he found them, off to the north in the mountains was another group, wild and free, eating fresh grass and watching out for dangers, the lead stallion questioned Alverana as to any predators in the area, or weather conditions that should be avoided, having nothing to report Alverana moved on. Reaching further away, he found a group of horses walking slowly through a forest, keeping careful watch for any strangers around them. Alverana left the distant group and returned to his own, focusing down on the horse beneath him. Finally, he broke the link and lifted his head.

"Kevana." he said, causing his friend to turn towards him. "I have found them, they are in a forest."

"How do you know?"

"The horses told me, they are walking carefully through an old forest, very alert for strangers."

"Where is this forest?"

"That's the only problem, the horses have no real sense of distance or direction, or maybe I'm just not reading the signs properly, perhaps that will come with practise."

"How many are there?"

"It is very difficult to tell, they are far away, the contact is very weak, but far away could be just over the next rise. I just have nothing to scale this against. I think there are fourteen horses in their group, not all with riders, but I could be wrong. I could even be looking at an entirely different group of travellers. But someone is definitely moving carefully through a forest."

"Could you get a direction to guide a search?"

"I don't think so, our directions don't really mean much to horses."

"What about their directions, can you make any sense of how they navigate?"

"Not really. I'm not being much of a help am I."

"Perhaps once we get closer things will be easier. Rest for a while. I'll have a talk to Worandana, see if he has any ideas." Kevana slowed his horse again to fall back down to where Worandana was having a deep discussion with Kirukana.

"We may have a way to track them, Alverana is still working out some problems but we believe they are currently walking through a forest, on very high alert. Like they are frightened of meeting someone there."

"How does he know this?" asked Worandana.

"This is where things get difficult, Alverana believes he has talked to the horses that they are riding."

Kirukana snorted and drew a deep breath.

"What have I said?" snapped Worandana.

Kirukana spluttered before speaking. "The word impossible will cost me my head."

"See, you can think before speaking, it's a habit you really should take to heart."

Kirukana nodded before continuing. "I have never heard of people talking to horses, at least none that got sensible answers."

"Better." said Worandana, he turned to Kevana, "I am attempting to train him, if he can stop the proclamations he might just keep his head a while longer."

"It might work, if he can do it when you're not around to remind him."

"I am here." muttered Kirukana, "I mean, talking horses, can no one else see how ridiculous this sounds?"

"In some ways Kirukana you are right." said Kevana. "but when Alverana tells me he has been communicating with the herd mind of the horses, then I believe him. No matter what you have been taught, we have evidence and that is enough for me. I don't need an edict from the council to tell me that something is possible, all I need is to see it happen. Here's a strange thought for you Kirukana, if the council have made one of their edicts, and you don't know about it, because you have been out of touch for so long, are you still guilty of heresy for not following the latest proclamation?"

Worandana laughed out loud. Kevana looked at him and frowned.

"I had just made a very similar observation, though mine was a little more extreme."

"Not sunrise again old man?"

"It always creates the best debates."

"You really need some new ideas now and again."

"I have plenty of new ideas, but someone just keeps declaring them heretical."

"Admit it Worandana, most of your 'new' ideas are actually old ones that most people have forgotten about."

"Many are old ideas put together in new ways, there are advances to be made, but it is not always easy for the leaders to handle all these new ideas."

"Like talking horses?" asked Kirukana.

"Yes, talking horses is definitely going to be difficult for many to accept, but it could easily be true, herd animals do have the ability to communicate within the herd, I have never thought that horses could over any distance, but I have no doubt they can communicate at close range. Have you?"

"What do you mean? I have never heard horses talking to each other?" asked Kirukana.

Worandana turned to Kevana. "For a person who deals with the esoteric on a daily basis he can be so literal." Turning back to Kirukana. "Have you seen a herd of horses running free? Have you ever noticed that when the herd decides to change direction, the whole herd does so at the same time? Have you seen flocks of birds performing the same feat in three dimensions? Tell me these animals aren't communicating in some way? It may be some way that invisible to us, but there is no doubt that they are communicating."

Kirukana thought for a while before answering. "I will concede that they communicate within their own species, but communicate with people? That is a huge step to take."

"Agreed. A huge step, but knowing that the communication occurs, is a small step, finding a translator, is the next, perhaps there exists such a translator somewhere in the human mind, one that most people never know about, one that takes special training to access, perhaps our own mental discipline gives us this access, who can tell."

"I don't believe it can happen, it's just not, er, something I can see."

"Don't forget the major part of our magic is belief, believe and it will happen."

"This is just too far from anything I have been taught, I just think like that." muttered Kirukana.

"Well that's not really a problem, if you can't think outside your current training, then you'll never make any new discoveries, all you have to do is believe the discoveries others make, which is what you have been doing all your life. It's a very small step for you, not only discoveries ratified by the council, but discoveries from other sources as well. Can you see that?"

"I think so, but to follow everyone's discoveries, that could lead to some serious errors."

"Agreed, learn from the mistakes and don't make them again, move on and learn new things. Doing this we can advance the magic of Zandaar, and increase his power. If we fail to advance, our magic will stagnate, and some smart and talented freelancer may come along and surpass us all. It could even be that Granger is such a one, in which case we are in some serious trouble."

"How can one man exceed the power of a god?"

"He doesn't need to, he only has to beat us. Our power is entirely our own, the only part of it that comes from Zandaar is the black fire, which is why it takes so long to conjure, and why it can only be called by those of sufficient rank, the ones Zandaar will actually listen to."

"Can't we just call the black fire down on these people?"

"Do you know where they are, and where they are going to be in the next half an hour, we need to be close to get an accurate target, which is why black fire isn't much use in battle, killing our own soldiers is considered a bad move."

"Didn't the abbot at Mount Indran call the fire down on Namdarin?"

"Yes. But he was an exceptional person, and he knew were the target was, he was outside the door of his office burning it down. His call would have been answered quickly, and accurately."

"So if we get close enough you can summon the fire to destroy them all?"

"I could try, but my request is less likely to be answered, I'm just not popular enough, either with the council or Zandaar."

"Why not?"

"I don't like the dogma enforced by the council, as you know, they know it and so treat me as a borderline heretic, they not quite summoned the courage to charge me as yet, but I am sure they will eventually, and they try to block any calls I make directly to Zandaar. So I live on my wits, and my own power, well, that of my decreasing number of subordinates."

"This whole thing is going to reflect very badly on you, isn't it?"

"Yes, but I'll go down fighting, and that is what the council fear the most, they are wondering how many of them I am going to take down with me." Worandana laughed.

"What if I was to make the request for the black fire?" asked Kirukana.

"You might stand a better chance than me, but can you perform the summoning, it's not an easy formula? Think about this, this group of thieves have between them a god's sword, another gods axe, Granger's staff, and the one that Gorgana took from us. What sort of destruction is going to occur if you burn these with the black fire? They could all explode, and that release could do untold damage. No, I don't think that is a good idea. The council will think the same, but Zandaar may not be so reluctant."

"Would Zandaar be happy with the destruction of the sword, or does he actually want it in his hand?"

"Who can tell. The watch over that tree has been there for centuries. All we know is that Zandaar wants the sword, but the council are divided."

"Whatever we decide here." said Kevana. "We cannot call the fire until we actually have a target, which we don't, this debate is pointless."

"No it's not." said Worandana. "I believe that Kirukana is finally starting to think. Anything that can promote that is always for the good."

"Until he turns us all in as heretics?"

"He may do that, but when he sees his own pyre set next to ours, he will understand."

"Sounds like a little too late to me."

"It's never too late to learn something new."

"I think that once the flames start licking around one's knees, there is nothing left to learn other than pain."

"True, but pain can be a great teacher."

"But Alverana hasn't actually got a location for them, only that they are in a forest, perhaps the forest of the elves, which still puts them days ahead of us, perhaps three, but only if we are travelling faster than they are, currently I don't believe we are, we need to be pushing on."

"Agreed, but how hard can we push the horses, or the injured?"

"Alverana seems to be recovering quite quickly, I'll talk to him, and perhaps we can move a little faster."

With this he pulled forwards until he was alongside Alverana.

"How goes it, friend?"

"Feeling better, ready for some hard riding, we have to catch them up, and I feel that we have to do it very soon, something bad is coming, something very bad."

"How do you know?"

"It's just a feeling in the air."

"Fine, keep a close eye on that feeling, I'm going to pick the pace up."

Alverana just nodded, Kevana kicked his horse to the front of the line, until he was alongside Fabrana.

"Time to move." Said Kevana. "Pick it up." Kevana kick his horse again, into a rolling canter, with the occasional gallop, when the terrain was suitable. They were running downhill through open scrubland, and so were making excellent speed, the green of the grass and the trees rushing past them, Kevana risked a look over his shoulder, to see the group strung out in a line behind the two leaders.

"Close that up, you're getting too spread out!" He yelled.

Alverana soon was right behind them, Petrovana moved up the column and took station alongside Alverana. Crathen pulled in behind Alverana, and Briana came up alongside. By this time the clerics realised that they were almost alone, Apostana was the first to reach the column, with Worandana next, leaving Kirukana taking up the rear. The new pace was such that conversation became a thing of the past, especially for the less skilled horsemen.

"Worandana." shouted Kirukana. The old man turned in his saddle. "I think that any further conversation is impossible, until we slow down." He threw back his head and laughed aloud. Worandana smiled and turned back to the front, concentrating on riding, something he knew that he wasn't exactly good at. Downhill they continued into the valley bottom, they reached the small stream, and turned downstream, it was in the general direction they needed to go, as far as they knew. The occasional group of trees slowed them down, but only briefly, in only an hour the pace was starting to show on the horses. They were blowing and sweating profusely, white foam falling from their flanks, and catching the legs of the horses behind. Kevana still didn't let the pace drop, running downstream, the open meadows made riding easy, but gradually the margins of the stream appeared to get wider, the ground more soft, the reeds higher and coarser. Very soon they were running along a greensward between huge banks of reeds, the growing scent of the bogs around them started to impinge on Kevana's senses. He pulled back on the reins, slowing the headlong pace until they were proceeding and a slow walk. The horses seemed a little happy as their breathing settled down to a more normal rate. Alverana pushed through to the front and walked alongside Kevana.

"We seem to be in a swamp."

"Obvious much?" asked Kevana.

"Sorry, but you were running so fast I didn't think you had noticed."

"The path looks firm enough."

"But we go where it wants, not where we want."

"But we don't know where we want to go."

"True, but I'd rather not have my course decided by someone else."

"It goes in the right sort of direction. South and east."

"But where to. We really have no choice at this point, we follow the path. Carefully." Alverana took the lead with these words, and stopped for a moment closed his eyes, focusing his other senses on everything that was around them. The smells of the swamps, the sounds of the birds and reptiles, the feel of the warm sun on his face. Slowly he moved forwards, still with his eyes closed, following the green path into the heart of the swamp.

CHAPTER FORTY

Kern in the lead as usual came upon a lone horseman, covered head to toe in green, his hood pulled forwards to hide his face, his longbow sat across his knees strung and ready. His horse rested quietly, occasionally shifting its weight from one foot to another, swaying from side to side. Kern signalled to others to stop and waved Namdarin forwards. Jayanne and Granger came forwards as well.

Arndrol stopped walking when his nose was almost touching the horse.

"Hello." Said Namdarin. "I am Namdarin of the house of Namdaron, we come in peace and seek aid of the elves. Can you guide us in this matter?"

"You say you come in peace but carry weapons of great power, why is this?"

"I have sworn an oath to kill a god, I am told these weapons are required for the task."

"Which god are you trying to kill?"

"Zandaar."

"There is no love for Zandaar amongst my people, even so, why should we help you?"

"Zandaar and his followers plan to make the whole world believers."

"We already have our own beliefs."

"Their plans take no notice of your current beliefs, you will follow Zandaar or you will die."

"The followers of Zandaar have been trying this for generations and have yet to make one convert."

"But how many have they killed?"

"Not as many as they hoped, nor as many as they would like, and far fewer than they think. We are a hardy people."

"Yet your numbers decline. Any deaths caused by the dark priests are reducing your numbers even more."

"How can you possibly help this?"

"It is our plan to destroy Zandaar, not the priesthood, not the city, but their god. Xeron has provided us with some weapons, and Gyara has told us that you have something that can help us. Can you take us to your leaders, so we can discuss these matters?"

"You expect to walk into our city carrying weapons of power?"

"We have no problems with elven kind, in fact we have had precious little contact with your people for many years, we have no wish to see the passing of the elves in our lifetimes, our short lifetimes, if we can stop the rapacious Zandaars, then there may be elves in these woods for many more years."

"Our numbers are declining, that is true, far too few are born, and far too many die, but the Zandaars have little effect overall, they leave us alone and we leave them alone, I feel they are just waiting for us all to die."

"We need to talk to your leaders, please take us there."

"If we refuse?"

"I believe that would be a mistake, for both our peoples."

While this conversation was going on, Gregor had dismounted and walked forwards slowly. He stepped between Namdarin and Granger, simply seeking a glimpse of an elf, something he had only heard of in books. As he came into view many things happened all at once. The elven bow snapped into the upright an arrow appeared at the string and the bow was pulled. Arndrol turned and put his body between the elf and his target.

"You bring a Zandaar into our forest?" yelled the elf. The forest around them suddenly creaked, as if a hundred longbows had been drawn. The wolf standing beside Kern ruffled it's mane to its fullest extent and growled loud and long, he was waiting for instructions, he needed to know which of the hundred targets so obvious in the greenery should be attacked first

"Hold." Came a shout from the forest off the track to the right.

A green clad elf stepped into view, threw back his hood, revealing long dark hair on a narrow head, the slightly pointed ears characteristic of the elves, large almond shaped eyes, with purple irises, and a narrow chin. He carried no bow, but a longsword hung at his side, the tip almost dragging in the dirt of the track.

"I am Gervane, why have you brought a Zandaar here?"

"My lord." said Gregor, falling to his knees. "I am an ex-zandaar, I have decided to leave that church, but have not found any new clothes as yet, I really didn't think it worth the effort until I have survived my brethren's attempt to kill me, I expect that to be sometime around sundown, my new friends have managed to keep them too tired to attack me for the last few days, but they must be rested enough to make an attempt come sundown."

"No one leaves Zandaar."

"I have, if I survive I may be the first to do so."

"How can we believe you?"

"What can I achieve by lying? You will know the truth, if any of the tales of your people are true. You have a truthsayer amongst you?"

"We do. Goldareth, come and read this black robed fool. If he lies, he dies."

"The others?" asked the first elf.

"They die too."

"How many will you lose?" demanded Namdarin, dropping the reins, and placing his hand on the hilt of the sword, Arndrol settled down, flexing knees and priming for the surge.

"Namdarin." said Gregor. "Stand down, I cannot fail any truth test they give me. For I tell nothing but the truth, that is one of the reasons I am in this tricky situation. I really struggle to tell lies. It's just part of my nature, and this was becoming a problem. Please don't worry about me."

"Gregor, you have chosen to be one of us, I would never have believed I would say this about a damned Zandaar. Gervane, you will die first, we will all die, but know this your world will end soon, and not by our hand. Stand ready." The last shouted as a command. Swords leapt to hand, Arndrol spat his bit, and shook his mane, Granger's staff spun over his head spitting blue sparks, and making ready for a huge discharge, the wolf targeted the first elf, and crouched ready to pounce. The sword of Xeron wove a blue pattern in the air. "Bring on your truthsayer and prepare to die!"

Gervane drew his sword and shouted. "Anyone shoots without my express permission will be dealt with most harshly." Facing mounted men, he knew things could go very badly very quickly. An elf came from the left side of the track, his bow strung but no arrow at the string, slowly he walked toward the kneeling from of Gregor, who despite all his protestations had a firm two handed grip on his staff, and the electric crackle of energy could clearly be heard. He was as ready as the others to kill before he died, or so it seemed.

Goldareth walked up to Gregor, now completely inside the group of armed and ready soldiers.

"Have you truly left the Zandaars, and do you wish no harm to elven kind?"

Gregor rose slowly to his feet, standing to his full height, his staff upright, one heel firmly placed on the ground, he glanced slowly around before looking into the elf's purple eyes. "Two questions, not good, one at a time is always better. I have left the Zandaars and I expect them to kill me sometime soon. I mean no harm to elven kind." He felt the inside of his skull itch, as if something was crawling around in there, a most uncomfortable feeling.

Goldareth turned to Gervane. "He speaks the truth, his fear is real, and his feelings are unmistakeable, there can be no doubt here."

The whole forest breathed a huge sigh of relief, as Gervane drew breath to speak, a single bow string thrummed, sending its messenger of death. Before the warriors could even start to move the heel of Gregor's staff struck the ground without moving, a surge of white light came from the staff, propagating in a circle it spread out covering the entirety of his group, it crystallised for an instant into a shell around them all, the arrow shattered against it. In the moment of it's shattering the shield collapsed, and along with-it Gregor.

"Patrol." yelled Gervane. "Stand down. On your knees. The one responsible for that arrow will learn the error of his ways, if he survives!"

Jangor pushed through the crowd, to the front. Surprised to see the elf on the path, on his knees, his bow on the ground in front of him and the arrow the same.

"Gervane. I am Jangor. I am a simple soldier, a simple mistake after far too much time spent with an arrow drawn, no one was hurt, I am sure that Gregor will recover from the energy expenditure. Let there be no excessive punishment for a slip of the fingers. What say you?"

"I say this is my troupe, and I will assign whatever punishment I see fit."

"Let us at least discuss this over a drink or two?" Jangor held his empty right hand aloft, a heartbeat later a flask was in the air, he snatched it, dropped from his horse and walked towards the elf. "What do you think?" Arndrol stamped a foot, he had been looking forwards to a fight, Jangor cuffed him on the side of the head. "Be quiet fool." he whispered. Gervane stepped forwards sheathing his sword.

"I think that a drink could be a way to cement a friendship."

"That's a fine idea, why didn't I think of it." laughed Jangor. "Here, or shall we go elsewhere?" He smiled up into the face of Gervane, who was more than five inches taller.

"Follow me, our home is some way but not too far for an afternoon stroll. Goldareth. Flanks and guards, let's have no more accidents." The elves vanished into the forest. Gervane and Jangor walked side by side along the path, the others following on horseback, though Namdarin did have to talk quite firmly to Arndrol, the horse was very unhappy that the fight never actually got going.

"Gervane, a stroll may be something different for us people of normal height."

"You short people just need a quicker pace, you can keep up." He laughed, as Jangor passed him the flask. Gervane uncorked the flask and took a small mouthful of the fiery spirit, coughed and stared harshly at Jangor.

"It's not poison, or if it is it takes a damned long time to kill a person." He took the flask back and took a large swallow for himself, wiped his mouth with the back of his hand and sighed hugely.

"What is it your people want from us?" Asked Gervane.

"I think it would be better to wait for that information until we have a chance to talk to your leaders."

"I am a member of the council of leaders, minor member, but member none the less."

"That could be useful. How would your people feel if we managed to remove Zandaar?"

"How do you mean?"

"We plan to kill him, or remove him from this plane, whichever works the best. Namdarin is all about fire and blood, I'd settle for a simple banishment spell, you know the sort of thing, burn some herbs, speak some words, shed a little blood, and the deed is done, Zandaar is gone, somehow I don't think I am going to get my wish, there is going to be blood and death and tears, but we aim to send him on with the others of the old gods, his time is over."

"How do you know this?"

"Namdarin swore an oath, then met with Xeron on the boundaries of death, there they talked for a while, it seems the old gods came to a decision that it was time they left, Zandaar even agreed with them, but reneged at the last moment, leaving him as the last of the old ones still here, his falsity means that the others though gone from this plane cannot pass on to a new existence until they can make him leave as well, for this reason Xeron made sure that his sword came into Namdarin's hands, I think he may have had something to do with the make up of this group, though I have no proof."

"I knew it was a weapon of some power, but didn't realise just who it belonged to."

"The axe that Jayanne wields is special as well, Granger has a powerful staff, as does Gregor, the rest of us are simple soldiers."

"Jangor, there is nothing about you that is simple. Gregor is not a Zandaar name."

"No. His name has been changed to something new, or more accurately something from the time before he was a member of the Zandaar priesthood. He is hoping that if he can think of himself as someone other than who they are looking for, they may just pass him by. It might work, if it doesn't he may die before we can do anything to defend him."

"He's sitting upright on a horse now, so he seems to be recovering."

Jangor turned and shouted. "Granger, how is Gregor doing?"

"He's feeling better, he almost drained himself completely with that shield magic, I really need to learn that one, I have given him a small charge, and we are all pulling energy as fast as we can, but we could really do with a nice big fire."

"Do you have fires in your home?" asked Jangor.

"We do after a fashion, though no wood is actually burned, we use the magic inherent in the structure to generate heat and light."

"Could we use some of that heat and light to charge our weapons?"

"I see no reason why not, but that isn't what you came here for, is it?"

"No. The bird god Gyara told us that one of your kings, holds something called a mindstone, that could be of great use to us in the upcoming battle."

"Our king carries no special weapons."

"This is where it gets a little strange. We have heard a tale that the green mindstone was used many years ago in a battle between the elves and men, Gyara says he is buried but not quite dead. Does that make any form of sense to you at all?"

"It does, the stone that you are after is part of his sword, it sits in the pommel much like the black stone in the sword that your other leader carries. How can that work? There can be only one. You can't have two leaders, one has to bc in charge."

"Actually, we work together very well, I am more of a military mind, he is far more volatile, he lives on his feelings, when he said that you would die first, he meant it. He called us to arms and we were ready. For me a fight that doesn't happen is one I've already won. We are very different, but the ways that we are the same make us an exceptional team. Had a battle occurred, Gregor would have held that shield until your first volley was spent, there would not have been a second, the wolf would have taken the elf on the road, Namdarin would have had your head in a heartbeat, Granger would have spread fire amongst your men, and to all the gods pray they are dead before Jayanne gets amongst them with that axe. I have seen how that thing drinks souls. We would probably all have died, but if one in ten of yours survived, then you did well."

"And I am taking this force into the heart of my city?"

"If your people offer us no harm, then we will harm none. We will walk away empty handed rather than start a war we cannot win. On this road we were threatened, this is not a good thing to do. There is at least one of the old gods on our side, though somehow I can't seem to trust Gyara, I feel that he or she, is hiding something."

"You don't even have a gender for this god?"

"This particular god, doesn't even have a permanent shape."

"I am so glad that our gods are so much easier to deal with. But stepping back a way, can you promise me that your people will not hurt any of mine?"

"I can assure you that if we are not threatened we will not respond with violence. We are peaceful, I know that this is hard to understand, seeing as we are soldiers after all, but we would much rather drink than fight."

"I understand, but I have been told that drinking usually leads to fighting with your people."

"Not mine. We are happy drunks, the most we will do with too much beer inside us, is tell you how much we love you and yours, just before we go to sleep. At which point just roll us into a corner, throw a cloth over us and call us a table." Jangor laughed.

The road around them was changing slowly, it grew wider and the surface firmer, the hardened mud was replaced with stone, small pebbles to start with but gradually bigger blocks, until it was like a road in any human city, but still there was no outward signs of an approaching elven city. The sounds of the forest slowly changed, it became less wild, the sounds of birds in the trees diminished, and were replaced by sounds that were similar, but not exactly the same. The high canopy of the trees became somehow thicker and greener, but more light showed through.

"We must be getting close to your city by now." Said Jangor. Grevane looked at him and raised his right arm, an open hand clenched into a fist. Thirty elves stepped onto the road alongside the travellers, Jangor looked at Gervane, his head cocked over to one side, his hand flashed to the hilt of the sword at his side.

"Peace brother, we have arrived, it is only fitting that you have an escort."

"I don't see a city, where is it?"

"Look up."

Jangor did just that, as he tilted his head back, it became obvious that there were many people looking down from the branches above them, so many narrow faces, staring down on the strangers. The trees above seemed to be connected by many broad branches, walkways that people were staring over the edges of. Higher above the walkways there were densities of branches that could be rooms, or meeting places, perhaps even courtyards, it seemed very strange to Jangor.

"This is truly amazing." said Jangor.

"This is our home, there are actually seven trees here, all growing together, there are many elves living here, I'm not going to tell you how many. Will your people be able to climb the trees, or should we have the baskets sent down?" He waved towards some steep ladders that reached up to the first layer of woven branches.

"Obviously the horses can't climb but all of us are relatively fit and healthy, so ladders aren't that much of a problem, unless we are climbing to the very tops?"

"The elders have been called, the great hall on the second level is being prepared, grooms will be here momentarily to take care of the horses." The group dismounted awaiting the arrival of the grooms.

"May I make an observation?" asked Jangor. Gervane nodded.

"This place is not very well defended, a shielded platoon could just walk in and set fire to the place."

"Uninvited they would never find it, the paths that lead here are protected and guarded, no force without an escort could get this far. The very wood itself is protected by many powerful magicians, making it burn would take far more than a small group could bring with them, and a large group would be met long before they got here."

"Are we a large group or a small group?"

"Your passage through the forest was noted, scouts observed, you are a small number of people carrying a great deal of power. There was some discussion as to how you should be met."

"Your scouts failed to notice the zandaar amongst us?"

"They saw only a man dressed in black, they didn't have one amongst them with the necessary sensitivity, that will not happen again."

"Out of the griddle into the fire." said Gregor. "And now into the forest fire. I'm not doing very well so far."

"You're breathing." said Namdarin.

"I have some hope that condition will continue." said Gregor.

Gervane started looking from side to side, as if searching for something.

"A problem?" asked Jangor.

"Something is changing, something powerful is changing. Archers stand ready!"

The elves had drawn bows in an instant, but still no target.

"I feel it too." said Granger. "I have felt this before."

"What is it?" demanded Gervane.

Granger turned slowly and looked at Jayanne. "The axe of Algoron." In a heartbeat Namdarin and Gregor were at her side, the sword of Xeron weaving a slow pattern in the air, Gregor's staff now dark as night stood upright. All the archers turned towards Jayanne. With a snap of the wrist the axe jumped into her hand and she screamed.

"Jayanne." shouted Granger. "Focus. Tell me what you feel."

"Hunger, howling hunger across the ages, hunger for the life of the trees, the seven. The stolen seven. Algoron is gone, his garden is gone, but the seven seedlings taken so many ages ago, still live, their progeny are the great trees of all the forests, they must die so that Algoron can truly rest."

"Our people stole no trees, these seven are as we found them, we helped them to grow, we felt their magic, but we did not steal them." said Gervane, still not calling on the archers to shoot.

"Long before the elves came the seedlings were stolen, ripped from the garden, and spirited away by the trickster."

"Gyara." said Kern, "is sometimes known as the trickster, this could be the reason she sent us here, perhaps she wants these trees killed for a reason, perhaps for the effect it will have on the elves, or for something we don't know about, Jayanne, look at me."

She turned towards him, he stepped right in front of her, totally unmindful of all the arrows now pointed at his back.

"Jayanne, you must focus, it is the axe that wants to kill the trees, not you, while your hand is on its haft, it is yours, not the other way around, it is your axe to control, take that control now. Gather your will, and subjugate it, it must be made to submit to your will, to your wants, to your wishes. Its instructions are ages old, give it new ones. What do you want from it, it is a simple thing, it only exists to destroy, give it a new target, give it a new reason to exist."

"Something changes." said Granger. Jayanne closed her eyes, and focused on the axe, Kern's soft voice and metered delivery helped her to reinforce the pattern in her mind, the simplest of instructions, a new task. Kill Zandaar. Kill Zandaar. Kill Zandaar. The axe started to resonate, the blade sang a clear tone, that built and built, until it was so loud that it was physically painful to all the people around, the elves started to move away from Jayanne, Gregor tried desperately to cover both ears with only one hand. Namdarin refused to remove one hand from the hilt of the longsword, Jayanne took the axe in both hands. The sound increased until finally it shattered into a scream that fled the grove. The sudden silence was almost as painful as the sound itself. Everyone within earshot stumbled at the absence. Jayanne didn't want to open her eyes, she knew the axe was destroyed, though the wooden haft still felt solid in her hands.

"Jayanne." said Kern. "Open your eyes." She did, and was amazed to see the axe still whole, somehow it felt a little different, but it's thirst for life was unchanged.

"Gervane." said Granger. "Speak."

"Suddenly the fear from the trees is gone."

"Jayanne. Speak."

"Now it wants to kill Zandaar. It's still unhappy about the stolen trees but not as unhappy as it is about Zandaar."

A new sound filled the grove, the sound of huge wings beating slowly, getting louder.

"Gyara comes." called Kern. Sure enough the dark bird slowly came into view, it stood upon the greensward it's wings blowing the grass in all directions at once. All the elves turned their bows towards the black shape.

"Gyara, what is your purpose here?"

"I have come to claim my trees, now the axe has a new task, I can come here without it finding out where they are."

"These trees belong to the elves now, you cannot take them."

"They are mine I stole them so many years ago, that damned axe would have killed them as soon as I came to them, it could always find me. I will have them." Gyara opened it's jet black wings, and called, seven twigs fell from the canopy, each with a small bulb of earth at one end. They dropped directly at Gyara's feet.

"Looks to me like you got the trees you stole." laughed Kern. "Sometimes I believe the universe actually has a sense of humour. Now you can start a garden of your own."

Gyara snatched the twigs in one claw and snapped it's wings forwards, started to fly away it's it usual manner, gradually it faded from view, not that anyone around was actually looking, the initial sweep of those black wings knocked everyone nearby off their feet, a few elven arrows scattered around the clearing, causing no damage, other than embarrassment.

As the people climbed back to their feet, Jayanne looked dumbfounded at the axe, then she turned to Granger. "Is it still Algoron's axe?"

"I think it is still the axe of Algoron, but now it has a new purpose, it is also yours. Does it still have a hunger?"

"Oh, yes, it still hungers for life, and it is exceptionally hungry at the moment."

"I suggest we find a nice big fire and feed it some energy, that might take the edge off its thirst for blood." While they were speaking an old elf came almost tumbling down the nearest ladder, his limbs were like sticks and his clothes hung on him like rags, after him came a group of younger, but not young elves. He ran straight up to Jayanne, his cloak flapping like a torn sail in the wind.

"How have you done this?" he demanded. Jangor looked to Gervane, only to find the elf on his knees, as were the rest of the escort.

"Gervane." said Jangor. "Introductions please?"

The old elf waved Gervane to his feet. Saying "Be quick about it."

"Jangor, Jayanne, this is the most ancient." Jangor frowned. "His name is lost in antiquity, he is simply most ancient, or eldest."

"Eldest." said Jangor. "What do you mean, we have done nothing that we are aware of, other than bring one of our weapons more under our control? Is that correct Jayanne?"

"Yes, it is now more mine than it was."

"The seven have lost a great fear. We have always known that there was something out in the world of which the trees were greatly afraid. You have taken away that fear, how?"

"Eldest. I am Kern. I am an old follower of Gyara, from the words exchanged with Gyara it appears that your seven trees were stolen many years ago from Algoron, by Gyara, and she planted them here. Algoron set the axe to hunt them down, but it couldn't find them directly it had to wait until Gyara actually came to them again, she obviously didn't do that. But the trees knew that Algoron had set an axe to find them. That is the reason for their fear. All the years that you have been looking after these trees the axe has been waiting, now it appears the waiting is done, Gyara has the seedlings she stole, and the axe has a new purpose. All in all a reason for celebration."

"The disquiet of the trees has been a topic of much conversation, amongst our wisest, but we never thought for one moment that it could be Gyara that was part of the problem. So the trees are now finally ours in their entirety?"

"I think so, Algoron is gone, he has no call over them, Gyara has her seedlings as she stole originally, and the axe is busy with something else."

"This is a great day indeed. Is there anything that we can do to help you in your obviously dangerous quest?"

Namdarin stepped forwards. "I am Namdarin, the quest is originally mine. There may be something you can help us with, but an open forum like this is probably not the best place to discuss it."

The eldest looked around for a moment. "Gervane, you know where to take them." Then he turned and scampered off towards the ladder, which he ran up with a total lack of any sort of fear for his own safety.

"Is he completely crazy?" Jangor asked Gervane.

"Not completely, but he does a very good impression."

"Please everyone." Gervane said to the group in general. "Follow me, we shall be meeting with the council of elders shortly, though I believe that any decisions they are going to make have already been decided."

Grooms took the horses, and the elven escort trooped off, following the horses, Jangor followed Gervane to the nearest ladder, the others followed along. Though the ladder was steep they had no real problems with it after only twenty feet, they stepped out onto a wide branch, one that showed the wear of many feet, here they could walk two abreast, there were hand rails to make thing easier for those with unsteady feet, the gentle motion of the trees in the breeze did feel a little strange, but not enough to upset anyone.

"Gervane. How much do these branches move when there is a real wind blowing?"

"I can't really say, we don't feel it, it's just a part of our world, something we are trained for from birth."

"How many in the council? Are there any allegiances or affiliations we need to know about?"

"This situation is completely without precedent, so things could go any way at all. The council is five, four of the major family heads and the eldest."

"We are probably going to ask for something they don't want to give, any idea which way they'll vote?"

"What gives you the idea they are going to vote on anything?"

"Isn't that how these things work the whole world over?"

"Not here."

"I don't understand."

"You'll see." Gervane laughed. They were walking up a broad pathway, one that seemed to made of three branches growing together.

"How can these branches all grow in the same way?" asked Granger.

"Do your people always ask so many questions?"

"I am afraid so." said Jangor. "We don't have the luxury of such long lives as your people, we need to know things now."

"The old stories tell that we found the seven trees, one in the centre and the others in a circle around it, the elders decided they were special and took them as our home, over the years we have taught the trees how to grow, and how to change, and how to protect themselves. We look after them and they look after us, no threatening force has ever approached our home, at least not until today."

"We had no idea about the history of your home trees, nor Gyara's involvement, nor Algoron's. Even so that appears to have been resolved, at least the eldest seemed happy."

The pathways were getting larger, now as wide as streets, and quite crowded with elves, some old, some young, some blatantly staring at the strangers. Though none made any attempt to approach them, or block their way, there wasn't even any talking going on in the trees, just the staring.

"Gervane. Why do they stare at us?" asked Jangor.

"Most of them have never seen your kind, they have heard about the barbarians outside the forest, but never seen them."

"They think of us as barbarians?"

"I am afraid so, the actions of your people, the way they breed until their numbers are too much for the land to support, the way they make war, to both reduce the numbers and expand their territory. The horrors you inflict on one another in the name of your various gods. Barbarian seems appropriate to me."

"As a soldier I have participated in many of these acts. But we also create art, and literature, we have many poets, and songwriters, we actually live in a very peaceful time. There are currently no major wars going on, and only a few small time bandits making any trouble at all."

"That may be the case, but the last time elves fought amongst themselves was so many years ago that almost none can remember, all our recent wars have been with your people."

"I agree, we can be difficult to live with, I hope that we never have to go to war with elves again. Your people are already struggling to survive."

"We approach the hall, are you ready to meet with the council?"

"We are as ready as we are ever going to be." said Jangor.

"It is customary for visitor to enter the hall unarmed."

"You seriously expect us to abandon our weapons before we go in?"

"It is the custom."

"This should be interesting." said Jangor, unbuckling his sword belt an propping his sword against the door post of the room ahead of them. The other soldiers followed suit. Gervane looked at Granger.

"You would deny an old man his walking stick?"

"I suppose not." Said Gervane, turning his gaze on Gregor. "You are not old." Gregor nodded and propped his staff with the swords. Gervane looked to Namdarin and Jayanne.

"You honestly want two weapons of the gods, left unrestrained by this doorway, when one of them has a proven thirst for the lives of your trees? These cannot be released surely you see that." said Jangor. "Jayanne?"

"Algoron's axe is still thirsty for the lifeblood of these trees, I cannot release it, who can tell what it will do. No. It must come with me."

Gervane simply shrugged and lead them through the wide doorway, the room was wide and long, the floor seemed to be woven from branches, so tightly woven that the were no holes in it big enough to snag a toddler's foot. There were many seats along the sides of the room, all of them filled, they walked forwards passing either side of the huge tree trunk that grew up through the middle of the room. At the opposite end to what seemed to be the only door, there were five large seats, these were not chairs, or thrones in the usual manner, like the smaller seats along the sides, they were grown from the wood of the walls, the five were taller and more ornate than all the others, but still wooden. The eldest was sitting in the centre seat, fidgeting, and chattering, he focused on the visitors as they came around the tree.

"Welcome friends." he called.

"These humans are armed." said the elf to the far left.

"Be quiet Loganar. Do you really want the axe of Algoron unattended by our door?"

"It is custom." said the elf on the far right.

"Galabrine." said the eldest. "Customs can be changed in a moment, or ignored for a while, be at peace my dear, these people mean us no harm." Galabrine bowed deeply, her bow caused Mander's breath to catch in his throat. Jangor's hard elbow soon restarted Mander's respiration, but the look froze his heart.

"People." said eldest. "These new friends have performed for us a service today that could not have been imagined by any, in all the years that we have been living here we never thought to release the trees from the fear of something that we couldn't identify, we have searched for years beyond count to find this thing, and these people simply carried it into our city and disarmed it. Who amongst us cannot feel the happiness of the trees? They are joyous in their hearts, their sap flows freer than it ever has, Gyara has lost her call upon them and the axe of Algoron no longer lusts for their death."

"I wouldn't go quite that far." whispered Jayanne, keeping a tight grip on the haft of the axe.

"We need to know how we can help these people along their way" said Eldest.

"Why should we help them?" asked the elf sitting next to eldest on his left.

"Calabron." replied Eldest. "My old friend, because it is right, they have helped us, even unknowingly, so we should help them, have no fear this seat will be yours before too long."

"New friends." said Eldest. "Tell the people of your quest."

Namdarin stepped forwards, Jangor stepped to the side.

"I am Namdarin, of the house of Namdaron. My house and family were destroyed by the black priesthood of Zandaar, they burned my house to the ground, with everyone in it, while I was away. I swore an oath to destroy them. Now that is what I intend to do, I have some friends who have tagged along for the ride, they know the possible fate that awaits them along this dangerous road. But still they follow, or sometimes lead. Along the road, we have collected the sword of Xeron, here upon my back, the axe of Algoron, which Jayanne carries, along the road we met with Gyara, she or he says that you have an artefact that will help us in our plan to destroy a god. Would you be willing to let us take this thing with us when we leave?"

"I have no problem with that." said Eldest. "You have liberated our home from a terrible fate, the axe of Algoron would have killed all our trees simply because Gyara stole them. Anything that we can give to help you we will."

"I hope so." said Namdarin. He glanced at his friends, Jayanne stepped away from him to give him some space, Granger casually lifted his staff, into both hands. Namdarin continued. "Gyara told us that in order to truly defeat Zandaar we need the mindstone."

"We cannot give them the mindstone." snapped the elf on the Eldest's right. "That is unconscionable. It is a major part of our heritage, we cannot just give it away because some strangers ask for it."

"I agree with you Tomas. We cannot just give this away, but we don't have to stop them from taking it."

"We can't do that." said Tomas. "The mindstone is part of who we are. We can't allow them to take it from us."

"Tomas, what use has that stone been to us for the last five hundred years? Why do we still not have a king to preside over our council?"

"We still have a king, he just sleeps."

"What good has he done for us?"

"He waits to rise and defend the city from our enemies."

"Where was he today, when the axe of Algoron came here looking to kill our trees? These people here abated that threat, not our king."

"We still can't just hand over the stone to them, it's not right."

"I agree." said Eldest. "I think that they should prove their worth, they have to take it from the king." A gasp ran through all the elves in the meeting place.

"You can't mean that." said Tomas.

"Why not? Our king sleeps as he has for so many years, in some ways he is the epitome of elven kind, he sits and achieves nothing, while he sits, so do we. We have achieved nothing in so many years, we have changed nothing, we are simply waiting to die, just like him. Only he can outlive us all, as he's isn't actually living."

"The only way they can take the stone from him is to end his life. You understand what that means?"

"Yes. If they are strong enough to defeat him, and take the stone, the king will finally die, and we will get a new king."

"Who will be the new king?"

"Are there any left of his line?"

"I can only think of one." said Tomas.

"Who's that?" asked Eldest.

"You know very well who that is, it is you."

"So, I change from being leader of the council as eldest, to being leader of the council as king. I don't see that as much of a change, do you?"

"But our king will be dead."

"The king is dead. Long live the king. Isn't that the normal order of things?"

"Why do you want this sudden change of title?"

"Really I don't, but for our people we need to move on, we need to change, or the world will move on without us."

"You think this is the only way?"

"Not the only one, but certainly the best, with a new king, we may be able to breathe a new life into our dying people, we need a new path and a new vision."

"It still feels very wrong."

"Yes, it does, but something must be done." He turned to Namdarin. "When your quest is finished, will you bring the stone back to us?"

"You have my word, if there is any way for the stone to be returned to you someone will find it. I don't expect to survive, I'm not sure that the stone will survive, but if any of us live through this, one will bring the stone to you, or whoever is king in your place."

"Thank you." said Eldest. "It would be better if this was started in the morning. After dawn you can take the king's mindstone, and in the afternoon we will either have some funerals or a coronation. Whatever happens, we'll have a feast to celebrate potential changes. Gervane, you will see to the needs of our guests, provide them with quarters suitable for them, whatever they need." Eldest jumped to his feet, as he walked towards Namdarin all the elves in the room scrambled to their feet. Eldest Took both of Namdarin's hands in his and bowed deeply. Namdarin bowed. Eldest stepped rapidly around the group and almost scampered out of the door. The other members of the council left in a more sedate and almost regal fashion, though none greeted Namdarin, or any of the others. Tomas approached Grevane.

"Give them everything that they need. They need to have the best possible chance tomorrow, I'd advise against too much drinking, and make sure they get plenty of rest. By the edict of the council they are under your care."

Gervane bowed but didn't appear happy about something.

"Is there a problem, my friend?" asked Jangor, quietly.

"Councillor Tomas has made me responsible for you, I will do whatever I can to help you, but I will also be held responsible for any improper actions of you and yours."

"I suggest we make this as simple for you as we can. We will camp in the clearing below, all we need is food, water and a fire, a very large fire. It would be helpful if someone could give us any information about your undead king, and I believe he has some guards."

"We have many storytellers who know all the tales of the undead king."

"It's not tales, what we really need is accurate information. We need to know about the enchantment that created his current state, we may be able to find a weakness in it and unravel it, I really don't want to go into a sword fight with a group of men who cannot be killed."

"They're not men."

"They're not really elves either."

"I suppose that is true as well. I will escort you down to the greensward and arrange for your gear to be brought to you, and then I will see if I can find the man that knows the most about the magic the undead king used."

"It might be better just to bring our horses to us, we will set up our camp and care for our own horses, we have no wish to be a burden to our hosts."

"I am sure I can arrange that."

"Our most urgent need is a huge fire, the bigger and hotter the better."

"I don't understand, it's not cold in our grove."

"No, but we have weapons that need to recharge, and a good fire is the easiest way to do that. Is that going to be a problem?"

"I don't see that as a problem, fire is fire, though ours are a little special. Please follow me I'll lead you by the easiest path. It's not as pretty as the way we came up, but it's smoother."

"Lead on." Said Jangor, making the hand signals that told the soldiers how the group should be assembled. Gregor and Brank were a little surprised when Mander stopped them from joining the line until almost they were almost at the end. They were released when only Mander and Andel were left behind them.

Gregor turned to Mander. "Why are we at the back?"

"Big hot staff, and a giant. Who's going to attack that?"

"You think we are in danger of attack here?"

"Some are very upset by the eldest's decisions, anything could happen, we just like to be ready. Why do you think Jangor suggested our own camp on the ground? There will be guard rota's for tonight, don't be surprised if something strange happens." Following Jangor and Gervane they were very soon on the ground, as the horses were brought into view, their packs still appeared to be undisturbed. Arndrol saw Namdarin, snapped his bit between his teeth, shook his head until the groom had no choice but to let him go. Androl came prancing across the green grass, his neck arched, a high stepping trot. Gervane looked a question at Namdarin.

"He's just a show off." Namdarin said as the horse stopped directly in front of him, and spat it's bit out into his hand.

"Are you sure this horse has no elven blood in him?" asked Gervane.

"Where I am from there are no elves, they are simply a tale from the distant past."

"It could be that is all we will be, in some ways Eldest is right, we need to change, but how I am not sure."

"I have been told that I need the mindstone, but that was by Gyara, so I'm not entirely sure." The grooms brought the rest of the horses, and soon departed, after Gervane had told them to bring lots of firewood. Whilst camp was being set up Jangor decided that their fire should be between two of the outer trees, and far enough from either of them to cause no harm, soon the grooms returned, and the fire was built. It was quite tall and wide. Kern pulled his tinderbox from inside his jacket and walked towards the fire to get it started. Gervane intercepted him and placed a hand on his shoulder.

"Let me." he said. Gervane stood in front of the fire, and held up his arms, he spoke briefly in a language that they couldn't understand, as he finished speaking the wood caught alight, flaring up into a large bonfire. "Is that big enough?" he asked. The heat was causing his face to redden.

"That should be just fine." said Jangor. "But we are going to need more wood to keep it going through the night."

"No you won't. Our fires are different from yours, they don't actually consume the wood. They give heat and light, but the wood remains. It is part of our magic. I go to find your story teller." Gervane walked away from the fire, back up into the trees.

"Granger." said Jangor. "Test this strange fire of theirs, let's make sure it is good enough to charge our weapons." Granger nodded and walked up to the fire, he pointed on end of his staff at it, opened the channel from the staff to the fire, the fire flared higher and hotter. He stepped back. He made some adjustments and placed the staff on the ground near the fire.

"Gervane is right." Said Granger. "Their fire is different, when you charge you weapons from it don't open the channel too wide, it just makes the fire bigger and hotter, so charge slowly, if you pull too much the whole grove could go up in flames." The other three placed their weapons near the fire and started charging them, slowly at first, then once the fire was stable, all four of them gradually increased the energy they were taking from the fire, until the fire was roaring but not in any danger of setting anything else alight.

"If we let these charge through the night we'll have a good reserve for tomorrows fight." said Granger.

"I want guards set through the night." said Jangor. "Kern sort the rota, I want one major weapon and one soldier on duty on a two-hour cycle. No-one leaves camp alone, latrine breaks in two's. Anyone unclear!" No-one spoke up.

Gregor approached Kern, speaking softly. "He's setting this camp like we are in unfriendly territory, why?"

"Because we may be. He doesn't like to take too many chances."

"I hope our hosts don't get too upset about an armed and wary camp in their midst."

"They can get as upset as they like, if they treat us right, we'll return the favour. Otherwise things are going to get very messy very quickly."

"Jangor would take on the whole city?"

"If necessary. It's what we do."

"I'm only happy that I don't have to ride that horse for a little while." said Brank.

"I'm sure the horse feels the same." chuckled Kern.

"Kern." said Gregor. "How long until sunset?"

"About an hour, why?"

"My former brothers have had a whole day to recover, I think they'll be making an attempt on my life fairly soon. Please don't include me in the guard duties for a few more hours. I'm going to meditate and shore up my defences if I can." Kern nodded, then said. "Granger, help him."

The two walked over to the fire and picked up their respective staves. They sat cross-legged facing one another, staffs across their laps holding hands, the sudden roaring from the fire attested to the fact that they were using a lot of energy for something.

Kern went over to where Namdarin and Jayanne were erecting the tent that they shared. "Jayanne. Is the axe going to be alright just sitting by the fire?"

"Yes. It still wants to kill the trees but has a much bigger need to kill Zandaar. It won't go wandering off on its own, at least not until Zandaar gets within range."

"Would it have before you changed it?"

"Oh yes. It was aware that the trees were here, though Gyara wasn't it would have started killing them very quickly, as it is currently sucking power from the fire, it would have been drinking the life from the trees, even without physical contact."

"Could it do that to people?"

"I don't think so, people are more active about their lives, trees are sort of passive, if that makes any sense. Or that's the way it feels to me."

Gervane came into view walking down a steep pathway with an elderly elf behind him.

"Jangor. This is Rohem, he is probably the most knowledgeable person here with regards to the king."

"Probably." snapped Rohem. "Probably! There is no-one else who comes even close to my knowledge of the king, at least no-one that makes any sense."

"Namdarin, Jayanne." Jangor called.

"Jangor." spoke Gervane softly. "Food and drink are being prepared, I will return shortly with these things, and some more people who wish to meet you all." Jangor nodded his thanks as Namdarin and Jayanne walked over.

"Shall we sit?" asked Jangor.

"Yes." answered Rohem, walking towards the nicely roaring fire.

"Not too close to the fire Rohem, that is likely to get a little hot and loud sometime soon." The elf frowned, which had quite an effect on his look, his thin arched eyebrows appeared to shuffle across his face and meet just above his long-pointed nose. Then they shuffled back.

"I don't understand." he said.

"Don't worry about it, just not too close." They all sat about ten feet from the fire.

"Right." said Jangor. "What can you tell us about the king and the magic he used to achieve his un-dead state."

"The king Grinderosch fought a hard battle against an enormous force of humans, we suffered so many dead that day, the king himself was sorely wounded, but the mindstone sustained him, and drawing energy from the enemies around him, any of his enemies bathed in the green light from the mindstone appeared to just stand still waiting to be killed, finally he forced a path through the surrounding forces and led the surviving elves back into the forest. He stood under the eaves of the forest while our dead and injured were removed from the field, no-one dared to interfere with the recovery, any that came forward were cut down by the green light. Once the field was cleared he left archers in the trees and then he retreated home to these very trees."

"Fine, we have a name for him and a watch out for the green light. What of the magic he used?"

"Over the next few months he had his funeral barrow built, it's a large earthen structure with stone walled rooms inside. The central corridor has eight rooms off each side, where the sixteen warriors sleep, the main chamber holds the king's bier, where he awaits the final battle to save our people. The sixteen were chosen for their skills as warriors, both sword and bow, all are masters, the king of course has his greatsword with the mindstone. As to the magic they used, it is believed that they took the potion of unending death and swore an oath to remain vigilant and ready to come to the aid of the people should the need arise."

"What is this unending death?" Asked Namdarin.

"It is the state they are in, their bodies don't decay as the dead generally do, they don't look well, but they function when called upon. When the reason for the call has abated they return to their undead sleep."

"How many times have they woken?"

"Only twice in all these years."

"Why did they wake?"

"On each occasion some adventurer had broken into the tomb to steal the mindstone. On the last attempt a large group attacked the warriors, two of the group made it out of the barrow, but were cut down by the warriors. Once they were dead, the warriors returned to the barrow. We went in the next day to remove the dead, some of the warriors were showing some damage, but their dried flesh didn't bleed, the king was unharmed his sword resting on his chest."

"Seems like you don't defend this place very well."

"It defends itself, anyone stupid enough to venture in dies."

"So, basically all we know is that they took some potion that suspends life, or death, or both, and that they will wake up when we try to take the mindstone. Will they awake as soon as we walk in, or as soon as we get within a given distance, or when we get to the king and his stone? Will they wake one at a time or en-mass?"

"We don't actually know." Replied Rohem. "They never leave any survivors for us to talk to."

"How long since they last awoke?"

"Two hundred years, or thereabouts."

"Even at a greatly reduced rate of decay their bodies must be slowing down by now. That may give us some form of tactical advantage. You said dried flesh, simple then we burn them. Even magically animated flesh can still burn. And while they are burning we chop them into kindling. I'll talk to Gervane when he gets back about lamp oil or something of that ilk. Thank you Rohem, your knowledge of the undead king has been almost useful."

Rohem jumped to his feet and stamped off towards the nearest of the trees. Muttering something about human ingrates. Jangor just smiled.

"Did you really have to be so rude to that old man?" asked Jayanne.

"I'm afraid so, he was such a pompous ass, the number one know it all, and he knew nothing of any value."

"I thought his information helped you to decide on a plan of action?"

"Undead soldiers, hundreds of years old, the obvious weapon is fire. Always fire." As he said these words the fire behind them sudden roared up into the air, the heat was so intense that they almost ran away from it. Once out of the searing heat they turned to where Granger and Gregor were now standing face to face, each holding his staff vertically in front of him, they appeared to be standing inside the fire, though they weren't actually burning. The fire seemed to be swirling around them. Equally the sword of Xeron and the axe of Algoron were now within the conflagration.

"Can you two help them?" asked Jangor, looking from Namdarin to Jayanne.

"I can't even reach the sword with my mind." said Namdarin, Jayanne simply shook her head.

"They're on their own." she said, over the roaring of the fire, which seemed to be building with every second that passed. The two within the blaze were unmoving, but equally unharmed.

"Kern?" asked Jangor.

"Sorry," was the gentle reply, "I can't reach them at all, that fire is really hot." He looked up into the branches above the fire, some leaves were turning brown, and smoking a little. Elves came running to the branches amongst them the eldest, a chant was set up, and the fire moved away from the trees, gradually following a path that left the leaves free to turn green again, they plumped up and fattened with new sap, and new life. The green of the trees spread slowly into the yellow of the fire, rapidly flooding the entirety with the green of new shoots and the smell of bursting buds. Even the sound changed subtly, it became the rustling of leaves in a wind, rather than the crackling of twigs in a fire. The protective force of the elves chanting forced the fire to spread out but not higher, pushing Jangor and the others further from their friends. More and more elves arrived to help the chant, protecting the trees and suppressing the fire.

In the heart of the fire, the two men stood face to face, barely visible in the swirling flames, both of their staves were clearly visible as vertical bars of light, one blue, one brilliant, almost blinding, white. The fire started to pulse, surging then, shrinking, surging then shrinking, with each shrinking phase the fire became smaller, but the surges failed to bring it back its previous intensity.

"It's going to end soon." Shouted Jangor, above the roar of fire. "Be ready they may need help." Suddenly, like a guttering candle the fire blew out, slowly the two men collapsed to the ground, Namdarin and Jangor rushed in, but were too slow to catch them before they reached the ground.

CHAPTER FORTY ONE

Alverana walked his horse slowly along the pathway, it wasn't straight but turned gradually from left to right and back again, the high banks of waving reeds each side restricted visibility to basically the width of the path. But it appeared to be going in the direction that they needed, so for now it will do. Gradually he felt that something wasn't quite right with this path, the turns though seeming random started to tend towards the east, the heat of the sun became more and more oppressive. The flies and beetles were swarming around them, the normal fragrance of the swamp somehow became a little more rotten, more like sewage than rotting vegetation.

"Kevana." The word snapped Kevana out of the somnolent reverie that had taken over his relaxed mind.

"What?" He whispered.

"Yes, somehow whispering seems appropriate, I don't like this path, it still leads the way we want to go, but I don't like the way it is changing."

"What do you mean?"

"I don't know it just feels wrong, there are more biting insects than there were a little while ago, and they are heavier and harder to discourage, there are more heavy cobwebs on the reeds, some are completely festooned."

Alverana's horse suddenly shied to the left and snorted, it took a few seconds for Alverana to get control again, in that time the horse had stepped off the path into the reeds, suddenly up to its belly in slimy mud and cold water, panic was only a moment away, Alverana spoke to it softly and coaxed it back up onto the path, where the horse just stood shaking. Alverana jumped off not letting the reins fall from his hand, still talking softy, re-assuringly. Blood was streaming from a cut on the horses front right leg, obviously some large biting insect had had a meal there, worse still, there were several large green leeches attached to legs and belly, they could be seen to visibly growing as he watched.

"I need malleable flame right now." He shouted. Holding his right hand up above his head. Worandana performed the minor conjuration in a moment and passed the flame across to Alverana. A single touch from the flame was enough to make the leeches release and fall to the ground, immediately looking for a new meal, only to find Alverana's heavy boot, stamping them into pink slime. Wiping the horse's wounds with as clean a rag as he could find, the bleeding of the first wound stopped, but the leech bites just kept on bleeding. Remembering a tale from his youth, he snatched cobwebs from the surrounding reeds and covered the wounds with them, the bleeding soon slowed and stopped.

"Whatever happens stay out of the water, there are some really nasty leeches in there." He shouted. "We need to make torches to keep the insects away." He grabbed handfuls of reed flower heads, full of seed and pollen. 'They'll burn nice and smoky.' He thought. Watching as the others followed suit. Once he had the heads twisted together and bound up with their own leaves he said. "Somebody fire me." Worandana conjured fire again, this time targeted for the torch.

"Kevana, are your people always this lazy?"

"Ask that when their swords are keeping the bandits off your back." The smoky torches went some way towards keeping the insects at bay, but they weren't entirely successful. The occasional one still settled for a swift meal, but no more horses went into the water.

"I am starting to get very worried about this path." Muttered Alverana to Kevana.

"I know what you mean, those damned leeches mean we cannot leave it, we are stuck going where ever this path leads, I wonder where it is taking us."

"Or to whom?"

"That too. Let's be as alert as we can, we can only hope to be good enough to take out any opposition that turns up."

"It's starting to get narrower."

"Perhaps we are nearing its end."

"We could always turn around and go back." Said Alverana.

"That would cost us half a day at least. We can't afford to lose any more time."

"Fine, then we blunder on regardless."

Their knees were almost touching as they rode side by side, the horses were struggling on the edges of the path. The reeds were leaning over the path and making the horses even more nervous, but this was concentrating the smoke and keeping the aerial biters at bay. As the path narrowed some more Alverana took the lead, hoping that his senses would give them any warnings that were needed. The path narrowed some more, until it was only as wide as a single horse and the footing started to get more than a little soft. Alverana's horse started tossing it's head the closeness of the water and the buzzing of the insects was starting to get to it. Alverana's soothing words helped, but only partly. 'Perhaps there is something else that is worrying the horse.' Alverana closed his eyes and focused on the other senses, the smell of the swamp had moved towards rotting meat, the sort of stench from the back of an abattoir, blood and guts slowly decomposing in the afternoon sun, the very thought of it made his stomach turn over. The buzzing of the insects seemed further away, there were still many around, but they were much quieter than they had been. Alverana turned in his saddle and whispered to Kevana. "Something is coming, and it's not going to be good."

"What?"

"I've no idea, but it's a meat eater, after a fashion."

"What do you mean?"

"I think it prefers its meat rotten, can't you smell it?"

"I suppose, but it's just a swamp."

"This is not a swamp, it's a trap, and we are all the way in it now."

"Stop." Kevana turned in his saddle, "Worandana, get up here, we have a large predator somewhere nearby, we are in its trap, reach out for it, find the damned thing, we need to know what it is and where."

Worandana dismounted and walked forwards, there was no way that two horses could pass without stepping into the water. He stroked the neck of Alverana's horse as he came by, though the horse was not to be consoled. He reached the front of the column, the ground underfoot more than a little soft, the grass looked like it was sinking while he watched.

"Kevana we may need to retreat in a hurry, the causeway is sinking. Alverana you are right, the stink of rotting meat is much clearer now."

"Turning is going to be very difficult, find it, and make it go away."

"I'll try." Worandana focused his mind on an ancient charm, one that he hoped would work in this case. Speaking the words of the charm and making the hand signs, he wove a pattern in the air, once it was complete he released the glowing symbol into the water ahead of them. In a few seconds there was a howling from somewhere off to the right, which was answered from the left. Ahead there were more howls, all the other sounds in the swamp ended, even the insects just dropped out of the air, only the mind-numbing howl remained. The noise started to get louder, or perhaps more worrying, nearer.

"Lightning everyone. Alverana left, Kevana right of centre, Apostana right, stand ready for my word." Shouted Worandana, above the rapidly increasing noise. Worandana held a lightning bolt in his right hand above his head, then held up his left hand, three fingers, two fingers, one finger, the left hand snapped down, the right hand snapped forwards, as did three others, four lightning bolts formed in the air and struck into the water, the whole causeway convulsed with the shock, almost threw the horses over, most of the sound vanished, only a distant howl could be heard and that sounded like it was moving away at great speed.

"I think that should see us safe for a while, even the leeches will be knocked out for a few hours if no actually destroyed. So let's push along quickly."

Already the causeway was rising slowly from the water, getting wider and firmer. Kevana nodded to Alverana as Worandana walked back towards his horse. "We need to look for resupply and more personnel." He said as he passed Kevana.

Kevana felt the pockets in the front of his robe, only one each side, one flame and one lightening left, nodding to himself, he was sure that Worandana was right, they needed some supplies and people would be useful. Alverana set off once Worandana was mounted, somehow the swamp seemed to be as quiet as a graveyard on an autumn night, Alverana shivered, despite the heat from the sun, he was cold. Very soon the path was wide enough for two horses, still very close to the level of the water, but Kevana was able to ride alongside his friend.

"I'm with Worandana, we need some supplies and a few more bodies wouldn't hurt." He said quietly, not wishing to disturb the peace of the swamp.

"I agree, once we're out of this mess, we'll look for a monastery, there has to be one nearby, hopefully not a large one."

Alverana simply nodded. Still not confident to pick the pace up too much they walked the horses along the greenway. Something hunched up out of the grass, it was large and green and for all its outward appearance it seemed to be a leech, but it's body was two feet across at the thickest, the end that could be considered the head, turned towards them, and raised above the ground, as if scenting the air, the 'neck' extended until it was level with the horses heads, questing towards the men, both pulled their reins down and tight, hoping to stop the horses from panicking. Both swept swords from scabbards. The darker green head swelled slowly, as the body of the thing shrunk, it moved closer to the men, and the head opened like a three petalled flower, a howl started to emanate from its foul smelling mouth, Kevana leaned forwards and struck on the fore-hand, Alverana on the backhand, the two swords passed each other like a perfect shear, the head was separated, and the sound died, the sack like body collapse to the ground and spilled green and sticky goo across the grass, twitched a few times then rolled slowly into the water.

Kevana reached down and speared the head with his sword, lifted it up, and had a close look, it still looked like a three petalled flower, with a central structure not unlike the pistol of any bee pollinated flower, however this pistol was slowly trying to climb up the sword to get at the man. A flick of the wrist and it dropped far out into the water.

"What, in all the hells are those things?" Asked Alverana.

"Dead." Shrugged Kevana.

"It wasn't too difficult to kill, though."

"No, but I bet it moves a lot better in the water, and generally in groups, then they'd be a real problem."

"This pathway is looking better, and the swamp is coming back to life, let's get moving." Said Alverana. Kevana just nodded, and they kicked the horses into a fast trot. A rapid glance showed that the others were keeping up, the path turned more south than east for a while and widened, climbing slowly above the level of the water, it gradually became so firm that the pounding of the horse's hooves start to actually make sound. After an hour at this pace they climbed out of the swamp, and up onto a level plain. Running south as the sun was approaching the mountains in the west.

"Alverana." Said Kevana. As he pulled rein and slowed to a walk. "Find us a camp site, we need to find and kill a traitor." Alverana nodded and kicked back up to a canter, turning uphill, Kevana frowned and pulled to a stop.

"Alverana is going to find us a camp site, we'll wait here for him."

"Have you thought about what I said?" asked Worandana.

"Yes. I agree. I'm almost out of silver, and I'm sure the rest of you are the same, in the morning we'll look for a monastery somewhere near, we should be able to pick up some silver and perhaps a few people. Between us we carry more than enough rank. Just so long as there aren't any bad reports of us out there."

"That's a chance we'll have to take. Our numbers are far too low to take on the 'thieves', they have far better numbers and their weapons could be more than a match for us."

"I think you worry too much old man, after this evening we'll have killed Gorgana, and a major weapon will have been taken from them."

"Only if we can find him."

"What do you mean?"

"I don't believe he would have taken this dangerous route if he didn't believe he could survive, he has a plan, and sadly I have no idea what it is."

"You probably knew him best, so you should be able to find him even from the most extreme range, with some support from the rest of us."

"That's what I mean, he would know that, he has something prepared for this."

"He can't change who he is. We'll find him and end him. Here's a novel thought, if you search for him, with the power of your knowledge and your people, can I ride like a horse along with you to use the power of my people to kill him?"

"Riding like a piggyback?"

"That's what I mean, you find him we'll kill him. Is this possible?"

"I've never heard of it being done before, but it could be possible. I fairly certain we should be able to act in some sort of concert, we've known each other fairly well over many years." Worandana looked down and the ground his brows furrowed in deep thought.

"You know who would be good at this sort of thing?" He asked looking up again.

"Go on."

"Gorgana. Tuning disparate groups into a concert would be right up his particular alleyway."

"He's not here, I thought that was the whole point."

"Yes, it is the point I am trying to make, we are going to search him out as a concert, what if his defence is a similar concert? He could have the entire group defending him."

"We have to try at least, we may be able to find out where they are, and what they are doing. Alverana's coming back." He pointed to the west.

"I have a stream and a flood plain for a camping place, follow me." He turned and galloped off, not even looking backwards. Kevana and the others followed, over the ridge and down into a small valley, there was a beautiful stream, and large flat span of grass more than suitable for a camp site, so suitable that there was even a charred section of grass where a fire had been recently.

"I wonder if the thieves camped here?" Asked Kevana of no one in particular.

"No." Said Alverana. "this fireplace is far too old. It weeks since there was a fire here."

Kevana glanced at the slowly falling sun. "I want camp set and food done, meditations completed before that sun reaches those mountain tops. Move!" He dropped off his horse and removed the saddle in a moment, dropping his tent and other gear before walking the horse off to a place where the picket line would be set, Petrovana already had one end of the line pegged down and was walking the other one out. Once it was down Kevana threw a running loop around it for his horse's halter. Then released the horse walking back to set up the tent he shared with Alverana, who's fire and cooking duties had him busy right now. All around him the tents were going up and the camp was taking shape. It only took an hour for the camp to be completed and food to be served. Before the sun had fallen behind the mountains everything was ready for the evenings proceedings.

"Kevana. Here's a question for you, there are only three of my clerics left, so can the three of us make a circle or is it a triangle?"

"Sorry I don't actually care, all you have to do is find him, my group will kill him." Looking around the camp, Crathen is of no use at all in this, training would take years before he could be even slightly useful. Kevana stared at Briana, caught his eye, communicating with only eye movements, he asked if Briana was willing to join with the clerics, a brief nod was all he needed.

"Briana, you can join the clerics for now. That makes the groups balanced, four members each. Worandana find this traitor, and we will kill him. Crathen, do something useful, make some tea for when we are finished, we'll probably need it. This is not going to be easy. Worandana, can you tune to me?"

"Yes. I can do that."

"So we tune together and set out to find Gorgana."

"I understand."

"You find him, we kill him."

"I understand. It's still not going to be that easy."

"Will you let me know when you have a target, or do we just tag along all the way?"

"It would be better if you stay here, until we have something for you to attack."

"I'm really struggling with this sort of thing. It's hard to understand being here but somewhere else. I'm sorry but I'm a soldier, I can understand a man hiding behind a tree, but a man being here and behind the tree at the same time is hard for my brain to get a hold of."

"I will send you a call when it's time to tag along."

Worandana turned to the three men that were going to be his circle. "We need to build a charge, then I will separate and go looking for Gorgana, unlike a normal ring, I want you three to keep building charges, once round then throw it at me, even though I am not actually here. Is that clear? I know the repeat charges will be small, but every little bit can help. Any one not understand?" There were no questions asked, so he assumed that they all understood. He turned to the other circle. "When we start building you follow suit, when I launch my search you keep the cycle building, you keep it building until I call, then you Kevana, pick up the next cycle and bring the whole thing with you to where I tell you. You three do as my circle will be doing, once round and send. Do you all understand?" The men in question simply nodded.

"And I'll make the tea." muttered Crathen.

"And you Crathen," smiled Worandana, "will make the tea."

"I want to be there when you kill this traitor." said Crathen.

"You don't have the training or the skill for this. Tea it is." Said Worandana.

"Right." said Worandana, softly. "Does everyone understand?"

The whole group nodded but said nothing.

"My circle, I am going to want absolute maximum output from you, I'm going to need an immense charge before I launch, so be ready for some fast and furious energy exchanges, I will only launch when I think that you have given all there is to give, and just that little bit more. Everybody ready?" Nods again. "I'll start." They all settled into two circles, both leaders started the energy cycles, Worandana's group, having more highly trained people in it, achieved a much higher rate and much higher output, in only a minute Worandana was ready to launch, so he did. Taking a massive surge of energy with him he leapt into space and set off vaguely east and south, calling Gorgana's name, hoping to make contact, along with the name he called to the staff that he had carried for so many years, it was an old friend, suddenly it was the staff that came into view, changed though it was, somewhere deep inside some part of it was still his. Somehow the man holding it wasn't Gorgana. The man was sitting cross-legged on the grass, the staff across his knees, facing him was another man, older, staff similarly placed, standing over them insubstantial, was a woman. She looked straight into Worandana's eyes.

"He is mine now, you cannot have him." Her voice echoed in his head.

Worandana felt another surge of energy from his circle, and converted it to fire, throwing it at the female figure. The campfire behind her grew rapidly both in size and intensity, Worandana could feel the heat on his face, the paired staves took on the same green tinged light of the fire, as did the woman, she expanded until the seated men were hunched between her legs, she stood over them, calm, her green eyes focused tightly on Worandana's astral form, he suddenly felt weak, then next surge from his circle arrived, and he called to Kevana. 'Kevana, bring everything that you can.'

In a heartbeat Kevana was there, he threw a massive bolt of energy at the one he believed to be Gorgana, the woman caught it in her hand, and absently tossed it right back. Kevana's shape faltered, flickered, almost extinguished.

"He is mine now, you cannot have him." she said again. Her form seemed to thicken as they watched, she became more solid, less transparent. Energy pulses from their respective circles arrived at almost the same instant, Kevana chose lightning, Worandana tried fire again, only this time they both aimed for the strange figure, she recoiled slightly, as they hit, but she didn't fall, she reached towards the invaders, green fire flew from her fingers and struck at them, it did little harm, but they knew they were under attack, slowly Kevana's arms and chest became engulfed in green flames, Worandana fared a little better he was managing to keep the fire from attaching itself to his arms, the next surge gave the priests enough power to cast off the green fire. Worandana set up a continuous attack, electricity flowed from his fingertips, trying to find a way passed the woman, into the two men below her, where ever the lightning probed she intercepted it, with green fire or her hands, she seemed to have no real issue absorbing all he could send, the next surge from Kevana's group, he tried something different, changing the energy into a river of cold water, directed at the fire in the background. For a moment the fire decreased in it's intensity, but soon roared back into the life, Worandana noticed the change in the fire, and a corresponding reduction the the woman's strength, with his next surge he followed Kevana's lead, only a steaming river of ice was aimed at the fire, again the fire reduced but rapidly returned, Kevana's next pulse another blast of ice, with exactly the same result, the two were expending their power simply to suppress the fire and the woman, but they had nothing left to attack their real targets. With a gesture the womanly figure engulfed the two seated figures with green fire, surrounding them with it's protective glow. With every ice attack it dipped and returned. Her voice boomed in their heads.

"Who is going to tire first? Leave now, while you still can." They could feel the power building in her as the fire behind her grew. The two priests glanced at each other and used the next surge to return. Their return shut down both circles. All concerned staggered, Briana fell over on to his back, gasping for breath.

"Is he dead?" asked Crathen. Worandana shook his head, and reached out for a cup of tea. Kevana hung his head, then looked up at Worandana.

"What just happened?"

"We got beaten, quite comprehensively. I don't know who that woman is, but she protects him now."

"She took that charge and just tossed it back at me, not what I expected to happen. Who is she?"

"I don't have a single clue, could he have been recruited by another god already?"

"I don't see how, and which goddess was that?"

"Her image doesn't match any that I have read about, but there was something very fundamental about her power."

"Could the image have been projected by the two men?"

"Perhaps, but to what end?"

"To distract and confuse us, an image they could both associate with, and concentrate their forces against us."

"Kevana, did you notice the fire, it was the same colour as her eyes, as were the staves."

"What does that mean?"

"The fire was considerably smaller when I first got there, it seemed to get larger and hotter as soon as I attacked her."

"So he has a fire goddess protecting him?"

"No. More likely they were taking energy from the fire and channelling it through her."

"So effectively, two of them beat all eight of us?"

"That seems to be the case."

"We definitely need more people." Kevana thought for a few moments. "We rest tonight and, in the morning, we reach out for a local monastery. If I have to conscript every able-bodied man, then that is what I will do. These people are getting far too strong far too quickly."

"So is that it, you're not going to do anything else." asked Crathen.

"No." replied Kevana, more than a little fatigued. "We were comprehensively bested by what I believe to be only two, count them, two of our opponents. None of the others were involved. Eight against two and we lost. We need many more bodies before we attack them again."

"How can I help?"

"The discipline for this sort of things takes years of training, so I am very sorry it is unlikely that you can be of any use to us at all, until we get within physical striking distance, then you can run onto their swords and distract them while we kill them, with all our gratitude."

"A little harsh." said Petrovana. "At least he's willing to help."

"Agreed." said Kevana. "You didn't choose to be here, so we should really thank you for all your help. I'm just a little short of, well, anything right now, patience, confidence, endurance, take your pick."

"Right." said Worandana. "Sleep now, new world in the morning." They all had a last drink of hot tea before going to their tents.

Kevana and Alverana crawled into the tent that they shared. Stripped their travelling clothes and covered themselves with their sleep rolls.

"Just how bad was that goddess?" asked Alverana.

"She took the blast that I took there, as if it was nothing, just caught it and sent it back at me. I didn't believe it."

"Was this like an energy hand off in a power circle?"

"Now that is not something I thought about at the time. But yes, I suppose much like a hand off, but I sent that as a blast of fire, it should have roasted anything it hit, even one of ours."

"What happened to that blast of hot fire?"

"I'm not actually sure, it came back to me, but had no power, it was simply a flare. So that damned green goddess pulled all the juice and then sent it back empty."

"But why?"

"Because she could. I have never felt so inadequate since the early training, when it was decided that I should be a soldier."

"You regret that?" asked Alverana, softly.

"Not really, can you imagine how highly strung either of us would be dealing with clerics all day, every day?"

"At the moment that is exactly what we do."

"Oh, how much fun is that?"

"Well, not much, but without them we'd never have made it into the mountain let alone out of it."

"True, but I don't have to like it."

"Agreed, but we do need them, and more like them, we are going to have to put up with them for a while longer, perhaps a long while."

"That's one of the things that worries me, do we need clerics, or soldiers?"

"What do you mean?"

"To be brutal, we can find them, we can track them, we can hunt them down and kill them, the clerics can track them, hunt them and kill them from a distance. Do we really need them? So far killing from a distance has been a complete failure, every time we have tried this something goes wrong. The longer this drags on the more I begin to believe that we need to make this a face to face physical confrontation, then, and only then we will win."

"Perhaps." replied Alverana. "They do have a powerful magician, or more accurately now two."

"And a new god, to protect them."

"It would be good not to have to deal with clerics, but we really have no choice, they are far better at dealing with the magicians."

"True I suppose, but we have to stop them taking too much control until we are actually in range, and I mean visual range."

"So we are going to find some more men, then just chase these thieves down?"

"Yes. It's going to mean some hard riding, and some long days."

"How will Worandana take this?"

"To be honest, I don't really care, the choices are simple, we need more men, both soldiers and clerics, this will put us some more days behind the thieves, so we will have some serious catching up to do, I feel that Gorgana has made this a little easier for us, if only by accident."

"Easier?"

"Oh yes. I think I can track the damned green goddess from half a world away, in fact I think I'm going to be lucky to keep the bitch out of my dreams."

"You want me to guard your dreams for you?"

"No, you get some sleep, hard riding tomorrow." Alverana simply nodded and turned away, as if to sleep. Though this was far from his mind, which spun round in turmoil, like a dog chasing it's tail, he knew he wasn't going to sleep much. Kevana was exactly the same, they lay back to back in their sleeping rolls, neither doing much in the way of sleeping.

"Wake up, sleepy heads." Came the call from outside the tent. Kevana failed to identify the voice, but rolled away from the warm body pressed against his back.

"Let's get moving." He whispered to Alverana. The two dressed and crawled out into full daylight, the sun well above the horizon.

"I thought we were going to be on the road early." Call Worandana, barely dressed himself.

"Well," said Kevana, "when did you wake up?"

"Just now."

"Who woke you?"

"Crathen."

"The rest of us are very tired after last night, Crathen is still fresh. Well done young man, some of these sluggabeds could have slept until noon."

"Who are you calling sluggabed?" Demanded Worandana.

"An old saying comes to mind, it's something about hats, I don't quite remember." Laughed Kevana, gripping his old friends shoulder affectionately.

"Anyone any idea at all where the nearest monastery might be?"

No one made any reply.

"Anyone even seen a map of this area?"

"I saw one many years ago." said Worandana, "but it was an old map then, so of no real use right now, not that I can remember it anyway."

"Looks like we are going to need a search, volunteers?"

"Why?" asked Crathen, "The city is south and a little west, and I believe the monastery is south of that, how hard can it be to find?"

"Sometimes I think we rely far too much on our magic." said Worandana. "Lead on Crathen."

"I'm not saying I know where it is, but even on a warm day like today, it's going to produce a smoke plume that can be seen for miles. Once we start to see the farms, all we have to do is follow the tracks, they'll lead to the city, where else are they going to go?"

"Well said young man." said Kevana, "Let's get this camp stripped down and get moving, we still have some thieves to kill." It took a short time to pack everything away and mount up.

"Alverana, Crathen." shouted Kevana. "Take point, let's see if we can find some friends before the end of today." The column formed up and set off at a fairly leisurely pace south and a little west.

It was almost noon before they came upon some cultivated fields, there was no one working them, but the cabbages were doing what cabbages do, growing slowly, adding a certain fragrance to the air. The track around the edges of the fields were quite narrow, but offered no risks for the horses, choosing the southerly paths whenever they could they made excellent time, though they found no one to give them any directions.

"Rest." Yelled Kevana soon after the sun passed its zenith. The horses were more than happy for the respite from the punishing pace, so were the men, they sat on the grass verge of a cross road, the horses feasting on the lush greenery, the men just resting.

"How far do you think we are from the town?" asked Kevana of Crathen.

"I'm not sure, I never actually went there, but the others were there and back in just over half a day, and our camp had no fields around it."

"Alverana, what do you think?"

"The roads aren't yet wide enough for carts to pass each other, so we are still a way out of town. If these clouds would blow away we might even be able to get a better indication of direction." As if Zandaar had heard him a gap opened in the rapidly flowing cloud cover, large fingers of sunlight reached down and clawed at the ground, Alverana scanned the area looking for any signs of a major settlement. Suddenly he raised an arm and pointed.

"There. The air looks thicker that way, either the town is there, or some farmer is burning the stubble off a field, but it's not exactly the season for burning."

"That's almost directly west." Said Kevana.

"And quite a way."

"You mean we could have ridden straight by and missed the town completely?"

"That is a possibility, but night would most likely have given away it's location. We'd have found it tomorrow at the latest, it's still going to be late today before we get there."

"We need to get there before the sun goes down," said Kevana, "the gates are likely to be closed after then, and not opened until sunrise."

"You can be certain of that," said Crathen, "it seems that Namdarin caused quite a stir on his way out of town, even brought a member of the city guard with him."

"So we may have some problems getting into the city?"

"I'd say so, but who can say that was a few days ago."

"Rest over." called Kevana, "let's not kill the horses, but I'd rather not wait all night outside this city." They all mounted up and set off in the direction that Alverana had indicated. In less than an hour it became obvious that they were going the right way, the paths became wider, they say more people working in the fields, more carts, and more houses. They avoided contact with the people as much as they could, farmers can talk for hours about a cow that died three years ago, this was time they didn't need to waste. As the city walls came into view the sun was still a fair way from setting, Alverana slowed the pace while there was still a way to go to the gates.

"Why so slow?" asked Crathen.

"Give the horses chance to cool down a little, perhaps the guards will be more trusting if they don't think we are in such a rush."

"Why are we in a rush, I thought Kevana wanted a monastery, not this city?"

"I think a night in a bed, and good food and stabling for the horses will be good for us all, and turning up at a monastery mid-morning, on cool horses, and not so travel worn, will give a much better impression than what you see now." He glanced back down the line, Crathen followed his look, the group did have a seriously stressed and dishevelled look about them.

"We do look a little desperate." laughed Crathen, Alverana slowed the horses down a little more and waved at Kevana, bringing him to the front of the column, the open gate now only fifty yards away. A guard by the gate finally noticed their formation, he looked in through the gate and then came back out to block their path with his spear, in moments more men came out to stand with him, two spears crossed was more than enough to block passage into the town, and more spears behind them.

CHAPTER FORTY TWO

Granger groaned even before Namdarin managed to turn him over, Gregor was completely lifeless. Jangor held a hand to his throat and found a slow pulse.

"He's alive." he declared. Granger looked around, somewhat bemused.

"Is everyone else all right?" asked Granger in hushed tones.

"Everyone is fine," said Namdarin, "but I don't think the elves are going to be very happy when they get down here, your fire tried its level best to burn down their trees."

"Move the fire further out, we are going to need it."

Mander and Andel, approached the sticks that had formed the basis of the fire, and finding them cold moved them further way from the trees. Elves started to appear all around, they had taken many pathways down from the branches, amongst the first of them was the Eldest. The other elves hung back in deference to the leader, not entirely sure what was going to happen.

"Now that was different." Said the Eldest to Jangor. "Whatever was happening there, we were simply defending the trees."

"I am sorry. We had no intention to put your trees in any danger, I certainly didn't think that the fire would get that big, it was certainly intense for a while." Jangor bowed slightly to the old elf.

"Well. I enjoyed that." Said the Eldest, looking round at all the surprised faces of his people. "I have never heard the trees call so loud for support, and it wasn't only in their defence either, they wanted us to help your people. Sadly, we were struggling just to keep the fire away from the branches, the trees themselves were pushing power into that fire. We have never seen this sort of thing before. It was so good to see that so many are still sensitive to the needs of the trees." Turning to the crowd. "Thank you, my people, I think the danger is passed, you can all return to your homes, but be ready there may be a further call. Well done to you all." Turning back to Jangor, the crowd just melted back into the trees, except for one, a 'young' female, though elves don't actually appear to age as humans do.

"Laura." said the Eldest, "you can return as well, I have nothing to fear here amongst these people."

"I am here for you, you will not send me away." Her bow of deference did nothing to reduce the imperative of her statement.

"Jangor. This is Laura, kin of my kin, somewhere back in time, she has become very protective of me in recent years."

"Decades you mean." She spoke clearly but quietly; her voice had the sound of small bells behind it. Jangor stared briefly into her large violet eyes, feeling an intense attraction, suddenly he turned away. With a shake of his head he turned back to the eldest.

"Are you sure there are no problems with your people? After all that was a large fire."

"No problems at all, and now you've moved its base I'll restart it for you." With a simple hand gesture, the fire started again, this time at a more manageable level. "How are your people?" asked the Eldest. Jangor looked round to see Granger climbing slowly to his feet, Gregor was groaning and slowly coming around, his right hand searching for his staff, when he found it his whole body suddenly tensed, a snapped intake of breath and a slow exhale, Gregor levered himself into the upright leaning heavily on the staff.

"That was insane." He said, staring at Granger.

"It was that and more." replied Granger, smiling hugely.

"Damn it." snapped Jangor. "What happened?" He turned around, "And what is going on with you two?" He caught both Namdarin and Jayanne with his eyes.

"What do you mean?" frowned Namdarin.

"Something that never happens." He paused and looked around for a moment or two. "Weapons." he shouted. Namdarin's hand snapped above his right shoulder, Jayanne's hand snapped, in its normal manner. Sword nor axe were where they should have been. "Fools." Snapped Jangor, parade ground voice shaking the trees. Namdarin's frown deepened, his shoulders tensed, tendons showing like cables, Jayanne's crouch deepened and her biceps grew under extreme tension. With a soft whistling sound both sword and axe left their places on the ground and raced to the waiting hands, almost as one they slapped into waiting palms.

"You were both separated from your weapons, any one could have run off with them."

Jayanne simply dropped the axe.

"Anyone?" She asked. "Do you feel lucky enough to try it?"

The hard green of her eyes locked into Jangor's, in a few seconds he looked away.

"That's a good choice." said Granger, "I'm not sure how the axe would deal with a strange hand, especially now that Jayanne has sort of tamed it." As it drifted gently back to her hand.

"Namdarin." he went on. "How are you for power?"

"Pretty good, not full, but plenty on tap." They both looked to Jayanne. She simply nodded.

"Well I am almost completely out." Said Granger turning the unasked question to Gregor.

"Just about dry." The pair walked over to the new fire and dropped the staves into it. The fire roared up into the night sky, too far from the trees to be any danger, but far too high to be comfortable for the people, so they moved away a few paces.

"Will somebody please tell me what is going on?" Asked the Eldest. Kern placed a brawny arm around the elf's skinny shoulders.

"Once it was established that no one was dead, there was a brief military discussion, about carelessness with weaponry, and now the gentlemen are recharging their staffs with the power from your wonderful fire." said Kern, quietly.

"Staves." Muttered the Eldest.

"Or what you will." smiled Kern.

Brank came and stood next to Laura. He looked down smiling, "Sometimes I think these people are crazy."

"Oh my, you're tall." she said, "How long have you known them?"

"I think mother filled my boots with manure when I was young." he laughed, reciting a joke told him so many times. "I've known these people less than two days, now that is so scary, not yet two days and we've been through so much together." He laughed and dropped to his knees so that he was nearer to her height, she was still looking up at him, but with less of a crick in her neck. She smiled, "They must be good people?" she asked.

"I believe so, they have honour, and a serious quest, but good is difficult to say, they have potential for extreme violence, but are generally honourable, or so I feel. No, they are good people."

"Do they mean my people harm." Her almond shaped eyes wide, her voice shaky and smooth at the same time.

"My dear," his voice lowered as he leaned down towards her, "I can't believe they mean harm to anyone other than Zandaar, and I don't mean the priests, Namdarin means to kill their god."

"For truth?"

"For truth, threatened they respond rapidly, within hours of meeting Jangor and Kern, Namdarin challenged an entire city to gain the freedom of his friends and myself. He didn't even know me then, I'm not sure he knows me even now, he needed to free his friends, I just tagged along for the ride."

"How can you trust him?"

"Have you heard of how we met Gervane and his patrol?"

"No."

"I'm assuming standard tactics here, we are stopped on the road by one man, the rest are concealed in the trees around us. They threaten us, Namdarin challenges, he's like that, Gervane steps forwards, Namdarin informs him that he will die first, and that we will all die, and if Gervane's force sets off home with better than one in ten, they should consider themselves victorious. His last words were 'Stand ready.' Swords were drawn, hell, even the wolf had a target ready, the man in the road was going to lose his throat before the wolf died. Gervane called for a truce before things got messy."

"Would you have died for him?"

"That would have been the most likely outcome, Gregor's shield would have stopped the first volley of arrows, there would not have been a second. We would all have died, the odds against us were too great, though many of your people would have died too. That would have been a very bad day."

"Bad for you?"

"Yes and no, bad for all of us. Namdarin has no wish to kill any other than Zandaar, if the priests come within range then they die, if they stay away he'll not actually hunt them down."

"Will you follow him until the end?"

"Most likely, Kern and I have a sort of brotherhood, I had to leave my previous employment, I was forced to kill a man who was related by marriage to the commander of the guard."

"Forced?"

"He made the mistake of threatening an old friend, a very old friend it turned out. Before he could carry out his threat both Jangor and I killed him."

"You killed him over a simple threat, was there no other way?"

"It seems I don't respond well to threats either." Brank laughed. He turned to the others, just as Kern returned to the group with his arm still around the Eldest.

"Gregor. What happened? All we saw was raging fire." asked Jangor, more than a little impatiently.

"Granger had suggested that I use the image of my mother to protect myself, we did this before we started out to come here, tonight we settled down to charge the staffs and reinforce this image, while we were doing this my old friends decided to attack, first Worandana arrived carrying a heavy charge, then Kevana came carrying even more power, that in itself is strange, the figure of my mother formed and took their attacks from them, without causing either of us any harm, they attacked her a few times then started throwing ice at the fire, they sensed that it was the source of her power, the harder they hit it the more power it gave, the mother figure bathed them in fire, which they threw off, with every surge of the fire I could feel the power of the elves pushing it away from the trees, only pushing it away not really trying to put it out, more concentrating it. Their attacks began to develop a rhythm, they were running entirely on the power coming from their circles, I knew they couldn't keep this up for much longer, so I made the figure speak to them, she asked who would tire first, and suggested they leave while they still can. They did."

"So what does that mean to us?" asked Jangor.

"I'd say," said Gregor slowly, "the only person missing from their attack was Crathen, he would have no skill for this, the whole of their group attacked us, and the two of us beat them."

"Not quite true." said Granger. Gregor frowned. "Look at it from their point of view, the two of us, a mystical woman, and a huge fire. That's what beat them."

"But beat them we did."

"Certainly."

"But what does that mean to us?" asked Jangor again.

"I don't believe," said Gregor, "that they'll try that again any time soon."

"I agree." said Granger, "they need more men before they can even think of that sort of thing again, probably a lot more."

"Brank." said Jangor, turning to the big man, "how far from the town, and how big was that monastery?"

"Maybe a couple of days ride, and I've no idea how big, never went there."

"So we are looking at three or four days before they even start after us again?"

"Most likely. " nodded Brank.

"So that gives us a few days breather, but we have a battle in the morning, so we need to get some rest, where the hell is Gervane?"

"Why do you want Gervane?" asked the Eldest.

"I asked him to find us some lamp oil, or something similar."

"That is not going to be easy, you've seen our fires, they don't even destroy the wood, so lighting oil is just something we don't use."

"He seemed to think he has something useful. I just wish he'd get here, I want to test it before we actually have to use it."

"I am sure he'll be here in due course, in the mean time I could have food and drink brought down."

"That would be very kind." said Jangor, "If it's not too much trouble."

"It's no trouble, I'll send word." The Eldest's big eyes closed slowly, after a short time they opened again. "Food and drink are on the way, as is Gervane, but he's not happy, I'm not sure why, but he's not."

"You can communicate without seeing the people you are 'talking' to." said Granger.

"Yes," replied the Eldest, "not over any real distance and only with those one knows well, it's takes skill and practice, but over time we get better at it."

"A useful skill." said Gregor, "One that the Zandaars are very good at. When we know the person we want to talk to reaching many days travel isn't difficult, talking to strangers is something else."

"Here comes the food." said the Eldest, waving to small group of elves carrying baskets. Behind these stamped Gervane, his face a stormy cloud. While the food was being laid out on the ground, Jangor approached Gervane.

"What is wrong my friend?" he asked.

"I am sorry, I can't find anything like lamp oil, we don't use anything like it, I thought the engineers, the ones that build our lifting gear, they should have some light oil, or at least something, but all they have is this grease, it's too thick and heavy to be of use, it does burn if it gets hot enough, but it's just not fluid enough." He turned one of the pots upside down and nothing fell out.

"Don't fret, we'll find something that will work. Have a drink to calm your nerves." said Jangor reaching for his flask.

"Try some of ours for a change." said Gervane, taking a flask from inside his jacket. Jangor popped the lid off it and took a large gulp, his eyes opened wide, he forced a swallow, the heat of the spirit burned his throat all the way to his stomach.

"That was mean." said the Eldest, "Spritz is sometimes far too strong for some of our own people, me included." Gervane laughed at Jangor's continuing breathing issues.

"Oh my," spluttered Jangor, "that is seriously strong."

"I think our distillation process goes a little further than yours." said Gervane, smiling.

Jangor stared at the flask in his hand, like it was a venomous snake. Then at the pots Gervane had left on the ground, then back to the flask, and the pots.

"That is an idea." said Gervane. "It's going upset some people's feelings, but it should work."

"It's going to upset my feelings, but we need to give it a try. Can you get some more and mixing vessels for us?"

"I think I'll let the top man do that." he turned to the Eldest, "Can you get us some more Spritz, say about three gallons, some buckets, and some wine bottles?"

"These people have a battle tomorrow, three gallons of Spritz will most likely kill them. Add wine and they'll certainly be dead."

"I think you have missed the point." said Laura. "They plan to turn your favourite drink into a weapon."

"You cannot mean that?" he whispered.

"I believe they do, some mixture of Spritz and grease will make an excellent weapon to end the undead soldiers, and perhaps even the king himself."

"But three gallons of Spritz? Does it have to be that much? That will take much of the stock, and days to replace."

"The poor old one." Laura laughed, "he'll have to make do with wine."

"Don't tell them about the wine." he looked from side to side rapidly. "You can't tell what they'll want to do with that, latrine cleaner perhaps."

"Personally," she said, reaching out to hold his hand, "Spritz is only fit for drain cleaner anyway."

Both Eldest and Jangor gasped at such a statement, Gervane threw back his head and laughed aloud, engendering stares from the others. "You people," he said between laughs, "may be completely crazy, but you're certainly not boring. Eldest you send the call for the supplies we need."

"Must I." he turned to Laura for support.

"Do it." she whispered. He closed his eyes slowly, after a moment he opened them again. "It's done." He slumped to the grass, looking for all the world like a lost puppy in the rain. Laura leaned down and kissed him on the forehead whispering. "You poor old elf." Smiling she turned to Brank. "I believe these people to be good, if crazy, you may all die." Brank slowly knelt before her, taking each of her small hands in his. He looked deep into her eyes, then spoke in a loud voice. "Do you want to live forever?" The answering shouts all around caused Laura to jump, startled by the shouts that all said the same. "No!"

"This is the way soldiers live, it's the only way we can live." Slowly she leaned forwards and reached up to kiss him, long and soft. When she broke away she whispered "Crazy." She turned away but held on to one hand. A small group of elves were walking towards them, loaded down with all sorts of boxes and things. They approached the Eldest.

"We weren't exactly sure what you wanted, or why you wanted it but I think we have brought everything you and your new friends could possibly need."

"That is not very polite." said the Eldest, without getting up. "These people are your friends as well, so please treat them as such."

"Apologies, to you and our new friends, the distillers are a little unhappy at the hit their stocks have taken, they are even now bringing an old still back into service, they know that no matter the outcome there is likely to be considerable drinking tomorrow."

"So long as there is enough Spritz for me, the rest can make do with wine."

"Hang on." said Jangor, "You led me to believe that Spritz was too strong for you, now everyone else has to make do with wine?"

"That." interrupted Gervane, "was a small joke, we all know that no one drinks Spritz like our beloved leader, I think he was trying to catch some of us laughing, but again he failed. Sometimes his sense of humour is a little strange."

Jangor turned to the group of elves. "Many thanks for the food and drink, please feel free to join us, we will be more than happy to share."

The elves exchanges glances then politely refused, Jangor shrugged as they walked away.

"It's not you." said Gervane, nodding towards the Eldest, "some of the people don't like being too close to him, he does have a propensity for handing out tasks, with absolutely no thought to what the people may be doing in their lives."

"I see. Their loss. Mander sort the food and drinks out, Spritz is for eldest only and of course our experimentation. While that is going on why don't you and I start with the experimentation?" Jangor said to Gervane.

"I don't know how I can help really, how hard can it be?"

"We may have to do some sampling."

"That to is true, let's be some way apart from the others, we don't want them getting hurt." Laughed Gervane. The two of them carried some supplies further from the trees, they really had no idea how things would go. Mander dropped a flask in the Eldest's hands, along with some food, mainly meat, bread and gravy. The food he basically ignored.

"It's gone quiet." Whispered Laura to Brank, leaning in close whilst sitting on the grass next to him.

"I don't expect it to last. These people even get noisy in their sleep."

"I think I am beginning to understand. Hey, you're not so tall when you're lying down."

"No, but I certainly cover a lot of grass." He laughed and reached towards her to kiss her again, she leaned towards him, putting her arm across his body and pushing him down onto the grass, as she laid alongside him, her feet were level with his thighs, she looked like a child next to him.

"How old are you?" he asked breaking the kiss and looking up into her eyes.

"I may be small next to you, but isn't everyone? But I probably have more years than you would believe."

"You may be surprised by what I can believe, a friend of mine, who it turns out is only part elf, recently told me that he was a hundred and thirty years old. I believed him with no problems, so you could easily be that old or forty, either way you have much more experience that I do at a mere twenty-six years, this is a daunting prospect."

"You are daunted by a child sized woman?" she giggled, rolling across on top of him and sitting more upright.

"You are not helping, sitting there staring down at me with those huge eyes."

"Who is this half elf?" she asked, wriggling against him, just to add to his discomfort.

"His name is Andreas, more like a quarter elf, please stop squirming like that it's most distracting."

"Mixed race children are very rare, not always a joy for the families concerned, but definitely rare." She leaned forwards and supported herself on her crossed arms on his chest, she stared for a moment then lowered her mouth to his. Mander walked up with food in one hand and a bottle of wine in the other.

"Brank. I know you are new to this group, but I am the one who chases the women."

Laura turned her head and looked up at Mander, then she slowly looked down to his boots and back up again before speaking. "You're too small and pale." Brank laughed loudly, Laura bouncing on his pitching belly. She settled onto his chest and kissed his neck softly. Gently he levered himself into an upright position, she swung her legs forwards, and gripped his sides with them.

"You're wide as well." She whispered. He held her close for a moment or two, then whispered. "Shall we eat?"

"I'm quite comfortable here." She said.

"You are starting to make me a little uncomfortable."

"I can tell." she smiled, then stood up, glancing down at the bulge in his trousers she turned towards the Eldest. There was a loud explosion, she screamed and dived back into Branks arms.

"Shush." he said, stoking her hair. "It's just Jangor and Gervane experimenting, I think they got the mix a little too hot that time.

"Sorry." Shouted Jangor, picking himself up from the grass, "It's a work in progress, we'll get it right before dawn, I hope." he laughed.

"Try drinking less of it." Shouted the Eldest.

"That might be an idea." said Jangor, turning back to Gervane, "A little less Spritz next time."

"I concur." replied Gervane, laughing. "I hadn't realised just how explosive Spritz is, I think I will make some recommendations about reducing the strength of it, it's just too dangerous."

"I think." said the Eldest loudly. "I shall recommend a new posting to the wastes of the far north, fancy being the new commander Gervane?"

"Sorry my lord, but I'd much rather not."

"Then you keep your recommendations to yourself, and so will I."

"Agreed my lord, just please be careful near an open flame with your Spritz in future. I'm surprised no one has been killed already."

Jangor went back to mixing and the others returned to their food and drink.

Laura sat down beside Brank, sharing a large plate of food, that was mainly vegetables and a right gravy, and a bottle of rich red wine. As he passed the bottle back to her she asked, "What do you think of our wine?"

"It's very good, but I don't drink much wine, I don't drink much of anything really, I have found that things can turn quickly ugly, so I prefer to keep my senses sharp. Jangor's the man to ask, he likes his wine, and seems to drink more than anyone."

"He's a little pre-occupied right now, perhaps I'll ask him later or in the morning."

Very soon all the food was eaten, and the wine was flowing slowly, the camp settled down for that quiet time before bed, Namdarin and Jayanne were sitting together, holding hands and saying nothing, even Mander and Andel had stopped bickering.

"Granger." Called Jangor, waving a small pot in the air, "Hit this with a blast of that fancy blue fire of yours." Granger's staff snapped up and pointed at the designated item. Jangor dived for the ground. "Not while I've still got hold of it." He yelled. Placing the pot on the ground and walking away, Granger waited for a nod, and on the signal released a small bolt of blue fire at the pot. There was a moderately loud thump, and blazing fluid scattered around the broken pot, burning hotly, a bright yellow in the deepening dusk.

"That'll do," said Jangor, "let's mix up some more before we get too drunk." Gervane just nodded. It didn't take them long to mix up several more batches of the highly inflammable liquid. All the time they were drinking the wine that the elves had provided. Gervane prevailed upon Jangor to try one he had never seen before, it was a strange looking pale wine, generally of the colour that would be called white, as in not red, but this one was most certainly green. Not a vivid green, but a soft and transparent green.

"We call it springwine," said Gervane, "It's the basis of Spritz, we make huge batches of it, by collecting the first rising sap of the spring, it is sweet enough to ferment without any additional sugars, this gives it its singular taste and colour. We tap the sap all through the summer as well, but nothing is as good as that first rush of spring."

"It's very good." said Jangor. "Different from anything I've every drunk, I can't really describe it, the only word that actually comes to mind is green, the stuff tastes green. What do you say Kern?"

"I've tasted it before, many years ago, and from a different forest, but green is the only word that fits."

"This is a real journey of discovery, beers, wines, and spirits galore." Jangor sat down next to Gervane, and they began to talk as soldiers often do of battles, campaigns and women, and let's not forget drinks. Brank and Laura were sitting outside the tent he shared with Gregor, making conversation about something and nothing, he was telling her of his life, his past and his friends.

"Tell me of this half elf you know."

"He's not half, maybe a quarter, his grandmother was an elf, daughter of Braid, I think, I'm not really sure, I don't really get names, stories of battle and wars, these I get, but names and families just seem to get away from me, anyway, Andreas father was half elf, he lived a very long life, by our standards, Andreas himself is a hundred and thirty years, an impossible age for a man, but it seems that a little elven blood goes a long way. "

"Is he a good man?"

"Oh yes, he has a family that he provides well, though sadly his children are all dead, not enough elf in them, but he cares for his grandchildren, even though they be in their dotage. They are only half his age, but almost done with this life, his great grands are doing well, and another generation in on its way. By all the gods!" he exclaimed.

"What is it?" Laura asked.

"When Andreas does eventually die, his funeral is going to be enormous, almost a quarter of the city are his relations in some way, if only by marriage. That's going to be a party and a half, and I'm going to miss it."

"He may still be alive when your quest is done."

"He may be, but there is no certainty that I will be." He lay back on the grass and crossed his hands on his chest.

"I may be no seer, but I believe you will survive, and that you will get back for Andreas' funeral, and then come here to tell me of it, and your quest."

"But you may not be here, you could have moved on, married with children and such."

"In your lifetime, somehow I think not. The only male I care about is over there pouring Spritz down his neck, trying to forget the things he could have achieved as king, he'll none of me. Even if you make him king tomorrow, he'll not accomplish half as much as he would like before he dies, he's of the line of kings, he was boyhood friend to Braids father, to him, your lives are as the mayfly."

"And to you?"

"That is yet to be decided." She smiled, her eyes glowing in the flickering firelight.

"I think it's time for bed." said Gervane staggered to his feet and stumbling over to where the Eldest was lying on the grass. He reached down, offering a hand to his leader, the hands clasped and the Eldest was drawn slowly to his feet. The Eldest looked at Laura. 'Are you coming?' he asked without the words being audible to the humans around them. 'No.' she replied. 'Gervane will see you to your bed, I'll stay a while, I think I'll try out this man, he appears to be nice enough.' 'Be careful, granddaughter.' said the Eldest. 'Too often are we moths to the flame of their passions, they burn so hot and so fast, I don't want you to be hurt.' 'Grandfather, or is that great grandfather, I am a big girl, I've tried enough lovers, I want to feel that passion that I have heard so much and so little about.' 'There is a reason it's not talked about, their love is a trap, a prison, a snare of short years and pain. Please daughter, do not go there.' 'Grandfather I will do this, I will experience this, why should you, or I, deny myself this? I'll give a smile when the pain comes, because the memories will be so bright that nothing can eclipse them.' 'Or,' said Gervane, 'he could be a very bad lover.' 'Whatever happens I'll tell you in the morning, when these humans go off to make grandfather a king,' She turned away and lay her head on Branks crossed hands. He uncrossed his hands and held her to his chest, where the slow beating of his heart filled her ears. Gervane and the Eldest wobbled together towards the trees, as they passed between the trees two ropes dropped from above, Gervane gripped one and tied the other to the Eldest's wrist, is a heartbeat they vanished upwards into the branches.

"Aren't you going with them?" asked Brank, dreading the answer.

"No," she whispered, "not yet a while." she smiled up at him, moving slowly upwards, until she was close enough to kiss him, which she did. Kern stood and attracted everyone's attention, except those currently kissing. Pointing to people, he indicated watch duties, Gregor and Mander, first, Granger and Andel second, himself and Jayanne, third, Namdarin and Stergin fourth. Namdarin waved at Kern, pointed at Jangor, Kern looked at Jangor, shrugged and ran his finger across his throat, Jangor was already dead. Everyone smiled and retreated to their tents, except for the designated guards. By the time Brank and Laura broke the kiss, the camp was empty, the guards had retreated from the fire light, whispered voices was all that could be heard of them, the brilliant green eyes of the wolf shone from it's station outside Kern and Jangor's tent, Jangor still didn't trust the wolf enough to allow it into the tent.

"Where did everyone go?" asked Laura.

"Guards are out of sight somewhere, and everyone else is in bed, we have a battle in the morning remember?"

"Why do you need guards?" she asked, her voice raising above a whisper.

"We are a military camp."

"In friendly territory."

"Agreed, however, there are factions within your people, who would much prefer that the Eldest wasn't made king tomorrow by his new friends. They made that very clear."

"I agree, but what can they do? If they attack you he will have them all killed, he has more than enough following amongst the people."

"But what happens if he dies tonight?"

"There will be a massive power struggle, there are at least three groups that would be fighting for control."

"Which will win?"

"Give me a moment." She closed her eyes. 'Gervane!' her mind fairly howled into the night, the wolf twitched, and looked around. 'Gervane!' 'I hear you, Laura, what do you want?' 'Our new friends have an idea that the Eldest may be in danger, they feel that someone may try to kill him, or them, there are a lot of people who would rather he not be king.' 'I'm way ahead of you, well Jangor mentioned it earlier, the eldest is surrounded by twenty guards, personally loyal to me, and certain members of the council, the ones most opposed to the eldest, have been conscripted as food tasters, they were quite upset about this, certain members of their personal guards are a little under the weather right now, but no one has been killed as yet. Do these measures meet your requirements?' 'Yes, thank you, I got a little worried.' 'Fret ye not. Everything is under control, now go have your fun and get it out of your system.' 'What if it doesn't get it out of my system?' 'I'll still be here to pick up the pieces later on.' 'Somehow Gervane, I find your devotion more than a little disconcerting.' 'I am who I am, of that you can have no doubt.' 'True, I suppose, talk in the morning?' 'Waiting is.' The mental link broke with a shock that surprised her.

"I have talked to Gervane, the Eldest is well protected, or so it seems, Jangor advise Gervane that he may be in danger earlier."

"He's an sharp man."

"So are you."

"I suppose, I'm just a soldier."

"No. You are far more than that, you pretend to be a simple thug, but you are much more than that, you are a clever man."

"I have found that being a thug makes life so much more simple."

"Life is never simple, this I know from personal experience."

"How can your life be complicated, your position is secure amongst your people, you have nothing to fear."

"I'm not too sure of that. I am of the Eldest's line, if he goes down, I could be in danger, I'm not sure that I am ready for that. I really don't want to think about this right now, please, just kiss me."

Brank pulled her towards himself and kissed her as requested, for many moments the kiss continued, tongues chasing each other, breath running fast and nasal, as the heat between them rose. Suddenly he pushed her away. Fear in his eyes.

"What's wrong." She whispered huskily.

"Sorry," he said, "You feel like a girl, a tiny small girl, a child, one to be protected at any cost, even with the cost of my own life, why does this feel so wrong?"

"Child!" She said, "you call me child, I have more years than your grandmother, I am pure breed elf, I am ninety of your years old. I'm no child! I may be small by your standards, but I am old enough to be your grandmother and you call me child?" She pushed his hands out the way and kissed him hard and fast, she climbed on top of Brank, even though her weight would have been no problem had he chosen to throw her off, this was a choice he was already finding impossible to make, gradually she slowed down, and reduced the pressure against his lips, lifting up her head, but still straddling his chest.

"Enough of your silliness?" His only response was to gently pull her head down for more kissing, the passion rising in him could no longer be denied, there was no way he could turn away from her now, he slid his hands slowly down her back, until they cupped the hard globes of her buttocks, his left hand stayed there massaging the tense muscles, while the right slid slowly up under her tunic, up her spine, feeling every bump and bony protrusion along the way, feeling her ribs moving with the intensity of her breathing, he slid his hand round towards the front, suddenly she sat up. He froze, for a moment frightened he had broken some taboo, with a single fluid motion she pulled off her tunic and cast it away, then dived back down for more kissing. Her small hard breasts barely hung under their own weight, his hand soon found them and stroked each in turn, he marvelled at the racing of her heart, which he could feel clearly. She leaned back again and attacked his shirt, somehow her brain had forgotten how buttons worked, the frustration on her face caused him to smile and lend a hand, not the hand sneaking slowly into the waist band of her trousers. As soon as the shirt was opened, and his wide and very hairy chest was revealed, she dropped forwards again and pressed her breasts against him, wriggling from side to side, she moaned in pleasure.

"Elves are almost completely hairless." she muttered, still wriggling. His hand snapped the fastener on her trousers and unlaced the front, before plunging inside. She moaned as his large hand forced it's way between her thighs, she pushed against it as it cupped her sex.

"I'd say you are right, almost completely hairless." She smiled and kissed him hard again, then lifted her lower body, until she was standing up bent at the waist, kissing him, his hands were forced to relinquish their grip, they could no longer reach the parts they were interested in, with a quick squirm and a shimmy the trousers and boots were gone. She stepped over and dropped down on him again, rubbing herself against the coarse hair on his belly, she sat upright, sliding slowly backwards and forwards, his hands found her buttocks again, and helped them forwards, but restrained their backwards motion just a little, gradually she slid, inch by inch up his hairy chest, until he reached up with his tongue and tasted her, she squealed at the touch, and pushed down onto his mouth, she writhed as she pressed herself to him, his tongue probing and tasting, circling and plunging, in only a few seconds she tensed and grunted as the pleasure overtook her senses, after many seconds shaking and quivering, she collapsed forwards, completely wrapping his head in her belly and thighs.

"Oh, my." She whispered, once her breathing was back under some sort of control, "that was wonderful."

"You do know it is customary to return the favour." he said, lifting her so he could kiss her some more. She broke away saying. "You taste different."

"I taste of you, that is why." She slowly cocked her head to one side as if deep in thought, then leaned forwards to lick his chin. "You could do with a shave," she said, "but you don't taste unpleasant, musky and salty, but not nasty."

"You've never tasted yourself on your other lovers?"

"Never."

"Why not?"

"That sort of thing just isn't done."

"Why?"

"I don't know, I have been warned about your passionate ways, it is told that you use it to trap elves and bind them to you."

"There may be some truth in that, if you've never tasted yourself on a lover, have you ever tasted your lover?" She blinked slowly her eyes flashing in the firelight, she shook her head.

"You may be old enough to be my grandmother, but at this game you are as a child, should I teach you, are you sure you want to learn?" Again, the slow blink and the flashing eyes. She nodded.

"Sure?" again she nodded, a little more emphatically this time. He pulled her down and kissed her some more, until she started to wriggle against his belly again.

"I need to be undressed." he whispered, sitting up and removing his shirt, she slid down into his lap, her large eyes opened wider than ever, she moved a little just to be sure, there was no mistake, Brank was most certainly excited. He smiled at her and lifted her, she put arms around his neck, and he stood up, her weight did nothing to inconvenience his motion, her thin legs wrapped around his belly as far as they could, he reached beneath her and released his trousers, and underwear, boots kicked off with some minor dancing. Lifting her with one hand under her buttocks and the other holding her head so he could kiss her, he sank slowly to the grass. Gradually he settled her down into his lap again, his manhood tight against her buttocks, her eyes opened wider than ever. "You need to be very sure about this, if you chose to run off home, I'll not chase you, I'll not think harshly of you, but I will most likely cry myself to sleep." She stared into his eyes for a moment, then reached up to pull his head down to kiss him.

"I'm sure, or at least I think I am." she whispered.

"If you're sure, move round and take a look, I'm not certain what you are expecting." She hitched up off him and looked down, seeing his nakedness for the first time.

"Oh my." She muttered reaching out to him. "You're not too long, but by all the gods you're wide." Her small hand failed to encircle his girth, with both hands she managed to encircle him, she slowly moved her hand up and down, the shaft, marvelling at the heat and the soft, yet solid feel.

"Lick it." he whispered, she stared at him wide eyed. "Do you want to learn how to pleasure a man, or an elf?" She nodded then slowly approached the monster in her hands, tentatively she licked the end. "All around the head." he whispered, she swirled her tongue around the head and dipped the tip into his slit.

"How does it taste?"

She ran her tongue around the inside of her mouth before answering. "Salty, musky and a little bitter."

"Bad?"

"No, different, not bad."

"Fine, now suck on the end and work your hands up and down." She dived down, and engulfed the end of his cock, sucking for all she was worth and rubbing it rapidly.

"Slow down, there is no rush, we have all night." She smiled briefly and returned to her task, more slowly this time. "Move your ass round here where I can reach it." he said, guiding her with one hand, there was no way the current action could become mutual, her body was just far too short. With a sudden thought he pushed away ideas of children and focused on grannies, though he had no experience of grannies such as this one, some of the whores from his past may have been grandmothers, but he didn't stay around to find out. While she was occupied he alternated between inserting two fingers into her tight opening and rubbing softly on her quite obvious bump. She tried to moan but there was something in her mouth.

"Is that good?" he asked, she looked back at him and nodded. "Please be careful with the teeth, it may feel hard but it's still only skin and quite sensitive." A more sedate nod this time. He went back to his ministrations and she wriggled against his invading fingers. He sensed her orgasm approaching as fast as his own.

"You might want to move your head." he said, "keep rubbing but move your head." She looked at him a little confused, then her orgasm took her, and feeling her body clench around his fingers sent Brank over the edge. He grunted several times and jets of ejaculate went everywhere.

Once her orgasm had subsided, she stared at him, her hands still sticky. She looked more than a little upset.

"Is there a problem?" he asked softly.

"Yes." she snapped, quietly. "I was hoping to feel that monster inside me." She slapped his shrinking penis to one side.

"Hey, I may not be a teenager any more, but give me a few minutes and maybe some more mouth action, and I'll be back again."

"Do you actually mean that?"

"Of course, do you find that so hard to believe?"

"Yes."

"Why?"

"Experience."

"What do you mean? I'm sorry if I'm stupid but you may have to explain in simple language for me."

"Well," she cocked her head to one side, as if considering something, "to put this in plain language, elvish male's recovery time can be days."

"You've got to be joking."

"No." she shook her head.

"I am so sorry." He laughed, not too loud, he didn't want to wake people up. "You need to get out more, for young human male's recovery time can be minutes, or sometimes seconds. At my age it can take a little time, but never days."

"For truth?"

"Truth, care to try again?"

He simply looked down, she followed his eyes, and saw that the monster was awakening.

"See," he said, "he knows when you're thinking about him."

She reached down and placed the head in her mouth again, feeling the beat of his heart, as the resurrection continued, soon she had to let some out of her mouth as it was completely full.

"It looks even bigger now." She whispered, "suddenly I'm not so sure about this."

"If it frightens you too much, then that isn't a problem, I will never force you to do anything you don't want to, we could sleep, or lay here all night playing finger games, or you could even share your discovery with a small group of your girlfriends. Entirely up to you." She looked him in the eyes, then slowly closed her eyes. When she looked at him again she whispered, "They are watching from the tree above." She crawled on top of him and kissed him, more to hide her face from her friends.

"Don't feel pressured by them, do what you want to." He whispered, stroking her hair with one hand and fondling her buttocks with the other. He kissed her again, slowly and deeply. She was getting excited all over again, her breath came in short pants, she couldn't tell if it was the audience that was exciting her or the thought of Brank inside her.

"Sit up and come this way," he muttered, "let me make sure you are ready."

She did as she was told, sitting upright then moving up to his head where he could make sure that she was wet enough for what was to come. She writhed on his face again, as he tongued her and fondled her breasts, she threw back her head and groaned aloud.

"Was that for the crowd?" he asked.

"Perhaps a little, but mainly for you."

"If you are sure you want to try this, now is the time." he whispered, stroking her hair.

"How should we do this?" she said very quietly.

"You better be on top, then you have control, I don't want to hurt you."

"Perhaps I want to be hurt?"

"We may see about that later, after you got used to me." He lifted her up and pushed down his body, she supported her own weight on her legs, and crouched over his member. Taking the head in her hand, she rubbed it against her opening, lubricating it with her freely flowing juices, she looked him in the eyes and settled downwards, her opening spread a little but not enough to allow him entry. Slowly she pressed down harder, gradually increasing the pressure. With a pop the head was inside, she froze, barely daring to breathe, he saw the tension in her body and the pain in her eyes, despite the delightful tightness her grabbed her by the thighs to lift her clear.

"No." she said, "just let me get used to this feeling, I've never felt so full, so stretched, it hurts a little, but it is a wonderful pain."

"It feels incredible to me too." he said, not really wanting to move her, but equally not wanting to hurt her. Her eyes locked on his, as she lifted slightly, then down again. He grunted, she whispered, "Oh my." She continued the slow and slightly painful process, each descent pushed more and more of him inside her, until eventually her pelvic bone touched his. "Oh my." she said again, "I've got all of you." she leaned forward to kiss him, but her body was far too small to bridge the gap, she made do with a smile and the fondling of his hairy chest and nipples. Slowly she started to rock backwards and forwards, the vice like grip told Brank that he wasn't going to last long, so he reached forwards and started to rub her clitoris, hoping to set her off first, she started to lift up and down on him, he was distracted by what he saw, as she moved upwards, her waist seemed to contract, as she moved downwards her waist expanded a little and her belly pushed outwards towards him, he had never been anywhere so hot and tight in his life, he started to grunt and push up into her descending thrusts, until the moment was upon them, she leant backwards a little, closed her eyes, and exploded, her body and mind blew apart, him the same, as he exploded within her, he felt as if someone was doing the same to him, she felt his jets filling her insides, and that her jets were doing the filling, the orgasmic maelstrom joined their minds dividing their individuality, coagulating their consciousness into a spinning spiral of sensuous delight. The mind link broke and suddenly they were each alone, though stilled joined in passionate embrace. Slowly Branks connection shrunk and fell out into the open air. He stared into her eyes, she looked back saying nothing, for there was nothing that needed to be said. Eventually he spoke.

"Was that what it felt like, were our minds joined briefly?"

"Yes. We can communicate with our minds, and occasionally a link is made in a moment of passion, but I have never felt anything so intense before, so completely consuming, it was like we were a single entity, if only for a few moments. I felt everything that you did. It was my penis pumping inside me, spraying my insides with my juices. This is insane."

"I agree that is exactly what I felt, I was both parties at the same time, giving and receiving, but wonderful and magical, an orgasmic rush that cannot be beaten."

"I was warned about the passion of humans, but I had to try it. Now I want some more."

"So do I." he whispered. She reached down and took his shrunken and slimy appendage in her hand working it up and down, to bring it back to life. A rope fell from the tree above them and an elf came swarming down it, she dropped the last few feet to the ground and almost ran over to them.

"Laura." she said. "What have you done?"

"Hi Vic, we're just having a little fun. You want to join in, as soon as I wake this up again?" she waved the penis from side to side, but it was showing no signs of wakefulness as yet.

"Laura, please rest a moment, and listen to me." Laura sat back and smiled at Brank, kissed him briefly.

"Speak." she said, lying alongside Brank with her head on his shoulder and her arm protectively across his belly, idly twirling the hairs around his navel.

"We heard what you intended," said Vic, "so we came to be nearby if things got too rough, five more of your friends are up there in that tree, when we saw the man you had chosen we couldn't believe it, he's huge. When you rode his face to orgasm, we couldn't believe that either."

"Believe it and try it, I think elvish males will need a little training." laughed Laura.

"The disbelief just keeps on coming, we watched you suck him to orgasm, more disbelief, no one ever does that, it's a senseless waste of seed. We were getting ready to return to our beds, and more disbelief, he's ready again."

"Excuse me," said Brank, "but he does know that you are talking about him, and thinking about him, he's sensitive to these things and could just wake up again."

"Oh." said Vic, "more disbelief, but we'll see. Anyway, we didn't believe you could get all of that inside you."

"I did." Smiled Laura.

"We noticed, and when you both came together the orgasmic mind storm you two set off was so intense that your friends in the tree are still unconscious, or were when I came down, one almost fell out of the tree.

"Why weren't you affected?" Asked Brank.

"I've never been good at that sort of thing, I think my mind is a little different to everyone else's. Just different enough so I have to focus really hard to make any sort of mental communication at all. Have you any idea how many pregnancies that sort of mental explosion could have triggered tonight?"

"My turn to not understand." Said Brank.

"There is thought to be a correlation between the strength of the mind meld and the likely hood of conception, oh." She looked hard at Laura. "You could be pregnant already, judging by the seed still dribbling out of you."

Laura reached between her thighs, scooped up a handful of the residue and wiped in on the grass, she shrugged.

"Laura. Have you any idea how wide the head of a half human baby is?" Laura shook her head.

"I have heard enough to know that far too many die in childbirth than do normally. Enough of our women can't handle the narrow heads of elvish babies. Let alone the fatheaded half humans."

"I know that many of my people are called fat headed, but that usually more to do with the way they use what is inside the head, rather than its actual size." Brank laughed.

"This is not funny." Snapped Vic. "If she is pregnant by you then she has a one in three chance of survival, two out of three die. Given her size and shape, that more likely to be one in five."

"Surely your doctors have potions or herbs, that weaken the seed, or make the planting ground barren? Our doctors have these things, though more than a little uncertain, and with some possible side effects."

"If such a thing exists it is never spoken of, any pregnancy is too valuable to our race."

"Even one that is only half elf?"

"That may be the deciding factor, we'll have to ask the surgeons, see what can be done."

"Please help Laura, I would hate her to die over a single night of passion."

"Single?" asked Laura.

"Yes." said Vic, "single. No more risks for you until we can be sure it is safe."

"But you don't know how good it feels."

"Actually I do, despite my inabilities, I am fully aware how good it feels to have that thing inside me spewing it's seed all over my insides. You're the one that has no idea, no idea how much I want wake that up and ride it to oblivion." She pointed at Branks still quiescent manhood.

"Not just you." Said a new voice. They turned to see an elf walking towards them.

"Acron." said Vic. "You too?"

"Yes, after that mental storm, I want to feel that inside me again."

"But you're male." Stuttered Brank. "You are, aren't you?"

"I was this afternoon, but after that mindburst, I am so jealous of these women and their more receptive parts, that I could be tempted to endure the pain for the pleasure. Are you ladies willing to share?"

"Hey," said Brank, "I am here, and not entirely sure I want to be shared, or even if I want to play this game at all." The elves exchanged looks.

"I am sorry." said Vic, "We have all gotten a little carried away in the moment, that mind burst was more powerful than any we have even heard of from the distant past. There are stories of a mind meld so strong that an entire tribe went crazy for so long

154

that many of them died, they didn't eat or drink, a cascade of mind storms just kept them rutting until they died."

"Not a bad way to die." said Acron, with a smirk.

"There are worse ways." said Brank.

"Can we trust that sanity will prevail?" asked Vic looking straight at Laura.

"Sanity." muttered Laura, looking away.

"Fine." Said Vic. "Acron, you're with me, let's leave these two to sort out their feelings, and go and see how the rest of our friends are recovering from that rather large jolt." She linked her arm through his and started walking him over to the rope she had come down. Seeing to it that he went up first, she followed into the lowest branches of the tree, where quiet, but indistinct voices could be heard.

"Well that was more than a little strange." said Brank, putting an arm around Laura, and pulling her tighter against his body.

"I suppose we are strange to your people."

"We have a saying, a stranger is only someone you haven't met yet. I believe we have met." he laughed softly, Laura smiled and squeezed him closer.

"Are you cold?" he asked.

"No, but suddenly the thought of an audience leaves me a little cold."

"Shall we retire to the dark of my tent?"

"Don't you share it with someone?"

"Generally, but I think Kern has arranged the sentry duties, so we won't be disturbed. Sometimes soldiers can be very considerate."

"I'm not sure about the dark," she whispered, "I may be frightened and have to hold tight to you."

"I certain that I can endure such an inconvenience, for your peace of mind." he chuckled. He climbed to his feet and reached down to Laura, he lifted her with one arm and sat her on his hip, much as a mother would carry a babe in arms, he kissed her softly and walked over to his tent, bending in through the opening he didn't release her until there was space in his sleeping roll to lay her down, this he did. Then he got down beside her, and covered them both with his blanket, that didn't smell too much of horses. She kissed him for a moment, then turned away, she pressed her back up against his chest, pulled one arm across her chest and the other down and across her belly. Her head was level with his, as they settled down to sleep, her buttocks were only just below his navel, and pressed hard against him. He knew that despite the exercise of the evening sleep was going to be difficult, her body pressed against him was just too exciting. Again, thoughts of children crowded his mind, and knowing her age didn't really help, in the dark and the privacy of his tent, she was still small. Eventually her gentle breathing lulled him to sleep.

She felt the change come over him as his body surrendered to sleep. His gentle snores felt strange against the back of her neck, strange but none the less comforting, now that the rush of passion had subsided she considered the possibility that she might be pregnant, she understood the risks of childbirth, and the greatly increased risk of a part human child, could she take that risk again for the joy of the passion? Now she had cooled down, she wasn't sure. Some of the things her friends had said started to come to the fore in her mind. Her friends up in the tree had been included in the mind meld, no that was wrong, they weren't included they were consumed by it, it took them over completely, Acron had said that he wanted to feel Brank inside him again. Which was very strange, as far as she was aware, Acron didn't have much in the way of sexual feelings for women, let alone males, such attractions were rare, but not considered to be unusual. Vic had talked about the mind meld, not that their experience should be called that, a gentle joining of minds this was not, it ripped through every mind within range, or every mind that was susceptible. 'I wonder what the range on that burst was?' She thought, 'I'll have to ask around tomorrow.' Still her mind refused to sleep, the possibilities just kept rushing around it in maddening circles, eventually her curiosity got the better of her, she reached slowly behind her, and slid her hand down his hairy belly, as far as she could reach, the slow movement timed to his breathing soothed her a little but that was not what she was looking for, gently she wriggled down his body, trying not to wake him, her reaching fingertips found the coarse pubic hair, and stroked it softly, but this wasn't what she was looking for further down she slid. Finally, she had the root of his penis in as much of her hand as could enfold it, even in its relaxed state she could barely enclose it in her small hand. There was a catch in his breathing, she froze, he breathed again, slow and smooth, she moved a little further down, just to improve her grip, just to hold the monster and dream of it, or so she told herself, even though she knew she was lying. She could feel his heart beating against her shoulders and in her hand, strong and slow, the hypnotic beat was slowly putting her to sleep, until she realised that her hand no longer reached around him, every heart beat made him a tiny bit bigger, her eyes opened wide in the darkness, her heart pounded in her chest, how can he recover this quickly? And still be asleep. 'Perhaps he is faking.' She focussed on his breathing and his heart beat, each the slow steady sounds of deep sleep, no hint of excitement, nothing at all to indicate the stimulation of his body, she was so surprised when his head brushed against the back of her naked thighs that she twitched, then clenched her body, she tried to relax but the tension in her muscles made her whole body shiver. Her hand released him, and he twitched against her bare buttocks. 'Oh!' She thought. 'What do I do now? How I want to feel that inside me again.' She felt his heartbeat in the pulsing of his body as it twitched against her. 'But dare I risk it? Another mind meld like the last one and I'm sure to get pregnant, if I'm not already. If I am, then there's no more risk.' The moment of indecision passed, she pushed him over onto his back, turned around, straddled his head and dropped back down onto his body. Brank woke to find her opening pressed against his mouth and the head of his penis in hers. He mumbled against her body, and almost threw her off, she released him momentarily. "Shush." she whispered, "Just enjoy." Then her ability to talk was taken away by his presence again. Lying on his belly, she stroked him with both hands, and licked him, and sucked him, as he returned the favour, she felt the juices start to flow and her breath catch in her throat, he started to moan, and to lick her faster and deeper, swirling his tongue all around her, then focussing on the small nodule that brought her the most pleasure, she mumbled and stroked him faster, he matched her pace, motion for motion, action for action, until they were moving as one, acting as one, feeling as one. He tasted himself in his own mouth, she felt her tongue on her own clitoris, the explosion of orgasm took them away, they shared the feelings and the moments, the intensity shared in their brains completely took their minds away, they joyously collapsed.

Sometime later he returned to consciousness, with a kiss he picked her up and turned her around, held her close, and kissed her again. With this kiss she reacted, her eyes snapped open, and stared into his.

"What was that?" He asked.

"The same as last time, I think, but without the risk. If you know what I mean?"

"I think I do, that was certainly fun. Did you enjoy it?"

"How could I not? The real question is did anyone else?"

"What do you mean?"

"Well, with our first experience, others felt the pleasure, shared in the moment, enjoyed the feelings, if this happened again, we could have a way to increase the fertility of my people. Would you be willing to help in this?"

"Certainly, but I do have a prior commitment as yet, my brother Kern has need of me, but once this quest is done I shall return, and help you in any way that I can. Right now, however, I feel that dawn is rapidly approaching and I need some sleep."

"Sleep my love." she whispered, turning her back to him, "Tomorrow I will ask the questions of the wise men, how I hope that this feeling is true." She settled down and fell into a deep sleep almost immediately.

CHAPTER FORTY THREE

Laura woke suddenly, to the pre-dawn sounds of waking birds, in the dim light of the tent all she could see was the huge wall of hairy back in front of her, she reached up and placed her hand high on his ribcage, felt the slow rise and fall and the steady thump of his heart.

"Oh, how I want him again." she muttered to herself, and the birds who didn't really care what she was saying. Gently she shook him.

"Brank." she said a little louder. "Brank wake up, it's time for me to go and you have a battle to fight. Wake up." He groaned and rolled slowly towards her, his arms enfolded her and pulled her hard against his chest.

"You are one of the most beautiful sights to wake up to." he said, kissing the top of her head.

"One?" she questioned, luxuriating in the pressure of his arms, her body moving sinuously against his.

"Fine," he whispered, "the most beautiful." She felt his excitement rising against her thighs.

"Again?" she asked.

"It's a morning thing."

"No wonder your people breed like rabbits."

"Such is the nature of man." he smiled down at her.

"I need to go, before things get too excited." she shrugged his arms off, and he released her.

"Will I see you later?" he asked, as she turned to crawl out of the tent.

"If you survive." she said looking back over her shoulder, her hair outlined in the light pouring through the opening in the tent. Her smile was hidden by the light but her small firm buttocks were framed by that very same light, she laughed and vanished. Kern was by the fire already cooking breakfast as she came into view, she smiled at him as she walked across the grass, collected her clothes and walked off in towards the trees, not bothering to get dressed. Kern's eyes followed her progress as his brows arched, questions unasked behind his eyes. A smile crossed his lips at the memories so engendered. Brank crawled into view, smiled at Kern, gathered his clothes and slowly dressed.

"What's for breakfast?" he asked.

"Bacon, eggs, toast, some tasty mushrooms, the usual, we do have a battle to fight this morning."

"Coffee?"

"In the pot." Kern waved at the pot on the edge of the fire, with metal cups nearby. Brank filled a cup, drained it and filled it again.

"Heavy night?" asked Kern.

"That's definitely one way of putting it."

"That's not going to cause us any problems with her kin, is it?"

"I don't think so, it could even be that they will be more than happy with the things we found out last night."

"Care to explain?"

"No, I think we'll see how things go before explanations become necessary."

"Fine, you can wake the others, a quick breakfast then we can go kill a king."

Brank turned away and walked amongst the tents, waking every one, Jangor he left until last. The old soldier crawled into view, looking more than a little dead himself.

"How are you feeling?" asked Kern, a huge smile on his face, he really didn't need an answer, but he was going to get one.

"My tongue feels like a worn out sandal." replied Jangor, "That Spritz is truly wicked stuff."

"So you'll not be drinking any more of it then?" laughed Kern.

"Don't be ridiculous." said Mander, "One day he'll poison himself with all that booze."

"One day?" said Andel. "More like every day."

"Enough." said Kern. "Eat. We face a battle this morning. Jangor do we have tactic for today?"

"Nothing major, I thought we'd wake them up, one at a time if possible, set them alight, then run them around for a bit, until they start to fall apart, then chop them into ineffectual pieces."

"Not much of a plan." said Namdarin.

"But it does give a level of freedom that is the sign of a good plan." said Jangor.

"A plan should take into consideration all the possible variables, and account for all possible outcomes."

"Our most important variable that we don't actually know, is how these warriors will react to fire, for most men, their first instinct is to get the fire out, it could be that these sleeping warriors wont feel the pain of the fire, then they become more of a danger to us, that's why I want to wake them up one at a time. We need to know."

"Well," said Namdarin, "I don't know how elves build their funeral barrows, but for a doorway to be secure, it needs to be small, if we can hold them in the door way, then that could give us the time we need to burn them down."

"Good as a secondary plan, depending on the shape of the door. But we still don't know how to deal with the power of the mindstone."

"Or even what it actually is."

"From the tales it causes the enemies to just stand still and wait to be killed."

"If Jayanne and I attack the king, keep him too busy to get to the rest of you, you can deal with the warriors, and we can deal with the king, how does that sound?"

"Good idea, but only if they are all out in the open, stuck in the doorway that won't work."

"How would the elves feel if we burned their king as well?"

"Who knows, I hadn't even considered not using fire on him. These soldiers aren't alive or dead, we need to disable them as quickly as possible."

"If the doorway is too wide, we'll let them chase us for a while and then chop them into small pieces, sounds the moment for Jayanne and I to start working on them."

"Sounds like a plan to me." said Jangor.

"Horses?" asked Namdarin.

"Fire, I think not."

"Perhaps you're right, I know Arndrol wouldn't have a problem, but the others, aren't as well trained."

"You mean battle hardened."

"That too." laughed Namdarin. "You know he's not going to be happy about being left out?"

"He'll just have to deal with it."

Namdarin laughed out loud and turned to where the horses were picketed, his mind jumped the gap to the horse and sent soothing thoughts. He broke the connection, and looked down at the wolf that was relaxed near Kern's feet. He looked at Jangor with eyebrows raised in a question.

Jangor shrugged. "Kern can see to that damned wolf."

"I will, he'll be no problem, though fire is a natural enemy to him, something ingrained in his basic nature, we'll just have to see how he responds, most likely he'll fall back to defend the horses." Kern reached down a ruffled the wolf's mane, the large head rose and a wide tongue lashed across Kern's wrist. Suddenly the wolf jumped to it's feet, shook it's mane out to it's fullest extent, and growled low in it's throat. Kern turned to look where the wolf was pointing, walking around the line of horses came a group of elves, Eldest flanked by Gervane and Laura, now dressed, behind them came a group of thirty, or so, bowmen, bows strung. Kern reached down and grabbed a fistful of mane. "Relax." He said. The growl stopped but the tension in the wolf didn't decrease by much. Jangor walked towards the approaching party, mainly to put a little space between them and the wolf.

"Good morning Eldest." he bowed to the elvish leader, nodded to Gervane and Laura. She ignored his greeting and walked around him, straight up to Brank, she jumped up into his arms and hung on his neck, kissing him firmly.

"Jangor." said the Eldest. "There are things we need to talk about if you survive today."

"So I see." said Jangor, with a quick glance at the couple. "Thanks for bringing some of your bowmen to help us."

"They're not for you." laughed the eldest. "They are here entirely to protect our trees. If you actions look likely to bring hot fire in amongst the trees they will do what they can to prevent it."

"They look to be a few short."

"They'll be using heavy wide blade arrows," he waved at Gervane, who produced one from his quiver, fully five inches from across the tip, heavy and obviously sharp. "These are for short range, designed to take limbs, not just punch holes in armour."

"So your warriors aren't wearing armour?"

"No. Defence wasn't seen as one of their problems, after all they can't die."

"We shall endeavour to keep them away from your trees, while we reduce their effectiveness, and I now feel much better that you have another defence, other than us."

"Remember, the archers are here to defend the city, if you all die and the warriors return to their tombs, we will not go after them."

"We'll be ready in a few minutes." said Jangor. The soldiers prepared their weapons, Jayanne and Namdarin, the same, though Namdarin decided that this was all going to be close quarters work, so he left his bow behind. The chill in the air was quite intense, both Granger and Gregor were grabbing the last dregs of power for their staves. Jangor handed a crate of bottles to Brank.

"What ever you do don't drop these, they won't ignite, but they could be an issue if friends get covered in the stuff." Brank simply nodded.

"Kern." said Jangor. "Guard Brank, and that crate." Again a nod.

They all looked round, there was a commotion where the horses were picketed, Arndrol had his halter rope firmly in his teeth and was twisting his head from side to side, the rope couldn't take this sort of punishment for long, it severed and fell to the ground. The other horses still firmly attached to the picket line, but now Arndrol was free. He came strutting over to Namdarin, and stood nose to nose with his friend. Snorting hot breath in the man's face. Namdarin shook his head, and unclipped the remnants of the rope from the halter, removed the halter and threw them both on the ground. Namdarin turned to Jangor and shrugged. "Looks like he's been missing out on a few recently."

"Let's hope he can keep his head, this is going to get hot and scary."

"He's a fool, but he's not stupid, he does know when to run away. Let's do this."

"Eldest." said Jangor. "Lead on."

Jangor fell in alongside the elderly elf, Gervane to the eldest's other side, and Laura, alongside Jangor. Behind them came Kern and Brank, the wolf to Kern's left heel, and Brank to his right. Brank's broadsword was drawn and resting across one of his huge shoulders, the crate tucked under one arm.

"Laura." he said, softly. "I don't think you should be involved in this." Her head snapped around and the look told him as much as the words spoken by the eldest.

"She has been so informed, at some length, and with many threats, her response was short and eloquent. She stays with the archers, and if things go badly the surviving archers will carry her to safety"

"Grandsire!" she replied loudly. "That is not what was agreed."

"Kin of my kin, I made no agreement with you. You will survive."

"And what of you?" asked Jangor. With the snap of an ancient and scrawny wrist a longsword materialised in the Eldest's hand. He looked Jangor in the eyes and spoke quietly, "Today we are brothers." Jangor leaned forwards and looked at Gervane "You need to get this old man out of here."

"Tried." Jangor's jaw dropped open, Gervane shrugged.

"Stergin, Mander." Shouted Jangor, without looking round. "On him." His raised hand indicated the target, two clenched fists striking breastplates told him that his orders were understood. He leaned forwards again.

"Doesn't he have a personal guard or some such?"

"Yes."

"And?"

"He sent them away, 'Go north one day then come back'. His instructions were very precise."

"What does that mean?"

"It means that something is going on here that I don't know about and I don't like that."

"Care to share?" asked Jangor looking straight at the Eldest. The smile said everything and exactly nothing at the same time. Their slow procession had carried them across the glade of the trees and they were approaching the eastern edge, they would pass between two of the great trees and on to what seems to be a road leading east. Before they drew level with the boles of the great trees, a forest of ropes fell from the lower branches and elves came swarming down, in their hundreds. The Eldest's bowmen tensed a little and moved forwards through the group, the wolf growled and moved to the fore, Arndrol came and took up station alongside the predator. Four figures came to the fore from the group of elves, members of the council all.

"What is the meaning of this?" Demanded the Eldest.

"We can't allow you to give away such an important part of our heritage." said Tomas coming to the front.

"Pray tell, why not?"

"It is ours, it is that simple."

"And currently it does us no good at all."

"How does giving it away help us?"

"Each of you have brought a large part of your personal guard here this morning, you plan to pit elf against elf, family against family, friend against friend, how does this help us?"

"We don't want to do that, but if we must, then we will."

"What is it that frightens you the most? The loss of the stone, or the possibility of a new king?"

"To be honest, both."

"I have something that will frighten you even more, I intend to do battle with the old king, if by doing so we both die, then you will have a queen." With this word, some of the bowmen the Eldest had brought with him captured Laura and carried her back with them. "Relax Brank." said the Eldest, "she is simply being moved to a place of safety." Turning back to Tomas, "how many centuries since a dark queen ruled here? If your actions result in my death, then she has the potential to be the darkest of queens." Laura struggles could still be heard. "She'll not be hurt." said the Eldest to Brank, seeing the big man's discomfort.

"Queens are as mortal as kings." said Brank, looking back into the milling crowd that contained Laura.

"In your culture perhaps, in ours no. The murder of a few soldiers is acceptable, but to deliberately kill a woman, is just unthinkable."

"You'd be surprised what some people can think." muttered Brank. The council members were huddled together, exchanging some rather heated words.

"What about your warrior women?" asked Jangor, more to give the elves time to sort themselves out.

"It is their choice, they choose to be warriors, they choose to fight, they choose to die. If the will to fight ever passes from them, then they return to the city, to live the more normal life of the women."

"Interesting." said Jangor. Tomas came to the front.

"It is decided." He called so all could hear. "We'll not hinder your plan, but neither will we help you. We'll not risk the emergence of a black queen." The eldest raised a clenched fist high over his head and opened his hand. There was a scream as Laura was released, she came running over to the Eldest.

"How dare you?" she spat in his face. "How dare you treat me like this?"

"I am sorry, but we needed to sort this out and this seemed to be the way that would create the fewest problems."

"How could you ever believe that I, I, could ever be a black queen?"

"All women have the potential to be that cruel, to be that lethal, to be that brutal. Feel the anger inside you right now, feel the roiling turmoil, if you choose to focus that outside yourself, then you could easily be the darkest queen we have ever had." Even as he spoke these words, she felt the anger turning inwards against itself, until it faded to almost nothing.

"Sometimes Grandfather I can really hate you." She turned away pushed through the front line, and walked up to Brank, pulled his head down and kissed him firmly. "We will talk later." she whispered, as she pulled away she noticed the crate, she shrugged, then walked back into the group of bowmen, as if she wanted nothing more to do with with this venture.

"Well that went better than I expected." said the Eldest to Jangor.

"You knew this would happen?"

"It was one of the likely outcomes, come on we have a king to depose."

The Eldest walked slowly towards the gathering of the four family heads and their guards, and as he expected they all moved aside to let the small group of strangers and bowmen through. Dawn was by now a long time in the past, the sun was clearly visible through the trees, the path that was slowly developing beneath their feet surprised Jangor.

"Do many come here?" he asked.

"Enough to create this path, or to make its creation worthwhile, I remember a time when this could become a muddy mess, until it was decided that it should be paved, rocks were brought in from all over the forest, some have more meaning than others, some come from old graves in the far north, some from riverbeds in the south, each carried and placed by one of our people."

"Quite an undertaking."

"We always seem to have plenty of time, perhaps it's down to our long lives."

"If we are successful today, what will become of this great barrow." Waving at the manufactured hill in front of them, still a fair way off but clearly visible, there was a small clearing around it, the path lead to a dark opening in the end nearest to them.

"We may use it as a resting place for dead kings in the future, rather than the undead that are here now."

"I would have thought there would be trees all around it, being elvish?"

"Trees just don't seem to grow well too close to the mound, grasses and certain flowers, manage but they grow slowly, and the ones that do are all powerful drugs, or poisons."

"Poison or drug is generally only a degree of dosage." laughed Jangor.

Jangor peered into the dark opening before looking back. "Somebody torch me." he said.

"You really ought to be more careful what you say." said Kern passing a lit torch, Brank shied away from the torch, his cargo of incendiaries made him more than a little nervous. The dark and narrow tunnel was partially lit by the flickering flames, not really wide enough, nor high enough to swing a sword, somehow it smelled a little strange, but he couldn't quite place it. The wolf poked his nose in then shied away, he knew what the smell was and didn't like it one bit, he moved back to the perimeter of the group, where Arndrol was standing, equally unsure of the smell that was drifting from the open mound.

"I'm going to take a quick look around, Namdarin, Jayanne, if I come out running please kill whatever is following me. There's no space in there for sword play."

"I believe the central chamber is quite large." Said the Eldest.

"I want to take out the warriors this side of it first. We take the king only when we have to."

Jayanne and Namdarin took up stations either side of the opening as Jangor went slowly inside, the dark stone walls looked like narrow bricks laid in coarse mortar, all sorts of irregular spaces and sizes, the overall effect was a little untidy, but certainly serviceable. Jangor came to pair of dark openings, again no doors, just openings, bracing himself he moved the torch into the one on his left, listening carefully all he heard was the crackling of the torch, no sounds from inside and nothing from the outside, it was almost as if a door had been closed to the outside world, so much so that he glanced back towards the opening, to see the anxious faces of his friends outlined against the brightness. He moved the torch furthor into tho opening, and then looked slowly inside, the strange smell was even stronger, not quite so subtle, laying on a stone platform was an elf, for all intents he looked as dead as they come. The fair skin of the elves was darkened with age, the bony knuckles of both hands gripped a sword hilt, the sword was placed on the chest point downwards, the hilt was long enough for a two handed grip, and the first six inches of the blade below the simple cross piece, looked wide and sturdy, shaped but not sharp, a further extended grip, the point came as far as the elves knees, too long to be a knife, but too short to be a longsword, like the one that Namdarin was slowly swinging in the strengthening sunlight.

"Damn." muttered Jangor, "That sword is perfect for close quarters work like in there narrow hallways." He reached further in with the torch and followed himself, closer examination proved that the elf was currently lifeless, no sign of breath or blood. He stepped out of the musty chamber into the one across the hallway. Exactly the same in that room as well, though the elf was showing a little more battle damage, one arm was gashed open from shoulder to elbow. 'I wonder how functional that will be when they wake up.' thought Jangor. Stepping back into the hallway, he walked further in, two more rooms, two more elves, same again. The pool of daylight was beginning to look an awful long way away as he walked further in, two more rooms, two more elves, one showing some serious damage to a leg, basically the thigh was opened from hip to knee. Back into the hall way. Looking back at the daylight, it seemed so far away, though he knew it was only forty feet. He risked a quick glance into the last two rooms before the central chamber, exactly the same result. More sleeping or dead elves. He almost ran to the exit.

"Well." he sighed once out in the open again. "just looking at them doesn't wake them."

"Did you look upon the king?" asked the Eldest, almost reverently.

"No. I figure, either entering the centre chamber or maybe a personal attack will wake them."

"So now what?" asked Mander.

"Brank, pass me a bottle." said Jangor, "I'll see if a little seasoning will wake them."

"You sure?" asked Kern, glancing from torch to bottle. Jangor shrugged.

"We need to know." Jangor turned back into the dark passage way holding the torch high in his left hand. With the bottle in his right he was effectively unarmed, this made him more nervous than ever, into the first opening he crept an sprinkled a little of the liquid on the sleeping elf, ready to run for it if he showed any signs of waking, again nothing. Jangor went back into the crypt and emptied the bottle all over the elf. No reaction. Seven more times he liberally soaked the elves, before retreating to the sunlight.

"Now what?" demanded the Eldest.

"Now we wake them up. Everyone ready. I've no idea how fast these guys are going to move, they might be normal elf speed, or we could be lucky and their years of sleeping could have slowed them down. I'm going to set fire to one, that should wake them up, if it doesn't we just wait until they burn out and go to the other end and repeat the process."

He went into the passage way and tossed the torch into the room to the left, then came running out while switching his sword to his right hand. The flames ignited with a soft thump, not quite enough to be considered an explosion, a deep moan filled the whole barrow, a blazing elf came into view, rapidly followed by the others, they seemed to look around for a few moments, then moved towards the waiting warriors, a second caught fire from the first, then flames spread rapidly back along the passageway a plume rushed forwards out into the open air, pushing Jangor and the other backwards, the intense heat, and the smell of burning flesh forced them away. Jangor slashed as the first one out, the heat and smoke made the strike difficult and weak, though he struck true there was little damage to the elf. The wolf howled and retreated further from the burning men, Arndrol went with him, torn between helping his friend and the fear of fire.

"It's like hitting an old tree." Namdarin yelled as the second came out into the sunlight. Namdarin's broadsword swung, a blue streak in the morning sun, the sort of stroke that would cut a man in two, it hit the second elf, and removed an arm, no more, the arm fell to the ground and continued to move slowly, grasping for anything that came near it. Jayanne's axe took the other arm from the second, with no sword to wield it still came on. Jangor was fencing with the first, managing to hold his own, "Take their heads." he yelled, as Stergin came up alongside, to help him, the other elves were stuck in the opening, pushing hard to get out,

Namdarin slashed at the second's neck, a good strike but not enough to sever the head, Jayanne followed his strike with one of her own, this time the elf's head fell in flame to the ground, it rolled back towards the passageway, still the elf came on, it's only weapon now the fire that was eating it away, Jayanne and Namdarin were forced to give way, as they fell back another burning elf emerged. The wolf dashed in, only to break away at the last moment and sprint out of range of the fire.

"Heart." Screamed the Eldest. "Take the heart."

Jayanne stepped across Namdarin's line, and swung her axe as hard as she could into the centre of the burning elf. The elf collapsed into a lifeless burning hulk, Jayanne screamed and staggered backwards, Namdarin stepped forwards across the fallen body, his sword beating the next elves sword aside, then taking first one arm, then a leg, as the elf toppled over, Mander was helping Jayanne to her feet.

"I'm fine." she shouted, "be careful of those hearts they are carrying a huge amount of power. It surprised me, that's all."

Namdarin plunged his sword into the fallen elf's chest, his turn to scream, but he was better prepared, he didn't actually fall over.

"Brank." shouted Jangor, "Up on top of the barrow, douse the ones I haven't as they come out, Granger, Gregor, with Brank." Brank had almost made it to the space above the doorway when the first non-burning elf came out.

"Not the king, not the king." shouted the Eldest, "he is mine."

Brank poured the sticky fluid over the next elf to come out into the open, and Granger sent the spark that lit him, Brank emptied his bottle over the next one and Gregor sent the flare that started the fire. Granger started adding to the fires of the elves when the others were trying to take limbs and heads and hearts, Brank kept looking for more elves to come out, he really enjoyed setting them on fire, watching them fighting and dying, was good, but the burning made all this so different from anything he had ever experienced before. 'I'm sure there should be at least a couple more.' he thought. Trying to count the burning and already dead. The Eldest was engaging the king, Jangor was helping him, he spotted some movement at the edge of the field, Laura was running towards him, the bowmen at her back, the bowmen were taking their firing positions, she yelled "Brank." He saw that the arrows were pointed at him.

"Down." she screamed, he spun and dropped taking the two magicians with him, he heard the bows released but didn't see any of the arrows, when he finally got his vision cleared, he saw that the three missing elves had come out of the other end of the barrow and climbed over the top, they were now struggling to move at all, their arms and legs were all pinned one to the other by the festoons of arrows that pierced them, arrows that just kept on coming, Granger sprayed the nearest one with fire, though the flames didn't burn quite so bright they were enough to slow the elf down, Granger plunged the end of his staff straight into its chest, right into the heart, his turn to scream, the influx of energy was so intense that he had to do something with it, a bright blue bar of fire leapt through the elf impaled upon the staff and tore the other two to pieces. Once Granger had suppressed the blue fire he turn to his friends on the ground, Brank had already made his way down, and was holding Laura in his arms. The warrior elves were mostly heaps of smouldering ashes, only the king was still active, he was trying to kill the Eldest, who was attempting to return the favour. The Eldest's skill with a sword was quite surprising to Jangor, his wrist was strong and fast, but the old king had the overall advantage that he didn't actually bleed, where the Eldest was definitely starting to show some of this.

"You cannot win, Eldest." said Namdarin. "much as you would like to, it can't be you, your sword doesn't have the power to end this creature." A simple nod from the old man and Namdarin stepped in front of the king, attacked his sword and made him turn away from the eldest. The large green stone in the pommel of the kings sword started to glow, brighter and brighter, until Namdarin was struggling to take his eyes from it. The eldest stepped in the way and took the kings sword upon his own, the green stone dimmed slowly until it lost its shine completely,

"So long as it is an elf that fights him the stone cannot achieve its full power, or any power really." said Laura. "The Eldest cannot keep this up for much longer do something."

"I can burn his heart form here." said Granger. Gregor hefted his staff as well.

"He carries more power than the others together, you want to handle that sort of load?"

"Axe or sword. Choose!" Shouted Jangor. Namdarin glanced at Jayanne then moved behind the king, as the Eldest forced him to turn, Namdarin drove the sword of Xeron into the king's back, right through his heart, Jayanne stepped close and touched the blade of the axe against the blade of the sword, hoping to share in the energy, and she did, they both screamed loudly at the sudden influx of power, but only for a moment, in less than a heartbeat the surge was gone. Grinderosch threw back his head and howled, dropped his sword, and slowly sank to his knees.

"Why have you done this?" choked Grinderosch, though he should have been dead by now.

"We need the stone." said the Eldest, "and we need to move on, we need a living King to lead us."

"There will be a price to pay, something moves in the darkness and it comes this way." Grinderosch fell forwards off the sword, in a matter of moments all the years of his non-life caught up with his body, it turned to dust, until it was only a stain on the ground. The bodies of the other warriors went the same way, their fires gradually extinguished, the Eldest dropped his own sword and picked up the sword of Grinderosch, the green stone in the pommel glowed brightly, for moment, then returned to its more normal quiescent state, a brilliant green, a little cloudy, but with a sparkle in its depths, like a lamp in murky water at the bottom of a well.

"Injuries?" Demanded Jangor. None spoke, he looked around, only the Eldest showed any signs of blood, a scratch to his belly and a shallow cut to his left arm. "Mander." he called. "See to the Eldest's wounds. Once that is done, we'll head back into the city. Let's see what sort of reception we get." It only took Mander a few moments to clean the wounds and bind them, while this was going on Brank returned to the top of the mound and recovered the crate it still contained two un-used bottles of the incendiary fluid, 'They might be useful later.' he thought.

"Eldest, how does that sword feel?" asked Jangor.

"Strange, and not. Alive and dead. Good and evil." the Eldest shook his head slowly from side to side. "I really don't know how I feel about it, or more to the point, how it feels about me."

"Perhaps it's a little concerned about regicide?"

"Namdarin killed him, not me, though I suppose I did make it possible."

"I cannot believe these guys have lasted this long," said Jangor. "Only you have any injuries, though a couple of ours did get close to being hurt."

"Perhaps it was my presence that slowed them down, I certainly prevented the mindstone from working as it should." said the Eldest. He turned the sword over and over in his hand, staring at the green stone in the pommel, the spark of light in its depths entranced the eyes, even though it wasn't actually active, it's hypnotic force could not be denied. "I never in my wildest dreams thought that I would be holding this treasure." he said to Jangor.

"Not only are you holding it, but it appears you are to be king."

"That is possibly even more frightening. What am I going to do?"

"I have no idea." said Jangor. "What are the biggest problems that your people face?"

"You mean other than your people?"

"Well yes." laughed Jangor.

"Our declining numbers, with every year that passes we are fewer."

"Please believe that I have no wish to cause offence to you or your people."

"If you have something to suggest please do so."

"This could be an idea that would never even be thought by you and yours," Jangor paused, looking deep into the Eldest's eyes, waiting for some indication, finally it came as a barely perceptible nod. "Select the most fertile of your people and mate them, in a few generations your population could be self-sustaining again."

"Bred like cattle?" whispered the Eldest.

"It's only a thought, I meant no harm by it."

"The problem could be that it is already to late for that to work, the most fertile have two children, the least none. These days a family with two children is rare, three is almost unheard of.

But there may be some progress that could be made in this way, we'll have to investigate it."

"There may be something that you can do as a people but that is for you to decide. I have no idea how your people will take to any of this, Laura may know more than you."

"Why do you say that?"

"She spends more time with the people, they are more likely to be open with her than with you."

"I'm king, surely all I have to do is tell them what to do?"

Jangor laughed out loud. "Eldest my friend, you've already been king for far too long." The Eldest simply frowned.

"Please explain."

"How about a tale from your own history, something you should remember, depending on exactly how old you are?"

"Go on."

"An elvish leader called Braid, had a meeting with a human general, they came to an understanding that a few hundred human soldiers would hid in the forest until something could be changed."

"I remember that tale, it was a few thousand troops, squatting in our forest for far too long."

"Details like numbers tend to move around depending on the age of the story, but that is not important, can you remember what had to be changed?"

"Was it the king's mind?"

"The two of them knew that changing his mind was never going to happen so they decided to change the king."

"Braid and this general decided to change a king, but you can't change king, they only change when they are...." The Eldest frowned as his voice stumbled to a halt. Jangor looked at Laura, Laura looked at Jangor and smiled.

"He'll get there," she whispered. "it just takes him a while some days." she laughed quietly, Jangor waited silently.

"Braid plotted to kill a human king, Braid and a human general? That's what you are saying?"

"Correct."

"Interesting, but I don't see the connection to me."

"And there he was, stupid again." Laughed Laura. She reached for the old elf and hugged him warmly. "You know we love you, don't you?"

"Will you please explain what all this means?" he pushed her off until she was held at arm's length.

"Well," she smiled, "the human king was doing something that his people didn't like, in fact he was going to get many of them killed, just to kill off a tribe of elves, so Braid and the general decided to kill the king, until they found one they liked. Do you understand?" They all watched as realisation finally shone in the Eldest's eyes, and his jaw fell open, then snapped shut.

"They killed the king, simply to change him."

"That is exactly what they did," said Jangor. "it took a little longer than they had hoped, but they did it. So, be careful what you expect your people to do, if they hate it enough, they'll change the king. Understand?"

"You mean my own people would kill me if they didn't agree with me?"

"It is one of the problems of being a king, generally kings don't get to retire."

"I'm going to need some serious guidance here."

"That is what your council is for."

"But I've spent most of my life simply ignoring them, why should that change?"

"Have you made any great changes in the way things are done?"

"Not really I suppose, in all my years the first decision I have made of any real import was to let you attempt to take the mindstone from the king."

"What happened?"

"They all turned out against me, it almost came to blows."

"That was open rebellion, had you given them some more time, say planned to take the mindstone in a few weeks, that would have given them enough time to arrange an accident for an old man."

"You think they would actually do that?"

"This is a standard tool of statecraft amongst our people, removal of inconvenient nobles is in fact a recognised trade in the human world. There are few practitioners, and hiring them is in itself risky, but there are some that are truly excellent at their chosen profession. One such, whose name is unknown, and is believed to live in the far west, specialises in de-fenestration. He is known simply as The Cleaner. I've looked into this one quite closely, just as a matter of professional interest you understand, I think he is a small group of maybe as many as three, or one man with a herd of horses he doesn't mind killing, he just gets about too much, alternatively he is being credited with a few real accidents. Another alternative that I have actually considered is that they're all accidents and The Cleaner doesn't exist."

"That sounds particularly gruesome, and people actually pay for this service?"

"Why gruesome?"

"It just sounds like a dreadful way to die."

"Is there a good one? Anyway it refers to a word in an obscure dialect, and involves a fall from a high place, usually a window, but not always, cliff top, battlement, wall. Fall or perhaps thrown. A short time for screaming then silence. Better than slowly bleeding to death from a belly wound."

"Somehow I don't feel any better about it. I think we should return to the city and see how my people feel about a new king."

"You need something before we do that." said Granger.

"What?"

"A name, all good kings have a good name, so what is yours?"

"Now that is something almost no one will remember." laughed the Eldest. "It's been so many years since anyone has actually used my name, I've almost forgotten it."

"Then perhaps you should choose a new one."

"I couldn't do that, it would dishonour my entire family. I'll just have to go back to using the name I was given." The Eldest smiled to himself.

"Old man," said Laura, "put us out of our misery and tell us!"

"It's a name with a long history, it reaches back into the depths of time."

"Tell us old man, before I brain you with your newly acquired sword."

"Laura, kin of my kin, are you telling me that you don't know my true name?"

"Give me your sword fool." She snarled.

"My given name from all those years ago is." he paused, she reached for the sword. "Fennion. I was called Fennion. And will be again."

"King Fennion." whispered Laura. "a name of some omen that is for sure."

"Explain." said Jangor.

"Fennion was one of the first elves that came here and set up amongst these trees. He was actually the one who saw the potential of these trees." said the Eldest.

"So," said Namdarin. "Fennion has returned and the race of elves will be great again."

"Perhaps, my namesake did come to a rather messy end."

"What do you mean?"

"Perhaps The Cleaner got him." Laughed Fennion. "The seven trees had reached a considerable height, but were a little spindly, thin and sparse, perhaps they had grown too quickly, he was high up in the canopy, convincing them to fatten their branches and to fill out the trunks, to grow more branches and carry more leaves, a sudden gust of wind, or perhaps The Cleaner, caused him to fall, by the time he reached the ground he was a thoroughly broken elf. The next king carried on the good work and the trees flourished as you see them now. We will have to see how the people accept a new Fennion to rule them."

"If you rule wisely and change things slowly, then they will accept you." said Namdarin, "Have you any children to take over when you die?"

"The nearest thing I have to offspring is Laura here." He waved in the direction of the small woman.

"You, only hours ago, were railing about 'Dark Queens', how can she be queen?"

"For our people the dark rulers are always created in blood and pain, the worst are the ones that kill to become queen."

"You actually allow that sort of thing?" asked Jangor.

"Sadly, the rules of inheritance are quite strict amongst our people."

"Even if the incumbent is murdered?"

"I'm afraid so."

"Perhaps you should do something about that."

"I can give that a try, but that will of course depend on the will of the people."

"I am sure they will see the sense in not allowing murderers to take power."

"I suppose we better go and face them now." Fennion reached out with his left hand to Laura, and held the sword in his right, walking slowly back to the trees, Jangor, Namdarin, and Jayanne, followed on behind the others fell in behind them, and the bowmen brought up the rear.

As they approached the circle of trees a fairly large reception committee was awaiting them, fronted by the members of the council. Tomas at the forefront.

"Well, judging by your new weapon we have a new king." Tomas called loudly, so that the crowd could hear him.

"So it seems." said Fennion, "unless you have a better candidate of the line of Grinderosch."

"You know very well there is only one other of the line of kings, and she's not ready to be queen." Laura released his hand and stepped backwards to stand beside Brank.

"I am sure that she will be by the time it is her turn. Though I don't think this old elf will last any serious amount of time."

"Don't think that we are stupid," replied Tomas, "everyone knows that the mindstone extends life."

"And you know that I intend of lending the stone to Namdarin here, to help him remove Zandaar. So it is most likely that I will be dead before the stone is returned, and long life goes to the queen."

"So!" shouted Tomas, "What will be your first command as the new king with no name?"

"I feel that we all deserve a party, a celebration, a coronation of some sort, a feast for this evening, as our new friends will have to leave very soon we should do this as quickly as possible. Just because you don't remember my name, doesn't mean I don't have one. I have been 'eldest' for so long, more years than any in the past, I am Fennion." A gasp ran through the collection of elves, one croaky old voice cackled loudly, the owner fell to her knees laughing loudly.

"Silence crone." called Fennion, a huge smile on his face. The laughing continued for a short time.

"I remember." she said, climbing slowly to her feet, with the assistance of those around her, "I remember how everyone laughed when your mother named you, how presumptuous, to think that a scrawny little runt like you could ever be a true Fennion."

"To be true." said Fennion, "I never believed I could be king, and when Grinderosch went into the mound, then I knew."

"But now you have changed all that, you have killed Grinderosch, and declared yourself king."

"I didn't kill him, these brave people behind me did, they ended his existence, I wouldn't call it life, or even the semblance of life, at best it was moments of awareness in ages of night. Their night is ended, their watch is over, now we must now look to defend ourselves, and our trees. Though these people have also removed the greatest threat to them. What say you old woman, will you dance with me to celebrate our new awakening, our new beginning," "Our new ending?" she interrupted.

"Ending indeed. The end of the line of Grinderosch, after me comes Laura, and she has no heirs. Who here would give her the heirs she needs to continue the great line?" There were murmurings amongst the crowd, Laura's right arm reached as far around Brank's waist as she could, his left hand rested gently on her left shoulder, his right on his sword hilt. A young elf pushed to the front of the crowd, and stepped forwards, speaking in a clear and melodic voice.

"I would be honoured to help the lady with her issue issue." The crowd laughed softly. "However I think she has already chosen for herself." He bowed deeply to Laura and Brank, before stepping back to melt into the crowd, a huge smile on his face.

"The people would never accept a half-elf as king." said Tomas.

"Laura will have no children from me." Brank's deep voice boomed above the noise of the crowd. "A half human child would kill her, I'll not have that happen." His grip tightened on his sword, his biceps bulged under tension, and his shoulder twitched.

"All this is beside the point." said Fennion, "this is a problem for many years in the future, now the pressing matter to hand is how big can this party be? I suggest as big as we can possibly manage, kitchens start cooking, brewers start with the selection of wines and ales for this evenings celebrations, distillers Spritz will be required as well. The party will start at sundown in the central glade, until then myself and my new friends will retire to the council chamber, council members, your presence is required, your personal guard are not, we have much to talk about."

Fennion stamped towards the crowd, which parted like the sea upon the prow of a ship, the others followed in his footsteps pushing the crowd even further back, he lead them to the central and major tree, they climbed slowly up the spiralling walk way, followed by the councillors but not the bowmen, they stayed by the pathway, blocking any from following, this was only a symbolic gesture, there were far more paths leading up to the council chamber. The path was short and steep, nothing the elves weren't used to, but Jayanne had to hang on Namdarin's arm, not that either of them minded that, Brank's long legs made it hard for Laura to keep up, until, she finally gave up, and jumped up into his arms, Namdarin laughed when he looked back to see them, she looked even more like a child, Jayanne smiled, Jangor was a little disturbed, Kern was more so, his frown triggered a raised eyebrow from Brank, Kern mouthed a word, later. Very soon they were in the council chamber, they passed the doorway, no one questioned the presence of their weapons, Fennion waved a hand signal at one of the door guards, in moments a long table was carried in, then some chairs to go along with it, the council members sat along one edge, Fennion took the seat at one end, Laura, the other. Jangor, Jayanne, Namdarin, Kern took the other side, the rest sat along one wall, of the chamber, knowing that their contributions would be minimal. The wolf that had followed as quietly as he could sat at Kern's feet, calmly watching everyone. Brank fluttered around like a lost butterfly, until Laura stood and waved him into her seat, then she firmly sat on his knee, staring a challenge at the council members, not one that any of them took up. She threw an arm around his neck and kissed him lightly on one cheek. She looked at Fennion and said.

"Speak old man. This is your game, play it how you will."

"Thank you, kin of my kin. Members of the council of elders, there is something you all need to understand, I know that as king Fennion, my reign will be short, I'm very old already, I'm going to give the mindstone to Namdarin, hopefully he will bring it back to us, once it's job is done. Then it can be used to help us, I was talking with our friends, after we had beaten old king Grinderosch, our biggest problem, other than the humans, as they pointed out, is our low reproduction rate. Have any one you any idea how this can be changed."

"We are people not cattle." Snapped Galabrine.

"I know that, my dear, even though we are a long lived people, our death rate exceeds our birth rate, we are a dying race. What can we do to change this?"

"If your new friends stopped trying to kill us all the time, we'd do a lot better." Said Loganar.

"Namdarin is going to try to end one of the major problems that we have, but even so, our battle losses in the last fifty years have been negligible. The problem is our lack of children. We need to do something to increase our birth rate, and we need to do it soon."

"Could it be." muttered a diffident voice, all turned to Calabron.

"Go on, out with it." said Fennion.

"Could it be that we are leaving it too late to start families, Laura here is almost typical, ninety years old and no husband, no children." He turned his face to the table, fearing that he had spoken too much.

"You could be right, Calabron." said Laura. "Though I disagree with typical, most women by the time they are my age have husband at least. It may be too late for me already."

"What do you mean, too late? I've known women have babies into their two hundredth year." said Galabrine.

Laura stared hard into Galabrine's old eyes, for a long time before speaking.

"I have no wish to be crude, but there is no other way to say this that will make you understand, after the mindstorm that we shared last night, on more than one occasion, I'll not have any children until Brank has left this world, and perhaps not even then."

"You cannot mean that." said Galabrine.

"Oh, but I can, and so can a few of my friends, they were close enough to get caught up in the mind meld, by close enough I mean they were in the lower branches of the tree and we were on the ground."

"That can't be true." Snapped Galabrine.

"Ask them. Even Vic, who is renowned for being as deaf as a stump, got caught up in the rush."

"No."

"I'd suggest you find yourself a human lover, if you weren't already too old. They may be considered to be beneath us, but their passion is undeniable, and unstoppable." She turned to Brank and spoke more softly. "I have been to see the healers this morning, before the battle, there are drugs that can prevent pregnancy, and they agree with Vic, the mindstorm that you, no, we, generated last night, could quite easily affect the fertility of any female that was close enough to feel it. Even an old stick like Galabrine." She leaned in close and kissed him softly.

"That cannot be right." Whispered Galabrine, looking straight at Calabron.

"I have heard whispers of such," replied Calabron, "obviously not spoken in polite company."

"When have you ever been in company that wasn't polite?" She asked.

"We are getting a little away from the topic in hand." said Fennion. "How can we take advantage of this potential improvement without embarrassing the more polite members of our society?"

"If you tell them you plan to get them involved in someone else's orgasmic mind meld, then most of them will simply stay away." said Tomas, "I know I would, and will."

"If any such plan is made," said Fennion, "then attendance of family heads will be compulsory. How can we expect the common people to participate if we don't?"

"You cannot mean that."

"Oh, but I do."

"And you may even enjoy it." laughed Laura.

"What do you mean?" demanded Tomas.

"Are you sure you want to know?"

"No, and yes, just tell me."

"My friends were above us in a tree, just watching to ensure I wasn't going to be hurt. Well that's what they told me. When our first meld hit, only Vic, deaf as a post remember, only Vic remained conscious, all the others passed out. A few minutes later a friend came down from the tree, he was more than a little unsteady on this feet, he explained that he desperately wanted those feelings again, he wanted those sensations again, and not the ones that Brank here was broadcasting, he wanted the feelings I was broadcasting, he wanted intensely to feel someone exploding inside him. Calabron we know that your inclinations have tended that way in the past, but this friend had never shown any attraction to men at all. We'll just have to see how he feels when the rush has faded. Tomas, are you ready to experience this sort of sexual intensity?"

"I have never felt that sort of intensity, even in my youth." said Tomas. Laura laughed.

"If what Laura says, and her friends report, is true, then you my old friend, could be in for a wild ride." Tomas coughed but said nothing more.

"How about this for a plan?" said Jangor, all the elves turned to him, not really believing that he had even spoken. "We're going to have a party tonight, there will be wine and Spritz, just let the party flow and see what happens, we do have a few human males here, who may be willing to offer their services, to advance the population of elven kind of course."

"An excellent idea." said Fennion, again elvish heads snapped round to stare at him. "I'd even go one step further, any family head suggesting that amorous youngsters take their action elsewhere will be seriously reprimanded, is that understood?" The elves simply nodded.

"Sounds like someone is planning an orgy." Whispered Mander to no one in particular.

"It could be interesting." Muttered Andel.

"What do you think wolf?" Asked Kern, reaching down to stroke the head of the predator, that was resting on his knee.

"What is that wolf doing in here?" Demanded Loganar.

"And when did he come in." asked Jangor.

"He's sitting with his friends, listening to some conversation, he came in when we all did, but even you Jangor, have become used to his presence, you didn't even notice."

Loganar jumped up and snarled. "Armed humans, and now animals, what is this place coming to? This is so wrong."

"Oh sit down you old fool." snapped Fennion. "Things need to change around here, and if that means embracing armed humans and terrifying predators, then embrace them you will."

"Who are you calling old? You're twenty years older than me."

"So you don't dispute fool then?"

The wolf emitted a soft but deep growl, Jangor shouted. "Gentlemen." before he continued at a much quieter pitch. "Please calm down, the humans are indeed armed, but they mean you no harm, the wolf is a predator, but more than happy to sit quietly amongst his friends, so long as you remain relaxed, shouting tends to make us all nervous. What say we calm things down some? Kern, is the wolf, ready to meet some new friends?"

"I think he can cope with a few more friends."

"Bring him to the elves, let him meet them." Kern stood slowly and turned towards the head of the table were Fennion was sitting, the table on his left, he patted his right thigh, hoping that the wolf had been trained to the standard signals and even remembered them, before he'd taken his first step the wolf was in position it's left shoulder touching the tall man's thigh, together they marched to the head of the table, then turned to face Fennion. As soon as Kern stopped walking the wolf sat. Kern looked down at the wolf and smiled. The wolf looked up and returned the smile, or the wolf like equivalent, his jaw dropped slowly open and his long tongue fell out to hang loosely.

"King Fennion are you ready to meet, er, Wolf?"

"I'm not so sure about that, he's a lot bigger when he's this close."

"Reach down with an open hand, present it so Wolf can sample your scent." Slowly Fennion did as he was told.

"Wolf this is King Fennion, he is a friend." Said Kern solemnly, Wolf sniffed the hand and then licked it quickly.

"That tickles." said Fennion.

"Now Wolf knows you and could find you in a crowd, far faster than any human or elf for that matter, if he classes you as a member of his pack, then he'll die to defend you, the down side is that he will expect the same from you. Are you willing to go that far?"

"I'm not sure if I want to be a member of a pack."

"Too late for that." Laughed Kern. "Anyone else want to meet Wolf?"

Most of the elves shook their heads, Loganar however spoke up, "I have no wish to be part of an animals pack, that is just ridiculous."

"As you will, elder Loganar." said Kern, "Anyone else?" he asked again. There were no takers, so he returned to his seat, with Wolf alongside him.

"I want to meet Wolf." said Laura, jumping off Brank's lap.

"Slowly." said Kern, "offer him a hand." Laura walked slowly towards Wolf, who's tail was waving slowly from side to side, she offered him a hand, Wolf looked even bigger standing waist high on the young elf, he sniffed and licked. She fell to her knees and flung her arms around his neck, holding him tightly for a moment, he sniffed her hair and licked her ear, before he dropped belly down to the ground, and reached up with his head, gently he gripped her jaw in his teeth, only for an instant then licked her face.

"Oh my, he's a big friendly boy." whispered Laura, ruffling his mane with both hands. Slowly she returned to her seat.

"That's something you don't see very often." said Kern.

"I never expected for one instant that he would go that far." said Laura.

"I thought he was going to kill you." said Brank, "but then he let go."

"Laura, how do you know about wolves?" asked Kern.

"I used to track them and watch them all the time, the greeting ceremony is quite common when hunters return to the pack. I've seen it so often but never thought I'd be a part of it."

"Will someone tell the old man what the hell is going on?" Demanded Fennion.

"The greeting Wolf just gave to Laura, was the same as a low status wolf meeting an alpha, highest status in the pack. Which means that wolf here regards Laura as alpha female, so threaten her at your own risk, he'll defend her at the cost of his own life, or yours."

"I'm not sure if I'm happy about that or not." said Fennion.

"I wouldn't worry about it, though your bowmen this morning could have had a really hard time. Laura, please be careful not to panic if you care about the people around you, Wolf won't be terribly clear about the difference between playing and fighting. Someone could easily get hurt."

"Perhaps my friends should remember that as well." She stared meaningfully at Fennion.

"Fine." said Fennion. "A new wolf pack has been created, with one of my family as a member, I'm not entirely sure how I feel about that, we have a plan for a large party tonight, a new king, and perhaps a new future, all in all a good day, I think. Have the members of the council anything to add?"

"I." said Tomas, "am not entirely sure it has been a good day, but we can only wait and see. "

"Agreed." said Galabrine. "There is still the matter of the mindstone, and how do you intend on separating it from the sword without breaking everything, it appears to be very firmly attached."

"I don't believe that can be accomplished." said Calabron.

"I think we'll leave that until the morning." said Jangor, "there's no rush after all."

"Until later." said Tomas leading the members of the council out of the chamber.

"Don't forget." said Fennion loudly. "The best beers and the finest wines, oh, and some food."

"What are we going to do until the party?" Asked Mander.

"You are a soldier." said Jangor, "Swords to be cleaned and sharpened, amour to be checked and polished, horses to be groomed, and now it seems dogs to be fed and watered. Any more stupid questions?"

"Can you never keep your mouth shut?" Asked Andel.

"Of course he can't." said Stergin, "any more than you can."

"I'll see to Wolf, and the horses." said Kern, he walked towards the door, and called, "Wolf." Wolf looked at Laura, then followed his other friend out of the chamber, and down into the glade.

Laura stood and took Brank by the hand. "Let me show you my city, it is most beautiful."

"Fennion." said Granger. The king jump to his feet. "Oh my." he said, "I had forgotten that you were there. What can I help you with?"

"Gregor and I have been standing quietly, we were not required for your deliberations with your council, we would like to investigate you old king's chamber, it could be that by meditating there we will be able to tell you more about him, and his warriors. Would this cause any problems?"

"Of course not, I don't need to tell you to be careful in there, there may be a considerable amount of residual power there."

"We'll be very careful, we'll try not to disturb anything, really we just want to feel the place, it could tell us so much." Granger bowed to Fennion and turned to leave, with Gregor on his heels.

CHAPTER FORTY FOUR

"Halt strangers." called the foremost of the guards. "What business do you have here?"

Kevana stopped the horses still far enough from the gate so the guards couldn't feel crowded.

"We seek a room for ourselves and stabling for our horses, that is all, we plan to be on the road again early in the morning, there is a monastery nearby we want to visit. Is there a problem of some sort?"

"We have had problems with strangers recently, there were some deaths."

"We are simple monks, peaceful and quiet, we won't cause you any such problems." As Kevana was speaking a tall man walked out of the gate, towards the guards, his uniform marked him as possibly commander or captain.

"Good afternoon gentlemen," he said slowly, "what is your purpose here?"

"As I was explaining to your man here, we are simple clerics looking for a night's rest, that is not under a hedge, before we pass on to our monastery, which is I believe south of here."

"Is your god Zandaar?"

"Zandaar is the light and the way, he is our guide and our defender."

"We have heard of your particular god, our people have enough gods of their own, they have no need of yours."

"We are not here to convert a city such as yours, we have urgent business elsewhere, we simply ask for a place to rest before we move on in the morning, do we ask too much of your fine city?"

"I am not sure, we have been warned about you, and yours, you can understand."

"Warned by who, we are a peaceful order?"

"A man came through here some days ago, and warned us that you are expanding, with the intent to take over the world."

"Would this be a man who stole something that belongs to our god?"

"No." interrupted Crathen, "it would be Jangor, Namdarin only came here later on."

"Namdarin a man with a blue sword?" Asked the captain.

"Yes," said Kevana, "he stole the sword of our god, so he's never going to speak highly of us."

"Actually." said the captain, "It was Jangor that spoke out against you, as a soldier I give his words much weight."

"We have no wish to cause any harm to your people, we only want a night's rest before we go after your soldier friends, we have to get that sword for our god. If we have to kill them then so be it, I know these words stand against us, but I am being honest. There is no love between us and Namdarin, I believe he caused you some problems as it was." Harvang stared hard at the sergeant.

"There was a problem, some died, but he showed himself to be an honourable man."

"Do we get the chance to prove that we can be honourable, or are you going to close your gates to us?" Harvang thought for a few moments.

"Jon." he looked at the sergeant, "guide them to the parrot. You gentlemen," he turned to Kevana, "can stay there tonight but be gone tomorrow. Be careful how you talk of Jangor or Brank, whilst you are there, both are well respected in the parrot, one for a long time, and the other for an act that some considered murder."

"I understand." said Kevana, his glance around his group said far more than words ever could. "We will be on our best behaviour, but would you care to explain how murder gains respect?"

"No." said Harvang, he waved the guards back, and as the pathway opened Jon lead them through. Kevana caught Alverana's eyes, the look was enough, Alverana nodded, he settled into his saddle, appearing to be almost asleep, Crathen stared at him, but got no response. The column followed the sergeant at a steady walking pace, through the heavy gate. Kevana held his place until the others had all passed, then he turned to Harvang.

"Would you care to join us for our evening meal? I would like to talk to you more."

"No, I'll be taking dinner with my wife. Jon will be more than happy to take my place, he has very young children that he would much rather be away from. Tell him I said he was to look after you." He waved Kevana through the now empty gateway.

"Look after, watch over, or guard?" Laughed Kevana, as he walked his horse passed the captain, he soon caught up with the others and followed them through the packed streets, heading slowly down the hill towards the parrot, he wasn't paying too much attention to what was going on around him, Alverana was taking care of all that. Crathen wondered why his friend had suddenly become so quiet, but didn't bother to question this, he was used to the peculiarities of his new associates. They crossed the square now emptying of vendors, market stalls all closed up and the clean-up crews carting away the detritus of the day, Alverana almost laughed when he saw the wooden parrot, with its slightly peeling blue paint. Jon turned down the small alleyway at the side of the inn, around to the back gate, a small gate but wide enough when opened for a mounted man. Jon hammered on the gate with a heavy fist, in only moments the gate was opened by a young man.

"Yes?" he spoke quietly.

"The captain has allowed these men to stay here for the night, please see to their needs. I shall be back shortly."

"I will do that."

"Gentlemen, I will see you in a little while, I have other things to do just now." He nodded to Kevana and left.

"Gentlemen," said the stable boy, "please come in, my name is Chris, I'll be taking care of your horses, if you'd care to follow me, and we can get them in their stalls for the night." He took hold of the reins of Alverana's horse and guided it slowly into the stable yard, it was not a large place, but would be big enough to hold their horses for a night. Chris paused long enough for Alverana to dismount, the others all followed suit, then he lead the horse into the nearest stall, Crathen lead his horse in alongside, the stalls were wide enough for two horses each, but there were only just enough for the riding horses, the pack animals would have to stay out in the yard, tethered to a long rail that ran along one side.

"Gentlemen, saddles on the rails and collect any luggage you wish to take inside, there is no need to unload the pack animals, and please don't worry about thieves here, we don't have any. I shall go and inform the innkeeper that he has guests, I'll be back shortly." He disappeared into the inn through the small back door.

"You heard the captain of the stable." Said Kevana loudly. "Let's have these horses prepared for the night, before he gets back, wouldn't want to embarrass him, now would we?" He laughed as he pulled his horse into a stall, and started to remove the saddle bags, then the saddle. Alverana checked the rail thoroughly, before he put his saddle on it, the rails had a curved top that had been sanded very smooth and varnished to a high gloss. They would certainly not deposit splinters in the bottoms of the saddles. Kevana was very careful about the placement of his saddle blanket, it covered the saddle completely, he squeezed between the horse and the stall until he was standing by the horse's head. He stroked the horses neck and its ears, before speaking.

"If that blanket is on the floor in the morning, and there are teeth marks in my saddle, and horse slobber all over it, then you, I, and a large stick are going to have words, is that clear?"

The horse nodded and flicked its ears, snuffling softly. Kevana patted him softly on the neck then made his way out of the stall, he crossed the yard to help Petrovana with the pack horses. Chris came back into the yard, with a larger man behind him.

"My name is Senjin, I'm the landlord here, welcome to the blue parrot, we have rooms enough for you all, they are small but clean, so long as you don't mind sharing."

"We are used to sharing, that will not be an issue for us, all we need is food and a place to sleep, though a bath would be appreciated, we've been on the road some time."

"Out house and bath house in the corner of the yard," he waved vaguely towards a nondescript door that Kevana hadn't noticed, "Chris with light the fire under the boiler, it shouldn't take too long for the water to be hot enough. I ask that you be frugal with the water, it is an expensive commodity in this town. Please follow me and we'll get you settled in." He turned back into the inn, Kevana followed with the others behind. Just inside the door was a narrow stair leading up to the upper floor, the first door they came to was marked "Private", the corridor they walked along ran along the whole length of the building, with small windows looking out over the stable yard.

"There are four rooms each with four beds, you may use them all, or as few as you wish, I don't expect to have any more guests this late in the day, the gates being already closed. Though there may be the odd one that isn't well enough to make their own way home, they usually get dumped on a bed to sleep it off. Food will be served either in the common room, or outside in the garden if you wish. Food is included in the room price, but drink is not, price for your party is four gold."

"Including breakfast?"

"Of course."

Kevana rummaged in his purse, and paid Senjin.

"Thank you, gentlemen, please enjoy your stay in the blue parrot." The tall man squeezed passed the monks and entered the door marked private.

"Three to a room." said Kevana, "the price of these rooms has wiped me out, Worandana you are paying for the beers, we'll meet in the common room in a few minutes."

Kevana, Alverana, and Crathen, took the first room, Petrovana, Fabrana, and Briana, the next, Worandana, Kirukana, and Apostana the third, leaving one room for any latecomers. While they were selecting beds and stowing their belongings in lockers at the foot of the beds, Kevana looked at Alverana and asked. "Tell me?"

"Prosperous town, walls are strong, gates are very strong, but only if they get them closed."

"I noticed that myself. Go on."

"The walls and gates could survive a protracted siege, but the farms outside would have to be abandoned, the city may survive but the community would be destroyed. I see no religious organisation at all, at least none with overall power, temples and shrines to disparate gods are all over the city, I counted no less than six temples on a single pathway, given this, and the size of the city, I'd estimate at least twenty-five different temples, maybe as many as forty, a small sample you understand. The guard is efficient, but somehow disturbed at the moment, perhaps the loss of some of their number and the departure of Brank has upset their balance. All in all, a complex but stable economy, ripe for the taking, with a standard take over method, this city could be ours in less than two years."

"Are we safe here?"

"I'd say yes, so long as we keep within their restrictions, otherwise, they could respond quickly and to our detriment."

"Fine, we will behave, and tomorrow we will leave, and when we get to the monastery we will file a target report, and get things moving to take this city, it could be good for Zandaar, and us in particular."

"Agreed."

"So you're just going to take over the entire city?" asked Crathen.

"Oh yes," said Kevana, "it's ripe for the taking, but we aren't in any hurry, two years, maybe more, we are in no hurry. This will make a great centre for the militant arm; the whole city is a huge castle."

"Except for the farms on the outside."

"We can work around that, massive stores on the inside, and we are only a few weeks away from other centres of military might. We only have to hold for three maybe four weeks and fifty thousand men are marching on the backs of the surrounding forces, not that anyone could amass a big enough force locally to be any issue for this town, once it is ours of course."

"Plan B?" asked Alverana.

"Depending on the location of potential supporting cities, this one could indeed be good for a plan B."

"Plan B?" asked Crathen.

"Simple really, the city gets surrounded by a hoard of howling barbarians, who chase all the farmers inside, then we offer to help the city under certain conditions, it's really surprising how barbarians assembling siege engines at someone's walls will make their beliefs so flexible, ten thousand black robed warriors chase the five thousand barbarians over the horizon, the city is saved, fifteen thousand black robed troops come back over the horizon and are welcomed as hero's, and a few new temples are built, everything returns to peace and tranquillity, only now we have a large following on the inside, and the farmers whose homes are surprisingly undamaged, are more than willing to be our friends. Six months and the whole city is ours. Plan B."

"So which do you intend for this city?"

"Neither, I'm just too busy right now to be involved in something so local, bigger fish to fry. Let's get down stairs before Briana drinks all the beer."

"Swords?" asked Alverana.

"Good point, swords stay in the rooms, belt knives only. Go and tell the others." Alverana left quickly and caught the others as they were going down the stairs, Petrovana was very unhappy about leaving his sword behind, but did as he was told, after many threats of murder and general mayhem should his sword go missing, his belt knife was almost short sword size anyway, and he certainly knew how to use it. Finally, they passed down the stairs into the common room as a group, into one of those silences that often occur when strangers enter a bar.

"Ah, gentlemen." called Senjin from his place behind the bar, "I have a large table set for you all in front of the fire, please take your seats and I'll bring drinks over and take your food order in a few moments." He waved in the direction of a long table with benches either side, more than big enough for the nine to sit around, many eyes followed them as they took their seats, Kevana at one end, Worandana at the other, after a few brief hand signals from Kevana the clerics ended up sitting with their backs to the wall, and the soldiers with their backs to the room, they were going to be relying on Kevana's eyes to warn them of any trouble in the room, they had barely seat themselves when Senjin walked over.

"Drinks gentlemen?"

"Two jugs of beer, and two bottles of wine." said Kevana.

"How many glasses for the wine?" Kevana gave him a cold, hard stare.

"One." Senjin's eyebrows raised a little at this, but no comment was made.

"We have beef or mutton for tonight, while you gentlemen are making up your minds I'll go and sort the drinks out." He turned away and returned to the bar. Very soon a young girl came over carrying two huge jugs of beer, followed by Senjin, who had a tray of mugs and two bottles of wine, and a glass.

"Fine, drinks have been served, what would you like to eat?"

"Six beef, three mutton, if you please." said Worandana.

"Certainly sirs, it won't be long, please enjoy your meals." Senjin and the girl walked slowly away, Briana twisted in his seat trying to get a better look at the girl.

"Briana." snapped Kevana, "face front! Keep yourself under control, we are here entirely on sufferance, do nothing at all to jeopardise that, do I make myself perfectly clear?"

"Yes sir." muttered Briana, "I only wanted a look she smelled good."

"She looked great." said Apostana, laughing gently.

"You're not helping." said Kevana. Apostana smiled and shrugged, his eyes sparkling in the lamp light.

"She still looks great." said Apostana, "she's coming back." Carrying plates she leaned over the table, and placed the plates in front of the men, guessing as to which wanted the beef stew she was carrying, she only guessed one wrong, as Senjin turned up with another huge tray, three plates of mutton and a basket of warm bread rolls, and two large bowls of steaming vegetables, these he scattered about the large table.

"She looks even better walking away," said Apostana, "the way those hips sway could break any man's vows." he laughed out loud, Briana turned his face downwards.

"She's a beautiful little flower is our Petunia," said a new voice, they all turned to see that Jon had arrived, "but she's more than capable of looking after herself, she numbers nettles and thistles amongst her brothers and cousins, she has nothing at all to fear anywhere in this town." He pushed his way round the end of the table and sat down between Kevana and Apostana, saying, "room for a small one?" He smiled at the monks and then called. "Senjin, mutton for me." then quieter, "I'm partial to a good bit of mutton, slow roasted with lots of sweet mint, that's how Senjin cooks it here. It's far better than eating at home, not that I can tell the wife that." Petunia came over with another plate of mutton and a mug for beer, she already knew what Jon would be drinking, with a swirl she was gone again. Jon filled his mug from one of the jugs on the table.

"How do you like the Blue Parrot gentlemen?" asked Jon.

"It's an interesting place," said Kevana, "only one question springs to mind."

"Go on, ask away." Smiled Jon.

"The landlord, Senjin, he's a tall man, by anyone's standards, but he's built like a rake, landlords should not be so thin. How is this?"

"He doesn't drink, well the occasional, and I do mean occasional, glass of wine, he has never been seen to eat a meal, he says he gets enough from his tasting of everyone else's food, and the barman is fat, so he doesn't need to be, or that's what he says."

"It's just a little unusual that's all."

"Oh, this place is that. It's always a good place to spend an evening, generally there are minstrels that turn up to sing for beer or pennies. Minstrels, so it's generally beer. Sometimes there's fools, telling jokes and taking falls, it's almost never boring, I feel that tonight promises to be interesting in new ways though."

"What do you mean?" asked Kevana between mouthfuls of beef stew, he noticed that Jon hadn't stopped talking long enough to eat anything, or even take much of a drink.

"I fear that Harvang, sorry, the captain, may have played somewhat of a cruel joke making you stay here."

"Say on." muttered Kevana.

"It has been said that you Zandaars are going to take over the world, and you've moved into the hills to the south, and that our little town may be next on your agenda."

"I can assure you that though our god is always looking for converts, your little town isn't anywhere in his plans at the moment."

"Jangor and Brank say otherwise before they were forced to leave town, and they have many supporters here." Jon laughed, finally scooping up a mouthful of mutton, mopping up the gravy with a bread roll.

"What does this mean for us?" asked Kevana.

"Basically, Harvang put you down in hostile territory to see how you would deal with it, he's a great one for field testing his men."

Alverana and the other soldiers moved their bench away from the table, just enough to give them some space to move.

"Relax. It's not going to come to combat, but it is likely to get loud, I'm glad you left your swords in your rooms, eat up gentlemen things are going to get exciting soon."

"What do you mean? Asked Worandana.

"Word is already out that the dark priesthood is here, as Jangor predicted. You can expect some resistance." laughed Jon.

"I am assuming he was talking about the monastery to the south, that is where we are going next."

"Recon party then?"

"How can the words of a stranger be valued so much? We are simple monks, travelling."

"First, he beat Brank, a sporting event that many would pay a month's wages to watch and beat him without killing him. Then he killed a man that really needed it, another sporting event, but over far too quickly from all accounts. Then on their way out of town, one of their party threw lightning bolts around like they were his personal playthings, and a slip of a girl killed a seasoned warrior in single combat, as she was instructed, 'Don't play with this one, just kill him, one blow.' Jangor told her, he smashed his sword on her axe, she gave him the opportunity to walk away with his life, he was goaded into carrying on, and died in moments, she chopped him completely in two. I am sorry, but the words and actions of these people carry far more weight here than you ever will."

"We will be here only one night and gone in the morning, early, hopefully." Kevana said, emptying his first bottle of wine and starting on the second.

The room slowly changed, it gradually became quieter, and a certain amount of space appeared around the monks and their table.

"Jon Carpenter, why are you sitting with these heathens?" Came a voice from the shadows.

"Andreas my old friend, you know me, I get all the good jobs, I'm babysitting the monks as they pass through our wonderful town, and you well know the name I go by now. My father was a carpenter, still is I suppose, but he has specialised his trade some, he now makes only spindles, hence I have a new name I'm Jon Turner, you know that."

"You hope to protect them from us?"

"No, I'm here to protect you from yourself, we really don't want any unpleasantness now do we?"

"You expect us to trust them?"

"No, I expect you to trust me, I'm here to make sure they leave first thing in the morning, and that they harm, or are harmed by, no-one, do you understand?"

"Harvang has lost his mind."

"I prefer the believe that the captain is looking after the needs of our city, when these people leave here tomorrow, and that is exactly what they are going to do, they will understand that a religious take over is destined to fail, and a military one will be far too expensive for them. All you have to do is play nice."

"Play nice is a good idea." said a voice from the back of the crowd, a tall man moved forwards, "Senjin," he called, "Wine."

"Good evening captain, I wasn't expecting you." said Jon.

"I know, you were doing fine, so I thought I'd join in, any objections?"

"None at all. Please take a seat, I fairly sure these soldiers can close ranks a little."

"We are simply monks." said Kevana as Harvang squeezed in between him and Alverana, nudging the others along the bench to make space, a bottle and a glass came over his shoulder and Senjin departed quickly.

"Please don't take us for fools, there are clerics here," he waved as one side of the table, "and there are military brothers here." Waving at the other. "The one not in black I am unsure of, but the rest of you give your selves away with every mannerism. Take this large fellow next to me, he must have a terribly itchy hand, have you seen a doctor about this? He needs to scratch it every few seconds with the handle of his knife, quite an impressive eating tool if I do say so myself."

"Alverana." said Kevana, "Relax."

"Alverana," said Harvang, "pleased to meet you, there is nothing to fear here. Andreas, come forward and meet some new friends." Reluctantly the tall man walked forwards into the light.

"Abomination!" shouted a voice, followed instantly by another.

"Kirukana. Be silent. Apostana cut his throat if he so much as squeaks." Apostana's knife was at Kirukana's throat in less than a heartbeat. "Apologies Andreas, this one is more than a little narrow of mind, but he is in some ways right, is he not?"

"Your god would regard me as such, but I am a man much as all the others."

"Andreas," said Harvang, "your secret is getting out, it's only a matter of time now, far too many know and more guess, but the call is yours." Andreas stared at Harvang for a moment or two, then spoke slowly and in a very clear voice, so there could be no doubt.

"From this day forward, I shall be known as Andreas Half-elven." There were gasps from around the room, and more than one voice saying, "I knew it." Andreas went on, "not so much half but not entirely man."

"Interesting," said Worandana, "I knew that such existed, but I never hoped to meet a person of mixed lineage such as yourself."

"The real surprise is how quickly your young man recognised me." Andreas said.

"The markers are clear, and sadly trained into those from Zandaarkoon from an early age, the shape of the head, the length of your fingers, the fingers almost the same length, and thumb disproportionately long as well."

"Why do Zandaars care so much?"

"I believe it is fear that drives them."

"Are you really going to have this man's throat cut with all these people around?" Asked Andreas looking hard into the eyes of Kirukana.

"I suppose we shouldn't, but he has a tendency to spout dogma without a moment's thought."

"Release him, what he has to say may prove interesting."

"That's unlikely." muttered Alverana.

"I can do that," replied Worandana, "but if you are offended by his words, you'll have to be the one to cut his throat." With a nod to Apostana, the knife vanished from Kirukana's neck.

"Well young man. Why is your god so frightened of men with elvish parents?"

"Zandaar is not frightened of anything."

"Really, what are the instructions laid down by your god when you meet a person such as myself?"

"The whole family should be cleansed."

"Now that doesn't sound too bad, some prayers and some burning herbs, maybe a gift for Zandaar, I'm sure that can cause no ill feeling."

"No, cleansed by fire, the whole family and their property burned to ashes."

"So tell me again how your god isn't frightened by people of mixed race."

"There is an old tale," interjected Apostana, "not spoken of much these days, it's an old, old prophecy, I can't quite remember it, there's something about an elvish rock, and a fire that will end the time of the gods. Do you remember it Worandana?"

"I've never heard of it, and that in itself is unusual. But why would that turn Zandaar against the half elven?"

"The elves will never leave their forests to attack Zandaarkoon, and their weapons are entirely their own, no human could use them, but mixed, they will leave the forest and could take the rock with them."

"That could cause some consternation amongst the council." said Worandana, "That might account for the scorched earth policy against half elven."

"Something else to think about." said Crathen, all eyes turned to him. "Namdarin has gone to the elves to find something called 'The Mindstone' a weapon he has been told will help him in his fight against Zandaar."

"Who told him this?" snapped Worandana.

"Gyara."

"Andreas." said Harvang, "Isn't interesting how these people throw the names of gods around as if they were their personal friends?"

"I'd say it was frightening, it's scary how such educated people can believe that their god cares for them in any personal way." Andreas shook his head.

"Zandaar cares for all his people, each and every one." snapped Kirukana.

"Even those converted at the point of a sword?" asked Andreas, waving at the soldiers.

"Yes, even those." said Kirukana.

"Somehow you lack sincerity."

"No." said Worandana, "he does actually believe what he says."

"And you?"

"Not so much, I wasn't raised in Zandaarkoon, I learned much before I went there, sadly Kirukana didn't have that luxury. If I'm not mistaken this may even be his first trip outside the city."

"That's not true." interrupted Kirukana, "I went on many a trip outside the city."

"Escorted?"

"Always, we went out into the surrounding villages, to meet the normal people, the farmers and the craftsmen, the people that life in the city depends on, and they all seemed to be very devout, true servants of Zandaar."

"They don't have much in the way of choice, being so close to the central city, do they?"

"Of course, there is a choice, there's always a choice."

"So these common people outside your city walls can worship any god they want, even Gyara?"

"That would be heresy."

"And there's only one punishment for heresy, death by fire?"

"That's right, the heretics must be cleansed by fire."

"Lots of choice then, worship Zandaar or burn."

"That is the way it should be, praise Zandaar." The other monks clasped their hands over their hearts and muttered "Praise Zandaar."

"It's amazing that you can even believe that this is right." said Andreas. "How many secret heretics are discovered every year?"

"It gets fewer every year, there are almost none some years."

"Kirukana." interrupted Worandana, "be careful, you are being led into a trap."

"I have nothing to fear from the truth."

"Exactly." smiled Andreas, "Surely the city itself is secure from the heretics?"

"Not true, still we find the odd one inside the city, sometimes high-ranking people."

"Surely these people must give up all their fellow heretics before they burn?"

"Actually, they generally burn professing innocence, and give up no one."

"Wouldn't you give up everyone to keep your family from the flames?"

"Certainly, but generally the only names these high-ranking heretics give are beyond reproach, simply bitter attempts to strike back at their accusers."

"So you are saying that the only way to avoid accusations of heresy, is to accuse someone first."

"I don't see what you mean." Kirukana looked confused.

"If your heretics have no fellow followers, then they are very rare people, most people pick up a religion from those around them, they have friends who follow their new god, not so in your cases. I think that your heretics were falsely accused, and then removed because they were inconvenient to someone in authority, but that's just the ones in the city, what about the ones discovered outside the city?"

"I don't believe your generalisation." said Kirukana.

"Answer the question anyway." said Worandana.

"The heretics are generally in groups outside the city, they pay lip service to Zandaar, but worship another god when they think no one is looking."

"Do you find many of these groups?"

"No more than one every couple of years or so, sometimes longer."

"And what do you do when you burn out half a village?"

"Faithful from the city move out into the village to take over the farms, and churches, the businesses and services."

"So whole towns can be converted by fire?"

"You could see it that way, but that would be heresy." snapped Kirukana.

"My mere existence is heresy, so why should I worry about what I think?"

"Our god is good for our people; any others are not worthy of his support."

"Young man you are deluded, your god wants the whole world, and he will burn it to own it. I will fight with every breath that I have to prevent him, if I have to kill every black robe that I see, then that is what I will do, after all they want to kill me."

"Old friend," said Captain Harvang, "these people are currently under my protection, you'll not harm them while they are here."

"I understand Captain, they are your responsibility."

"Only until they leave town, if you want to hunt them down after that, feel free, you might even find some to help you, but I'd much rather you didn't, I think the world has a surprise for them fairly soon."

"What do you mean?"

"You didn't see the fight at the gate, you didn't see Namdarin and his blue sword challenge the entire city, nor what the woman's axe did, or the magicians staff spitting lightning, these are serious people, if they find a weapon from the elves, then Zandaar could actually be in danger."

"From what I have seen here today," said Andreas, "he needs to be, these people will take the world, if we want it or no."

"You are probably right my friend, let's hope that the world wants something else." said Harvang.

"Gyara has a different plan." said Kirukana.

"Silence." said Worandana.

"No, Kirukana," snapped Harvang, staring hard at Worandana, "please say on, what does the trickster intend." Apostana's knife appeared at Kirukana's throat again, Alverana's at Harvangs.

"This is interesting." said Jon, looking at Kevana to his right. "If you and yours spill blood here, then this is where your quest ends, how does Gyara feel about that?"

"Actually, Gyara is unsure, so failed to commit. Stand down." The last shouted to the whole table, knives reluctantly returned to belts.

"So what did Gyara have to say?" asked Jon, gently, his eyes half hooded, Kevana snared by his look.

"Be quiet." said Worandana. Kevana glanced briefly at his old friend before turning back to Jon.

"Gyara said that both groups have the ability to end all life, and release him from servitude to this world, so he'll not take sides."

"What form did Gyara take?"

"Huge black crow."

"It is known that in this form Gyara tells no lies, often not the entire truth, but no lies."

"What does this mean to us?" asked Kevana.

"That's simple." said Harvang. Kevana's head snapped to the left. Harvang whistled, a platoon of the guard came marching into the bar.

"Stand guard. The only person allowed through the cordon is Senjin, and perhaps Petunia, everyone else is blocked. Gentlemen your safety in our town is now assured, latrine and bathhouse trips will be escorted, you will not be alone, your doors will be guarded when you sleep. You will come to no harm in my town, you have my word, I'm sorry about the additional restrictions, but your presence does seem to create a certain amount of tension. When you leave tomorrow, I suggest you advise your brothers in the hills to the south that this city should now be considered hostile territory, I really can't guarantee the safety of un-announced visitors"

"I understand." Kevana muttered glaring are Kırukana.

"Senjin." Called Harvang, "More wine and beer if you please, this party seems to have taken a turn for the worst. Someone sing us a happy song." He turned to Kevana, "You must have had an interesting journey to get here. You must have a tale or two?"

"We certainly have, it started off so well, then the cold came, the memory of that cold makes me shiver even here in front that roaring fire, I can feel the creeping fingers of ice reaching down my spine, before we crossed the mountains, we were attacked by a pair of snow demons, you can laugh, I can't think of anything else to call them, they were like bears, only with very long legs, they ran on four feet or upright on two, they threw rocks at us and tried to knock us from our horses, we managed to get past them but it was a close thing, they were the most fearsome things I have ever seen outside a nightmare, though recently they have been turning up there as well. Before the horses had their breathing back to normal we came upon a temple of Gyara, Alverana here had some experience of this so he performed a summoning, that was something I had never seen before or even heard of, the huge black bird slow appeared out of thin air, he sensed the we were a threat and counter attacked, he killed one of our people."

"We were no threat," interrupted Alverana, "he just didn't like the fact that we may actually consider ourselves as such."

"So what did Gyara say?"

"After he killed Helvana, we had a short discussion, he refused to help us, he said that he couldn't take sides."

"But he'd already helped Namdarin." said Crathen.

"What do you mean?" demanded Kevana.

"Gyara said that he needed the elven mindstone, without that he couldn't defeat Zandaar."

"I thought I had told you, it was Gyara, that told Namdarin he needed the mindstone."

"I don't remember that, so Gyara sent Namdarin to the elves, to get this weapon of theirs."

"Yes. And I believe that he is there now, acquiring it."

"When we attacked Gorgana, I felt trees all around him." said Worandana.

"Namdarin and his group are at the city of the elves, attempting to take a great weapon from them what are the chances of the elves letting them take a weapon from them?" asked Kevana.

"Who can tell? They may even volunteer this weapon." said Petrovana, "It's even possible that they may be glad to get rid of it. After all, a god killing weapon is going to attract a serious amount of attention, not something they really want."

"Petrovana, have you ever heard of this weapon before? I haven't."

"We really need to move on at speed," said Kevana, "we have to intercept them before they get to Zandaarkoon. I don't want to waste a night here, if we ride through the night we can be at the monastery before dawn."

"And good for nothing, our horses will be dead on their feet, and so will we." said Worandana. "We ride at first light and we are not going to kill our horses getting there. Is that clear?" Kevana nodded then stared at the table top, picking at the surface with a fingernail.

"You must have more tales for us?" asked Harvang.

"I have another tale for you." said Alverana, he lifted his mug of beer, and drank a large draft, before refilling it from the jug on the table.

"Say on, please." said Jon.

"This is great beer, and we know where it comes from, we passed through the village where it is brewed, only a few days ago. Our journey there took us through the passages in the mountains, where we came up against a huge animal, it was in the tunnels through the mountains. Have you heard of it?"

"Passageways, or animals, I've heard of neither."

"I have no idea how long we travelled through the tunnels under the mountain, it certainly felt like days, but without the sun we just couldn't be at all sure, we knew there was a large predator in the cave system somewhere, I could see its tracks, and they were very large indeed, but had no idea whether it was in front of us or behind, I wasn't even sure which I preferred to be true. Sometimes I wanted to sneak up behind it, sometimes I wanted to hear it behind us, the not knowing was the worst part, I couldn't tell how old the tracks were or even if there was only one, there could have been two, this thought started to prey on my mind. I could tell from the changing quality of the air that we were getting close to the exit, I could smell the green of the outside, finally the tension became too much, I passed the torch to one of the men behind me and started the attack prayer. Around a bend the tunnel opened up into a huge cavern, our enemies were in sight, a fair way off fighting a huge snake, and I do mean huge, we moved to attack, the clerics started hurling fire and lightning at the snake, it turned to attack us, giving our enemies time to escape, we could only see some of the snake, it's head was wide enough to swallow a horse, the first third came down from the foggy roof of the cavern, and struck at us, sword blows would keep it away, but did little or no damage, one of our number threw his knives at it, they stuck into its neck behind the head, but with the attacks against its head I don't think it really noticed, leaving the others to continue the attacks I withdrew and ran off to the side, out of its line of sight, then ran up and climbed the stairway of knives, ran up to its head and drove my sword down just behind the head, hoping to sever the spine and kill the thing quickly, it sort of worked, but then snakes don't have much of a central nervous system, the rest of it was still quite functional, it slammed me up against the roof and threw me off, that's where the lights went out for me, but it appears I was successful, it died, it took a while, but it did die."

"That's quite some story." said Harvang.

"And exactly as it happened." said Kevana.

"Your team seems to do very well. Coming up against Namdarin and his group is going to be a little different."

"We know that already, but we have plans in place."

"You're going to need more men, and even with a lot of them watch out for the woman with the axe."

"I've heard something about her, but somehow I don't quite believe it."

"Oh, believe it," said Harvang, "she's better than you will ever believe, I lost a valued sergeant to that damned axe of hers."

"What do you mean?" asked Kevana.

"My turn for a tale, well, Jangor and Brank killed a sergeant called Jackis." There was a general cheer from the room. "As you can see he wasn't a popular man around here."

"He threatened to kill me." said Andreas.

"I understand and have no doubt about that." smiled Harvang. "Anyway, back to the story, Brank came back to the gate carrying the dead body that had been Jackis." Again, a cheer. "Much of the guard had turned out, even my wife was there, you need to understand that Jackis was her brother, she was screaming about hanging the murderers from the nearest tree. You know how women are. Something changed in the crowd that had gathered, people were coming to the front and walking into the empty space that people always leave when they think a battle is going to happen, a man with a long sword on his back hilt above his right shoulder, a woman in a cape made from a single white bearskin, and an old man with a long wooden staff, the man came to front and declared that the men were travelling under his protection, he drew his longsword, blue blade and black stone in the hilt flashed in the sun, he challenged the guard to single combat to win their release. The old man spun his staff above his head and lightning scattered around the square. My wife instructed a sergeant to take the challenge, he stepped forwards. Then the woman in the white cape stepped forwards, 'Let me, my lord.' she said. Jangor looked at her and said, 'Don't play with this one, one stroke.' she nodded and turned to the sergeant, flicked the cape from her shoulders, hefted the axe casually in one hand, she actually smiled at him, and waited. He didn't really know what to do, Namdarin looked a little nervous, his sword twitching in his hand, eventually the sergeant attacked, somewhat tentatively, she caught is attack on the face of her axe, again and again, she did exactly the same thing, she never countered, she never even moved, she caught every one of his blows on the face of the axe, until finally, she turned the axe, his sword hit the edge, and shattered. 'Yield.' she said. One of the other men threw a sword into the centre of the field. 'Pick it up.' yelled my wife. The woman stared at her, then the sergeant reached for the sword on the ground, he came up swinging into the attack. She blocked his attack with the face of the axe, and made her only attack of the entire fight, his breastplate flashed into sparks as her axe tore through it, she turned and walked away, my wife screaming for her to come back and stop being a coward. Then the sergeant fell into two discrete piles. Namdarin whistled, a large white horse pushed its way through the crowd, with two others in tow. The woman picked up her cape, and mounted her horse, the old man pulled himself into his saddle, Namdarin looked at me and asked if I would honour the agreement, I simply nodded, Jangor and his friend, mounted their horses, Brank came over and asked for a horse in lieu of pay, and mounted a pony that was brought, last Namdarin mounted the huge white stallion, they trooped out through the gate, the woman walked her horse slowly over to where my wife was standing, 'You killed a man here today, not me.' She walked her horse slowly to the gate, Namdarin turned before he got to the gate, his horse reared up on its hind legs and screamed a challenge, then turned and left." Harvang turned to Kevana, "Perhaps now you understand the nature of the people you are up against, I suggest that if you want to live, you turn around and run for home. Any other course is going to lead to your deaths."

"We cannot," Kevana said quietly, "we have been tasked by our god, if our deaths occur then so be it. We cannot turn aside from this trial, but we will be improving the odds very soon."

"How do you plan to do that?"

"We shall be picking up some more men, and some more weapons from the monastery."

"If they follow you, then some, or all, may die."

"Live or die, our duty is clear."

"It's a hard road you walk." Harvang muttered.

"But I don't walk it alone," replied Kevana, "we are never alone."

"I think that if you wish to survive, you should race to Zandaarkoon and call out the whole of your army. However, that elvish weapon improves that sword, it's going to quite formidable."

"I can't do that," Kevana said, softly, "It's my duty to take the sword to Zandaar, that is exactly what I will do."

"Then stop chasing them, go to where you think they will be."

"That is the problem, if they take to the river, then they could easily pass us by."

"If they take the river, then they'll have to leave their horses behind, once they've done that, they may as well ride the river all the way to Zandarkoon, so all you have to do is search every southbound boat." Laughed Harvang.

"No." Crathen said, "Namdarin won't leave his horse behind, he'll ride far enough south, so the boats are big enough to carry their horses, gives them more flexibility when they get close to the city as well."

"True." Harvang said, "they are a team, he might just leave the horse with the elves, if they prove to be friendly, but he'll not just sell it, it's family."

"How far south will they have to go to find boats that big?" Worandana asked.

"Perhaps a hundred miles, maybe more."

"So." Kevana interrupted. "Five or ten days south, then another five or ten on the river, and we have to intercept them somewhere along this path?"

"That just about sums up the task ahead of you." said Harvang, "But you do have the advantage of your magic to track them, don't you?"

"That's almost as physically hard as tracking them down on horseback, and there is the outside possibility that they may find some way to hide the sword from us."

"Will Zandaar be able to feel the sword getting closer?"

"Yes." said Worandana. "He'll sense it for sure, he may not be able to tell if friend or foe is carrying it, but he'll know it is coming."

"Are you certain?" Kevana asked.

"Oh yes. Once you get close enough, even you'll be able to feel it, it has a certain presence on the magical plane."

"How close?"

"For me, perhaps a quarter of a mile, for you, maybe a hundred paces." Worandana laughed aloud.

"Thanks friend." muttered Kevana, glancing around the table at the smiling faces. Smiling Alverana stood up. Havang frowned at him. "Latrine." muttered the big monk. Harvang nodded.

"Someone else go with him, safety in numbers and all that." then he glanced at two of his guards and so doing designated them escort. Fabrana stood and moved to follow Alverana. The guard opened up a path to the rear doorway and the two moved along it, the locals seemed a little restive, but made no attempts to interfere.

"I think," Kevana said, quite loudly, "we'll forgo bathing tonight, given the tension in this town, we can wait another day, until we get to the monastery."

"Thank you for that." Harvang replied, "That will make things a little easier for my men."

"I still find it hard to believe that the people in this town would attack soldiers like us, simply because we are hunting people they met, or more likely, heard about, on one day?"

"They made a big impression, in that one day."

"I am fairly sure that if you had tried to stop them leaving many of your people would have died, Jangor is a warrior, and Namdarin even more so, he's got nothing left to lose."

"I don't think that is exactly true." Crathen commented.

"What do you mean?" Kevana asked.

"Rightly, or not, he believes Jayanne to be his."

"And you plan to take her away?"

"That is correct."

"I think you had better be sure he is dead first." Said Harvang.

"I'm hoping that these monks will see to that."

"If she gets in the way she is going to die as well, you do understand that?" Kevana declared.

"I'll do what I can to see she's otherwise occupied."

"You plan to take on her and her axe?"

"I'm hoping it won't come to that." Crathen almost mumbled.

"You seem to me to be somewhat of an outsider in both groups, how did that happen?" Asked Jon.

"That's a long story." Laughed Crathen.

"Have you got something better to do?"

"I suppose not. I had been given a task by a Baron Melandius, he offered me one hundred pieces of silver for the head of a minor brigand."

"We met Melandius," said Petrovana, "he was quite rude to us."

"That was later." Kevana said. "Sorry Crathen, please carry on."

"I was heading north where I was told this Blackbeard had his base. I heard a group coming towards me, along the same narrow defile I was taking, so I moved off the path to hide amongst the rocks where I could watch them and not be seen, I was hoping that Blackbeard would be with them. Of course, he wasn't. They stopped, one pointed at my tracks in the snow, looking down they were far too obvious, one pointed vaguely in my direction, then Namdarin lifted his bow, nocked an arrow, pulled and released in one smooth motion, I dropped to the ground, only just before the arrow would have hit me. You won't believe how fast those arrows fly. There was some discussion, then the arrow drifted slowly passed me returning to Namdarin's hand, Jayanne unbound her hair and let it all fall loose, she spun the binding around her head a few times, I was curious, stupid and curious, the strap suddenly went somehow loose, and the lights went out. I woke up being carried down the hill. I have to admit there was little fight in me at this point, pain and flashing lights in my head, but no fight." Crathen paused to drink some of his beer.

"She used a simple sling." said Alverana, sounding a little surprised. Crathen just nodded. "Nobody uses slings any more, arrows have a far better range, and a crossbow will punch a hole in plate armour."

"All that is true," Crathen continued, "but her pouch of suitable stones is refilled at every stream she passes. Arrows take some time and skill to make, crossbow bolts even more so, all she needs is a strip of soft leather and a streambed. Shall I continue?" He didn't actually wait for an answer. "Jangor explained to Namdarin something about how a man with an arrow in his head doesn't often answer questions. He then asked me what I was doing. I told him of the quest given to me by Melandius, he said that Blackbeard was actually a member of their party, I looked around, and reached for my sword, Stergin's hand held my wrist so I couldn't draw, then they showed be a bearded head in a bag. I told Jangor how much silver Melandius had offered for that head, they all started laughing. Jangor said, 'He offered us one thousand, and expected us to die, we killed most of Blackbeard's men, and there were nearly thirty of them.' 'Who killed them?' asked Namdarin. 'Fine, you and Jayanne killed them all, we just collected the head. We are on our way to Melandius' house to claim our reward, would you like to tag along?' That is how I ended up with Namdarin's group."

"That doesn't tell us how you ended up, with these monks?" Jon asked.

"That's an entirely different story." Interrupted Kevana, "one that we are not going to hear today." His glare around the table made it very clear to all that no one was to tell of Gorgana's defection. Slowly he came to his feet, "I need a little walk." Harvang rose, "Would you like some company?"

"Have I a choice?"

"Not really. Please follow me." Harvang's simple gesture passed command to Jon, as the two walked away from the table, through the much more relaxed guards, the whole room seemed a lot less belligerent, together they walked to the corner of the yard earlier indicated by Senjin, the door opened on to a well-lit room, ahead of them were three small bath tubs, set against one wall, an elderly woman was emptying a large bucket of water into the one nearest the fire, she glanced up at the two men, put her bucket on the floor, took off her robe and hung it on a hook near the tub and climbed slowly into the obviously hot water.

"Does her openness shock you?"

"I'm a soldier, I've seen naked people before."

"Not all religions are so tolerant."

"More soldier than religious."

Harvang nodded and turned to the other door that lead off the main room, this one opened into a much smaller space, still well lit, two oil lamps hung from the rafters, ahead was a bench like affair with two large holes, to the right a sloping gutter that went down to disappear below the bench, to the left a small table with a basin and a ewer of water, a towel hung on a peg on the wall and a hard cake of soap in a small brown dish. Harvang walked to the gutter and unbuttoned his trousers, there was more than enough room for Kevana to stand alongside him, which he did. As the two stood side by side Kevana sniffed, then sniffed again, Harvang looked at him and smiled.

"You're going to make me ask, aren't you?" Kevana asked. Harvang nodded, smiling.

"Fine, that's a damned pit latrine, it's too deep and we're too close to the river for it to be anything else, how come it doesn't smell?"

"That's an interesting question." Harvang replied, turning away, splashing some water on his hands and walking slowly out of the door, Kevana very much on his heels.

"Good night Dottie." He called to the old woman in the bath, a raised arm waved.

"Yes you are right it is the most simple of pit latrines, a really awful job when it needs emptying, but it does have a large chimney, one that goes clear to the roof of the building. The place does come with a warning though, never sit next to someone when it is windy outside."

"Why?"

"When the wind is blowing hard across the top of the chimney, then the draw on it can be quite intense, it's not unheard of for both parties to be stuck in their holes until help arrives. There is a tale, how true it is I cannot say, that on one blustery night a rather thin lady was only restrained by her shoulders and knees, her companion was unable to lift her out, and had to go and get a couple of strong men to pull her free. Again, how true, I have no idea."

"This is certainly a very strange place."

"All places are strange until you can call them home."

"I suppose that is true, but as a soldier I really have no home, I serve."

"I understand that, if you were ever to leave the service of your god, then you could easily run a garrison like this one, or even a much bigger one, I know it's very unlikely, but it is a thought."

"I shall keep that in mind, though I think it's not going to be at all likely, I will most likely die in service, this is after all what soldiers like us are for. Do you see yourself retiring?"

"My situation is safer that yours, I spend almost no time in the field, our walls are so good that almost no one will risk attacking us, can you imagine the loses from attacking our walls?"

"Your town doesn't have anything in it worth that much, but sometimes raiders will operate on a rumour. Just look at those walls, they've got to be protecting something."

"When our town was founded, they were turbulent times, so a great deal of effort was put into the design and building of the walls."

"But still a river runs through?"

"You've seen the quality of our gates?" Kevana nodded. "Well the valves that control the river are even more complex, we can block water coming in, and going out, occasionally we even test them, if we shut both gates the river flows round the east side, it runs almost along the wall, any besiegers that side are in for a wet time." He laughed out loud.

"What about water supply?"

"We have seven good wells inside the walls, in a time of war these are confiscated by the watch and water becomes free for all that need it."

"You mean it isn't free for the people now?"

"No, the water belongs to the people that own the wells, river water is always free, but not always so nice to drink."

"I just have some difficulty with people actually paying for water."

"It's not massively expensive, but it is a regular payment to be met."

"Somehow I don't think any attacking force is going to succeed unless they get inside before the gates are closed, and then hold the gates, is this part of the reason for our escort tonight?"

"It may have been a factor, but not a serious consideration, I don't believe that your small group, no matter what sort of skills you have, could hold the gates for long enough, even the lightest of horse troops would need almost an hour to get to the gate from the nearest point of concealment, and yes I do know where that would be. There's a valley off to the north it runs east west, you could hide a thousand horse in there, but you didn't, I may be a simple provincial captain, but I'm not stupid."

"Harvang, no one would ever suggest that you are that, some of your people are not happy with our presence, but they understand your need to know what we are doing, and we are passing through, with the dawn we will be riding out of your south gate, in a week a momentary excitement, in a month forgotten completely."

"You don't know these people, your visit will be the talk of the town for months, once the dark of winter sets in, and it's not far off now, they'll talk of little else, well your visit, the death of Jackis, and battle for the gate, I dread to think how big these tales will be come spring."

"Shall we go back inside? My people may be getting a little worried."

"Of course. Please follow me." Harvang turned to the door just as it opened and Worandana, Petrovana, and two guardsmen came out.

"We missed you." Worandana said softly.

"Just been chatting." Kevana stepped aside so they could pass, then walked in through to the bar where the others were still sitting.

"We were beginning to get worried about you." Alverana said, as Kevana sat down in his chair.

"Just shooting the breeze, it's an interesting town."

"I'm not at all sure I like it." Alverana stared hard at Harvang, who smiled.

"Well we'll not be staying long. Anyone not been to the latrine get it sorted out very soon, once that is done we are all retiring for the night, I want exercises and breakfast completed before sunrise, I expect to be through the gates as soon as they open. Anyone unclear?" A few groans were all the answers he got, as Worandana returned two more stood to be escorted outside.

"We're going to bed soon." said Kevana.

"Fine." replied Worandana, "we need to be on the road early."

"Senjin." called Kevana, "more beer and more wine, last drink before bedtime." A wave from the bar was all the answer they got, until Petunia shouldered her way through the cordon of guardsmen, carrying a large tray with a pair of jugs and two bottles of wine. She carefully balanced one edge of the tray on the end of the table, passed the two jugs down to the men, and handed the two bottles out, to Kevana and Harvang.

"I'll have a taste of that wine." Called Worandana from the other end of the table.

A bottle passed down the table, Worandana, took a sip straight from the bottle, then a much bigger sip.

"That's quite a good wine, not what I expected from a place like this." he nodded slowly then passed the bottle back up the table. Harvang smiled as the bottle passed him, back into Kevana's waiting hand.

"You know something about this?" Asked Kevana.

"Be glad that I do." was the laughing reply, "Imagine the dregs that would have been served to the men hunting Brank." He paused to let the idea sink in, then continued. "I couldn't let that happen, instructions were sent to Senjin, and he has followed them most admirably though that is not the best from his cellar, it is far from the worst."

"Hey Senjin." He called. "Remember that Arcian red you picked up real cheap a few years ago?" Jeers and laughter from around the room.

"Of course." came a voice from the darkness of the bar. "I've still got a couple of bottles left, if you've got a horse's backside that needs a wash." More laughter.

"Oh my, that was a classic." Smiled Harvang. "It's not often that Senjin gets taken, but that time he most certainly was. He was on a buying trip, many days south, he's been struggling to find a decent red wine, and his boat back was waiting, up come these merchants he's never seen before, and they offered him some good red, good price too, as they needed to be moving on. Pick any bottle from any case, he was told, and he did, one of the merchants picked up the bottle he selected and opened it, they both tasted it and toasted it, the deal was struck, the cases unloaded onto Senjin's boat, the cart wandered slowly away from the dock. They must have switched the bottle between lifting it from the crate and opening it, because every other bottle in all twenty cases was absolutely dreadful. Senjin is not wrong, they are barely fit for washing a horse's arse." Kevana joined in the general laughter of the bar.

"One little mistake," came a voice from the dark, "one little mistake, one time, and no one ever forgets."

"How come he's only got a couple of bottles left?" Whispered Kevana.

"If he thinks the customer is drunk enough, he'll sell them a bottle at full price for the good stuff, they'll not notice. Which is another reason not to get too drunk in here." Harvang didn't talk too quietly.

"I heard that." voice from the dark again. "I've almost never done anything like that, I use it to fortify some of the weaker dark beers, you can't really taste it, but it does have a bit of a kick."

"Of course, Senjin, of course." Laughed Harvang.

"Looks like it's time for us to go to our beds." Declared Kevana, watching Fabrana and Kirukana return from the latrine.

"There's an old naked woman in there." said Kirukana, quite loudly.

"You certainly spent enough time making sure she was so." Laughed Fabrana.

"Have these people no modesty?"

"You may find this as a bit of a surprise," Fabrana went on, "most people take their clothes off to bathe."

"Enough." Snapped Worandana. "Time for bed." Those still seated stood, Alverana grabbed a jug and his mug from the table, Kevana a bottle.

"I'll bid you good night," said Harvang, "I'll be back before dawn, Jon, choose three others to stand guard with you for the night watch."

"I get all the good jobs." laughed Jon, pointing at three of the guards.

"Two should be enough to guard the one stairway." said Alverana.

"Given the quantity of beer drunk tonight, I'd say there will be more trips to the latrine tonight, two to guard the stair and two to guard the drunks." Laughed Jon. "The rest of you will be back here before sunrise, escort duty is not finished until the ecclesiastical gentlemen have left the city."

"Good night captain." he said, as he led the visitors out into the back yard and up the steps to their rooms.

Kevana, Alverana and Crathen went into their room, to their various beds, Alverana checked his roll and was certain it had not been disturbed, the small feather he had left on the top was still there. They stripped and went to their beds, as they pulled the blankets up to their chins they each sighed, it had been so long since they had slept in real beds.

CHAPTER FORTY FIVE

Granger quickly descended the steep walkway that lead to the central glade, his short but rapid strides took him to the path towards the barrow at quite a rate.

"Hey." called Gregor. "What's the rush? We have permission of the new, as yet uncrowned, king."

"I'd really like to be the first to enter, anyone else may just disturb something, and that could actually be dangerous to them, we need to make sure there are no residual energies that could cause problems."

"You think the place may be booby trapped?"

"It's not beyond the realms of possibility."

"Then stop being so slow." The younger man laughed as he started to run along the path to the mound, rapidly outdistancing his elderly friend. Gregor slowed down so that Granger could catch up, though he did have to work quite hard to do it, by the time they both arrived at the entrance to the barrow they were quite out of breath. They were met by two of Fennion's bowmen.

"Halt." shouted one bowman. "No one is allowed entry."

"Fennion has sent us to check the place out, we need to find out if it has any magical traps or even some simple mechanical ones, before the general populace are allowed access."

"That is why we are here, Fennion tasked us with guard duty, we have to stop people getting hurt in there."

"And he has sent us to make sure it is safe, would you like to lead the way inside?"

"No. We'll let you go inside and secure the place, if you need help scream loudly and we may be tempted to come inside to help you."

"Sounds like a plan to me." said Granger, "how many people have you turned away?"

"Only the one."

"Who was that?"

"He was Androlian. Captain of the personal guard of Tomas."

"That in itself is interesting, but of no real moment right now." said Granger. "Will you allow us access?"

"If it is Fennion's wish that you investigate the mound then we will make sure you are not disturbed."

"That's good, while we were talking with the council it was decided that there will be a large party tonight in the central glade, we should be finished with the investigation in time for you and your men to attend. If you can keep the untrained away for a few hours that would be appreciated."

"We will secure the entrances so that the staff bearers can complete their work." The elf saluted and sent his companion around the barrow to tell the others guarding the opposite entrance.

"Please step back a little way." said Gregor, to the guard, who did exactly as requested, apparently he had no wish to challenge the barrow in any way at all. Gregor turned to Granger, "How do you want to do this?"

"We just need to be sensitive to the place, feel out its existence, and then kill it."

"How do we do that?"

"I was hoping that you might have an idea."

"I don't have a clue. Let's just walk in like we know what we are doing, confidence is the key." said Gregor.

Granger smiled and lead the way inside. The dark soon closed in around them both, they came to the first of the side rooms, it contained almost nothing other than a stone bier, which looked so much like a tomb that Granger tried to see if the top could be opened, either it was too heavy for him to move, or it was one solid piece of stone. The sides were engraved with images of trees, and the foot had something that may have been a name at some time, though time had taken its toll, it was completely unreadable. Upon the wall at the head of the bier was a bas-relief of a very stylised tree, and a star above it. There was a considerable amount of smoke staining of the walls and the ceiling, after all this was where the fire had been started, but no real damage. Granger looked at Gregor and shrugged, as if the room had nothing more to tell them. Gregor backed out of the room and turned into the one across the passageway, the only change here was that the engraving on the foot was different, and the star on the tree was in a different place.

"I wonder what the significance of the star is?" Asked Granger.

"It's on a different branch of the tree, perhaps he comes from a different family, maybe the branches represent the families. We'll ask Fennion when we get back, can you feel any power? I'm getting nothing."

"I'm only getting some sort of echo, like the power has only recently gone, but that would stand to reason, I'd have thought it would have been more than it is though, those warriors were carrying an awfully large charge."

"So either they have been carrying that charge since they entered this tomb, or they have been charging from somewhere in here."

"That is exactly what I think, we need to find that source, if it exists and shut the thing down, or someone else may find a way to tap it, and that could be disastrous in the wrong hands."

"It could be another source like the lightning stone, it might even be an offshoot of the same one."

"It's a very long way to the lightning stone, it's very unlikely to be an offshoot, but it could be something similar, we have to find it. Perhaps it's in the platforms themselves."

"Are you suggesting we lie down on them?" queried Gregor.

"I'm not sure, I'm not getting any feeling from this one." Granger said, running his hand slowly across the surface, the roughness of the stonework, somehow felt a little out of place. "What do you think about the surface, I can't feel any tool marks in it, but it's not like it was eroded by wind or water?"

"Hang on a moment." Gregor went back into the first room and picked up the torch that Jangor had used to ignite the warrior that was sleeping there, the sudden surge of flame had blown the torch out, there was plenty of life left in it. He relit it as he walked into the second room, holding the torch low beside the bier, so that it's light would exaggerate the imperfections in the surface. The low angle of the light showed a pattern of lines and shapes.

"I'm seeing star shapes at head, heart, a really big one there, belly and groin, and lines or channels leading to the head." Granger said, moving to the head of the bier, Gregor moved the flickering torch to illuminate the end in a similar manner.

"Wide channels leading down into the ground." Granger said, softly. "I'd suggest channels to carry the power and stars to focus it, each on a power centre for the human body, as described in an ancient religion, I assume that elves are somewhat similar, sometimes I wish that I had brought all my books with me."

"Whatever the purpose of these diagrams, the power comes here from somewhere else. Main chamber?"

"Most likely, but let's not rush, we'll have to check all the rooms, come on." Grange lead the way out of the second room, and back into the passageway, together they entered the next room towards the centre.

"Can you feel it?" asked Gregor. "The power is definitely stronger in here." Granger merely nodded, looking up he said. "Star is in a different place again, another family?"

"Perhaps, the channels feel sharper in here." said Gregor holding the torch down and looking across the surface, "I believe they are actually glowing a little in the torchlight." Granger bent over to view the surface.

"Definitely, there is still power flowing in them, but it is fading quite rapidly. Let's move on." Into the next room they went.

"The star is in the same place." said Gregor.

"There are only eight branches and sixteen warriors, so some have to be the same." replied Granger. "I can see the channels glowing without the torch in here, and the power is quite strong. Now here's a thought." He slowly moved the tip of his staff over the centre of the biggest star, gently he lowered it, reaching out with his mind to open the channel to the power, his mind could feel it, but it kept wriggling away from the contact, he chased after it, following around in circle as it tried so desperately to avoid him. Gregor could feel the tension in the old man's mind, and the battle that was going on, slowly Granger's mind surrounded the power in the stone, and focused it into the centre of the star where his staff was positioned, waiting, suddenly the bridge was made, and the power started to flow. Granger sent a thought to Gregor, 'Join me' Gregor moved his staff to the centre of the circle and opened it to receive the power that was flowing, steady but hot, the power flowed into both staves, gradually the stars and the channels in the surface of the stone started to glow even stronger, actually eclipsing the light from the flickering torch.

"Enough." whispered Granger, "Break the link." He snapped his staff away from the central star, a small flash jumped to the point as the connection was severed, Gregor did exactly the same. The star was actually scattering light all around the room, Granger looked at Gregor and muttered "Wow."

"Indeed." replied Gregor. "This is better that the lightning stone, it's more controlled, more difficult to open the channel, but far more controlled in its delivery, I like it."

"We still have to find some way to shut it down."

"Agreed, let's move on." He lead the way into the next room, the same as the others, star in a different place, but here they could see the glowing of the stars on the bier.

"We've both taken a large quantity of energy from the field in this mound, and now it seems to be running in charging mode." said Granger, "I wonder how long this will last?"

"You want to wait around until it fades?"

"Not really, we need to get this thing sorted out quickly. Neither of us is short of power right now, so let's go and turn it off."

"Fine." Gregor said, leaving the room and going to the entrance to the central chamber.

"Oh my." he said, not actually entering. The room they were facing was considerably larger than the others, though it had little more in decoration than the rest. The tree at the head of the bier had a star on every branch, and these stars were lighting the room. At the opposite end of the oval room, was another tree, only this one was constructed in three dimensions, though the branches seem to be made of stone, and the stars on the ends of the branches were glowing crystal.

"This is definitely the centre of the power that kept the warriors in their sleeping state." said Granger.

"And fed them power to awaken them."

"I don't sense any power sealing the doorway."

"You go first then." laughed Gregor. Tentatively Granger stepped across the threshold, the harsh light picked out his grey hair and turned it almost white, he crossed to the foot of the bier, again the name on it was faded by time, but could have been the name of the king. He turned and waved Gregor into the room.

"An oval shaped room like this," he almost whispered, speaking just loud enough to be heard over the rustling of the non-existent leaves on the tree, "there are two centres, the king's heart would have rested at one, and this tree at the other." They turned to face the tree.

"I agree." muttered Gregor. "The tree is the power here, but how do we shut it down?"

"Notice how one of the stars is much darker than the others?"

"Yes, it's much less than all the others."

"If the stars represent the great families of the elves, then the darkest one should be the line of the king, after all he only has two surviving relatives."

"Agreed, but how does that help us."

"If these stars are feeding on the power of the great families of the elves, then this in itself could be affecting they reproductive capabilities. The smallest being the line of Grinderosch, now almost extinct. The stars appear to simply hang on small wire loops, I suggest we lift them off the branches, what do you think?"

"Do you want to try that?"

Granger stepped up to the tree, and selected the darkest of the crystalline stars, he reached for is slowly with both hands, as he approached he could feel the hairs on his arms lift and tremble, a gentle sizzling noise gradually increased as he neared the star. Suddenly he stepped back.

"I can feel it, it's going to discharge if I touch it."

"The loops that hang the stars are simply that, hoops of metal, pick them up with a staff, and then put them down on the floor, hopefully they'll discharge into the floor and cause no damage?"

"It would have to be mine, the metal on yours might discharge them into the person holding it."

"Agreed." Gregor stepped back to give Granger some space to manoeuvre.

Slowly Granger inserted his staff through the hoop on the darkest star, there was some noise from it but no discharge. It took some wriggling to get the star off the branch, but it did eventually slip free, as it came clear of the branch the light went out inside.

"Ground or bier?" asked Gregor.

"Ground, I think, we don't know what is going on with these stone platforms." Slowly he lowered the dark star to the ground, it touched with no obvious affect, and lay on its back after he withdrew the staff. Tentatively Gregor reach out to it, there was no noise, no tension, no flickering, even as he touched it with bare skin, nothing.

"It's completely dead, nothing, I can't feel anything from it." he said.

"Let's try one of the more lively ones." Granger manoeuvred the end of his staff through the loop, he nodded at Gregor to take the other end, together the removal was easier, it's light went out as it came off the branch, then joined the other on the ground. The two looked at each other and set about removing all the other stars. As the last one came off the tree the room was plunged into darkness.

"We didn't think about that." Laughed Gregor.

"Stand still for a while, there is light coming down the corridors, but it will take a while for our eyes to get used to it." Gradually the room appeared to lighten as their eyes became used to the darkness. Soon they could see enough to put the last of the stars on the ground. Granger moved his staff so that was above the kings resting place, right over the star that would have been below his heart.

"Nothing, there is no power here now."

"I'll check a couple of the other rooms." said Gregor, walking out into the corridor and blocking the light for a short time. Then he blocked the light again as he crossed the hallway. In only moments he returned.

"All dead, not even a hint of an echo."

"So, what do we do with these stars?"

"We can't destroy them, we should give them back to the families they belong to."

"How do we identify them?"

"Perhaps the elves can do that, maybe it doesn't even matter, one star to each of the eight family lines. Let the elves sort it out. We've released these great jewels, they can dispose of them any way they choose."

Granger nodded, conjured a small light at the tip of his staff, looking around the central chamber in the soft blue light he could see the representations of stars on the ceiling, glowing a soft silvery pattern, group like none he had ever seen before.

"These don't look like the stars in our sky?" he said, glancing at Gregor.

"I've never really studied the stars, they're only important to heretics and sailors."

"Heretics?"

"Sorry slipping back into old ways of thinking. There are some that believe the stars hold the secrets of all our lives, I have never been one that subscribed to that particular belief."

"Neither have I, but these patterns are very different from the ones I see in the sky."

"Perhaps they aren't an actual picture of the sky, but randomly placed blobs of silvery paint."

"You see the people that created this space doing that? Scattering paint about?"

"Well, I suppose not. Just look at the detail on the tree, and the carving or engraving of the energy pathways on the stones" Granger looked back at the tree just in time to see a branch fall to the ground.

"It appears to be falling apart." he reached down to move the stars away from the falling tree, one by one the branches fell to the ground and shattered into dust, when the last one fell the top of the trunk started to turn into sand and fall down to the ground, in only a few minutes the great tree had been reduced to a pile of sand on the floor.

"That's a shame." said Gregor, "that was a very nice tree."

"And now it's purpose is over."

"Other than taking these stars back to the elves, I think our purpose here is over as well."

Granger nodded, then he relit the almost spent torch and stood it up in the sand, that had so recently been a stone tree.

"Thread them onto my staff, we should be able to carry them between us."

"What if they touch? They could do almost anything."

"No, two of them are already touching and I can feel nothing from them. Without the tree and the energy pathways and whatever magics were used when they were installed, they are probably harmless."

"It's that probably that I don't like."

"We don't have long before that torch fails completely so let's get to it." said Granger, easing his staff through the loop on the nearest star. One by one the eight stars were positioned on Granger's staff.

"Suddenly it strikes me." said Gregor, "They look so much like the stars that children draw each with eight points, longest axis vertical, next horizontal, and the intermediates shortest of all."

"And they are still quite tall when you take into consideration the loops they hung on."

"Let's see if we can lift them." said Gregor once they were all on the staff, he propped his staff against the king's bier, and gripped Grange's staff in both hands, together they lifted the staff and its cargo. With the staff in their hands and their arms straight down from the shoulders, the points of the stars were still dragging on the ground.

"That won't do." said Granger. "Turn around and face the staff as I do." A bemused Gregor followed Granger's actions. "Now lift the arms and let the staff slide down to the crook of your elbows." Now they had the staff high enough to stop the stars dragging on the ground and supported by two arms at each end.

"This is all well and good, but my staff is over there, and I don't have any way of picking it up." said Gregor.

"We can't leave that behind." said Granger. "It's carrying far too much energy to fall into untrained hands."

"Power." said Gregor.

"Power, energy, call it whatever you want."

"You miss the point."

"Explain for a stupid old man then." snapped Granger.

"When you killed that warrior, was that a gain or loss."

"I threw energy out, to burn the other two, and still came out with an overall gain, so much that it actually hurt to force it into the staff."

"Power. Why should we carry all this weight when your staff has so much power?"

"I am sorry that I am such a stupid old man." Granger closed his eyes and reached into his staff with his mind, slowly tapping the power there to lift itself and its load of stars. Gregor, felt the weight lessen, until he could lift the staff with one hand, he reached out and picked up his own staff, placed it carefully along Granger's, then started transferring power into Granger's staff, the weight almost vanished completely.

"Now that makes a lot more sense." said Ganger. "Let's take these to Jangor, he'll want to make a presentation of them to the elves."

"Not the worst idea you've had today." laughed Gregor, lifting the staffs onto his shoulder with one hand and whistling a merry tune. A quick glance over his shoulder and he started walking down the corridor toward the daylight, and thinking of lunch, that could not be far away.

"What have you got there?" asked the guard as they walked into the sunlight.

"I believe these to be the central power of the tomb." answered Granger. "They will be presented to King Fennion at tonight's celebration, he can decide their disposition. I suspect they will be returned to the families they originally came from. You can consider the tomb safe now, as far as we can tell it no longer has any power at all."

"That's good news, I'll send a runner to the king, see if we can get permission to stand down this guard duty. Thanks." The guard seemed very pleased as he waved one of his men off to the city, the man proved to be a runner indeed, he was back in the city before the magicians where even half way to the central glade, and he was on his way back as they passed between the outer ring of trees.

"What is this?" demanded Jangor as the laden pair approached.

"We think these crystals may belong to the great families of the elves," replied Granger, as the pair lowered their burden to the grass. "I think you should return them at tonight's party."

"Could they be of any use to us?"

"I don't think so, they were suspended on a stone tree, and were suffused with power, power that they passed on to the sleeping warriors, once we removed them from the tree they went dark. I think their power is firmly rooted in the tree and the people here."

"They look to cumbersome and heavy to be of much use to us any way."

"Oh, they are that. It's cost us a great deal of power to get them here, I need to get my staff out of them and to get some power into it." Jangor and Gregor helped remove the stars from Granger's staff, however there was no fire currently lit, so he made do with taking heat and light out of the air. Kern walked up as Granger was planting his staff in the ground, in a nice warm puddle of sunlight, it turned black as night and fog started to crawl slowly down the length of it, spreading a cool pool that gradually made its way down hill towards the stream on the south side of the glade.

"The horses are fine," said Kern. "Even that brute of yours." he laughed, looking at Namdarin, who was sitting outside his tent next to Jayanne, they weren't talking just holding hands. Namdarin smiled, then returned to his thoughts. "These elves certainly know how to look after horses." he went on to Jangor. Jangor turned to Namdarin and Jayanne.

"Hey." he said quietly, they both looked up. "You could at least pretend."

"What do you mean?" asked Namdarin.

"You can hear the sound of Stergin and that damned whetstone of his, Mander and Andel are cleaning their armour, you two could at least pretend that your weapons need sharpening, that your arrows need checking, we all know that they don't, but you could at least pretend. Try to look like you are doing something." Namdarin laughed, but stood, in a flash the sword was in his hand.

"In the interests of the moral of the group I will do what I can." He said, he ducked into his tent briefly, returning with a small whetstone of his own. He unrolled it slowly from the leather cloth it was wrapped in.

"Damn, it's dry." he muttered.

"We have plenty of water." said Jangor.

"I prefer to use oil on my whetstones, it's not as readily available but gives a better finish."

"I have this lamp oil I took from Melandius's house, try that." said Jangor taking one of the small bottle from his belt pouch. Namdarin accepted the bottle and sprinkled a little of the almost colourless oil on his whetstone, it soaked straight in, so he added a little more, until the surface of the stone was shiny with the oil, slowly he ran the stone along the edge of the sword, it made very little noise, but appeared to polish the edge quite considerably, in only a few minutes one edge of the great sword shone like the best quality mirror, very soon the other edge was the same, Namdarin merely touched it with his thumb to test it and it cut the skin immediately.

"That oil really helps, I've never had a sword this sharp before." Namdarin said swinging the sword from side to side and listening to the clear whistling sound it made. Stergin looked round to see where the noise was coming from, then walked over.

"That sounds really sharp."

"Here try this." said Namdarin, passing him the whetstone. After only a few passes Stergin was surprised by the improvement in the edge of his sword.

"What is this?" he asked.

"Lamp oil rather than water, looks like it gives a very fine edge, not sure how quickly it will take out the nicks of a sword fight, or how hard this edge will be, but it certainly will cut anything it touches." Namdarin passed him the bottle so he could lubricate his own stone.

"How long does an oiling usually last?"

"Wrap the stone tightly in leather it can last for weeks, the leather becomes a reservoir for the oil."

Stergin nodded and oiled his stone some more, before handing the bottle back to Namdarin, who in turn handed it to Jangor.

"No, you keep it." said the soldier, "I've not found a use for it yet."

"You have your own sword."

"Yes, but I give it to Stergin to sharpen, he's far better at it, and I believe he actually likes to do it."

"There is something about sharpening a sword, something really calming, I find it helps to focus the mind." said Stergin, "It gives the hands something to do while leaving the mind free for other matters."

"I'm going to sharpen all my arrows." said Namdarin, he glanced at Jayanne, the question un-asked. She thought for a moment then nodded, and went to get her quiver, which she passed to Namdarin and returned to her place on the grass.

"Looks like I've got the sharpening duties." he said to Stergin, who laughed out loud, and took Jangor's sword. A short inspection was followed by a snort of derision.

"Have you been chopping trees with this fine weapon?"

"Those damned warriors were like trees."

"How many times do you have to be told, joints, not bones?" at this point he stamped off to set about the damaged sword with some gusto, even the oil did little to reduce the noise of his whetstone. Jangor turned to Namdarin.

"He always says things like that, some of us can chose high or low, I can't pick shoulder, elbow or wrist, but that's just not good enough for Stergin, it's part of the reason he is so good a swordsman."

"I'd not like to come up against him in battle." said Namdarin, sitting down on the grass and removing all of Jayanne's arrows from the quiver, checking the first one against the sunlight, he honed the edges only briefly, and returned it to its case, soon to be followed by all of its fellows.

"Not only does that oil improve the edge, it increases the speed, it's a marvel." he said to Jayanne as he returned her refilled quiver. She smiled and rolled to her feet, both Namdarin and Jangor stared at her as she bent over to return the quiver to the tent, as she turned back Jangor snapped his eyes away, but Namdarin did not, he continued to look at her figure even as she came towards him. Her hand snapped to one of the knives in her belt, in a fluid continuation the knife was drawn and, in a flash, came forwards towards Namdarin, Jangor started to move, hoping to prevent any bloodshed, as her arm reached the end of its course, the knife turned over in her hand and presented the hilt to Namdarin.

"You may as well do these." she laughed, looking at Jangor staggering to his feet.

"Please don't do that." he said, settling back onto the grass. "My nerves are bad enough in this place."

"What's got you so jumpy?" Asked Jayanne.

"Only a couple of hours ago the people of this city were on the brink of rising in open rebellion, is that not cause enough?"

"That rebellion was defused by Fennion."

"The overt rebellion, I agree, Fennion appeased the council with his words, what about the ones that didn't hear his words, or hearing them chose to ignore them? Now is the time for the hidden rebellion, now is the time of the assassin."

"You think that is a serious danger?" demanded Namdarin.

"Not serious I suppose, these elves are the most tightly controlled people I have ever met, the word of the king is instant law. It only takes one hothead, one malcontent, one disgruntled teenager and it all goes up in smoke. Once that fire is lit, it's very difficult to put out, impossible without major bloodshed. So, yes I am worried."

"Do you think it will come to a head at this party Fennion has planned?"

Jangor stared hard into Namdarin's eyes.

"Drink, food, dancing. Drink, strangers, dancing. Drink, food, drink. What do you think?"

"Said like that, it's definitely a recipe for disaster. Though I don't think we are in any danger, to change everything all they have to do is remove King and heir."

"Do you think they would?" Asked Jayanne.

"I don't know them well enough to judge that." said Namdarin.

"Me neither." answered Jangor. "We'll just have to be on our guard." He climbed slowly to his feet.

"Listen up people." he called and waited for them all to gather round.

"It's possible that the situation here could descend into bloody rebellion tonight. Any rebels have two choices, they take all of us, or they end for all time the line of Fennion. I can't believe in this society they have enough rebels willing to die to kill us, but it only takes two knifes to kill Fennion and Laura."

"To kill Laura, someone would have to climb over a dead Brank." laughed Stergin.

"Agreed," said Jangor, "and very unlikely. We still need to be ready, so drink slowly, laugh quietly, and stay awake, don't eat anything that you haven't seen someone else eat, poison has long been a favourite of assassins."

"I find it very hard to believe that elves would stoop to assassination," said Granger, "let alone the indiscriminate nature of poison."

"We just have to be aware that there are some in this city that are seriously upset at the actions of their new king or even his existence. I think we all need to get some rest before the party, it's could be a long night."

"Right." said Kern. "Guards?"

"Yes and no. Let's have someone awake at all times, no patrolling, no standing watching, just sitting and relaxed. We don't want our hosts to think we are nervous. Sort out a relaxed and informal rota." He looked at Kern, leaving him to make the arrangements. "I'm going to get a little sleep, someone wake me up in a few hours." Jangor crawled into his tent and was snoring in moments.

"I'll take the first watch." said Kern, "Namdarin you next?" Namdarin simply nodded, he knew he'd pick someone else when he got bored. Kern went to sit with his back to a tree, where he could see the whole camp, he settled down with Wolf alongside. Wolf was resting, he seemed to be almost asleep, but his eyes never stopped moving, and his ears jumped at the slightest sound. Namdarin stood and sheathed his sword, he reached down with one hand to Jayanne, she took it and came slowly to her feet following his pull. Together they walked north through the glade, hand in hand, not a word spoken, soon they were gone from sight, obscured by the trees, first the massive trunks of the outer ring, then the smaller trees growing outside the city.

"It's so quiet out here." Jayanne whispered, looking up into Namdarin's eyes, just as a flash of sunlight lit the black stone in the sword hilt above his head, the dark light scattered around his head, almost like a shattered shadow.

"It is hard to believe we are so close to a city of a kind."

"But their city is so natural, it's simply a part of the forest, it can only be found when it wants to be." She reached with her left hand to hold Namdarin's right, he took it gently as they walked together.

"You know that a gentleman should always keep his sword arm clear when escorting a lady?"

"But if I changed hands then you'd be blocking my axe arm." she said gently swinging the axe forwards and backwards, the head just clearing the ground, but sweeping through the grass, with a quiet rushing sound.

"I've just noticed something." whispered Namdarin, deliberately not looking at Jayanne.

"What?"

"I'm not certain, but with the axe hanging from its strap it not dragging on the ground."

"And your point is?"

"This morning, when we were fighting the undead warriors, you had both hands on the haft and swinging it at those elves."

"Yes."

"You had more haft between your hands, for the leverage, and more haft above your top hand, for striking power, than the axe currently has. I think it changes shape, depending on what it is currently doing, in battle it gets bigger, when not it shrinks."

"Surely that is not possible." she whispered.

"Remember the fight in the town where we picked up Brank?"

"Yes. I don't think I'll ever forget that, the axe really wanted to hurt him before he died."

"Your strike cut him clean in two, and he was not a small man, he must have been at least a foot from front to back, the axe is currently perhaps as much as two hands wide, nowhere near enough to have made that strike."

"And I was standing almost a sword length away from him at the time, so you are certainly right. I have a question."

"Go on."

"Why are we whispering?"

"So, the axe can't hear us?"

Jayanne threw back her head and laughed out loud, "We're whispering in case an axe has ears?" She leaned in against his arm and turned her face up to be kissed, he obliged at some length. Before their combined temperatures rose too far he broke away and gasped a sudden breath.

"Damn woman, you are just too much, you drive me wild."

"Wild enough to abandon your current course?"

He let go of her hand and turned away for a moment, before turning back and looking down into her eyes, the green flashing in the dappled light through the trees.

"No, I cannot turn away from the course I have set, Zandaar must be stopped, he is evil and must be removed from this world, before he takes it all for himself, he will not stop until it is all his."

She picked up his hand and continued their walk away from the city, after a short time, she stopped, and turned to him.

"I will follow your cause until it's conclusion where ever it leads." She smiled and turned away, walking slowly and swinging their joined hands in so many ways like a child.

"What have I done to deserve someone like you?" He asked, his voice barely above the sound of the wind in the leaves.

"That has yet to be decided," she smiled, "it could be that I don't deserve you."

"You are young and beautiful, smart and resourceful, caring and considerate, you are far too good for an old man like me."

"You're fishing for compliments, stop it."

"No, you should have a young man, someone vital and loving."

"I believe that a young man however vital couldn't be as good for me as you have been."

"You could be settled into a quiet life, with family and children, not riding around this world with a bunch of madmen committing random acts of butchery."

"There is no way I could ever have children without you to show me the way," she lifted his right hand to her mouth and kissed it softly, "and I don't think that random is the right word, rapists needed killing, and a lesson had to be taught, I wonder if Harvang's wife actually learned something on that day."

"We'll never know that unless we go back, and I have no intention of doing that."

"Who can say where we are bound once this is completed."

"I like to believe I could return to my home, but I don't believe that is going to happen."

"I think that Fennion would grant us sanctuary, especially if we bring back the mindstone."

"Could you live out your life here? Trees, elves, and Fennion?"

"I'm not so sure about that, the new king is likely to become somewhat of a pain, if we came back here I think we would immediately become members of the council, or the kings advisors, no, too much like hard work, let's not come back here."

"How about the village where the lightning stone and Anya are?"

"That could be a place to stay, but not for the long term, we really don't have much in the way of skills that could be useful there."

"So, we go back to your home, and Morgan, he'd welcome us with open arms."

"You want to be a miner? Somehow, I don't see you grubbing in the ground, and something you must be aware of, you have convinced Morgan not to sell to the Zandaar priesthood, but they'll still be getting silver from third parties." Namdarin nodded. "Once we have removed Zandaar himself, then the value of the silver is going to crash, there could be some hard times ahead for my home town."

"Perhaps, but the silver found there is still special, and worth more than ordinary silver, after all it doesn't tarnish, so for jewellery it's still valuable."

"Yes, but it will have travel much further, so the value will be reduced, could be hard times ahead."

"I'm sure they will survive."

"But do you want to work that hard to make a living from mining?"

"Probably not, I can think of many better things to do than grubbing in the ground."

"Perhaps you could sign on as guard for silver shipments, that would pay quite well, at least if you were good at it."

"That might be a good career for me, these dreams are nice to think about, but we have to survive Zandaar for them to have the slightest chance of becoming reality."

"But you at least harbour a dream of us being together after this is all over." she smiled up at him and leaned in for another kiss, this one lasted considerably longer, until he pushed away, his breath catching harshly in his throat, "I think we need to be getting back to the others, have you any idea which way it is?"

"I can follow our tracks back, even if you can't, but do we really need to go back so soon?" Jayanne grinned and her green eyes lit up in the dabbled sunlight coming through the canopy of the trees. "Even if I lose the track, you can call on the horses or Wolf to come find us, so what's the hurry?" she let the axe slip from her wrist and sank slowly to the ground, he resisted her pull for a while, but eventually gave in, following her to the ground, for more kissing, and so much more.

It was some time later when they started to put their clothes back on, both more than a little tired from their exertions, tired, but sated, at least for a while.

"We came this way." said Jayanne indicating a depression in the grass, and some disturbance in the leaf litter of the forest.

"You sure?" he asked, gathering his thoughts to reach out for the horse herd mind. She shrugged and grinned, straightening her tunic and picking up the axe for the first time in a while. She flinched as the haft made contact with her skin.

"What's wrong?" he demanded, looking around for enemies hiding in the light undergrowth of the forest.

"Nothing." muttered Jayanne, "Sometimes it creates a sudden rush of energy, if it's been out of contact for a while."

"Does it hurt?"

"Not as such, it's just a surprise more than anything. I try to be ready for it, but somehow it's always a shock."

"I wonder why that is?"

"Maybe it doesn't like to be alone."

"Well it's not alone now. You sure about the way back to the city?"

"I say it's that way." she waved an arm, challenging him to say something else.

After only a moment's thought he was certain that she was right, Arndrol was in the same direction and Wolf was there as well, though Wolf was already moving. Together that set off along a path that looked like two sets of footprints side by side and moving slowly. They were both convinced that they were heading in the right direction, until they felt a disturbance in the forest coming towards them, there were alarm calls from the birds and silence from the other animals, the wave of silence was suddenly all around them, and a large wolf came into view, smiling as only a wolf can, long red tongue lolling from his mouth as he came to halt in front of them, he sat down and yipped merrily, his wagging tail swept clean the tracks on the ground that they had left.

"I only asked where he was, not for a guide." Namdarin said, waving for Wolf to lead them back.

"Perhaps he was bored and fancied a bit of a run."

"Well we can't be that far from the city it took him very little time to find us."

"He's following a scent he knows very well, over easy terrain, wolves can move at quite a speed, after all they hunt horses in the wild."

"He doesn't seem to be at all tired, he's prancing around like a puppy."

"He's happy to see us and knows he doesn't have to run back."

She took his hand again, and they walked back towards the city, following Wolf, who was ranging off to the sides of the path chasing whatever scents he found, but always back in a few moments to check on their progress, which just never appeared to be fast enough for the impatient canine. He'd scamper off along the track, turn and stare at them, trying to hurry them along, Namdarin and Jayanne laughed at his antics, but saw no reason to hurry, walking at a moderate pace they walked back through the outer ring of trees, into the heart of the glade, only just after midday.

"Where have you two been?" asked Jangor.

"For a walk in the forest, it's truly beautiful, not sure how nice it would be on a cold and windy winters day, but today, with the sun shining, and only enough breeze to stir the leaves, it's been a nice time."

"Did you call Wolf, he certainly set off at one hell on a pace?"

"I wasn't certain which direction we had come in, so I reached out for the horses, and Wolf, just to get a direction to come back, I didn't mean for him to come to guide us."

"Well he did," said Kern, "one moment he was sitting peacefully, the next he looked up, ears scanning all around, he gave one of those little barks of his, and off, in a moment he was gone from sight."

"Well we're back now, have we missed anything important?"

"Not really, we are simply waiting until the party tonight. Speaking of which, have you any idea how you're going to get the stone out of Fennion's sword and into yours?"

"Not a one, I've looked long and hard at the stone in my sword and can't see any way it is going to come out easily, remember the guard in Melandius's house, I hit him quite hard with the pommel stone, and it is still as solid as it was. If Gyara says we need the stone, then there must be a way to get it, but what?"

"Maybe the stone's themselves know the way, perhaps we simply have to bring them together?" Granger suggested, looking round.

"If all else fails, what have we to lose?" Laughed Gregor.

A familiar face was walking towards them.

"You people really do know how to stir things up." said Gervane as he drew near.

"What have we done now?" demanded Jangor.

"Word is that you have stolen the family jewels?"

Jangor laughed heartily.

"I don't see anything funny here."

The others joined in with the laughter, Gervane's serious mien did nothing at all to quieten them.

"I am sorry." Laughed Jangor, "but I believe there is a little confusion here."

"Then clarify." snapped Gervane.

"Amongst our people the 'family jewels' are a euphemism for the genitals of males, and I don't see that we have stolen any of those," he looked at Jayanne, "at least not for some time."

"It's been a while." Jayanne giggled.

"I asked for clarification not more confusion." said Gervane.

"Jayanne went through a phase of collecting the 'family jewels' but only of men who had raped her, and if they were lucky she killed them first."

"Are you people insane?" Gervane was getting more and more angry. "Those family jewels there." He pointed to the row of crystals on the ground.

"Ah." said Jangor, "now that begins to make some sense. Granger and Gregor collected them from inside the barrow, they believe there were the power that kept the warriors in their undead state. My plan was to present them at tonight's party, Granger thinks they belong to each of the major families, though there are eight crystals and only five representatives on the council, and we've no idea how to tell which families they belong to, no markings that we can discern. Have a look for yourself."

Gervane approached the crystals slowly. "It's been so many years, we thought they were merely legends, but these are the family jewels." A snigger from Andel, and a stare from Jangor. "I thought that they were real, but there was no record of them disappearing, though I suppose, once they were in the barrow, no one was going to go looking for them." He knelt down beside them reverently, and reached out gingerly, as his hand neared the crystals one of them flickered into life, as he snatched his hand away it went dark again.

"Try that again." whispered Jangor.

Gervane reached out to the crystal that had flickered, again it came to life, once his hand was near it.

"Are you a member of one of the major families?" Jangor asked.

"Yes, mine is one of the most populous, if not the greatest."

"Then now we have a way to identify which crystal belongs to which family." said Jangor, "That'll make things so much easier. Gervane, do you need to go back to your people and tell them not to worry, or can we keep this a little surprise for them?"

"It's a long time until the party, have you any idea how upset they are going to be by then?"

"That'll make the surprise so much better, they'll be convinced we are simple robbers by then, and when the family heads are presented with their crystals, sorry, 'jewels', they'll not have any idea how to respond. Can you imagine the looks on their faces?"

"Tomas will have a fit, on the spot, oh my, that is just too precious. You got any Spritz left?"

"I believe we may have a little somewhere." laughed Jangor, reaching into a pack beside him he pulled out a small flask, and shook it tentatively, "there's some but not much." With a flick of the wrist he passed the flask to Gervane, then pulled another one from the pack. "This one's better." With a twist he flicked off the cap and raised the flask to Gervane. "You call it."

Gervane thought for a moment, "To elders and fits, may they each enjoy the other." They both laughed and drank, Jangor got the two actions a little mixed up and ended up with a serious coughing fit.

"The trick," said Gervane, "is not to breathe it, you're supposed to drink it." He laughed even harder.

"I know that." coughed Jangor, "but sometimes I get a little confused."

"It's his age." said Stergin. A glare from Jangor only made Stergin laugh all the more.

"Have you any idea when this party will start?" Asked Kern, stroking the head of Wolf with one hand.

"It'll probably be before sundown, but not by much, sunset is an important time for our people, many rituals and ceremonies start with the prayer for the new day."

"So, we have some time then?" Asked Jangor, hefting his flask.

"Yes." Answered Gervane.

"What did you say earlier?" Asked Kern, looking hard at Jangor.

"I know," muttered Jangor, "I'll drink slowly, small sips, long time apart."

"Your rules." said Kern.

"I know, you don't have to labour the point."

"What rules?" asked Gervane.

"There was almost an open rebellion this morning." sighed Jangor.

"And?"

"It is possible that with two thrusts of a sharp knife the line of Fennion ends tonight."

"Who would do such a thing?"

"Tomas, any of the great families, none of them are happy with the current situation."

"I'd have his head in a heartbeat."

"He won't do it himself, stupid, he'll have some paid lackey, paid and expendable, and thereby dead, lackey."

"There'd be war amongst the families."

"Are you sure about that?"

"Actually, now I think about it, probably not, how would it go? 'Crazy person commits atrocity, deepest sympathy to all concerned, I'll be in charge now'"

"Actually persons, sadly dead before they could talk."

"Persons?"

"As has already been pointed out to me, the only way anyone is going to stick a knife in Laura, is to step over a dead Brank, and that is not going to accomplished easily or quickly, there will be noise and blood."

"The party will be here in the central glade, what about a couple of archers?" Gervane looked up into the branches.

"Shit." shouted Jangor. "Gervane, please light me a big fire." Gervane frowned but gestured in the direction of last night's fire, a surge of green flames jumped up. Jangor nodded. "Gregor, Granger, get your staffs charged, and I mean charged, Gregor teach Granger that barrier spell you used, you have only a few hours to do it."

"What's wrong?" asked Namdarin.

"Why didn't I think of archers?" shouted Jangor, looking up into the low hanging branches of the trees.

"Crap." muttered Namdarin. A glance at Jayanne was all it took, together they walked to the now raging fire and dropped their weapons in the verges of it. The fire sank momentarily then surged to even greater heights.

"We may not be able to shield, but we may be able to take an arrow out of the air."

"That's a plan, Namdarin and Granger you're on Fennion, Jayanne and Gregor you take Laura. This is going to be some party. Damn." He stuffed his flask inside his jacket and stamped over to the fire and back, he drew his sword, and made a few practise passes with it. It whistled softly as the air rushed over it. He glared at the sword, then found Stergin with his eyes, "It whistles, it's not sharp enough, fix it." He tossed the sword in Stergin's general direction and turned back to the fire before the swordsman had snatched it out of the air. Jangor's pacing did not get any more relaxed, as he passed from the camp to the fire and back. The raging blaze reddened his face and the expectant faces did nothing to improve his temper.

"Crap, shit and more crap." he shouted. "Too much cover, and not enough time to set things up properly, what I need is a seer."

"Please," said Gervane, "define for me what you mean?"

"Someone you can sense danger, someone who can feel people's thoughts before they act, the magicians I have don't do that. Do you?" the snapped question brought only shaken heads. "Have you such a one Gervane?"

"A truthsayer may be able to do such a thing, I'll ask for Goldareth to come down to talk to us." Gervane's eyes lost their focus, and looked into the depths of the forest, finally he spoke. "Goldareth is coming but he is some distance away, it may take him some time. Can you relax a little? All this pacing is making my neck hurt." Jangor snorted but dropped to the grass beside Gervane.

"I'm sure we'll sort something out." said Gervane. "if the worst comes, then the sword and the axe take out the arrows, and the magicians make sure the archers don't get a second shot."

"That may work, but only if there are two archers, if there are more then many will die."

"There may even be no archers, and mad assassins with knives even."

"That would be good, but given the reactions this morning I don't see it, do you?"

"It's not likely, but I can hope, surely that good sense will prevail?"

"If anyone is going to cause trouble it's going to be Tomas, do you agree?"

"Certainly, not the largest, but certainly the most powerful family, and he has a serious hate for your people, I've no idea where it comes from, but he does."

"Do you know of a member of his family that we can borrow for a moment or two?"

"Yes, Goldareth is already on his way here."

"Then I have a plan that may just pull his teeth before anything goes badly."

"What do you mean?"

"Nothing is certain yet, but across the glade I see trestles being lowered, for tables and food, and stillages, for barrels of beer. The party is going to be held down here in the glade, and I am certain that the royal council will want to make an entrance."

"Oh. You can bet your life on that, there'll be the whole procession thing, fancy clothes and fancier music, a sedate walk as the major players take centre stage."

"The king will be in the centre, and his chief advisor to his right, he daughter to his left?"

"That is the most likely format for the king's party. With the other members of the council behind."

"Our front line will be Namdarin in the centre to meet the king, the sword of Xeron riding high above his shoulder, to his right Jayanne, to face Laura, Jayanne will pull Laura out of the centre and keep her moving, Brank will follow, Laura should be safe. I will face Tomas, and I will present him with his family jewel. If things go badly after that, I'll feed him his family jewels hopefully before he dies, and that's a trick I learned from a lady."

"Who you calling a lady?" asked Jayanne, everyone laughed except for a confused Gervane, who frowned a question at Jangor.

"Perhaps I'll explain." said Jangor, then he shouted. "Granger." The old man came over. "How long could you and Gregor hold that shield magic if you were feeding the staffs from the fire directly."

"Not long it's a massive drain, certainly not more than a few breaths."

"Then we take out the council, and hold King and daughter hostage, those that are left escape under threats to the king."

"It's a plan of a sort." said Gervane, "not something I am happy with, but militarily speaking it's workable. Desperate, but potentially workable, let's hope it doesn't come to that." He raised his flask to Jangor, who followed suit.

"You do know," whispered Gervane, leaning close to Jangor, "if things go that badly, you'll never leave the glade, archers will put arrows through your heads before you've gone a hundred paces."

"I know, but they don't need to. Let's hope that your people see some sense."

Gervane nodded and raised his flask again, Jangor did the same.

"How do you know Tomas will make his move at the first meeting?" Gervane asked.

"He can't wait because it will be very difficult once our groups are intermixed, that would be better for the knife wielding assassin, but you're right, elves won't do that, it'll be archers, and it has to be as soon as we all meet." Gervane nodded and took a sip from his flask, stared at it, shook it, and dropped it on the ground, he reached out and took the one from Jangor's hand, had a sip then passed it back. Looking up he saw someone walking towards them. "Here's Goldareth."

"Goldareth." said Jangor, "please sit with us a spell." The elf sat still a little confused.

"I have a question for you," he continued, "if there was an elf up in the lower branches of this tree, and he was pointing an arrow at your head could you feel it?"

"Not in any precise way, I'd need to know who and where, and more likely why?"

"So, you can't feel that, how about emotion, can you detect emotion at a distance in a person you can see?"

"To some extent, again why?"

"There is a chance that someone on the council is planning something very unpleasant for the party tonight, someone may be planning to kill the king, and his line." said Gervane.

"That's not be difficult, two arrows, one heartbeat, new king. The only one that could even think such a thing is Tomas. You believe he has planned something?"

"It could be." said Gervane.

"If you could feel his emotion when we meet and give us only a single heartbeat of warning that something bad is going to happen, then we can take care of the rest."

"I should be able to do that, the intensity of the emotion, be it fear, or excitement, would broadcast quite strongly, if I could get a couple of my brothers involved we'd do a lot better."

"Have you some you can trust? If any of this leaks out the plans will be dropped and the king will die when we aren't here to protect him."

"Surely the plan is to keep the mindstone and give back the family jewels?" Gervane laughed this time, Jangor just smiled. "Did I say something funny?" asked Goldareth.

"No." said Gervane, "It's a human translation that makes that a little funny."

"Come with me." said Jangor getting to his feet, and offering a hand to Goldareth, he took him to a blanket with something under it. He lifted the blanket.

"Oh, my stars." muttered Goldareth.

"Find me the one that is Tomas's and I will present it to him later, we have no intention of keeping these things."

"How can I tell which is ours?"

"Just wave your hand near them yours will light up." "There it is." Jangor pulled the lit star from the pile and placed it on the top, then flicked the blanket back over them.

"You don't mind if I give that to Tomas, do you?"

"No, and that will certainly trigger an emotional response if he has set anything in motion."

"All we need from you is a warning, our magicians will put up a shield, that should stop the first volley of arrows, then we will be in a position to defend the King and Laura, if it turns out that we are the targets, then things are going to get very bloody, do you understand?"

"I think so, let's just hope that your fears are groundless."

"Here's hoping." Jangor raised his flask and drank, passing the flask to Goldareth.

"My brethren approach," muttered Goldareth, "I'll take them aside and explain the danger that you believe exists."

"You don't believe?"

"I don't want to believe, we have only just acquired a living king, to kill him so soon is just wrong in so many ways." Goldareth nodded and walked off to meet his fellow truthsayers. Jangor returned to where Gervane was still seated on the grass, he passed the flask down as he settled.

"Do you think they'll be of any use?" he asked.

"Who can tell?" said Gervane, "This is far outside their usual activities, normally they are in contact with those they are testing, it certainly going to be a new challenge for them."

"Is there anything else we can do before the party this evening?" Asked Jangor.

"Other than warn Brank, I can't think of anything." said Gervane.

"I wonder where he is?"

"He's with Laura, so he's safe, and so is she."

"I'd really like to warn him before it all kicks off."

"I'm sure he'll be quick enough on the uptake, he's a professional after all."

"He'd be quicker if primed."

"Agreed, let's hope he shows, but I wouldn't count on it, Laura is not going to want to let him out of her sight."

"I know." Jangor shrugged, "How long until sunset?"

"A couple of hours."

"Time to get dressed then."

"It'll take that long? You have a clean shirt in your pack?" Laughed Gervane.

"Now that is a point. I think I have some laundry to do." He stood, passed the flask to Gervane, "Go easy, this evening could be exciting." Looking round he called. "Mander, rig some clothes lines, we have some washing to do." he wandered off to the pack horses, and recovered some of his dirty clothing, to be joined at the stream by most of the others, a couple of hours beating dirty underwear and shirts against the rocks in the stream would certainly be enough of a warm up for any battle that was to come at sunset.

CHAPTER FORTY SIX

There was only the merest touch of pre-dawn light coming through the unguarded window when Alverana woke up. He threw off his blankets and rolled out of bed, the tiniest shake was all it took for Kevana to wake, he nodded towards Crathen, and Alverana went to wake him, this took considerably more force, but Crathen did eventually wake, he sat up. "It's been far too long since I had such a good night's sleep." he stretched and rolled out of bed.

"Go wake the others." said Kevana. Alverana nodded and opened the door. He laughed softly, as the guards in the hallway jumped to their feet.

"Good morning gentlemen." Said Alverana, "Sorry did I wake you?"

"Morning." Jon laughed. "It's been a very quiet night, no intruders from below and none of yours moving either."

"That's about to change." said Alverana. He entered each room briefly, and was greeted by groans and moans. He returned to the first room, and saw Crathen getting dressed, "Don't bother with that yet," Crathen looked little confused, "underclothes only, exercises first, then you can get dressed."

"If you're travelling with us, you may as well join in, it will help with your overall fitness and your integration into the group." said Kevana.

"I suppose I should really." said Crathen, realising that he had no choice.

They trooped out of the room together, and down the stairs to the yard where very quickly the rest of the group gathered. The guards separated, two to the outer gate and two to the door to the inside.

"I have spoken to Senjin." said Jon. "Breakfast will be served shortly in the common room."

"Thanks." replied Kevana. "Alverana you lead the routines."

Alverana put them all through a sequence of exercises nothing too strenuous, but enough to let them all know they had been doing something. Crathen was the hardest hit, he'd not done this sort of thing in many a year. Once the exercise session was completed Kevana spoke loudly.

"Latrine, wash, dress and pack. Then breakfast. Move it people." In only a few minutes packs were ready to be loaded and they all went into the common room, where a hearty breakfast was awaiting them, Jon and the guards joined them, after all it had been a long night for them, and one they'd not been prepared for. Kevana was a little surprised to see jugs of beer on the table.

"Jon, beer not water for breakfast?"

"The water here is quite drinkable, but beer which is boiled as part of its processing can be cheaper and actually cleaner. Hence beer. If you're heading south only drink from feeder streams to the west, the eastern swamplands have some rather unpleasant denizens that like to infest the human body, occasionally causing painful deaths."

"Anything like the leeches in the swamp to the north?" asked Alverana.

"I wouldn't know." replied Jon. "I've never been that far north."

"Take our advice," said Petrovana, "Don't."

"I'll do just that, if I can, but I don't always get to decide where I go." he shrugged his shoulders and waved his arms around meaningfully. Kevana laughed, looking around he noticed that one of the guards was missing.

"Someone gone to inform Harvang?" he asked. Jon simply nodded. "We need to be outside the gate before the sun comes up, is that going to be a problem?"

"I don't see why, the captain will be here in plenty of time, he can authorise the early opening on the gate."

"Can't you do that?"

"Of course, but why step on the captain's toes, for some reason officers can get a little touchy about juniors exceeding their authority."

"I have noticed that actually." Laughed Kevana.

"I hope you gentlemen had a good night's rest." said Harvang as he came in through the back door. "Your escort is waiting to take you to the gate as soon as you are ready."

"I for one had a good night's rest." Kevana said, "How restive are the natives this morning?"

"As I expected they are all tucked up in their beds. There are no bloodthirsty mobs awaiting you procession to the gate, much as I expected, once they have sobered up, and settled down, they'll be no problem. Southgate has already reported no people there at all, and yes I checked."

"As I would have done, it's far better for there to be no surprises." said Kevana, "We shall be only short time, can you open the gate ahead of sunrise for a change, we really need to be outside before the sun comes up?"

"Of course, I'll be more than happy to help you on your way." Harvang said, with a blank face, Jon smiled.

"What you really mean, is that you want us out of your responsibility as soon as possible." Kevana smiled, Jon laughed, Harvang only nodded in agreement. Kevana looked slowly at the window facing the river.

"It's getting very light out there. How long to the gate?"

"Walking perhaps a quarter of an hour, at a gallop, not recommended but half that, shortcut across the river, definitely not recommended half that again. I'd prefer a sedate walk to the gate, makes less noise, less disturbance, less likelihood to blunder into anything unpleasant."

"We still have plenty of time then." said Kevana. "I think we have a window of about half an hour. What do you think, Worandana?"

"Oh my. I hadn't thought of that." Replied the older man. "Half an hour should be more than enough." He stared into space for a moment or two. "You plan to synchronise the morning prayer, and so give us both a direction for the monastery, and perhaps some people to go with it. I find it pleasing that sometimes you can surprise even me." Worandana nodded, before looking out of the window. "I think we'd better get a move on, if we can get our rhythm established first, then the synchronisation should be easier."

"Eat up people." Snapped Kevana, "we ride immediately." He snatched a few slices of thickly cut bacon, and a warmed bread roll, which his stuffed in his robe, before getting to his feet.

"Worandana, have you paid the bar bill for last night?" Asked Kevana, obviously in a hurry to be moving.

"Don't worry about that." interjected Harvang, "the watch entertainment fund can see to that for you."

"By 'watch entertainment fund' he actually means the monies provided by the city to entertain visiting, er, dignitaries. But far more often to pay his bar bill the week before payday." Laughed Jon. Harvang only glared at the younger man, it was clear there was going to be some payment extracted for this 'joke'.

They all went out into the stable yard, packs were loaded onto horses, and the riders took their seats, Jon opened the rear gate of the inn, and the horsemen walked slowly out into the street, surrounded on all sides by mounted men of the guard. Jon and Harvang walked through the gate and mounted horses held for them by their subordinates.

"Let's move out." called Captain Harvang, not loud enough to upset the locals, but enough to be heard over the sound of hooves on cobbles. "Jon clear the road." Jon Turner forced his way to the front and set off out onto the street that followed the river down stream, the rest of the troop waited until he was far enough ahead before setting off at a slow walk, they wanted to give Jon enough time to be sure the road was safe for them. Kevana and Alverana at the front of the column of monks, with two guards in front and outside, two by two the column went with guards flanking and Harvang behind. After a few minor side streets they turned left into a street that lead to a bridge over the river, the bridge was only wide enough for one cart at a time, and the grooves in the road bed showed just how wide the cart wheels ran, not that there were any carts at this time in the morning. Once they were down off the bridge they turned right into a main road, it was wide and clear, the houses were so obviously rich and prosperous, homes to merchants and lords. A few servants were moving in the street, tending the small front gardens of the houses, and performing indeterminate tasks, a guard standing by a well waved as they passed, while he supervised an old woman filling a large clay pot, brown and unglazed. Each house they passed had a path alongside that lead to a stable yard, or some such, these all terminated in a tall and sturdy wall. After they passed a few of these houses they turned left into much wider road, ahead was the south gate, which looked just like the north gate they had come in by, the gate guards were there as was Jon, still mounted, talking quietly to a tall man on foot. As they approached it became clear that the man was Andreas.

"Andreas." said Harvang, "What are you doing here at this time in the morning?"

"I am simply here to ensure that these, monks, leave our town, and don't forget anything."

"What could they possibly forget?"

"One or two of their number could be left behind, or they may just forget how welcome their people are here."

"I have counted them, there are none missing, and I am fairly certain they understand how you and the others feel about them."

"I am sorry, but I just don't trust these people, they have agendas that we are unaware of."

"I am sure, but they are leaving right now. Guard open the gate." The gate guards looked a little confused, they weren't supposed to open the gate until the sun was visible, and they could be sure the outside was clear of enemies.

"Open the gate." shouted Harvang again.

The guard on the gate looked up at the man on the wall. "Is the outside clear?"

"As far as I can see, there is no one out there at all." was the reply.

The gate guard looked at Harvang again for confirmation, a grimace was all he got, he lifted the bar from the inside, the mechanism withdrew the heavy steel bolts from their slots on both sides of the gate, two of the guards started pushing against the gate, as the first guard reached for a steel bar, he placed this under the roller and levered it upwards forcing the gate to roll out along its tracks. Once it was moving it rolled smoothly open until it was wide enough for a cart to pass through.

Kevana coughed quite loudly, and having attracted Harvang's attention, stared at the ground in front of his horse. Harvang followed his eyes and saw exactly what he was looking at. Deep impressions in the dirt, the signs of heavy horse hoof prints, a heavy horse working hard, at this place, on a regular basis, pulling something heavy, perhaps a gate.

"I shall be having words with the crew on this gate once you have left."

"That could be a good idea."

"If you hear any strange sounds once you have left, please ignore them, sometimes soldiers seem to struggle with the simplest of concepts."

"I fully understand. I thank you for all your help, I am sorry for any inconvenience we have caused." said Kevana before he turned to Andreas. "I thank you for your tolerance, and hope that you come to understand that we mean you and yours no harm." Andreas nodded and they both ignored the gurgles from Kirukana, that sneaked past Worandana's knife. Kevana and his people passed slowly through the gate, out onto the road south from the city, there were carts in the distance approaching but the gate should be shut long before they arrived. With a simple instruction from Kevana the monks dismounted and gathered on the road from the gate, the surface was flat and clear, more than good enough for their purposes. Facing south they watched carefully for the sun rising to their left. Even as the red disk of the sun appeared above the mountains in the distance, Worandana started the morning prayer, the chant that he hoped would link them to the men from the monastery to the south, suddenly their chant skipped a beat, and fixed to the standard rhythm, they continued the chant for a short time, until Worandana indicated that he had the information he needed, he held his right hand high in the air.

"I have a name and a direction." he said.

"Mount up." said Kevana, "Let's ride, Worandana point and push the pace, the horses are rested, and properly fed, we can pick up some time." The monks all climbed into their saddles, and set off south from the city, at a fast canter, towards many carts that were going to be waiting for the gate to open. The drivers of the carts were a little confused to see riders coming from the city before the gate should be open. Though none of them saw fit to attempt to question the riders as they passed, not that they would have stopped anyway. When the road and the river turned westwards, Worandana looked for a shallow place to cross the river, then their path would not be pushed too far from its intended way. They splashed across a gravel bar and turned slightly east to bring them to the monastery as quickly as possible. The sun grew gradually higher as they crossed the plain, the ground grew firmer as they moved away from the river, occasional small trees and shrubs started to grow up around them, as they pounded through the rolling terrain. At the top of a particularly long and steep rise Kevana called a stop, the horses were sweating quite hard, and the riders were beginning to tire.

"We'll walk them for a while," he shouted, the line was strung out over quite a distance, "they need the rest."

"So do we." muttered Petrovana, to no one in particular, even so this gained him a hard look from Kevana. The group of riders closed up their ranks, and the horse's heavy breath filled the air with steam. The bright sun and lock of wind was doing nothing at all to help the horses cool down.

"The horses need water." said Alverana.

"So do we." mouthed Petrovana soundlessly.

"They can drink at the next stream we cross."

"Didn't Harvang warn against streams this side of the river?"

"He did say something about run off from a swamp, after the climb we just made, we have to be above the level of any swampland in this area, we must have left that behind an hour ago at least, I'm sure we'll be safe."

"How much further to the monastery?" asked Alverana, looking at Worandana.

"I'm not sure, you know how confusing distances can be, but we do have some more climbing to do, it's in the foothills almost directly south from here."

"Did you get any impression as to how big this place is?" Kevana asked.

"The abbot felt like a young man, and the impression I got is that this is a very new monastery, maybe they are still building the place."

"We'll find out when we get there, let's just hope they are able to help us."

"If they are building the place, then they should have some temporary people on site, we should be able to steal a few of those, without affecting their progress too much."

"I'm more interested in their stocks of silver. We're almost out."

"I think that generally for new start a fair size stock goes in with the builders, in case they have any problems with the locals."

"So they could have a fair few to spare." Kevana smiled, hoping to decimate the monasteries stores before they left. "Alverana." he called, "How much longer do these horses need to rest?"

"The more time we can give them the better they'll be able to run, the less time you give them to rest, the sooner they'll need to rest again. The choice is yours, of course, but seeing as you don't actually know how far we have to go today, I'd not push them too hard this early."

"Fine, they can have some more time, but not too long." The slow walk up into the foothills continued. It didn't take long for the horses to recover from the early morning push, but the terrain was becoming so rough that anything above a trot would be too dangerous, climbing steadily they came to a sudden plateau, a flat expanse that seemed to be at least a day's ride wide, and ahead came to a low pass between two high peaks, there was a column of smoke rising from the pass, too far away to tell exactly where in the pass it was, but close enough to be only a short ride.

"I'm assuming that the smoke is where we are going," called Kevana, "So everyone pick up the pace, I want to be there before noon." He kicked his horse, and simply expected the others to follow, which of course they did. Pounding across the plateau it was only a few minutes before they were passing cultivated fields, now mainly empty, harvests having been completed. As they approached the compound Kevana noted that the walls weren't stone, wooden fences instead, still quite solid but barely over six feet high, judging by the height of the watcher on the wall, there was a walkway on the inside, an alarm bell was ringing quite insistently, only to fall silent long before they were close to the wall.

"Bruciana." Called Worandana. "We have come as I said we would."

A face appeared over the parapet, and merely glanced at the assembled riders. There was no doubt in Bruciana's mind that these were indeed brothers, though he'd never had morning prayers disturbed in quite that fashion before.

"Open the gate." he shouted. "And welcome brothers, our house is yours for as long as you need it." The noise of heavy bars being removed was obvious before the large wooden gate opened slowly inwards, Kevana frowned a question at Worandana, it didn't need to be asked, but it was certainly unusual for the gate to be closed, and barred, during the day. A rapid glance about showed that no one was working the fields around them, also strange. Kevana shouldered his horse up against Worandana's. "Something strange going on here." He muttered, Worandana nodded, but said nothing. Side by side they walked their horses through the gate. All around the alertness of the whole monastery was clear, many of the residents were already arrayed for battle. Bows were strung, hands rested on sword hilts, the tension in the air was palpable. The moment that all the riders were in the central courtyard the gate slammed shut and the heavy wooden bars fell into place, arrows went to strings, bows were pulled, and swords were drawn.

"Crap." muttered Alverana. Kevana turned to his friend, "Relax. Worandana can deal with this." The frightened faces around the yard told him that were not truly soldiers, nor for that matter, mystics of any real power.

"Is there a problem?" called Worandana, a hand gesture as he moved his horse forwards towards Bruciana caused his clerics to form a loose pattern around him, with release of his clenched fist Kevana sensed the surge of energy start moving through the formation, a glance told him that the monks of this monastery had no idea that this was even happening.

"There have been reports of your groups, and as far as these go the worst possible situation is for you to have joined forces."

"Is that the worst possible?"

"Not exactly."

"Then tell me." Worandana's reply was a little stilted, he was passing on a large load at the time.

"If Worandana is wielding the sword of Zandaar, and Kevana's renegades are backing him, then kill on sight. Have you the sword old man?"

"If I had what would you do?"

"The instructions are to kill you all if necessary."

"If we had the sword," interrupted Kevana, "he would not be holding it, I would. Then again have you forgotten that no man can touch the sword?"

"Perhaps someone else forgot that, in their hurry to get the word out?" asked Worandana, looking straight at Bruciana. "Had you forgotten as well?" Bruciana glanced from side to side, then focussed on someone standing beside the gate. Kevana spun his horse around, now he had Bruciana's second in his sight. Kevana walked the horse slowly towards the suddenly frightened man, the others of his team were making themselves space in which to move and selecting targets if this was to come to battle, badly outnumbered they intended to make a good showing of themselves.

"I don't know what sort of soldiers your people are," said Kevana looking at the second, standing in front of the gate, a short sword in each hand, "but mine have been tested in battle, we have lost many friends on this mission. Worandana is by now carrying enough power to burn half of you, and I'm sure we can take the rest. What sort of soldiers are you?" He reached forwards with his left foot and tapped the horses shoulder, the horse kicked the cobbles of the yard hard, a shower of sparks scattered across the yard. The second stepped back against the gate.

"We're not really soldiers," said Bruciana, "nor are we clerics."

"What sort of monks are you then?" Snapped Kevana, spinning around and showering sparks everywhere. He walked the horse forwards until it was almost touching the leader. He glanced at Worandana and could tell that he was now struggling to contain the power in his circle.

"Really we're miners."

"Then I suggest you stand your troops down, if this comes to blows, then you and yours are going to die. You must have seen power cycles in operation, Worandana has been charging now since you closed the gate, he's struggling to hold it in, you need to make a decision and do it soon, and I do mean soon. What's it going to be?" Kevana snapped his left fist into the air, as it came down swords leaped from scabbards, Alverana fell from his horse and rolled into two men knocking them over and coming to his feet sword in hand. Petrovana had his sword to the second's throat before he even managed to move. Briana, Crathen, and Fabrana stayed mounted, swords drawn, covering various options.

"You are not renegades then?" asked Bruciana, quietly.

"We are simply brothers seeking help in our task, your threats make us very uneasy."

"I believe these to be friends," called Bruciana, "stand down." Swords dropped, bows were slowly released, people started to relax, then Worandana threw a huge column of fire up into the air, the thunderous roar made all the local monks fall to the ground, the horses twitched, but that was all, Kevana smiled, and dismounted, he stepped up to Bruciana and offered him a hand to help him back to his feet. Shakily the younger man accepted the assistance.

"Would he really have used that fire on us?" he whispered.

"If you had attacked us, certainly. Most, if not all, of your people would have died."

"We are supposed to be brothers; how can this have happened?"

"It's a long story, far too long, but no one was hurt, no harm done. Please tell me what reports drove you to this dangerous course?"

"A rider came through five days ago, he said that Zandaar's sword was loose in the world, and that Kevana's group should have it, and that Worandana's group had vanished from their assigned task, the thought was that the two may have taken the sword and be working against Zandaar."

"But we knew that no man can touch the sword."

"It seems that may not have been completely true."

"We were given the instruction that the sword could not be held by any man, now you have been told we may be using it, and we know as a fact that a man can touch the sword without dying, because Namdarin now carries it. We intend taking that sword, and giving it to Zandaar. Will you, Bruciana, help us in our holy duty?"

"I feel that I should, but I am unsure how I can help you."

"Simple, we need clerics and we need silver, can you lend us some?"

"Men we have aplenty, but how much use they will be to you I have no idea, silver we have some, and almost no use for it, so that is not a problem."

"Have you no skilled clerics here?" demanded Worandana.

"We are miners, we serve god by mining gold. We have little use for mystics here."

"Surely all your people have been through the training?"

"Of course, but the ones sent here have little skill with the mysteries, and similarly combat, strong backs, strong hearts, devotion to Zandaar, and dare I say it, slow minds, that is who we get here."

"So what, pray tell, is the purpose of this mission here?" snapped Worandana.

"I told you, we are miners, we dig gold for Zandaar."

"I always thought gold was mined by crazy old men in desolate wastelands." said Kevana.

"See the mountains behind us?" Bruciana waved an arm vaguely over his shoulder. Everyone looked up and the high and snow topped peaks, that appeared to sprout precipitously from the plateau. "Well, through them runs a river, it reaches this plateau and turns west, during the spring melt it floods quite extensively, and deposits large quantities of silt in the bends and wide, slow parts of its flow just around here, somewhere in those mountains it cuts through a good deposit of gold, and this gold drops out in the silt, we mine the silt sifting out the gold and send that on to Zandaarkoon, in a good year we can send six hundred pounds of gold to the capital."

"Oh my." said Petrovana, looking around the gathered monks, "have you any idea how much that is worth? It's a veritable fortune of each and every man here."

"We don't care about that, we serve our god by providing gold for his purposes, we don't have to fight, other than a few crazy old men trying to steal our gold, we don't get to throw mystical power around like our personal playthings, we live our lives and bend our backs for our god, our service is pure."

"I can't argue with that." said Worandana, "but we need your help, I'm looking for volunteers to join us, I'll train these in the mystic arts, or Kevana will train them in the arts of war, which ever they are best suited for, Bruciana can you recommend any for us?"

"What does Zandaar need gold for?" asked Crathen. Many heads turned to look and frown at the young man. "I'm sorry if the question sounds impertinent but it stands." Moments passed, people glanced from one face to another, some wondering why this question had not been asked before.

"Bruciana." said Worandana, "Who exactly do you send this gold to?"

"The council member in charge of our endeavours is Axorana." muttered Bruciana, Kirukana choked. Worandana snapped his head around to focus on Kirukana.

"Who is this Axorana?"

"He's the leader of one of the factions in the council."

"Your sponsor?"

"No, but certainly the one who's offered the most gold for my services."

"So he's using the gold from here to finance his own ends. I feel an urge to shut down his mining interests right now."

"Even if we do that." said Kevana, "He'll have a new batch of miners here within the month, it serves no purpose."

"Hang on." said Bruciana, "did he just threaten to kill us all?" Pointing at Worandana.

"He did indeed," laughed Kirukana, "for a change he's not threatening me."

"And he still expects volunteers?"

"Well," said Kirukana, "the volunteers aren't going to die here, they may die somewhere else, but not here, and not today."

"As I have already said, we are miners, we are not mystics, we are not soldiers, we sift silt for the gold it contains.

"Then it is time you learned some new skills." said Worandana. "Anyone here interested in something other than back breaking work?" His hard eyes scanned the assembled men, pausing for a moment on each one. That instant told him everything he needed to know, there were four men that were interested in something new, something different, something more challenging than digging silt and grading it. "That is good enough for me, you four be ready to ride in the morning, the rest of you," a waved arm indicated his own and Kevana's people, "see to the horses and get some rest and food. Bruciana you do have enough rooms for us all?"

"Yes, some of mine will have to double up and so will yours, but that's no hardship."

Worandana handed his reins to Kirukana he almost herded Bruciana into the main building with Kevana on his heels. Just inside the main door was a small room that acted as armoury, three walls were lined with weapon racks mostly empty as all the monks were armed, the shortest wall, had two large chests each with heavy locks. Worandana indicated the one on the left.

"How did you know?" asked Bruciana.

"There's a lot of silver in there and I can feel the cold from here."

"That chest is always cold."

"How did you come to have so much silver here?" asked Kevana.

"Axorana thought we would need it, probably because the other chest is full of gold. I'm expecting a troop of soldiers in the next few weeks, they come to take the gold to Zandaarkoon and often they leave us silver to help with our defences."

"We'll take a small portion of your silver, it will help us in our quest, and I'll spend the rest of today teaching you how to use it.

Once word gets out just how much gold you have here, then you're going to need to defend yourselves, there are robber bands that could take this place in only an hour."

"I've heard of them, but I think they are afraid of the military arm of our faith."

"Fear is often overridden by a chest full of gold."

"The report we got says that you were supposed to be investigating the destruction of a monastery, but that you appeared to given that up to join with Kevana here?" Bruciana cringed as soon as the question had left his mouth, fairly certain he had committed some sort of offence to either or both.

"Indeed." Laughed Worandana. "I was investigating the destruction of a monastery, bigger than this one, more men, stone walls, high tower, and permanent lookouts. One man invaded the monastery, and killed everyone inside, one man, alone. He has since acquired a group of friends, a varied group of friends, he has soldiers, and a magician of some power, and worse still, one of our own has joined him. He has some impressive weapons, not just the sword, a bow whose arrows always return, the woman who rides with him has an axe of some magical property, one man is now a formidable force, but we will hunt him down none the less. If he was after gold, he would ride through this place of yours without breaking stride."

"If he's not after gold, what is he seeking?"

"As far as we can tell, vengeance, it seems someone called the black fire down on his house and killed everyone, now he has sworn to kill Zandaar."

"So you know where he is going?"

"We'd like to stop him before he gets to Zandaarkoon."

"That would be for the best."

"Are you stalling for some reason?" asked Kevana, "Open the chest."

"Sorry, I just don't even like opening it." Bruciana unhooked a key from a chain around his neck, and bent down with a click the lock released and he opened the chest, the rush of cold air was palpable, a brief rush of fog poured from the chest and rolled slowly across the floor. As the heat in the room slowly burned back the fog, two large bags appeared in the chest, one red, one yellow.

"Someone is very serious about defending this place." Muttered Kevana.

"But not serious enough to train the people manning it." whispered Worandana, "that just doesn't make sense, unless Axorana was unaware as to the actual skill levels of his people?"

"I come from a mining background, as do all the people assigned here, we were only questioned about our backgrounds, I had the most experience, so I was designated 'abbot' of this mining camp, you have no idea how frightened we all were when your thoughts intruded on our morning prayers. Your name created all sorts of panic, and you were coming here."

"Not frightened, or panicked enough to open this chest."

"No, not that frightened." Bruciana opened the yellow bag.

"Stop." said Worandana. Bruciana froze and looked back over his shoulder.

"They're cold, very, very cold, if you touch them with bare skin they will burn. Use gloves, heavy gloves. Has no-one every explained how these should be stored?"

"Not that I can remember."

Worandana shook his head slowly and sighed.

"If you put a large number in a small space, like this many in a bag, in a box, they each try to take energy from their neighbours, in doing so they get cold, and over time they get really cold, as they are now, to use them you need skin contact, so these are useless until they are warmed up. Tip a few out of the bag and let them warm up on the floor." While Bruciana was following the instruction Worandana went on. "Put them in small bags, no more than ten to a bag, put the bags in trays with wooden dividers, that way they don't get too close to each other, you don't put your gold in big bags do you?"

"Well no, if a bag breaks, you can lose an awful lot of gold very quickly."

"Treat your silver the same, in big bags it is useless. Go and get some of the bags you put your gold in, and we'll take these somewhere to warm them up, you have a forge for melting your gold, don't you?"

"Yes, most of the gold we find is small particles, so we melt them into rough bars, Axorana sees to the purification and casting into coinage. We don't use the forge every day, but it never gets truly cold." Bruciana left the room.

"I've never seen so much silver in one place." said Kevana.

"Nor me."

"Why is Axorana stockpiling silver here? It's too far from Zandaarkoon to be of use, it just makes no sense to me."

"Perhaps, he's making as much money from the silver as he is from the gold, by taking these out of circulation in the capital he's pushing up the price of the ones still there. Once the price gets high enough he'll recall these and sell them quickly before people notice how many there are on the streets. More important question is 'why does he need so much money?' Could there be some major manoeuvring going on in the council?" Bruciana returned with an armful of small cloth bags and some gloves, he fell to his knees and started bagging the small pieces of cold silver.

"Bruciana, how long have you been mining gold here for Axorana?"

"Four years, though we didn't get much gold out in the first one, it took a while to get the sluice working properly, we are hoping to get a second sluice working in the spring, construction is almost complete, once winter sets in in the mountains the river slows down and the grading equipment doesn't work too well, we go back to the old ways during the winter. We can still produce a fair amount of gold, it's down to personal skill then, we actually have competitions to see who can find the most gold in a day, or a week, or a month. It helps to keep the men motivated."

"Isn't your percentage enough motivation?" asked Kevana.

"We don't keep any of the gold, it all goes to Zandaar." Bruciana's glare said far more than his words.

"Apologies," said Worandana, "we simply assumed that you'd be keeping a small percentage for yourselves, this is the normal practice, especially amongst miners working for someone else. That is all by the by anyway, let's get this silver bagged and warmed up so that I can start to teach you how to use them." Worandana smiled and pulled his gloves from his belt, and knelt down to help Bruciana. In a very short time there were three bags of each type of silver, again Bruciana left to get more bags and presumably deposit the filled ones in the forge, or at least somewhere warm.

"If we take ten of each for all of our group it will make almost no inroads into the stock here."

"Agreed," replied Worandana, "there must be the best part of three hundred of each here. Will tens be enough?"

"Granger blasted one out of the air with the power of his staff, and took the second one away from me, Gorgana presumably can do the same, but can they take two at a time?"

"I wouldn't have thought so, it takes a great deal of focus to snatch one away from its master, two should be impossible."

"Should?"

"I've never tried it, it's not even something we actually train either."

"Perhaps we should?"

"We are the only people who use these weapons, and we should train for the time when we are fighting amongst ourselves?" Worandana's raised eyebrows added a certain emphasis to the question.

"I suppose not," smiled Kevana, "it's not the sort of thing the council would want to suggest could ever happen."

"Am I mistaken," said Bruciana, from the doorway where he had been listening for a little while, "or are you saying that even after these weapons have been sent, they can be taken away from user and turned against him?"

"Not exactly," replied Worandana, "they have a very short life, deflected aside is possible, but to turn one completely around would take far too long."

"But it could be turned aside to strike a brother standing near?"

"That is I suppose possible, in which case don't surround an enemy and then start throwing fire or lightning bolts around. And that brings another thought, when you are hurling fire at an enemy don't worry about the safety of a brother standing nearby, this could cause the weapon to change target, they are controlled entirely by the thoughts of the user, you must keep your thoughts focused only on the enemy."

"I'm not at all sure I want to learn how to use these at all." said Bruciana.

"I'm sure that you will be fine, after all you're only going to be using them for the defence of your mine. You're not going to fighting ex-Zandaar monks, like we are."

"I'm very glad about that."

"Kevana, go and see to the supplies, I think fifteen is about right, and check out the ones that gave the impression that they wanted to join us. Bruciana lead us to a place where we can throw fireballs and lightning without causing any major harm to anything important." Kevana went into the courtyard and spoke to the first local he came across.

"Bruciana is learning about the silver, who is his number two?"

"I am Miclorana, I'm as near as you'll find to number two around here."

"That's great, we need to sort out beds for the night, some small supplies, and I need to talk to the ones that indicated to Worandana that they are interested in joining us, have you any idea who they might be?"

"He said four, the four most likely will be no problem, I'd even be happy for them to be gone."

"What is their problem with this posting?"

"They showed some aptitude when tested, and joined in an effort to get away from the mining villages they were born into, they were doing fine when suddenly training stops and they are assigned here, back in a mining village. Admittedly mining here is easier than most mines, we don't rely on gold to buy food, we do grow some of our own, but the majority of the supplies come in on the caravans, they take away the gold we find, but a bad season doesn't leave us hungry, the supplies still come in, so long as there is some gold for them to take away."

"That really make no sense to me, if the mine isn't producing gold why keep funding it?"

"The only time we don't produce much in the way of gold is through the winter, and the first two weeks of spring, in winter there's not enough water in the river, and in spring there's far too much. Next spring, we have a plan though, we are going to catch the peak of the flood and run it into large settling ponds, so that the sediments with the gold in will be captured all around us, we won't have to go too far to dig it up and sift it."

"So the fields that no one is working outside the walls are going to be the settling ponds?"

"That's right."

"I foresee a minor problem."

"Go on."

"For a portion of the year there is going to be standing water around your monastery?"

"Yes?"

"Standing water becomes stagnant water, breeding ground for biting insects and all the diseases they bring. I cannot imagine deliberately creating a swamp around my home."

"I hadn't thought of that, I'm not sure that Bruciana did either, this could be a problem."

"Especially when you have to wade through this swamp to dig out the sediments for sifting, you may not have to go far, but the journey could be quite perilous."

"I'll have to talk to Bruciana about that."

"Don't disturb him now, he's busy learning from Worandana, and that can be a task and half, the old man has very little tolerance for people who don't learn quickly. Just advise him that once the spring flood has abated dig some narrow drainage channels to let the water out slowly. That way the gold will still be there, but not the water. Possible dust storms in the summer, but I'd rather that than hordes of mosquitoes."

"I'll do that."

"I suspect that you're not one of the ones unhappy with being here?"

"I quite like it, the work is hard and monotonous, but small risk and good perks."

"Perks?"

"Only Bruciana believes that all the gold goes to Zandaarkoon, three or four times a year each of us finds a reason to go into town for a couple of days, hang on a decent drunk, or spend time with ladies of rent-able virtue. With the amount of gold this place produces it's an absolutely negligible loss."

"That makes it even more important that you learn how to defend yourselves. It's only a matter of time until the riches of this place become known in the wrong quarters. Introduce me to the malcontents and then go and find Bruciana and Worandana."

With a rapid tour round the compound Miclorana introduced Kevana to the four who had reacted to Worandana's offer, one changed his mind as soon as Kevana approached him, the others seemed to be glad of the chance to get out of the place, their position was much as Miclorana had described, coming from mining communities the last thing they wanted to be doing was grubbing in the ground. It turned out that Davadana and Strenoana were adequate bowmen, and Astorana was good with a sword, all three were young men, new to the priesthood, and unhappy with their assignments. Kevana questioned them about their experience of power circles, and silver weapons, knowledge they had some but experience little, searching they had heard of, but never attempted, or experienced.

"Damn it, what are they teaching the youngsters these days?" Snapped Kevana in a loud voice.

"I thought we had made it quite clear, or weren't you listening?" said Astorana. "After six months training we were graduated, named, and assigned here."

"So by the standard process your training was far from complete?"

"Definitely, we were sent here because of our mining backgrounds, which is not something we are happy about."

"That's good. I suggest you go and find Worandana and Bruciana, training is going on, introduce yourselves to Worandana, I have other things to do right now. Don't forget we'll be riding with the dawn, up until that point you can still change your minds. If you have any reservations about joining us, I suggest you speak to the other members of our party, they can give you a clearer picture of what has happened, and what we hope to happen." Kevana turned away and walked into the courtyard, over to where Alverana was dealing with the horses.

"Have we some volunteers?" asked Alverana.

"Perhaps, they have things to decide, but we may have three new bodies for the mill."

"Skilled?"

"There's nobody skilled here, but Worandana will take on their training, let's just hope we get them too far away to run home when things get hard for them." Laughed Kevana.

"But they're never going to be real clerics and that is what we need."

"Agreed. But if it comes to actual combat, they can go in first."

"That's not exactly the right attitude, is it?"

"I know, but what other purpose do they serve?"

"As leader it's up to you to give them purpose, isn't it?"

"Alverana, my dear friend, sometimes you can be a real pain. Let's go and see what else we can scavenge from this place." Together they walked over to the forge and collected some of the small cloth bags that were near the moulds that the rough gold was cast into. Kevana led the way to the armoury. Alverana looked down into the open chest, where the large red bag was still undisturbed.

"These people know nothing." he said.

"That is exactly what they have been telling us." said Kevana passing over a bundle of the small bags. "fifteen to a bag, remember gloves, we'll take them to the forge to warm."

"Fifteen is rather a lot."

"Yes, but decided by Worandana, perhaps he's expecting some rapid usage, by way of training?"

"How many bags?"

"One of each, for each member of our party, including the three new ones."

"That's two hundred of each, that's an awful lot."

"They'll still have a hundred or so of each here for defence, and seeing as they haven't used any in the four years this camp has been in operation, I don't believe they are going to be stressed."

"Fine." Muttered Alverana, kneeling on the floor, and counting flames into the bags.

"I'll go and see what I can raid from their larders." Laughed Kevana, as he walked out of the door. In the courtyard he saw the horses being unloaded and herded into stalls in the stable, noting that the stable was not only too small, but didn't hold enough horses for the men in the camp, so they couldn't all leave in a hurry, some would be on foot. Strategically a serious error, for such a small group. Someone wasn't at all concerned about their survival, at least not long term, badly lead, under-supplied, almost no training, "This place is a joke." he whispered, "and a very bad one." He stamped through the main building, and out of the back door, into the mining area, he kicked the back door quite hard as he passed through it, only a few splinters fell from the rickety structure. "Yet another joke." he said. Off to his left he could hear Worandana's raised voice, it sounded like things were not going well with the training, ahead were the grading and sorting mechanisms that performed the mining operations here, these appeared to be of the highest quality, solidly built, and properly maintained, for first time since he arrived he was actually impressed.

One sluice line was in operation and alongside it another was almost complete, two men were watching the sluice line and four were working on the second, forming the woodwork that made up the grading tables. While Kevana was watching as one of the men on the operational line scrapped a slurry off one of the tables, and dropped it into a flat round metal pan, he added some water and gently swirled it around, almost no dust became suspended in the water, and the particles in the pan appeared to have the right density and just that glitter to be gold. He emptied the pan unto a pile of similar dust, where the water trickled through and evaporated in the warm air of the afternoon, leaving a golden mound that was to be melted into ingots.

Turning to his left he followed the sound of Worandana's voice, until he found the practice area, Bruciana was currently facing the wrath of the elder monk. It appears his abilities were seriously lacking, even his parentage was in question.

"Worandana." Called Kevana, as he approached. "We don't have time to deal with his history, we need to be on the road tomorrow, just fix his deficiencies and make him operational, he's unlikely to meet any serious opposition, only a few brigands who are seriously impressed by a few lightning bolts and some fire balls. Unless, of course, the people we are chasing come this way, then they may be in some trouble."

"You teach them then." Snapped the older monk.

"Sorry, I'm a soldier, sword play and such yes, but this magic stuff is just beyond me." Laughed Kevana, he turned to the young men who planned to follow them. "You need to learn this, the rest of your training will be on the road, we may be going into battle fairly soon, so learn fast and learn well."

"We'll try." said Davadana, looking a little downhearted, he hadn't thought it would be this difficult.

"It's not that hard." said Kevana, "Belief and visualisation, believe it, and see it, and it will happen. This is why these weapons were created, their magic is easy to use and easy to learn, some of the other magics not so much, but this is the simplest, even I can throw lightning and fire around with the best."

"Yes." said Worandana, "but you still lose control of the fire sometimes."

"You wait until you throw a fireball against Granger, then you'll find out how hard this can be."

Worandana snorted. Kevana went on, to the newest recruits. "Men with swords, bows, woman with axe, these are fine as targets, our enemy has two magicians armed with staffs, if you throw fire against these men, then they will send it back against you, one of them did that to me, and though I'm not very skilled, I'm better at this than you are."

"Kevana." snapped Worandana, "go away." Kevana turned back towards the rear gate and kicked it again as he passed through. Searching the compound, he found Miclorana in short order.

"How are the accommodations going?" he asked.

"We'll have rooms for you all sorted very soon, food and drink will be served fairly soon, the mid-day meal is currently cooking, there should be enough to share, but we can't be sure, we weren't expecting a party as big as yours."

"Didn't Worandana explain how big our party was when he made contact this morning?"

"He may have done, but as soon as he identified himself, Bruciana panicked, he wasn't even sure when you would get here, just that you were on your way. Let's say that morning prayers turned into a serious toilet time."

"What do you mean?"

"He almost shit himself, it was only a few days ago when the report came in about your groups, then you turn up on our doorstep, invading morning prayers to tell him, oh my, that really shook him to the bone, he wasn't even aware that long distance communication like that was possible, he thought it had to be a arranged times between defined people, not just some random guy interrupting our morning ritual."

"Worandana used the rhythm of the morning ritual to find you, I wasn't at all sure it could be done, but he managed it."

"By Zandaar did he manage it. We could all hear him, his voice echoed around all our heads, then the whole thing just fell apart, we couldn't stay within the pattern, two of our number actually fainted."

"Worandana is one of the most powerful of our mystics, but even he can be beaten sometimes. Our enemies are in themselves quite powerful, and they are not going to give up easily, Namdarin has sworn to kill Zandaar."

"That's heresy. No one can kill a god."

"Be careful how you use that word, Worandana is somewhat tired of it right now, something to do with it's over use by one of our group."

"Which one?"

"Kirukana, he's very set in his ways for one so young."

"That seems to be the order of the day in Zandaarkoon, I've only been here for half a year, and I was so glad to get out of the capital, failure to conform to the latest ideals can soon become fatal."

"What if you are recalled?"

"My skills are best used here, so it's unlikely, but if it happens, I'm running. I'm not important enough to chase with any seriousness."

"Do not tell that to Kirukana, there will be a fire laid in no time at all."

"I'll not, where are you going when you leave here?"

"I'm not entirely sure, we need to catch up with the thieves, but if we keep chasing them I feel that we'll never actually catch up, we'll always be behind. A guardsman from the city just north of here suggested we try and go to where they are going to be, that way we might actually get ahead of them, but I don't want to risk losing them. Have you any ideas?"

"Nothing that is in any way certain. River or road, really your only choices, if they are going to Zandaarkoon, have you given any thought to the idea that they might be going somewhere else?"

"None at all, where could they be going?"

"Well they have a god killing sword, perhaps they will look for a god to wield it?"

"And where would they find that?"

"I have no idea, perhaps there are still gods in the icy northlands, or the eastern deserts, there are tales of dragons in the extreme east, if you can cross the deserts."

"I don't want to even consider that sort of thing, we could be chasing them forever."

"What of Gyara? She's rumoured to be active still?"

"Oh she's that, she killed one of our number soon after we started chasing that damned sword."

"You faced her in battle?"

"Not as such, we had a power circle charging for defence, she tore it apart and Helvana took the brunt of the blast, simply a demonstration of her power."

"So she's not interested enough to help either side."

"She's waiting for something to happen, but she's not sure which side will make it happen."

"I suggest you head south at speed, there's a place where the road and the river run side by side for some distance, if you get there first then you'll know how they are travelling."

"We believe they are currently in the elven forests."

"If they can't find one of the old elven gods to wield the sword, then they'll have to head south. You could be waiting for them, it's a few hard days riding, first east then south to Angorak, the river passes it on the west and the road on the east, only miles apart. All you have to do is be there first."

"If we station ourselves in Angorak, they'll either pass us quickly on the west, or slowly on the east, either way we can be ready for them."

"It's probably the best chance you'll get."

"Which other way could they go?"

"The direct routes are the river and the south road, they could go further east and then approach Zandaarkoon along the coast, no shortage of traffic on those roads, and not so heavily policed."

"But would they know about these options?"

"I've no idea." he turned away and yelled. "Crathen." The young man responded instantly to the summons. Walking across the courtyard, "Yes?"

"Does Namdarin know of more than one route to Zandaarkoon?"

"Not as far as I know, he knows it's south along the river, apparently he went that way once in a dream, so that's most likely the way he will go."

"Right." said Kevana, "We'll head for Angorak, and stop in one of the outlying villages on the north side, and wait for them to come to us."

"Sounds like a plan to me." said Miclorana.

"Crathen," said Kevana, "round up Alverana, and see to the horses, I want them in top condition when we leave here. Miclorana, I know you don't have anything like enough horses for your entire complement, but I am going to need some for the three men who have decided to come with us."

"I'm sure that will be no problem, I'll go and sort three relatively good horses for you, you can't have the best ones, Bruciana wouldn't stand for that."

"So long as they can ride, that will be good enough for us." Kevana turned to Crathen. "You have been given a task, why are you still here?"

"Sorry." muttered the younger man, turning away.

Kevana felt a little strange, for the first time in a long time, he had nothing to do, he stood in the middle of the compound and turned slowly around, watching the people all around him busy about whatever business they had, until the morning he had nothing to do, tasks had been assigned, food preparation was underway, after a few moments thought, he decided to do something that was unusual, he walked slowly in to the chapel, sat down on one of the long front benches, after several moments starring at his shoes, he slowly raised his eyes to the symbol above the altar. Focusing on the fire, and the lightning, he felt the whole room lurch suddenly as the symbol started to turn, even though he knew this was entirely within his own mind, his hands gripped the edge of the bench, the symbol of Zandaar spun faster and faster, until the centre turned slowly black, blacker than the deepest night, it spread slowly until it consumed the entire disc, and started on the wall and the altar, the black sucked on Kevana's mind, pulling harder and harder, Kevana discovered that his body couldn't move, with some effort he fought to close his eyes, slowly his eyelids fell, but the spinning blackness did not abate, it pulled him in even more strongly, Kevana felt that his mind was being pulled down a dark well, deeper and deeper he fell. With a mind wrenching twist he suddenly stopped, his fall had ended, but he still had no idea where he was, feeling tentatively about he noticed that the darkness was slightly less in one direction, moving without walking he approached the lighter section of this place he now inhabited, he couldn't bring himself to name it, neither room, nor hall, nor cave, nor plain, in the depths of his foreboding he knew that this place did not exist, to admit that would be to taint himself with the same description. The light became more general, more pervasive, a source-less grey illumination, that showed nothing more than more grey. Gradually the grey coalesced into a face, a head, a body, a man?

"Kevana." whispered a voice, reeking with the stench of an open grave.

"I am he." said Kevana, desperate to appear more confident than he was.

"I have seen."

"What have you seen?"

"You will bring me my sword. Your way is hard, but almost done, I will make it harder, and cause you some pain, but rest assured, the auguries have been cast and you will bring the sword to my temple."

"Will my men survive?"

"That is of no importance, the sword will come to me."

"And what will you do with it?"

"I will send the rest of the old gods away, they will leave or die."

"What of the new gods, the younger ones?"

"They are of no matter, they will be absorbed, they will become part of the true faith, what small powers they have will be mine."

"What of Gyara?"

"The trickster will stay, but his powers will be greatly reduced, he has little power of his own, it comes entirely from his followers, as their numbers decrease, so does his power."

"That is good to hear, I was a little worried, some of the things she told us were frightening."

"He, she, it matters nothing which guise he uses, his power is seriously limited, no matter what he says."

"Can I take this news back to my people? They will be so glad to hear it."

"Of course, faithful warrior, return now." With a simple gesture Kevana's consciousness returned to his body, not in the gentle manner it had left, but in a moment, an instant of mind destroying pain, Kevana screamed once and fell to the ground, and into darkness.

CHAPTER FORTY SEVEN

By the time that evening approached Namdarin, and the others were dressed in the cleanest clothes they had, weapons shined and sharpened, even Wolf had been bathed and dried, not something that he enjoyed, though the chasing around certainly got his blood pumping, in the end he made his opinion very clear, after the best part of an hour, running round and still dry, he suddenly stopped and howled briefly, before strutting into the shallow water and lay down, allowing Jayanne and Kern to see to his bathing. Once the two had decided that Wolf was clean he was allowed to stand up again, with a toss of his head he strutted into the middle of their camp and in the manner of canines everywhere, he began to shake the water from his coat, the shake started with his nose and progressed along his body, all the way to the tip of his tail, showering water everywhere, a quick roll in the green grass and another shake and he is dry, with a huge wolfie grin on his face, looking at all his friends cowering from the shower he had just given them.

Janqor walked over to where Gervane and the group of truthsayers were gathered.

"Have you got anything?"

"Nothing worth reporting, there is a lot of tension in the trees above, but that is only to be expected, there is a coronation and a celebration to be enjoyed, if the is anything above that we cannot feel it as yet, you may not get much of a warning, you know that?"

"A heartbeat or two should be enough, just so long as you can tell us what and where?"

"We will do what we can." Gervane turned back to his small group, together they sat in a circle on the grass holding hands, heads bowed, deep in concentration, the time was near when their talents could save the lives of Fennion and Laura, though they could cost many more lives. Gradually the number of elves in the glade increased, it was clear that the time of the ceremony was approaching, Jangor became more and more anxious, he was surprised just how many elves there were, he couldn't believe that so many lived in this small city, though as he thought about it, he actually had no idea how big the place was.

"Jangor." called Gervane, softly. The old soldiers hand snapped to his sword hilt, as he turned towards the elf. "Will you relax, you're causing so much disturbance that we can barely feel the lower branches." Jangor nodded and turned away, blowing a slow breath, trying to calm, both his nerves and his heart.

"They are coming." Muttered Gervane, falling back into the focus of his group, whispering together they reached into the crowds, hoping to find nothing of interest. Jangor assembled his greeting committee, he took the centre position, holding the crystalline star in both hands, suddenly he hated this star, he couldn't just throw it on the ground, but to draw his sword he would have to, and by then it would be too late. Namdarin to his left, bow dangling loosely in his left hand, and Jayanne to his right, the axe of Algoron hanging from her right. Approaching came Fennion in the centre, Tomas facing Namdarin, and Laura facing Jayanne, Laura had a soft smile on her face, and Brank just over her left shoulder. Slowly the two groups came together, only ten feet separated them when Gervane jumped to his feet and screamed. "Arrows and knives. Arrows and knives." His raised arms indicated the direction of the archers, the magicians shield snapped into being, a shimmering white haze, two arrows shattered against it, as the shield and Gregor collapsed, the bow of Morgandy spoke it message of death, Granger's staff sent a column of raving blue fire up into the branches, it took the archer in the chest, this was no bolt, it was a raging fire that followed him as he fell burning all the way to the grass. Jayanne pushed between Laura and Fennion, a rising backhand stroke took the falling arm with the knife, Jayanne regarded the head taken by the follow through as simply a bonus. With a powerful backwards blow of his large right arm Brank struck the last knife wielder, then engulfed Laura in his arms and took them both to the ground, her small frame completely covered by his own, as the knife man recovered to press on with his attack there was a flash of grey and black, it struck the man high in the chest and knocked him to the ground, a flash of white teeth, and a snap of powerful jaws, a crunch and a fountain of blood that dwindled quickly. A deep resonant growl as the only sound in the glade, the only motion Wolf twitching his grip, just to be sure his prey didn't suddenly get up and try again. A new sound was heard, a sword slowly sliding from its scabbard, the sword of Xeron rose from it place upon Namdarin's back, and the point settled into the hollow of Tomas' throat. The tableau held for many heartbeats.

"Do you really think it was him?" asked Fennion.

"He's the most likely." said Jangor, "he's next in line, isn't he?"

"There would be an election and these things are never certain, of course it would have been easier with a survivor to question."

"Sorry about that, I was hoping that at least one would survive, but then we had no idea how many there would be, had there been ten on the ground here, things could have turned out very differently. I actually hoped that one would survive." Jangor pointed at the elf that Wolf still had not let go of. "I was expecting Brank to take that one, without time to draw a sword the elf would have been broken but not dead."

"Do I take his head?" asked Namdarin. "the sword isn't heavy, but it is more than a little thirsty."

"I don't think so." said Fennion, "his family will no longer be first in the council, they will be last, there is no real evidence against them, but the trust is broken, they have a long way to come back, Calabron, you and yours will now be second in the council, is this acceptable?"

"Yes, Lord Fennion. We will be honoured to take this place in the council, at your side."

"May I speak?" ask Tomas, trying hard no to move, lest the sword open his throat.

"Speak." said Fennion.

"The blood shed here today is not of my doing, I know nothing of this at all, I will step down as leader of my clan, and I will remove my sons from the line of succession, we shall be placed last in the rolls of honour for our clan."

"No. Father." came a cry from the crowd. A slight and seemingly very young elf pushed through the assembly. "They are stealing our power, giving it to this geriatric fool, he has no line, no name, no heritage, he is no-one." Tomas looked Namdarin in the eye, a single tear rolled slowly down his narrow face, Namdarin nodded and withdrew the sword. Tomas turned, nodded slowly to Fennion, he walked slowly towards his son. Brank climbed slowly to his feet, releasing Laura, and standing her upright. He placed his finger on her lips, he turned her to face the action, Wolf saw her and finally release the dead elf, he walked slowly to Laura, sat at her feet, stood up on his back legs and placed his paws on her shoulders, gently he took her jaw in his teeth then licked her face before dropping to the ground and sitting beside her. Laura was a little disturbed by her bloodstained face, but did nothing at all to clean it.

"Are you responsible for this treachery?" Demanded Tomas in a loud voice, so that many could hear.

"Yes, father. We can't give away our power to these fools."

"Where those your friends?"

"Yes, they were supposed to end this stupidity, and they failed, they were killed by those animals."

"They didn't fail, they paid the price you set for them. Our family has paid the price that you set for us, and now I must pay the price, do you understand?"

"No. The power should be ours, take it from these fools and animals, they aren't even elvish."

"The power isn't ours, it never was or will be, this is the power of the king. Can you understand?"

"No."

"I am sorry my son, but the price must be paid."

"I don't understand."

"I know, and I am sorry." Tomas was standing very close to his son, his left arm around his son's shoulders, so close that the son couldn't see what was happening, Tomas slowly pulled his belt knife, and thrust it forwards, into his son's belly, turned it upwards an straight into his heart. Tomas watched as his son soundlessly died in his arms, with a kiss to his forehead he let the body fall to the ground, two screams of anguish came from the crowd, two forms pushed through the crowd, to the edge, but no further. Tomas stared briefly into the weeping eyes of an elderly elvish woman, he turned the knife over in his hands and gripped it firmly with both hands, placed the point against his heart, his whole body tensed briefly, with a howl he threw the knife away. Slowly he turned and marched over to where Namdarin was standing calmly watching.

"My lord Namdarin, please do an old elf a final boon, I cannot take my own life, end it for me please, I cannot bare the shame or the pain."

Namdarin looked deep into his eyes for an instant, then the sword of Xeron leapt from its scabbard into his upraised right hand. Namdarin turned his shoulder into the stroke to make it as simple as possible, no risk of a second strike being needed.

"Stop." yelled Fennion. "I forbid this, there has been enough loss of life today, too much blood spilled, no more." Namdarin dropped the wrist, and the sword vanished back into its scabbard, the black jewel high above Namdarin's shoulder. "You two." he continued waving in the general direction of Tomas' family. "Take this old elf aside and show him that there is still love in this world." He waved them forwards. "Who is second for the line of Tomas?" he called, looking around for a response. "Who is second for Tomas?" he demanded.

"I am," said a quiet voice, very close. "I am Torral, eldest son, and now only son, of Tomas. I am second of our clan. What is your will my king?"

"Torral," whispered Fennion, "I am so sorry for your loss this day, there are no words that can ever convey the depth of the sorrow caused here." He turned and waved Jangor forward. "Jangor has something he was going to present to your father, but he is in no condition to receive it right now, so the honour falls to you." Jangor stepped forwards and presented the star crystal to Torral.

"I am sorry for the loss you have suffered today, it was never my intention to cause such harm to your people, please take this crystal, I believe it belongs to your family line." he held it out. Torral looked at it suspiciously.

"I was told you would be keeping these as well." said Torral, loudly so the assembled people could hear.

"We have come for the mindstone, and we hope to return it, if we live, if we die, I apologise for that in advance, the crystals will be returned to their rightful families as soon as they can be identified."

"How can they be identified?"

"Reach out and touch it."

"How will that help?"

"Look kid, it ain't exactly light you know? I'm an old man, and I could drop it. Didn't your mother ever teach you about gift horses?" Torral looked around even more confused.

"Torral." snapped Fennion, "touch the crystal." Torral reached out tentatively, as his hand neared the crystal it started to glow, when he touched it, it flared brighter than the sun on a summers day, but soon settled down to just brilliant white light, illuminating the entire glad.

"That will do for me." said Jangor, "take it, it is yours. The rest are over there, at our camp," a wave and Stergin removed the blanket that covered the rest of the stars. "Family heads please collect your stars, I have no idea what will happen if you touch a star that is not yours, so exercise some caution, they do light up before you actually make contact, but be careful please." Jangor bowed towards the crowd, and then to Fennion.

"Smarty done." whispered Fennion to Jangor, "Smartly done." then much louder he went on.

"This is supposed to be a party, a celebration, but I believe there are a few housekeeping tasks that need seeing to first." he glanced quite pointedly at Torral.

"House Tomas." shouted Torral, "this is our mess, clean it now." he bowed to Fennion.

"I think he'll do well." said Fennion to Jangor.

"He shows promise, but he needs to work on his projection."

"What do you mean?"

"Now." said Jangor letting loose his parade ground voice that had people close by ducking, and the house Tomas running to remove the various corpses. Jangor turned to the elves trying to pick up the burned corpse that had fallen from the tree. "You men. Use a blanket." A hand signal had Stergin running with a blanket to help the struggling elves, every part they tried to pick up broke off, Granger had really done a thorough job of kIlling this one.

"See what I mean." said Jangor softly to Fennion. "Projection." He smiled. In very short order the glade was clear of all evidence of violence other than a group of three people huddled together crying and Laura's bloodstained face.

"Daughter." said Fennion, "Are you well?"

"Other than this lummox almost crushing me to death, I'm not hurt, well, only my pride, I could have taken that youth in my sleep."

"Possibly, but a lesson was learned by all today, threaten Laura and the wolf will find you."

"What does that mean old man?"

"Even when these people leave, and they must, and the wolf will go with them, you will still be protected by him." Fennion knelt down and pulled Wolf into his arms, and hugged him long and hard, Wolf's beard plastered blood over both of Fennion's shoulders. He looked up at his daughter. "None will threaten you, for fear that this beautiful animal may be hiding in the undergrowth. You are safe even when I am gone."

"Let that not be for many years." she whispered, more a hope than a belief.

Fennion turned to the gathered elves.

"Music." he called, "nothing miserable, something light and happy, servers, beer, wine, spritz, get it moving now." music started, and people came rushing around with trays of beverages. Fennion, turned to Jangor, "Projection?"

"Not bad for an old man." Laughed the soldier, snatching a bottle of wine and a flask of spritz from a passing tray, he pulled the stopper from the spritz with his teeth and spat it to the ground, took a quick swig and passed the flask to the king. While the king was taking a large draft from the flask, Jangor gave the stand down hand signal, his men all relaxed a little. Namdarin turned to Fennion, "You need to talk to your people, you need to get them on your side, especially the younger ones, or these rebellions will keep on happening." Fennion simple nodded and thought for a while, Jangor waved at Granger, and pointed at the prone figure of Gregor.

"He'll be all right, it took a lot to hold such a large shield on his own."

"You were supposed to do that together?"

"We reasoned that there would be two archers, and that Namdarin would be hard pressed to get them both after the shield failed, so we decided that he take the shield and I take the archer that Namdarin didn't go for first."

"If you're going to change my plans, you could at least let me know."

"There really wasn't time, the truthsayer called just as we made the decision."

"Well, go and see to Gregor, be certain he is going to live at least." Granger took the bottle of wine from Jangor and walked over to the collapsed figure in black. Jangor looked from one empty hand to the other, then Fennion placed a flask in his right. He smiled at Jangor, then turned to the crowd of his people.

"My friends." he called. "This has been a very strange day, so much has happened, some of it good, some not so. The old king, the undead king has been ended, and a new, well, not so new, king has taken his place." he paused briefly, hoping for some reaction from the people of the forest, a single voice raised in laughter. "If we are to survive in this world we have to be able to embrace change, the sun still comes up, but the seasons change, the sun still goes down, but the years change, the moon is never still, it changes all the time, but it is still here, we need to be like the moon, the only permanence in this world is change. The undead king and the council had so much inertia that change was almost stifled, sadly, I played a large part in that, I was wrong, I was stupid, I need to change, we need to advance, we need to progress, or the world will leave us alone to die. I wish I had a real plan, but I don't, well nothing engraved in stone, I believe that any plan that is too solidly fixed is doomed to fail, I plan to make my leadership as fluid as possible, if any of you have an idea how to improve our chances of survival in this ever changing world, then please come and talk to me, I will always listen, be wary though, the humans have a saying 'be careful what you wish for.' it refers to the fact that sometimes wishes have a tendency of turning out badly." Fennion paused, reached out with his left hand, Jangor immediately understood and slapped the flask of spritz into it, Fennion took a sip, then passed the flask back. "My people," he continued, "we need to emulate our human friends, not only do they embrace change, they deliberately affect it, they make it happen in their own favour, they force the world to conform to their needs, we need to follow in their footsteps. The first thing we need to do is to reverse the decline in numbers that we are currently experiencing. Does anyone disagree? Speak now, and speak loud, old man, a little deaf." He turned away, and towards Jangor, whispered, "How am I doing?"

"Looking good, they'll either go along with you or kill you." laughed Jangor.

"Thanks friend!" Fennion turned back to his people. "I'm hearing no negative voices, so I'll assume for now that you will all go along with my way of thinking. To that end, for now at least, I declare party time, let's try to forget the unpleasantness of today and have a little fun. I mean no disrespect to house Tomas, they have suffered some serious losses today, that cannot be trivialised, I wish there was some way I could reduce their pain, but only time can do that for them, there is something we can all do for them, and that is to move on from today's issues, we need to, not forget, but not hold the actions of a few malcontents against the whole family, they need to be able to rise above this, they need our help, and our love, now more than ever, we have to come together as a people, we need to challenge this world and make it our own, the old ways have worked so well for so many years, but the forest is changing and we need to change with it, or force the change along paths that suit us, that meet our needs, and help us to survive. My people can we do this together?" he paused, hoping for a reply, a few nods through the crowd was all he got. "Can we do this?" a little louder, more nods, a few muttered replies. "Can we do this?" he shouted, suddenly the entire body of elves responded, fists raised, and a resounding "Yes." shattered the air.

"We can start by having a bit of a party, our new friends, have given us a new king, returned some long lost family treasures, and given us the incentive to change, we only need to follow their lead, music, food, wine, let the celebration begin." he turned his back on the crowd, and looked at Jangor.

"Isn't there some sort of ceremony for the coronation of a king amongst your people?"

"It's been so long, and we really don't need all that pomposity right now, perhaps once you are gone we will get around to formalising the new king, but I see no need to rush it, they already accept me, that is good enough."

"Are you certain about that, it only takes one sharp knife in the dark?"

"No, the time for assassination is passed, your people foiled it, no one will try that again."

"Then find yourself some bodyguards, Torral has much to prove, drop the task on him."

"I'll think on that tomorrow, for now it's happy faces all round, can you do that?"

"I shall give the command, but the effect may not be as good as them actually being happy."

"Just tell them to relax, the time for battle is passed."

"I hope that you are right." Jangor attracted the eyes of Mander, who walked slowly over.

"Give the word, stand down, the king says the time for battle is passed." Mander nodded and walked over to each of the men, the news caused hands to move from sword hilts, wine and spritz to be drunk in earnest, and smiles on faces. Only Brank was still cautious, he was not going to move away from Laura, his nervousness was being sensed by Wolf, who also refused to stand down, he stood to the side of Laura, his great ruff standing proud, the occasional resonant growl deep in his throat. Laura jabbed Brank in the ribs with an elbow, and cuffed Wolf gently on the head.

"Will you two relax, nothing is going to harm me now, now get me some wine."

"Shouldn't the serving maids bring it to us?" muttered Brank.

"They would, but you two are frightening everyone, so go get us some wine, and relax."

Kern came over and looked down at Wolf, he dropped a cube of meat, Wolf took it in the air.

"You have done well today, my friend, now you can relax, come." The big man said slowly, never breaking eye contact with Wolf. Wolf looked up at Laura.

"I'll be fine, you go and rest." she stroked him and ruffled his ears. Wolf gave a puppy like yap and went to stand beside Kern, then followed the man as he went in search of some food, Brank returned with a large jug of wine, and two mugs, he offered one to Laura, she emptied the mug and gave it back to him for refilling, eyebrows raised but he filled it for her.

"Now what's going to happen?" he asked.

"It's a party, there will be drinking and eating, singing and dancing, and who can tell what the rest of the night will hold." She took him by the hand and walked slowly into the crowd of elves, looking for some of her friends to introduce him to.

Jangor was getting a little worried about Gregor, he was still lying on the ground, with Granger administering to him, so he walked over.

"How's he doing?"

"He's very tired." said Granger, "he drained his staff into that shield and much of himself, we are recharging now, he should be back on his feet in a few minutes, but it could be a day before he's back up to full strength."

"The shield is a great piece of magic, but not if it's going to take one of you out like this, I'd suggest you find some way to modify it, or stop using it completely."

"I agree." muttered Gregor, "it works but, oh, does it hurt."

"Good." said Jangor. "Well done anyway, and get some rest, we're going to be moving on in the morning. Granger, have you any idea how to switch the stones in the two swords, I've had a good look at them, and the pommels seem to be similar, but slightly different sizes, and I can find no way of removing either stone."

"I'll give it some thought, I can't believe that either Gyara or Xeron would destroy either sword or make one man wield both. I wish I had my books. There might be something in one of the older volumes."

"You'll just have to work from memory."

"There are yet times I wish I'd never left my cave."

"I'm fairly sure the Zandaars would have found some way to winkle you out of your valley and killed you."

"That is true," said Gregor. "it only took us a few hours to breach that scree, it would not have gone well for you, I'm sorry my friend, but you would have died." He drank a good draft of wine and climbed to his feet, "Let's get some food." Together they walked slowly over to the tables loaded with food of all sorts, soon they were tucking into everything in sight, they had no idea what most of it was, but they were desperately hungry, and thirsty, many of the elder elves approached to ask questions about the magic they had used, and the power they held.

Fennion and Jangor were sharing a bottle of wine when Gervane approached.

"My king." he said.

"News, Gervane?" Asked Jangor. Both elves looked at him, Jangor simply shrugged, the habit of command is one that is hard to break.

"My king, the heads of all the families, both major and minor, have made it very clear that they will follow the lead of house Tomas should any more stupidity like today's be even planned again, certain younger members have been taken into the north woods for some obedience training even as we speak, if you listen carefully you can hear the lessons being learned at the end of the lash."

"By the gods," whispered Jangor, "I hope you aren't creating a resentment that's going to bite you on the ass in some time yet to come."

"No." said Fennion, "once they have learned obedience, they will be despatched to the far northwoods, survival rates aren't high there, or the south ranges, where the barbarians always come from, mortality is always high amongst the primary defenders."

"Would the barbarians be my people?" Laughed Jangor.

"Of course."

"You take the lash to your own people and call us barbarians?"

"Of course, your ways are different, the way we see it, for every one that feels the lash a hundred learn how not to feel it."

"Brutal, but no doubt effective." Jangor shook his head and passed the flask of spritz to Fennion. Who passed it on to Gervane.

"Hey, this is empty." objected Gervane.

"Then see to it." laughed Fennion.

"Jangor my friend," laughed Gervane, "is there any way you can take our wonderful new king with you when you leave?" then he turned and went to get some more spritz, laughing aloud as he went.

"Somehow." said Jangor, "I think that things here will settle down quite nicely, your families seem to have everything under control."

"As you well know my friend," said Fennion, "Control is an illusion, when things want to get loose they will, and generally in ways that no-one ever expected. But I think we shall be free of conflict for a while, the longer the better, we can only hope that the families will come to accept the new order in time, the shorter the time the better."

"I agree, your trees are happier, Gyara no longer has a hold over them, I'd like to say the axe no longer lusts for their blood, but we know that is not the case, Jayanne keeps it in check, and that will have to do for now, once we leave the axe will cause less disturbance, things should be much more relaxed."

"Let's hope that is true, here comes my grand-daughter, she doesn't look happy." Jangor smiled as she stamped up to him.

"Will you tell this arse to relax?" Pointing with a jabbed thumb over her shoulder at Brank.

"What's the problem?" asked Jangor, smiling gently.

"He keeps threatening my friends, he never let's go of his sword hilt, he's drawn the damned thing twice already, just because someone reached into his pockets, his own pocket, not someone else's."

"Brank." Laughed Jangor. "I am sorry Laura, but he takes his duties very seriously, he sees you as under threat of assassination, you should probably consider yourself lucky to be still walking around." He paused, she frowned.

"He'd much rather hide you under a large stone and sit on the thing, to make sure no-one could get at you. He will relax, but it may take a while, I suggest you feed him some beer, or better still get your friends to feed him beer, he's much more relaxed when he's got a few beers inside him, but he's not the one you need to worry about."

"What do you mean?"

Jangor simply pointed across the central glade, to where Kern was leaning casually against a tree, a mug of beer in one hand, at his feet was Wolf, his large yellow eyes locked solidly on Laura, he came to a tense crouch, belly just clear of the ground, waiting a command. Laura looked into the adoring eyes, she slapped her thigh, Wolf launched, grass flew from his clawed feet, by the third spine spanning surge he was a full speed, only a couple of seconds later he was sliding to a stop on four stiff legs, grass tearing and scattering on the breeze. Wolf stood up on his hind legs, placed his front paws on Laura's shoulders, gripped her jaw briefly then licked her face enthusiastically. She pushed him off, and followed him to the ground, where she threw both arms round his neck and hugged him. She stood and pointed towards Kern, Wolf understood immediately, and trotted off to be beside his other friend, where he settled back down onto the grass. A sort glance at Kern, then his eyes locked straight onto Laura again.

"See." said Jangor, "He'll not slow down if someone is attacking you, he'll hit them at full speed, and if they are very lucky they may still have a head after he's gone past." Jangor turned to Brank.

"Relax, there are others on guard, and they are just as effective as you." Brank nodded. Laura turned to him, "Can we go and talk to a few of my friends, without you getting nuts?"

"Sorry." muttered Brank, "but I worry about you."

"I am perfectly safe, as Jangor and Wolf have just demonstrated, so leave them to worry about those things."

"I suppose." He reached out and took her tiny hand in his. She lead him slowly away, to where a group of her friends where eating and drinking, one of them passed Brank a jug of beer, he didn't bother with a mug or anything, he just drank straight from the jug, until it was empty, he exchanged a glance with Laura, and checked that Wolf was still watching, then wandered over to the brewers tables for a refill, this time he picked up a mug. He returned to Laura's group of friends, and offered refills to those drinking beer, the others could look to their own devices. Brank was having a hard time at this point, he had a jug of beer in one hand and a mug in the other, and no hand left to hold Laura with, he noticed that one of Laura's friends had a spare hand so he put the jug in it and smiled at the owner, somehow the elf in question felt no wish to question his sudden acquisition, nor the serving duties that went along with it. Brank stood alongside Laura, he wanted to put his arm around her waist, but that was too close to the ground, he would have to bend over too far. He settled for putting his hand on her shoulder, which was much more comfortable but somehow wasn't right. Laura turned to him, looked up into his eyes, and then jumped up into his arms, well, arm really, her legs gripped him around the waist, his hand snaked down under her bottom, to support some of her weight, her arm reached up around his neck, and she settled in place like a toddler on a mother's hip. Her huge smile said all that needed to be said, though Brank was uncomfortable with the situation, he had Laura in one hand and beer in the other, no way of drawing his sword quickly, this made him very nervous. He glanced around the glade to where Kern was leaning against the trunk of one of the outer trees, he seemed to be deep in conversation with an elven woman, at the big man's feet lay Wolf, yellow eyes and ears focused directly on Brank. Brank smiled at Wolf, who lowered his chin to the grass, but didn't break eye contact. Still on alert, still watchful, still ready.

"I like being up here." said Laura, whispering straight into Branks ear, which she then licked. Brank shivered and turned to her.

"Why?"

"I almost never get to look down on my friends, they're all so much taller than me, but from here they're really short, and I can feel every breath you take, and every beat of your heart, you turn me on so much, are we going to have some chance to get together later?"

"Only if you can guarantee that you won't get pregnant."

"The elders tell me that the herbs I have already taken are always effective, no woman with this much inside them has ever conceived."

"That will do for me, if you are sure?"

"I'm sure." she leaned in close and whispered, "drop me on the floor and do me right now."

"Can you imagine what the families would say?"

"Yes, and I really don't care."

"We really need to wait a while, the more we can get all together, the better, what do you think?"

"I agree, but I know how quick you can, oh my, I'm going to have to say it, reload."

"Exactly, the more of your people we can reach with the first mind meld, the more we can get with the 'reload', and beyond that the more we can get with the reload of my human friends."

"That's all well and good, but I want mine now."

"Relax my tiny elfin darling, you are going to get yours, and probably far more beyond."

"Now." she whispered.

"Later." he laughed, loudly.

"I hate you." she muttered, trying to get down.

"No' you don't." he said, her half-hearted struggles failed to convince him. So, he smiled broadly, then kissed her. She writhed, her pelvic bone pressed hard against his hip, the kiss deepened and the pressure increased, his tongue tangled with hers and she clenched her body against him, suddenly she became rigid and groaned into his mouth, her legs gripped him so tight he struggled to breathe, his mind was swamped by that all-encompassing joy, and he knew that she was broadcasting again, he fought to maintain his footing, the last thing he wanted to do was fall on her. She lost the grip in her legs, and Brank had to take her whole weight on one arm, as she leaned back he stretched the opposite leg out, lowering their collective centre of gravity, and increasing the stability of the whole. He finally had enough consciousness to look around, three of Laura's friends were on the ground twitching, as he scanned further afield, he caught the eyes of an elder elven woman, she caught his, her eyes rolled backwards, and her knees failed, and still Laura was shuddering against his hip. Slowly she came down from the orgiastic surge, she opened her eyes, and reached up to kiss him again. His head snapped backwards.

"Are you sure?" he asked glancing pointedly around. Laura saw her three friends on the ground, and the elder in the arms of her man, who had no idea why she had suddenly lost the ability to stand up.

"Yes." she mumbled. "kiss me, these people need to know how good this feels."

"But I wasn't involved in that one at all." he muttered, kissing her softly.

"I know," she answered, "Think how much better it is going to be when you are."

"That really is scary." She smiled and kissed him again.

Jangor grabbed Fennion's arm as he staggered. "Are you ok?" he asked, looking around for some threat.

"That would be a yes," said the king quietly, "and a no, and a maybe, and a whoa."

"Please make some sort of sense."

"Have you any idea what it feels like to be caught up in your own grand-daughters orgasmic pleasure?"

"That would be a no."

"Fine given that you have been so ensnared, and the question is, are you ok?"

"That would be a yes, and a no, and a maybe, and a whoa, I agree with you."

"See what I mean?"

"But Laura is there, with Brank, fully clothed."

"Exactly, have you any idea just how frightening that is? She has broadcast an orgasmic surge like that without his physical involvement, he was effectively only there."

"Is this a good or a bad thing?"

"Same answer set, yes, no, maybe, whoa." laughed Fennion.

"It looks like this is going to be an interesting evening."

"It could be so, let's go and meet some of the worthies, if you are up to that?"

"I'm fine with meeting new people, but I'm no diplomat, I'm a soldier."

"It's actually a soldier I need, just now."

"Why?"

"How the hell do I carry this damned sword?" he slapped his hand against the hilt at his hip, the sword bounced, and the tip dragged into the grass and didn't want to let go. Jangor laughed aloud. "It's not that funny."

"Oh, but it is. You've never had to carry a longsword before, you have realistically only two choices, change the way the scabbard attaches to your belt, give it a secondary strap, to lift the tip of the sword above the ground, this will of course give you a steel tail that follows behind you by about two feet, it can be awkward turning in doorways, and takes some getting used to. Second option, rig it to a baldrick as Namdarin uses, takes some practice to draw from there, but it gets in the way far less, it's still difficult to sit in a chair whilst wearing it, but it doesn't interfere on horseback."

"There is a third option." said Fennion.

"Go on, please."

"It hangs on the wall in the council chamber, I'm never going to be able to wield it as it should be, so why pretend?"

"Laura may be able to pick it up, but her legs are far too short to be able to use it. Really you need a tall strong man for a longsword."

"Someone like you perhaps?"

"I don't think I'm tall enough, I'd still be catching the tip on the ground, it takes a great deal of training to use a longsword with any finesse, it's not really designed as such. Namdarin or Brank, now they'd be good with a sword like that."

"We do have some tall warriors that should be able to manage it."

"No. It is more important as a symbol of your power, you can't just pass it around to the nearest soldier."

"But Namdarin or Brank would be acceptable?"

"Yes, they helped you win that sword, but I wish you luck trying to get Namdarin to give up his sword." Jangor laughed. "Let's go and talk to him, if we meet your worthies as a group they'll be even more impressed, or perhaps frightened. Come on." He turned and set off towards the black jewel of Namdarin's sword clearly visible above the heads of the crowd, Fennion followed him and stumbled over the sword at his hip. "Damn." he mumbled,

Jangor laughed softly. They caught up with Namdarin and Jayanne, they were moving slowly through the throng, arm in arm, looking for all the world like a relaxed couple on a stroll, Jangor held Fennion back for a moment.

"Notice anything?" He whispered.

"Two people arm in arm."

"Her right arm around his waist, his left around hers, two young people in love?"

"Aren't they?"

"Yes, but are they looking into each other's eyes? No, her bow hangs relaxed in her left hand, well, almost, relaxed the string would be down towards the ground, not tucked in against her elbow, half a heartbeat and that bow is nocked and aimed, another half, it's drawn and loosed, his sword is drawn and starting its first man splitting downstroke. Let's go meet them, slowly."

"Namdarin." said Jangor. The pair turned towards the king and the soldier. "Fennion would like us to meet some of his people, in a sort of professional capacity, is that all right with you?"

"That's good, the tension in this crowd is falling quite quickly, still getting the occasional hint of tension, but individuals only."

"Every society has its predators, they all get nervous when a bigger, meaner dog, starts peeing on their trees." Fennion laughed out loud.

"Let's go meet some of the meanest of those." Fennion said, leading Jangor by the arm, hoping that the other two would fall in behind, he put his right hand high in the air and called, "Wine." Servers came rushing over, Fennion and Jangor snatched a mug each from the tray, Namdarin snagged two, one for himself and one for Jayanne, she put her bow up, cross body, and sort of comfortable. She took her mug of wine and sipped, a small nod and another sip. Jangor nudged Fennion and whispered, "They're a bit slower now, two heartbeats and bodies start falling." Fennion smiled, and pushed through the crowd, he had seen a small knot of faces he knew far too well. All the council members, were gathered together, talking quietly.

"How are the greater families doing now?" Asked Fennion, loudly.

"We all have a few malcontents, they are being educated now, better they learn rather than die. House Tomas has suffered some losses today. At the hands of these barbarians." Fennion's hand snapped to his sword hilt, and tried to draw it, for some reason the sword failed to draw, he looked down then back up, to see Namdarin's blue sword already at the old man's throat. Two paces to the right Jayanne stood with an arrow to her lips ready to release.

"Namdarin," said Fennion, "my friend, please put up your sword and let me deal with this old fool, Jangor, help me with this damned thing."

"Safety strap, release it, then draw." Jangor reached across Fennion's body and released the strap, the sword could now be drawn fairly smoothly. Fennion rested the sword on the old man's shoulder, "Damn this thing's heavy, I'm going to need some practice." he muttered, then spoke much louder. "These are our friends, and they do not like to be called barbarians, even if that is exactly what they are, call them barbarians and they will act like barbarians, and more lessons will be learned. The question you need to ask yourself is 'will my second treat these barbarians better once he is promoted to first?' care to find out? But it will be too late for you to find out, you'll be dead."

"I apologise to you my king and to our new friends, they bring so much change, so quickly, it is difficult for an old man like me to keep up." He fell to his knees, Fennion carelessly let the sword turn so the edge was cutting into the man's skin.

"Friend Namdarin, do you accept this man's apology, or will you accept his head?"

"Apology accepted." said Namdarin.

"Wine." yelled Fennion. "This is getting to be a habit." He attempted to return his sword to its scabbard and struggled. "Jangor, please." he muttered. The old soldier showed him how to line the sword along his thumb and slide it into the scabbard, then snap the safety strap on so it wouldn't fall out.

Kern was enjoying himself, he was kissing an elfin woman, she was kissing him, they were fondling each other enthusiastically, his hand had slipped up inside her tunic, her nipple hard against his hand, when Wolf stood, and gave a warning yip. This was certainly an alarm sound.

"Timing Wolf." He whispered. "You sure?" He looked down, Wolf was on his feet, his mane fully extended, and a deep growl in his throat, a continuous rumbling. Kern kissed the woman again briefly, "I am sorry my dear, but something comes, and I believe I am needed." He kissed her again and stepped away from the tree they had been leaning against.

"Jangor." he yelled. "Wolf is worried, something comes."

"Were away?" Shouted Jangor.

Kern looked down at Wolf, "Where?" he whispered, Wolf stood facing north.

"North side." Yelled Kern, starting to run that way, Wolf at his heels, the gentle breeze was blowing into his face as he ran.

"To arms. North side." yelled Jangor, "Get your people to safety." he snapped at Fennion, then he started pushing his way through the crowd, towards the northern perimeter of the glade. Namdarin and Jayanne hot on his heels, Fennion could be heard shouting orders as they went to north. Jangor glanced back and could see a massive bottleneck of people trying to get up off the ground, into the trees, he came to a halt standing between the two trees at the most northern edge of the glade, Kern came up with Wolf, Mander, Andel, Stergin, followed in quick secession, Wolf was still bristling and growling deep in his throat.

"Shit." Snapped Namdarin, "I've left my bow in the tent." Jayanne tossed him her bow, and quiver, then released her hair.

"Get me some light." Yelled Jangor, looking into the dark was making him nervous. Bright torches started to spring up behind them, Granger and Gregor arrived, still not looking at their best, but ready to join the fray. Gervane and his group of guards came running up.

"Sorry Jangor," he said, "we were without arms, this was supposed to be a peaceful celebration." as thirty elvish bowmen took up positions behind the men.

"What are we facing?" Demanded Jangor. A quick glance at Namdarin was all that was needed. Namdarin's eyes unfocused for a moment.

"No horses." he reported. At this point Wolf settled back on his haunches, raised his head, and howled for all he was worth, the deeply resonant sound filled the glade, and the surrounding forest with a primeval challenge, that reached back a million years, and created echo's all around. Then it was answered, voices responded, many voices, all across the northern approaches.

"How many?" shouted Jangor. Looking straight at Namdarin. Namdarin's eyes unfocused again, he made the link with Wolf, and then on to the other wolves. In a flash he broke the connection.

"That may have been a mistake," he said, "they now know we have only one wolf, and that the rest are merely people, and they are many, for some reason that is not a single pack, there are at least three packs out there, and they want Wolf, there's maybe fifty of them all told."

"That's who you are." said Kern looking down at Wolf.

"Explain fast." demanded Jangor.

"Taken as a cub, trained to hunt wolf packs, they all know him, they all want him dead."

"If we give them the wolf, maybe they'll leave us alone." said one of Gervane's bowmen.

"That magnificent beast saved my grand-daughters life," shouted Fennion, "where were you? They can have you before Wolf."

"Crap." Snapped Jangor. "Namdarin, Jayanne take them at extreme range, start knocking them down as soon as you can. Fennion, you control the bowmen, I want co-ordinated volley fire, starting at fifty yards out, bowmen pick you targets, heads and hearts, fast as you can. Foot soldiers and magicians watch the flacks, these animals aren't stupid. Stand ready, they are coming."

Yellow eyes started to glare in the dark, bouncing through the underbrush, only to vanish again before anyone could launch a weapon at them, tense moments.

"Namdarin, Jayanne." called Jangor, "once the volley fire starts drop back behind the line and defend the archers. Mander, Stergin, left flank, Kern, Andel right flank, Kern try and keep our Wolf out of the mix. Fennion, don't you have any more troops than this?"

"They are coming, I can feel them." shouted the king. Jangor turned to see mounted elves riding towards them.

"Are you crazy?" Yelled Jangor. "Dismount! We are fighting wolves here, get those damned horses off the field, swords only, defend the archers. God's preserve us." Namdarin's borrowed bow started to sing its song, Jayanne's sling the same, the whack of stones on heads, the thunk of arrows through chests were the only sounds, gradually the yelps of injured wolves became more prominent as they came closer. A fierce glance from Jangor to Fennion, and the king spoke.

"Archers draw." Shouted the king.

"Namdarin, Jayanne fall back." Yelled Jangor.

"Shoot." yelled Fennion. "Draw." "Shoot." "Draw." Each command on consecutive heartbeats. This pace was emptying the archer's quivers, but nowhere near as fast as the wolves were dying. Jangor glanced to both flanks, the occasional flash of blue fire told him that any flanking wolves were being burned by the magicians, Kern was having a different problem, he had both arms round Wolf's neck and was struggling to restrain him.

"Cease fire." Called Jangor, "Cease fire." The archers lowered their bows. There was one wolf left, huge, grey, old, wise, running across the field. Jangor turned to Gervane, "Who's your best man?" Gervane pointed at one of the archers near the centre of the line.

"You." said Jangor, "I'd prefer it if our Wolf stays alive, if things go against him, kill that grey bastard." The elf nodded. Jangor looked over at Kern and shouted "Release." Kern let go and Wolf set off across the field like a black and grey streak, he came in low at the big grey, as the grey lunged forwards, Wolf tipped his head back and hit the grey at full speed with his breastbone, as the two rolled over and over, the grey was so stunned that he didn't even notice that Wolf ripped his throat out with one tremendous snap of his jaws. As the grey lay dying Wolf sat on his haunches and howled, howled for all he was worth.

Jayanne let the axe fall from her hand to dangle on its strap, and nudged Namdarin in the ribs, he looked at her, wondering what she wanted, hoping.

"Those were my arrows, and you shot them, now go get them back." She turned and started back to where the food was still spread out on the tables. Namdarin looked at Jangor, who laughed out loud. Namdarin slowly walked down range, to collect the arrows he had shot at the wolves, followed by a group of elves, equally distressed at the cost of arrows. Not all the wolves were dead, some needed a coup de grace, from a sharp knife, to put them out of their misery. Gervane was walking amongst the corpses, shaking his head.

"What's wrong?" asked Namdarin.

"These wolves only come south when the weather is really bad, it's not been that bad, so what sent them south."

"More to the point, what pulled three packs together to attack a city, or were they after something else? Ah, that's one of mine." He bent down to pull an arrow out of a wolf, the head of the arrow showed between the wolves ribs, Namdarin had given up trying to pull arrows by now, if the head was showing just push it on through, they'd take a little more cleaning, but it was easier to pull through and did less damage to the arrow.

"Namdarin." said Gervane quietly. "This wolf has no arrows in him."

"Check the head, you're looking for an unusual depression."

"Found it, just above the right eye, but what caused it?"

"Jayanne, and her sling." Gervane looked back over the field of the battle.

"But we're at least eighty paces from the battle line."

"It may have been one of her early shots, we both started shooting at about one hundred paces, but these guys were moving fast."

"How many did you hit?"

"I shot ten arrows, and I have found nine, I'm going to call one lost at this point, if I'd had my bow I'd have shot perhaps thirteen or fifteen arrows and lost none."

"Returning nine out of ten is a good score, perhaps the other one crawled away to die."

"I'm not going to spend any time looking for it. Do your people eat wolf, or use the skins?"

"Not really, though there is an awful lot of meat here, and some fine furs. I'll talk to Fennion about sending out a retrieval party in the morning, but for now we have a party to attend." Gervane's parade ground voice came next. "All right, everyone back to the city, let's see if they are ready to receive the conquering heroes. Keep your eyes open for strays."

Gervane and Namdarin walked back into the torch-lit glade, with the elven bowmen following, the torches seemed harsh as they were walking towards them, Namdarin wondered for a moment how they must have looked to the extra sensitive eyes of the attacking wolves, it can't have been easy for them, but why did they even try? He shook his head, knowing that the answer would always be hidden.

Jangor slowly walked up to where Brank was standing with one arm around Laura, and Fennion very close.

"Why weren't you on the front line?" Demanded Jangor.

"I figured it would be mostly bow work, and I didn't want these two getting stuck in the panic to get back up into the trees, anything could have happened in that mess." He nodded in the direction of the main pathway up from the ground, it was still a logjam of people, even though the word had been given that the danger was past. "Wolf did well, didn't he?"

"I think that is what he had been trained for in the past, maybe it was his scent that brought these wolves against us."

"So, he was trained by someone north of here to hunt wolf packs?"

"It's a possibility, they were northern wolves."

"I suppose we'll never know."

"Friend Fennion," said Jangor, "how does a warrior get a drink around here?"

"Drinks for the conquering heroes." Yelled Fennion, "Music, food, dancing and drinking, that is what we all need now. Let's show these barbarians how to party." The elves were more than a little nervous to start with but once the drink started flowing and the musicians started playing, then they became gradually happier, more and more carefree, Laura was never far from Brank, Kern and Wolf retired to the edge of the glade again, Kern resumed his conversation that had been disturbed by the arrival of the wolves, Namdarin and Jayanne were arm in arm as normal, not really dancing but swaying to the music occasionally, Mander, Andel, and Stergin, acquired female companions, or more accurately had them assigned by Laura from her group of friends. Granger and Gregor retreated together from the lighted area, a jug of wine and a flask with them. Jangor and Fennion worked the crowd together, generally with Gervane somewhere in close attendance. The party progressed at an unusual pace, it was almost as if the celebrants were worried about further disruptions, Jangor met and talked quite extensively to many of the family heads, both he and Fennion made a point of seeking out Tomas, to offer condolences for the losses his family had suffered that day.

"Tomas my old friend." Said Fennion. "Please try not to be too sad, I know that it is hard to lose a son, even harder the way you had to lose yours. I am so sorry that it had to happen this way."

"Tomas," said Jangor, "I am sorry that my people have caused you and yours so much distress today, you have proved yourself to be a great leader, I understand why you chose the action you did, you most likely averted a civil war, many more deaths could have been caused. There is only one possible problem, you may have created a martyr, you'll have to watch out for the youth following ideals of this young man, or more likely someone manipulating those ideals for their own ends, you're in for an interesting time."

"I thank you both for your words." said Tomas. "I feel that my actions today make my continuation as head of this house somewhat untenable. House Tomas will soon be house Torral, which is probably for the best, I have lost any enthusiasm for the politics of leadership, though Torral has an advantage, he has no sons." Tomas left the rest unsaid.

"Father." said Torral. "If you stand down as head of the house, and I am elected to take over, which is by no means certain, then I shall change my name and house Tomas shall carry on." he turned to Jangor. "I shall watch the young, and the old, our people shall not fall prey to the manipulations of those simply seeking power. So many don't understand that this sort of power is an empty purse. Spend it, go broke. Eat it, go hungry. Seek it, go mad. I only hope that I never have to take the sort of drastic action that father did today."

"My son." said Tomas, "this is as much my fault as anyone's, I should have been more observant, I just couldn't believe how far things could go, and how fast. You'll have to be much more vigilant than I am."

"House Tomas," said Fennion. "Is in good hands whichever of you is in charge, I have every confidence that you will be a major force in the coming years, shaping the future of our people." He bowed to both elves.

"My king." said Tomas. "Jangor, is that general, colonel, or captain?" Fennion laughed loudly

"Venerable Tomas," said Jangor. "Simply Jangor, those ranks mean nothing to me." His smile huge and happy.

"Fine. Jangor it is. I have been paying attention to what is going on tonight, I have noticed that two female members of the house Tomas appear to have allied themselves with your men, is this acceptable, or would you like me to remove them?"

"Tomas, dear Tomas." laughed Jangor. "This is not an alliance, it's a party, we will be leaving in the morning, though the way things are going, it's more likely to be after lunch, if these females decide that they want to come with us, they will be told in no uncertain terms, that they should stay here, life on the road with blank shields like us is no place for women of any race."

"That makes me feel a little better." said Tomas, "but what about the redhead who is with you?"

"Jayanne, oh my, Jayanne is special, very special, she carries the axe of Algoron, she loves Namdarin, she is savage in ways you will not believe, the very first time I saw her, she was naked and covered from head to toe in other men's blood, you call us barbarians, she can be far more barbaric than the rest of us. On that first day I saw the results of some of her battles, on that field there were men with their own severed penises in their mouths, I am in no way certain whether they were dead before this happened. They raped her, they had it coming, but Jayanne is most certainly special. Your ladies may be in for a fun night, but they are staying here. Is that all right with you?"

"Jangor, your words make me happier than you can know."

"Happiness," said Jangor, "is all we wish for the world, but as soldiers we seldom see it." Jangor bowed to Tomas, and turned away, leaving the elder to his own thoughts, and Torral with a strange look on his face.

"Father," said Torral. "That is, I believe a very good man, he is a soldier, and a killer, but none the less a good man at heart."

"That is his load, that he must carry through his life, but I agree, he carries it well. Let's drink some more, until the world goes away, then we don't have to deal with it until tomorrow."

"Is that wise?"

"Tonight, I don't believe wise is an option." They walked slowly arm in arm to the distiller's tables, spritz is definitely the best way to chase the world away, if only for a few hours.

CHAPTER FORTY EIGHT

Fennion and Jangor wandered through the crowd apparently aimlessly, but Fennion had a person in mind, he glimpsed her and turned Jangor towards her.

"Hail Galabrine." he laughed.

"Hail Eldest, sorry my king Fennion." She smiled hugely.

"Jangor," said Fennion, "meet the beauteous Galabrine, I know you've seen her in the chamber, but meet her personally for the first time." Jangor faced the lady in question and took both her hands in his, he bowed low and kissed both palms, he looked up into her eyes and spoke.

"Hail most beautiful lady of the elves of the dark forest." he rose slowly but didn't release her hands, staring into the almond shaped, soft grey coloured eyes.

"With my three hundred years I look like the caricature of a witch that your people use to frighten children into behaving themselves."

"I have heard that an artist can paint a picture of a person, and show her as she is today, a good artist can paint a picture of a person and show her as she was in the glory days of her youth, a great artist can paint a picture of a person and show her exactly as she is today, but make the viewer see as she was in the glory days of her youth. A single glance into those gorgeous grey eyes tells everything about the fire that burned there not so many years ago." He kissed her palms and released her hands.

"My lord Jangor, you are the most silver tongued of demons, so much so that even I may be tempted to try the sexual prowess that has been rumoured about your people in the last day."

"Beautiful Galabrine, I am no lord, simply a soldier, and sadly such prowess, if it ever existed in me, is many years in my past, however name one of my younger companions and I will have him present himself to you, he will meet and exceed any demands you may make until the cold light of dawn drags us from this place, onto the road to death."

"Jangor." said Galabrine, she smiled, then she howled with laughter, once she settled down she continued, "given a little time, I could surely come to love you, you are the most quintessential of rogues, you would even delegate the task of loving me to one of your young men, any of your young men, just so it wouldn't interfere with your drinking. You are both wonderful and wicked at the same time, I can see why people like you, love you, and follow you. For me such dalliances are far in the past, perhaps even as far as your sum of years."

"Compared to you, we are as the flowers of the fields, we flourish briefly, then we are cut down."

"Jangor." Galabrine stepped up close, and took his hands this time, a brief look of terror filled his eyes. "My love." Terror upon terror. "May I speak frankly?" Seeing no way to answer in anything other than the affirmative he nodded, dread filled his heart. "Jangor, my love, don't talk crap. In your short life, you have loved more, wanted more, hated more, needed more, and lived more than I will if I live another three hundred years. Your lives burn so bright and so hot, I could never hope to keep up with that. Fennion, take this demon away before I live out the rest of my life in the time before dawn." She threw her arms around Jangor and hugged him tightly. She kissed him briefly on the ear, and whispered, "You are a very bad man."

Jangor kissed Galabrine on the ear and whispered, "I believe that all you have to do is be near someone experiencing the orgasmic event." He pulled away and bowed, quickly before turning away.

Fennion simply followed Jangor as he walked away, once they were clear of Galabrine's gaggle of friends he asked. "I know you whispered something to her what was it?"

"A gentleman doesn't divulge his conversations with a lady."

"Gentleman? And that ain't no lady."

"I'm still not saying, let's just see how things progress later. Who's next in your next in our list of your people to meet?"

"I think Loganar, he's the eldest of the council other than me."

"Has he any history I need to know about?"

"Not really, his family is one of the oldest, but not the largest any more, their average age is high, their youngest generation is as small as mine."

"So, their family is on its way out?"

"Pretty much, their birth rate is so low that I think they are done, unless they do something remarkable."

"Lead on, let's go meet this Loganar, and see if he is as wise as his age suggests he should be." Jangor laughed. As they pushed their way through the crowds Jangor noticed something, not something unusual, at least not for human parties.

"My friend." he said, "Do your parties usually progress at this rate?" He indicated a couple dancing and kissing, fondling and groping. His hand up her tunic, on her breast, her's down his pants on his buttocks.

"No." said Fennion, "not normally, this sort of thing would be reserved for much later, and in private. Perhaps this is the influence of our people?" A quick look around showed Mander nearby, in almost the same situation, though his pants were down, and her hand was not on his buttocks.

"You need to watch out for that one." said Jangor, "He's a real fast worker, he'll see to that woman, and maybe three or four more before dawn, he'll not be worth shit tomorrow, but his smile will last a month."

"You are exaggerating surely?"

"I'm not entirely sure, looking around this place, he could quite easily turn into the fox in the hen house."

"I do not understand that reference."

"A fox gets into a hen house and it kills all the hens, it cannot possibly eat them all, but it kills them because it can."

"So, what are you saying?"

"He could quite easily fuck every female in your city or die trying." Jangor laughed loudly.

"This is a joke?"

"How many ways do I hope so? Where is this Loganar?"

"Most likely north east corner, his family mainly have their homes in that tree. He'll be holding court beneath it."

"North east it is, just get me away from Mander, I have no wish to be involved in his fun."

"Please don't take this wrongly, but I don't believe you are sensitive enough to pick up the orgasmic rush as our people are."

"Oh, by the gods, I hope you are so right."

"There's Loganar now. Let's go meet him."

As they approached Jangor noted that Loganar looked if anything older than Fennion, his limbs were thinner and more attenuated, the muscles showing as strings beneath the skin, his face was a tracery of lines and his brows were so long they hid his eyes.

"Loganar my friend." called Fennion as they wended their way through the phalanx of family members that were surrounding the leader. "Are you well?"

"As can be expected considering the upheaval all around us." Loganar's voice sounded somehow much more youthful than he looked, though he showed no sign of getting up from his seat, to greet his king. As if by magic two chairs appeared, one either side of Loganar. Fennion took one and Jangor the other.

"How do you feel about the world ahead?" asked Jangor.

"I feel the world has no longer any need of my family." Jangor smiled at Fennion.

"Pray tell, why is that?" asked Jangor.

"I have two great-grand children, two."

"Surely each generation should produce more and more children?"

"Not so for us."

"How many grandchildren pairs do you have, if I may be so bold?"

"I have five grand marriages, they are all here now, ten elves and between them two offspring. No matter what I say they won't see that the family is doomed."

"Then I ask a simple question, what the hell are they doing here?"

"What do you mean?" Demanded Loganar.

"I have been told that there is a link between fertility and the orgasmic mind meld broadcast by your females."

"I have heard that, but it is so rare, it almost never happens."

"Well." said Fennion, "Earlier tonight I got caught up in my own grand-daughters orgasmic broadcast, now that was disconcerting."

"I don't understand." said Loganar.

"Neither do I, she was fully clothed, and riding on his hip like a toddler, he's a large man, but the broadcast was unmistakeable and very frightening."

"Why were you frightened?" snapped Loganar.

"Because I've never felt that before." said Fennion, "and to realise this was my own grand-daughter's orgasm I was feeling, was very scary. If you don't believe me, get your ass out from under this tree, and go hang around where the humans are. Jangor how many?"

"Seven human males from my party, and they have no shortage of elven females, after last night's events between Brank and Laura, these females aren't hoping to get pregnant by human males, but are hoping to increase the chances of their friends getting pregnant. Loganar, this is going to sound really bad, but there is no good way to say this, you need to get your grand-pairs, out on this field, they need to be making love in a slow and easy way, waiting for that orgasmic surge from the females with the human males, and this just gets more and more difficult to say, do not despair when the human males, oh god, how do I say this?" Jangor looked at Fennion, who only shrugged. "Fine, this is how it is, believe it or not, I care not. When a human guy fires his first shot, that is not the end, reload time for really young guys is instant, for older guys can be minutes, but not hours, and definitely not days. My guys will be rolling again in moments, and your girls orgasmic surges will not be far behind. Fennion here's a weird thought, in the future, set up two or three males for each none fertile female, then use their orgasmic mind melds to get the fertile ones pregnant."

"That sounds like a good plan, only one problem, please define none fertile." said Fennion.

"Human females have a lunar cycle, sort of matched to the major moon. They are fertile for certain days of that cycle."

"As far as we can tell," said Fennion, "fertility is at the whim of the gods, no lunar cycles, no wishes, nothing other than the will of the gods."

"Oh, here's a thought." said Jangor, he looked straight at Fennion. "In your memory someone changed the way parties are celebrated amongst your people? Has someone suggested that some things should be private not public? That public displays of affection are somehow outré, and should be hidden from the public eye?"

"Actually, now that you mention it, yes, many years ago, one of the major family's religious leaders decided that these things should be kept private, it took a few years, but his perpetual whining got everyone to toe the line, and then he died."

"He sentenced your race to death." said Jangor, "get things sorted out and you'll be fine. But tonight, be ready to ride the wave, it's going to be crazy." Loganar closed his eyes.

"Fennion," said Jangor, "has he gone to sleep?"

"No, I believe he is thinking about your proposal. Give him a little time, and his decision will be made."

"How much time, my flask is getting a little low." Jangor took another drink, then turned the flask upside down, to indicate its actual state. One of Loganar's kin swapped flasks with Jangor, Jangor smiled. Loganar opened his eyes.

"Grand children, do as this barbarian suggests, go join the party and engage in the depravities of these ravagers."

"Grandfather, you cannot be serious, you want us to rut in the fields like animals and barbarians?"

"Yes, I do, and furthermore, children you will do the same, I want at least eight babies conceived this night, this will be test of this barbarian's theory. If it works, we shall be able to replenish our population in only a few hundred years."

"Father, I have to admit that I am not happy about this, but it shall be as you say, but who will care for you while we are away?"

"I shall sit here under my tree and observe the festivities. I am sure someone will pass by with a cup of wine for a lonely old man occasionally."

"As you will father." suddenly Loganar was alone with Fennion and Jangor.

"There has always be some pride amongst the family Loganar," said Fennion, "obedience is their watchword."

"I think you may has set the test a little high." said Jangor.

"Perhaps." replied Loganar, "but at least they're going to give it a try, if only they can get over the shyness that they have built up over the years. Fellow barbarians a toast, to the rebirth of the elves."

Fennion and Jangor raised their various drinks and smiled at the old elf, Gervane came towards them with Calabron in tow, along with his second and the seconds wife.

"My king." said Gervane, "Calabron would like a word."

"In a minute." snapped Calabron, "Loganar what have you done? It looks like your entire family has joined this party and they are all naked."

"Shyness?" Jangor smiled at Loganar, who laughed in return.

"Yes Calabron, and aren't they beautiful?"

"Perhaps, but what are they doing?"

"Hopefully having some fun, and getting me some grandchildren, and some great-grandchildren, and something else you may not want to know, had my wife been still alive, we'd be over there with them."

"It's revolting and disgusting behaviour, you must put an end to it."

"You are too young to remember that these are exactly the sort of parties we used to have when we were a flourishing race, you may have noticed, we no longer flourish."

"You cannot be taken in by these barbarians, they wish to corrupt our entire way of life."

"You, Calabron are wrong, they are actually returning our lifestyle to the way it was a hundred and more years ago."

"I'd say it's more like two hundred." said Fennion.

"The family Calabron will have nothing to do with this sort of debauchery."

"Let me guess," interrupted Jangor, "the religious leader that decided sex was dirty and should be hidden from view was of the family Calabron?"

"Yes and no. The family was called Kalan, at that time."

"And it was Kalan himself that made these decrees?" asked Jangor.

"Yes." smiled Fennion, looking straight into Calabron's eyes.

"Now for the hard question, how many children did Kalan bring to the great elvish nation in this forest."

"None." laughed Loganar. "There were rumours."

"Those were completely unfounded and never proved in any way." Snapped Calabron.

"So" said Jangor, "to summarise, Kalan found a small group of likeminded, most likely males, to share their sexual encounters behind closed doors and convinced the rest of you to follow suit. No wonder this guy was a leader, sounds like a really charismatic elf."

"This is entirely scurrilous speculation, many years after the events, none of this can be proved."

"I don't require proof." said Jangor. Slowly he stood, he turned from Calabron, looked straight passed the second, and stepped up to the seconds wife, he took both her hands in his, and stared into her eyes.

"My name is Jangor, you are?" his voice soft and gentle.

"I am Garwene."

"Beautiful name for a lovely lady, Garwene, do you have any children my dear?"

"None, though we hope and pray, and we keep trying."

"I protest this interrogation of my subjects." shouted Calabron.

"Silence." Snapped Fennion, nodding to Jangor to continue.

"You keep trying," Jangor's soft voice went on, "I'm assuming your lovemaking brings you some pleasure."

"Yes." Garwene whispered, snatching a rapid glance at her husband, before being trapped in Jangor's eyes again. The husband moved towards Jangor, Gervane's hand on his arm restrained him.

"You want to feel the orgasmic rush that Laura and her friends did last night?"

"Yes." she whispered.

"Ridiculous, there's no such thing." snapped Calabron.

"One more word and I'll have your head." said Fennion, so quietly that it was almost inaudible.

"Do you think this mind linking may increase the likely hood of pregnancy?"

"After fifty years of trying, I'll try anything."

"You don't look more than twenty-five years old to me, if you go and find Laura, and hold her hand I am sure that you will feel that mind meld, sometime tonight Brank is going to take her there again." Jangor glanced over Garwene's shoulder. He released her hands, took gentle hold of her shoulders and turned her around, he put his mouth next to her right ear. "Better yet, see the man on the ground, that's Mander, I think his companion is likely to be the first tonight."

"He's doing something unspeakable." snapped Calabron.

"Shh." Said Fennion.

"If you think that's unspeakable, then you really do have a lot to learn." said Jangor. "Garwene, run to her she's going to need someone very soon, hold her hand and look into her eyes." With a gentle push he sent her on her way. Jangor turned to the others, "Mander doesn't say much, but I'm told he has a skilled tongue." Gervane again restrained the husband. Jangor waited until Garwene was knelt beside the woman, holding her hand, the woman's eyes opened to stare into her new companions. "Mander." he snapped, a face looked up from the task it had been enjoying.

"Yes boss." said Mander, looking more than a little nervous. Jangor held his eyes for a few seconds before speaking.

"Send her." The look of surprise on Mander's face lasted almost a whole second, before the face dropped back between the white thighs, and the tongue swirled around the prominent parts of the woman's genitals, he sucked hard on her clitoris, tonguing the end as he did, her thighs twitched, her body trembled, her hips jumped upwards against him, the thighs suddenly clamped hard around his head, and she grunted loudly, her free hand reached up and grabbed Garwene's head, and pulled it down, their lips met and the kiss went on and on, gradually the trembling stopped, Mander emerged from the head lock, Garwene released the kiss and the hand, she staggered to her feet, and wobbled over to her husband, she threw her arms around his neck, and let him carry most of her weight.

"Well?" he asked.

"Her kiss felt wonderful, her, her, her mind just exploded into mine, I felt her tongue in my mouth and his in me." Her hands went to her lower body. "It felt absolutely the best ever, and I want more." She kissed him, then pulled him away towards the ongoing party.

"Well Calabron." said Fennion, "looks like your second is off to the party, perhaps you should go find your wife, and join the rest."

Mander looked up into Jangor's eyes, Jangor gave him a small nod. Mander smiled and switched around, he looked down into the elves eyes, and paused, waiting for permission to continue, from Jangor's vantage point it was obvious that such permission took very little time coming. Mander's hips plunged downwards and the woman's groan could be heard over the noise of the party.

"My king." said Calabron, "I'll have no part in this disgusting display, and I will not allow any of my family to participate."

"Your second already has a jug of wine in one hand and his wife in the other. They are going to be enthusiastic participants, and I am certain that many will follow their example, I do have one worry."

"Only one?" asked Calabron.

"One major, if half our women get pregnant all at once, who's going to look after me?" Fennion laughed loudly, and Jangor joined in. Loganar remained in his chair, watching the party unfold, while Calabron stamped off to round up as many of his friends as he could.

"Loganar." said Jangor, "I'll go fetch a jug of wine for you before we wander off, will you be alright here on your own?"

"I am sure I'll be fine, I do have a little concern though."

"Pray tell."

"That woman over there, who looks like she's well on her way to another orgasmic experience, she's not a broadcaster, she transmitted by touch to Garwene, I'm suddenly worried about a group of strong broadcasters somewhere in the middle of that morass of sexual energy, what if one broadcaster, say Laura, who is quite a strong one apparently, what if she triggers another, and another, and another, there could be a sort of cascade that could possibly set the entire field off in one gigantic surge."

"That may be possible." said Fennion, "Calabron's going to struggle to hide from that."

"But it could disable the whole city." said Jangor.

"We aren't under any sort of attack at the moment, and by the morning not many of those currently having fun are going to be able to walk as it is." said Fennion. "I reckon we are going to be lucky if a third of our population is functional come sun up."

"Fennion." said Jangor, "Let's go get a jug for Loganar, and continue our tour of the party." Together they went to a now abandoned vintners table, grabbed a jug and took it back to Loganar, the elderly elf accepted their gift with a huge smile on his face, and waved them on their way. They walked slowly around the perimeter, until they came to the tree where Kern was deep in conversation with a middle aged elvish woman, well, plenty of tongue action, but not many words being spoken. Jangor looked down at Wolf. "Are you the only one on guard tonight?" Wolf lifted his head briefly then rested it back down on the grass. Kern broke the kiss and turned to Jangor.

"Everything all right my friend?" he asked.

"Seems to be going well, you're not going to just fade away tonight, are you?"

"You know how I feel about crowds, but if I do fade, I'll not be alone."

"You'll take Wolf with you?"

"Yes, him too." Kern went back to kissing. Fennion and Jangor continued their tour, they got to the southern end of the glade and one of the huge fires that was burning there, this was one of the major sources of light for the whole party, on the southern side of the fire were two men sitting on the grass. From the party they were completely invisible against the glare of the flames. Jangor sat beside them.

"You two should go and enjoy the party, you may even have some fun."

"Our energy levels are very low," said Granger, "we are recharging."

"Gregor, are you feeling better?" Asked Jangor.

"I'm fine, thank you, but very low on energy as Granger says."

"You're a young man, you should go and enjoy the party, you never know you might get lucky, and find some frisky wench."

"If I did, I'd only embarrass myself, I have almost no experience of these things."

"Always time to learn." said Fennion.

"Granger," said Jangor, "you can't have had much contact with women in that cave of yours, get out there and give it a try?"

"I'm far too old, for that sort of party, I'd frighten off all the young people, they'd run away screaming."

"Well," said Jangor, "keep some sort of watch then, I don't believe there's any danger coming, but we never can tell. We just talked to Wolf and he seemed quite relaxed. There's food wine and beer on the north side, have a walk and keep an eye open." Jangor climbed to his feet, and the tour continued. They came upon the group of tents, Namdarin and Jayanne were sitting together near the fire, holding hands, they had observed the two approaching.

"Namdarin." said Jangor, "quick favour, check the horses, do we have any strangers in range?"

"It's night, horses should be asleep."

"Please try."

Namdarin's eyes got the unfocused look that they do when he's communicating with the animals.

"All the horses are here, ours and the elves, there are no others in range, but they could be asleep."

"That's good, Granger and Gregor are hiding behind the big fire, Kern is across the other side with Wolf, the rest are in the thick of the party, keep an eye out will you?"

"We will watch as we can." said Namdarin, though the smile on his face told a different story, Jangor knew as he walked away that those two wouldn't be seeing much beyond each other in a very short time.

"Does he really communicate with horses?" asked Fennion.

"All the evidence tells us this is true. He calls them back when they've run off, he knows when our enemies are approaching, he even communicates with Wolf, that's how he convinced Wolf to join us, well him and Kern's knowledge of animals. It's a useful skill."

"You are definitely unusual people."

"I suppose." said Jangor, as he paused on his slow walk back towards the tables, still laden with food and drink, looking around at the party going on around, many of the people now naked, many dancing, some both, some making love on the ground, and not just the younger ones, some of the older elves were joining in with the youth.

"This party is progressing far faster than normal." he said to Fennion.

"So, your parties don't go off like this?"

"No, even the wildest of parties, don't go this fast, I believe this may be something to do what happened last night, word Laura's experience spread, and people seem to want the experience for themselves, so things are heading that way at some speed."

Jangor looked around at the number of naked people, some dancing, some engaging in sexual activities. "My friend," he went on, "I have noticed a small anatomical difference between our two peoples."

"Keep it to yourself for a little while, I think someone is about to complain." Fennion nodded his head in the direction of an elf, she was slowly forcing her way through the crowd towards them, a bottle of wine in one hand and a large stone container in the other, the bottle was obviously open, the stone was closed with a large wooden stopper. Jangor looked at the woman approaching, he was unsure of her age, though she didn't look young, he couldn't actually decide how old she was, her face was slightly lined, and her mouth had a serious turn to it. She came to a stop in front of the two, she nodded briefly at the king and passed him the bottle of wine. With the now free hand she pulled the stopper from the stone jug, and passed it to Jangor, he sniffed delicately at the mouth of the jug, his eyes went wide, he slowly tipped up the jug, and took a tentative sip, as tentative as a man can get with a half-gallon stone jug. He looked at her for a moment before speaking.

"How does Wandras get to be here? It's a long way from home."

"My long dead husband had a taste for it, so this is private stock. I have a favour to ask."

"Sweet mistress Mariacostte," said Fennion, "how can I help you?"

"Not you fool." she snapped. She turned to Jangor. He stared at her briefly and took another sip from the jug.

"How can I help you?" She looked him straight in the eye.

"I'm getting on in years, even for a long-lived race such as ours." She paused, glanced at Fennion, then looked back at Jangor. "Before I die I want some fat human cock." Fennion spat wine everywhere, coughing and laughing all at the same time. Jangor was stunned, Mariacostte never looked away from his eyes for a single moment, eventually Jangor spoke.

"Surely madam, you would prefer one of the younger men, not an old guy like me?"

"No, I want a man more commensurate with my own age, I'm well into middle life." Again, Fennion spat, coughed and laughed.

"Shut up fool." she snapped. "Not one of those young men, will you help me."

"I'm an old soldier, I drink, and I fight, loving is not my forte, surely you can see that, pick one of my younger men, I'll make sure he presents himself for your pleasure, and if he fails to perform to your expectations, I'll have his head."

"No. I want a mature man, not a boy."

"Fennion, please help me here."

"I am sorry Jangor." laughed the king, "if Mariacostte has made up her mind, then there is no power in the world that can change it, you may try some form of trade though."

"I don't understand."

"I am fairly sure that Mariacostte doesn't drink Wandras, that jug has been here for a good few years, perhaps you could trade services for Wandras?" He laughed loudly.

"You want me to whore myself for booze, and you're my pimp?"

"If that's what it takes, I've known Mariacostte many years, she can be determined, very determined." He looked at the lady in question thoughtfully for a moment. "If I remember your husband was actually opposed to the match for a while, well a few years, he even moved to a mining camp in the cold north, until she tracked him down and brought him home, or was that to heel?"

"Fennion, you aren't helping here." said Jangor.

"Actually, I don't plan to, your fate is sealed. I suggest you go gracefully to the gallows."

"Brother won't you save me from the gallows pole?"

"No, take this wonderful elven dowager and send her to the moon."

"Who you calling dowager fool?" Snapped Mariacostte

"I am sorry, but you are no maid." Fennion smiled.

"That's a fact." Mariacostte laughed, then the smile dropped, "Jangor will you prove to me the efficacy of human loving, or will you run like a frightened rabbit?"

"Jangor, your call, the integrity of your whole race is in the balance here?" asked the king.

"I don't believe that I have any choice here." said Jangor, "Where would madam like this travesty to happen, I feel the choices are all yours?"

"I think we need to be amongst all the young people, let's us show them how this is done. What say you?"

"I say welcome to the house of love." He stepped up and leaned down, he kissed her softly, then with more passion, he enfolded her in his arms and pulled her in tight against him, the kiss becoming more and more intense. His left hand didn't let go of the jug, he slowly backed off, broke the kiss, and looked at Fennion. Then he looked around, then picked out the person he was looking for. "Gervane" he shouted, a gesture with the head told the elf what he wanted. Gervane worked his way through the crowd of people that where paying no attention to him at all. Jangor spoke to him softly. "I'm busy, king is yours, watch him." Gervane nodded, knowing that the protection of the king was now his, Jangor returned to his kissing, Mariacostte's arms came up around his neck, and pulled him in even tighter, slowly she lifted her weight up and he stood up straighter, she lifted her legs and wrapped them around his hips, his right hand fell to her bottom and helped with the lift, the left never let go of the stone jug. He briefly opened his eyes to watch Fennion and Gervane head off to the tables, laughing to each other. Jangor slowly crossed his ankles and sank cross legged to the ground, her body pressed against his chest, she settled into his lap, again he leaned slightly away from her and whispered, "Are you sure you want to do this, a younger man would be so much better?" She looked at him sternly. "My prowess in battle," he went on, "has been complemented many times, but on this particular field I have no measure of my performance, and I have no wish to disappoint."

"Jangor." she responded, wriggling slowly backwards and forwards, "if what I feel below me is actually you, I cannot be disappointed, so stop whining and put that mouth of yours to better use." she pulled his head down and kissed him firmly, her tongue fencing with his inside his mouth, he was surprised by the strength in her thin arms, his right hand slid slowly up her back, and to her neck, he stroked her neck under her hair, as he forced his tongue into her mouth, swirling and twisting, he felt the wiry muscles in her neck tense and twitch, he touched the hanging lobe of her left ear and slowly pinched it, her whole body jumped, had he been able to, he'd have smiled, he stroked his hand up the outer ridge of her ear, all the way to the pointed top, she shivered in his lap, her breath was catching in her throat, she trembled again. Jangor's left hand finally abandoned the stone jug, and went to her waist, and slid up inside her tunic, her tiny waist, warm soft flesh, then upwards to her prominent ribcage, he could feel the ribs moving as air rushed in and out of her lungs, she leant away from the invading hand, giggling she pulled away.

"Tickles." she smiled, moving back in to kiss Jangor some more, he pressed his hand against her chest more firmly, feeling the bumps of her ribs as it passed upwards to the mound of her breast, he rolled the nipple between his thumb and finger, teasing it into a prominent bump, surrounded by smaller bumps, she moaned into his mouth as he squeezed the whole breast with his large rough hand, her hands released his neck, and reached down to the hem of her tunic, in a flash it vanished upwards and was thrown away, she kissed him again and started working on his shirt, the large heavy buttons were hard for her shaky fingers, so he helped with one hand, not letting go of the breast with the other, moulding and fondling as his shirt came undone, in an instant his right arm was out of it, his left hand released her for a moment to pull itself from the restraint of the shirt sleeve, both his hands found her breasts, as they kissed again, her hands fondled his chest, her fingers entranced by the course hairs that grew there, then her fingers found a bare place on his ribs, a white line curved round his chest, an old scar, she explored it by touch alone, her eyes were closed and the kiss ran on. Slowly she moved her hands down towards his belly, the powerful muscles of his abdomen covered by a layer of fat, softening the overall effect, they arrived together at his belt buckle, struggling and fumbling, she grunted in frustration, he took her hands and lifted them up around his neck again, she took some of her weight on those arms and he used the power of his heavy thighs to lift them both straight up into the air, her legs snapped around his waist again, his hands snapped the belt buckle, and caught the sword hilt as the pants fell down, he kicked off his boots, then his trousers, and finally his underclothes, now naked, but still with an elven woman hanging from his neck and a sword in his left hand, the sword fell and thrust itself into the ground, next to the stone jug. Naked now he sank to the ground again, she settled back into his lap, her eyes snapped open as his manhood pressed against her, she wriggled against him, just to be sure what she was feeling.

"Jangor." she whispered, looking into his eyes.

"Yes, Mariacostte."

"Will you taste me, like I saw earlier?"

"If you wish, will you return the favour?"

"Oh my," she paused and looked around, there was all sorts of sex was going on around them, she looked back at him, "yes, I've never done that before, that sort of thing has been frowned on around here for a good many years, I'll try."

"Fine. Stand up." he muttered. She stood slowly, not certain what was going to happen next. Jangor released the catch on her skirt and it fell to the ground, he slowly unbuttoned her trousers, as they came open it became clear there were no more garments under these, he pulled them down, and off one leg at a time, her shoes went with them, she was now naked in front of him, her feet either side on his thighs, he stared up at her body, amazed at just how little body hair there was, the merest dusting on the mound of her sex, he looked into her eyes for a moment, then leaned forwards and kissed her mound, exploring the scent and flavour of her, his tongue gradually invaded her slit, spreading the plump lips, and releasing even more of her scent and taste, she reached down and pulled his head in tighter, pressing him against her, she spread her legs to make his access easier, he lapped at her opening, slowly first, then quicker and deeper. His hands gripped her buttocks, pulling her tighter against him, his right hand slide between her thighs and his middle finger slowly invaded her womanly centre, all the way in, with one smooth motion, his tongue concentrated on the hard nodule at the top of her slit, swirling around it and then flicking across it, she groaned and trembled, his middle finger started running in and out slowly at first then faster, suddenly it was joined by his index finger, Mariacostte grunted, Jangor was surprised by just how tight and wet she was, her hips twitched, pushing against him, her breath was harsh in her throat, Jangor knew she was getting close, her musky juice was running down her thighs, faster than he could lap it up, her buttocks clenched and she suddenly screamed as her whole body went into spasm, Jangor thought for a moment that she was going to fall, then her knees locked, her hands pulled his head even harder into her crotch, her hips pitched forwards against his face, now his thoughts turned to suffocation, but after several heartbeats she started to relax, gently she pulled his head back, he withdrew his fingers, she settled slowly into his lap again, Mariacostte kissed him softly tasting herself on his lips, gradually her breathing came back under her control.

"Are you all right?" he asked when she broke the kiss.

"I'm fine, that was wonderful. I'm going to find the ass that convinced us that this act is disgusting, revolting, repulsive, degrading, and all those other adjectives, I'm going to find him and cut his dick off, then feed it to him before he dies."

"Too late." said a voice nearby, "the story spoken behind closed doors, is that one of his young boys grew up, and did just that, this was all hushed up at the time, he was after all an influential member of our community."

"Anyone tries that sort of influence again, cut his dick off." Snapped Mariacostte, she turned back to Jangor, "where were we?"

"You are going to return the favour." he smiled and kissed her, slowly exploring her mouth with his tongue. She leaned back.

"I've no idea how this works, you'll have to show me." she whispered.

"It's not complicated, be careful with the teeth, sensitive parts, lots of hand and tongue work, don't forget the balls and ass, just do what you think I'll like, go slow and easy, there is no rush." he smiled at her, she kissed him again briefly, then got off his lap, she looked down at his rampant manhood, amazed at the size of it, it was nothing like as long as those of elvish men, but it was considerably wider, she thought about getting it in her mouth, and shuddered, she knelt beside him, and touched it with her hands, even her long fingers couldn't encIrcle it, she stroked it slowly from top to bottom and back again, glanced at Jangor, who smiled and nodded, she slowly reached down and licked the end, the salty, musky slightly bitter tang, was different but not unpleasant. She managed to get the head in her mouth, swirling her tongue around it, sucking gently, her hand working the shaft, slowly sinking she stretched her jaw and engulfed more of the hot rigidity, until it reached the entrance of her throat, she could force it no further, she had less than half of it inside her, she worked her hand down the shaft and further down to fondle the heavy balls in their loose furry sack, she rolled them gently around and was amazed by the softness and weight, she hefted them and then slid her hand further down, along the ridge to his puckered opening, here she circled it and listened to him groan in pleasure. She pulled her hand back up to work the shaft, and withdrew her mouth, now her tongue was free to swirl around the head, and probe the opening in the top, the saltiness intensified, his musky scent filled her nostrils, as her hand worked faster and she sucked harder, she wanted something no elven male could give her, she wanted to taste the very essence of man, his hips started to twitch, pushing upwards into her mouth, his groans became louder, her saliva poured down his cock, adding to the lubrication, sensation, and the speed of her hand, he grunted loudly and pushed his hips high in the air, forcing his manhood right up to her throat, then his essence sprayed the back of her mouth, she swallowed, another spurt of thick salty, musky, slightly bitter spend filled her, she kept swallowing trying to keep pace with his emissions, she marvelled at the quantity he had for her, the gush became a dribble and she had time to savour the taste, the tang, and the texture, she swirled it around in her mouth, swallowed most, then turned around to kiss him and share the flavour of him, his tongue rushed into her mouth, as they kissed, she could still taste her own flavour on his lips. She fell onto his chest.

"You had better be telling me the truth about your recovery time, or I will be very upset." she muttered into the damp mat of hair on his chest.

"I said you should try a younger man, but I'll be back in due course. How did you enjoy that?"

"I've never felt anything like it, done anything like it, or tasted anything like it, I loved the saltiness of you and the muskiness of me on your lips, I will treasure this night for the rest of my life."

"I am sure there is more to come, looking around I don't think your orgasm triggered anything else."

"I must not be a broadcaster, not that many of us are, sharing by touch is much more common, so I have heard, the old tales, from the times before all this was suddenly locked behind closed doors."

"So, this sort of party used to be more common?"

"According to the old tales."

"Perhaps they should be again."

"I agree." Mariacostte looked at the two people next to them on the ground, they were equally naked, he was on top, rocking slowly backwards and forwards, the two women's eyes met, and moments later their hands.

"How are you feeling?" Asked Mariacostte.

"I feel wonderful, this is so much better than skulking behind closed doors." She looked back into the eyes of her man, then reached up with her spare hand to stroke his face. Jangor looked at them and then passed them.

"Perhaps," he said quietly, "you should try what Laura is doing." He nodded with his head to indicate the direction. All four looked across, separated from them by a few people were Brank and Laura, he was lying flat on his back and she was bouncing up and down on top of him.

"Oh my," said Mariacostte, "can you see the size of that thing? It's huge. How can she take all that?"

"Looks like she's certainly enjoying herself." said the woman, she glanced meaningfully at her man then rolled him off, onto his back and mounted him just as Laura was, she began slowly rocking backwards and forward, up and down, twisting her hips in a random manner. Jangor observed her technique for a short time then spoke.

"Mind if we join in a little?" Her eyes flew wide, shocked.

"If it gets too much just tell us to leave." She glanced at her man, lying on the ground, his eyebrows simply raised, she nodded tentatively. Jangor knelt beside her and slowly kissed her, softly at first then harder as she responded, he struggled to maintain contact when she was moving up and down, but the back to front and the swirling motion were easy. He slowly broke the kiss, and smiled at her, her breath was short, she smiled back.

"You taste different." she whispered. He nodded, then looked at Mariacostte. "Kiss him." he said, Mariacostte blinked, Jangor nodded, she leaned down to kiss the man, then Jangor repositioned her, on her hands and knees, she looked back over her shoulder at him to see him kissing the woman again, she kissed the man hard and deep, plunging her tongue into his mouth and swirling it round his, she was getting quite excited kissing this man she barely knew, she still didn't have a name for him, but his face was familiar, he was responding similarly, one hand found her breast and started to fondle it. Jangor positioned himself behind Mariacostte, and slowly thrust his rejuvenated member into her, she grunted at the intrusion and would have fallen forwards if not for his grip on her hips, he paused for a moment or two, so she could get sort of used to the invader, then he started moving slowly backwards and forwards. Jangor leaned to his right to kiss the woman who was riding her man more quickly, he picked up his pace to match hers, harder and harder he plunged into Mariacostte's tight body, he took the woman's left hand and placed it on Mariacostte's backside, and put his own right hand on the woman's, feeling the muscles moving under the skin of her small globes. She broke their kiss and stared at Jangor.

"I can feel you moving inside her, like you are inside me, this is very strange." She whispered.

"Good or bad?" Muttered Jangor.

"Oh, good, very good, very, very, good." Her breathing became more ragged as she rode her man harder than ever, Jangor could tell she was close, as was Mariacostte, her thighs were trembling, somewhere nearby there was a howl, all the elves suddenly froze, their bodies so tense that they vibrated like plucked guitar strings, Mariacostte was so tight that he felt like he was trapped in a velvet vice, unable to move, then the rush of joy hit him, his brain overloaded and he pumped all the semen he had in a few short seconds, the howl was repeated by many more elven voices and one canine. Mariacostte fell forwards releasing Jangor as she slumped down, he reached down, yes, she was still breathing, a hand on the chest of the woman next to him told him her heart was beating, the man below them on the ground the same. He spun slowly to his feet, unconsciously his left hand wiped the residue from his manhood and rubbed it on his left thigh, his right hand snatched his sword from its place in the soil, turning he saw that all the elves in the glade seemed to be in the same state, stunned, immobile. Namdarin and Jayanne came running towards him, both naked, but armed, sword and axe at the ready.

"What happened?" shouted Namdarin, Granger came into view, his staff turning slow circles over his head, Brank was climbing to his feet with an immobile Laura in his arms, he held her on his hip like a small child, casting around for an enemy to fight. Over by the buffet tables, Fennion levered himself to his feet, waving a broken bottle of wine in the air.

"This hasn't happened to me in years." he yelled.

"I'm sure you've broken more bottles than most of us have drunk." laughed Jangor loudly.

"I'm not talking about the wine." he pointed at the slowly spreading wet patch at his crotch. "Not since I was a teenager." Groans and moans started to come from the elves on the ground, they appeared to be waking up. Laura flung her arms around Brank's neck and kissed him on the ear, she couldn't reach his mouth.

"That was wild." she said loudly, a feeling that was commonly voiced amongst the newly awakened. "I need a drink." she nudged Brank towards the tables, though she showed no intention of getting down from her comfortable position. Jangor started to feel just a little foolish, with a sword in his hand. Mariacostte stood beside him, took his left hand in her right and offered him the stone jug, Jangor looked at the jug, then his sword, jug, sword, the sword fell once more to stand upright in the grass, he took the jug from her, and she pulled the plug for him, he tipped it up to his mouth and took a huge draft, coughing as the spirit burned down his gullet.

"What the hell happened here?" Demanded Namdarin.

"I believe this is the sort of thing that happens at an elvish orgy," said Jangor, "they have a sort of mental link that is intensified by orgasm, you have to ask them. Well Mariacostte?"

"Certainly, not just orgasm, any sort of intense sexual activity, through contact even, we can feel the things that the others are feeling, it's confusing sometimes, when I was kissing that man I could feel her riding him, like he was me, when you kissed her, I could feel that like you were kissing me, but it was him kissing me, and you were kissing her."

"I can see that as getting confusing, so what did the man feel?"

"Everything, we could all feel what was happening to each of us, he could feel her riding his cock, and he could feel you kissing her, as if you were kissing him, he could feel me kissing him because I was, and he could feel you moving inside me, as if you were inside him."

"I can see that being difficult to deal with."

"Some never can deal with the pleasure, perhaps that is one of the reasons this sort of practice was stopped."

"So, what caused the final overload?"

"Laura, simply Laura, she's a very powerfully broadcaster, her orgasm involves everyone around her, and everyone they are touching, and if any of them are broadcasters, they go off as well, it's a cascade event, tonight it took everyone in the party, even Fennion joined in the collective orgasm, he seemed really impressed."

"Not everyone, us humans, though we did experience orgasms, they were our own and personal, in no way collective, somehow, I feel more than a little jealous, we've missed out on something, something different."

"Think on this, every elven male here has had an orgasm, even Fennion." she laughed. "They are done, over, history, until tomorrow, human males are something else, or so they say."

"We'll have to see about that." Jangor laughed aloud, took another swig from the stone jug, he looked around the crowd. "Looks like the emergency is over, let the party continue. Namdarin and Jayanne, thanks for your rapid response, I think you can go back to your own entertainments, Granger, you can investigate this strange phenomenon, you can question people, in the morning." Granger laughed, leaned on his staff for a moment and then turned away. Jangor looked around for the rest of his people, Kern was already fading back into the trees, wearing only shirt, Mander in the thick of things, an elven woman on each arm, Andel, lounging in the grass, Stergin on the edge of the group, with an elf of his own, finally Jangor spotted Gregor, he was on the northern edge of the crowd, and only identifiable by his heavy staff, which he waved in the air before turning to kiss the woman beside him, Jangor had never seen him in anything other than black, in the pink was something else. Jangor threw back his head and laughed so hard that the trees above seemed to shy away, he roughly pulled Mariacostte to him with his left arm and kissed her so hard that her knees started to fail. Jangor suddenly felt like a teenager as his member started to fill again. All around he could see elves slowly leaving the party well the males at least. As the elf that he and Mariacostte had been playing with started to sidle away Jangor put a hand on his arm and whispered. "Please stay."

"Why? She is right, one shot wonders, it's just the way we are."

"Perhaps we can use your empathy to help overcome this little issue."

The elf frowned a question.

"Maybe, at least try." The elf nodded and hugged his wife around the waist, pulling her to him, and kissing her, he was prepared to leave the field and allow her fun to continue, if Jangor could find some way to include him, then he was ready to try it.

"Jangor." said Jangor pointing to himself.

"Argorane." said the elf, then he nodded towards his wife, "Celestine."

"Please to make your acquaintance." said Jangor laughing and kissing Celestine.

"I think we are already more than acquainted." she laughed.

"Argorane." whispered Mariacostte, she seemed unsure of herself.

"I'm missing something here." said Jangor.

"He's a very high-ranking member of house Tomas, I didn't recognise him without his usual colours."

"Yes." laughed Argorane, "I tend to wear a particular set of colours, and it seems people don't see the face, it's a useful tool."

"How so?" asked Jangor, passing the jug to Argorane.

"When I walk through the city in my green and gold, with my hair pulled tightly back as it is now, everyone knows me." he paused to drink, coughed slightly, stared at the jug as if it was a poisonous snake, "when I walk abroad in drab grey, with my hair forwards and roughly curled, no-one recognises me." he laughed and took another slug from the poisoned jug. He passed the jug to Celestine, he released the binding from his hair and shook it loose, it fell below his collarbones in softly curled ringlets.

"See?" He reached over to pat Celestine on the back as she was choking on her first taste of Wandras.

"Now I know you, in both your guises." said Mariacostte.

"I can easily invent a new one." He laughed, he leaned slowly down and kissed Mariacostte, she returned the kiss, enthusiastically, pressing her body against Argorane. Jangor reached over and kissed Celestine softly. Then smiled at her, sliding his hand slowly up her bare back, he felt her shiver as his fingers passed between her shoulder blades, he kissed her again.

"How do you plan to help us males with our problem?" asked Argorane, when Jangor looked back at him.

"First off, lose the serious, lovemaking should be fun never serious, second off, I have no idea at all, when you kissed the lovely Mariacostte here what did you feel?"

"Just me kissing her."

"Fine, now relax and kiss her again." Argorane frowned but did as he was told, Jangor stepped up behind Mariacostte and started fondling her backside, stroking the soft globes, and the sliding his hand underneath between her slim thighs, he slowly slid his middle finger up inside her womanly opening, she groaned into Argorane's mouth, not breaking the kiss.

"Argorane." whispered Jangor, "feel what she is feeling, focus on what her senses are telling her, feel my fingers inside her, feel the excitement growing, I can feel it, can you?" He felt the tension building between the two and he twitched his head at Celestine, she came towards him and they kissed. He leaned back and whispered in her ear, "This may be difficult for you, but here goes, stroke his ass with one hand and put the other where mine is, inside Mariacostte." She frowned at him. "This could be the way to give your menfolk a second wind, it's no use if I have to be here, you have to be able to do it, please, I can feel her getting closer." Celestine nodded, her right hand stroked Argorane's buttocks, and her left slid under Mariacostte's to replace Jangor's.

"Argorane," said Jangor, "focus on what the women are feeling, feel their excitement, feel the tension building, feel their hands, their lips, their fingers." Jangor was hoping to stimulate some sort of reaction from Argorane, in only a few moments he was not disappointed. Slowly Argorane started to rise again, his manhood started to fill out, heartbeat by heartbeat it plumped up, twitch by twitch it lifted. Jangor stroked Celestine's tight bottom, he pressed up behind her, he kissed her neck softly and whispered. "Bend over and suck him, see if you can keep him hard." He felt her tremble. "If you won't I'm sure that Mariacostte will." he continued, sensing her reluctance. Celestine pushed Jangor backwards with her arse as she bent over at the hips, in an instant she had engulfed her husband almost to the root. Jangor stepped back, and picked up his jug, had a drink. He was beginning to feel a little left out, but there was something he needed to do first. He looked around and found Brank he was deeply involved with Laura.

"Brank." he called, not too loud, but loud enough for Brank to look up. Jangor pointed to his own eyes then at Argorane. Branks eyes opened wide, he took Laura's head in both hands and turned her to see what was happening. Her eyes went wide then wider. Laura stood and slowly walked over to Jangor.

"Was he involved in the first orgasmic event?" she asked quietly.

"He was as blown away as everyone else, except for us humans of course."

"Are you sure?"

"I had to check his pulse to be sure he was still alive."

"This is unheard of." She smiled, and knelt beside Celestine, Laura kissed the older woman on the ear and whispered something that no one else could hear. Celestine backed off her husband's member and passed it to Laura, who inhaled it as far as she could, her head bobbing as she worked it. After a minute or two she withdrew and passed the cock back to Celestine. With a huge smile she stood and turned to Jangor. She reached up and pulled his head down, so she could kiss him most thoroughly, one hand gripped his manhood and stroked it slowly.

"You have done something unheard of, thanks for this, you have shown us the way, we can never thank you enough. If you survive your current quest come back here, the women of this city will ensure that you die with a smile on your lips, and a bulge in your pants." She walked back to Brank and talked briefly to the women along the way, most of them ran off, spreading the word, until a tidal wave of women overran the males at the refreshment tables, dragging them back to the centre of the field. In small groups they set about learning what it took to get their men erect again, Jangor watched this going on for a short time, then he decided to get in on some of the action, he looked at Celestine's slender backside and stroked it with one hand, then slid that hand under between her thighs, he slowly push a finger up inside her, she was so wet, with her own lubrications and Argorane's deposits, she groaned and pushed back against the invader, she moaned when a second finger joined in, her sound muffled by the blockage in the mouth. The vibration in her throat triggered a similar response from Argorane, and on to Mariacostte. Jangor removed his hand and Celestine backed up looking for it to return, only to be surprised by something a whole lot bigger, Jangor slid slowly into her and pushed her forwards, until she wasn't able to go any further forwards, at least not without choking. Jangor picked up the pace until his balls were slapping against her mound on every thrust, pushing her higher, her grunts and groans were doing amazing things to the other two. Jangor reached forwards to hold her right breast as it swung under the impacts of his hips against her backside, he rolled the nipple hard and felt her heart beat faster and stronger, Celestine's legs started to shake, Jangor kept pounding into her tightness, suddenly her whole body clenched, her vagina gripped Jangor so tightly that he couldn't move, and the other two went equally rigid, their breathing stalled and their shared experience set Jangor off, even though he was actually outside it. He grunted loudly, and filled Celestine, as Argorane blew straight down her throat, reflex alone prevented Celestine from drowning. Together they all fell to the grass, in an uncoordinated pile. Jangor panting like a dog in a drought, the others slowly came back to their senses, Jangor passed the jug to Argorane first, Mariacostte grabbed Celestine by the head and kissed her enthusiastically, her tongue invading Celestine like a spear, Jangor laughed when he realised what she was after, Mariacostte wanted a taste of Argorane, even if it was diluted and second hand. Once their frantic kiss was over Mariacostte took the jug and had a mouthful of Wandras, then passed it off to Celestine, who gave it back to Jangor without drinking any.

"Was that good?" asked Jangor. The three elves looked from one to another, unsure who should speak first. Finally, Argorane decided to speak, whilst all around them more and more groups were successfully achieving resurrection of elvish maleness.

"That was amazing." he said, smiling hugely. "I could feel everything that was going on, when Laura took me in her mouth was astounding, but when you entered Celestine, that was just too much, I barely managed to hold on until Celestine went over the edge."

"Mariacostte?" asked Jangor.

"It was wonderful, I have never felt so good, not ever. Are you sure you have to go in the morning?"

"I have to go, but how early it's going to be I have no idea, we still have things to do. Celestine?"

"I have never experienced anything like that, it was awesome, to get my husband able for the second time in so short a span was special, to share him with Laura, more so, then your little surprise, that just filled me up all the way to the brim."

"Not quite the brim, but that would be too much for today I think." Laughed Jangor. "I'm hungry, shall we go and see if there is any food left?" He stood and reached a hand down to Mariacostte. She held up a hand and allowed him to pull her up, as she came to her feet she snatched up the stone jug with her free hand. Hand in hand they picked their way through the scattered bodies, towards the food tables, the crowd there was thinning out as more women convinced their men to re-join the party. Jangor was happy to see more and more elvish men getting their second wind, 'Perhaps this could be the turn around these people need.' he thought.

"Look around." muttered Mariacostte. "If only a few get pregnant tonight, this could see the rebirth of our nation."

"I was thinking exactly the same. We can only hope."

"And it's all because of you and your people."

"More like Laura and Brank, they set all this in motion."

"If you hadn't come here, then none of this would have happened."

"Then perhaps you should be thanking Gyara, she sent us here."

"I'd rather not be beholden to the trickster, thank you very much."

"The whole sequence of events that has brought us here, it's just life, it's how it works."

"Let's hope that new life stirs in this glade tonight."

"I'm fairly confident that many things are stirring tonight." Jangor laughed aloud, Mariacostte joined him, as they arrived at the buffet tables Jangor noticed Loganar still sitting in his chair watching the festivities, a huge smile on his face. Jangor picked up a bottle of wine and went over to the elder, Mariacostte followed.

"You look like you are having fun, old man." Smiled Jangor.

"It's certainly been an interesting night." Loganar took the bottle and drank a good-sized draft.

"Did you get caught up in Laura's first broadcast?" Jangor took the bottle, drank then passed it to Mariacostte.

"Only a little, the effect was quite light this far out, but it was something I'd not felt in far too many years."

"Would you like your chair moved closer to the action?"

"No, somehow I think my presence in the thick of things might put some of the younger ones off, and it really is them we need involved, not ancients like me. How are you enjoying tonight Mariacostte?"

"Great Loganar, this man has been a true revelation, I have never experienced anything like this, and I hope it isn't over."

"You are looking fine my dear, I'm sure there is more fun to be had this night." His candid gaze suddenly reminded her that she was naked. She blushed and attempted to cover herself. Jangor took back one of her hands and pulled it towards himself, he looked down and smiled at her.

"I am sure there will be more fun, and not too long to wait." Laughed Jangor.

"I need something to eat first." She looked back at Loganar, "would you like something to eat?"

"Only you my dear, but I fear that will do neither of us much good." He smiled and looked over her shoulder at someone who was approaching, his smile vanished in an instant.

"Loganar." snapped Calabron. "You have to do something about this debauchery, it must be stopped."

"Calabron." said Loganar, softly. "No, my involvement is small but still enjoyable, I will do nothing to prevent these young people having a good time."

"It's degrading for our entire race. It must be stopped." Calabron looked round at the people who had been talking to Loganar. "Mariacostte, cover yourself, you are a disgrace, you will take no further part in tonight's disgusting behaviour." Mariacostte grabbed Jangor's arm and held him still.

"Lord Calabron." She said quietly. "I will do exactly as I wish, I suggest you go back to chasing little boys, no one can believe that you actually managed to have children, but then they don't look too much like you."

"How dare you speak to me like that?"

"It's not actually that difficult. You are such an awful person."

"You filthy whore." Shouted Calabron, again Mariacostte snatched Jangor's arm. "You have no place in the family Calabron."

"Lord Loganar, it seems I am suddenly orphaned, would you care to adopt an abandoned child?"

"Lovely Mariacostte, you will always have a place with clan Loganar." said the elder.

"Many thanks my lord." said Mariacostte, she looked back at Calabron, and pointedly released Jangor's arm. Calabron stared briefly at Jangor before turning away and strutting off with his head held high. Loganar laughed out loud, almost falling from his chair in paroxysms of joy.

"What, pray tell, is so funny?" asked Jangor, once Loganar had calmed a little.

"Surely you can see the irony of that confrontation."

"No."

"Oh Jangor." smiled Mariacostte, she reached up and kissed him firmly, "for an experienced soldier, you can be very naive. He was terrified by the size of your weapon."

"You may have noticed that I am unarmed." Loganar was laughing so much that he couldn't even attempt to answer.

"No, my love you are so well armed, with weaponry that he would normally want so much, but I think you frighten him."

"Now I think I see what you mean." said Jangor. "Loganar, how many of your people feel like Calabron?"

"No more than one in twenty, not a really significant quantity, but as the birth-rate has fallen, it has started to show as a problem."

"Many of your women feel the same about men?"

"Not many at all, there are a few that like both sexes, not many that have totally forsworn men."

"Well, if tonight's experiment proves to be successful, then open parties like this should become more frequent, hopefully your birth-rate will return, and the decline will stop."

"Let us hope that is so." Loganar agreed firmly.

"Shall we re-join the festivities?" asked Jangor looking down at Mariacostte.

"I think we've done enough to show the people the way, I feel like something a little more private."

"We can go to my tent, I think Kern is going to be away all night."

"That sounds good to me." her smile made Jangor laugh.

"I'll need my sword and that jug of Wandras, so we'll pick those up along the way." He turned back to Loganar. "Good night Lord Loganar, I hope this party meets all of your expectations." He bowed solemnly.

"Good night Jangor." nodded Loganar. Mariacostte took Jangor's hand and lead him slowly away.

ABOUT THE AUTHOR

My name is Michael Porter, some call me Roaddog.

Formal training for writing, I have exactly none, I did start reading early, generally before breakfast, I actually learned to read before I started school, many thanks to mother for all the hours she put in. Of course this wasn't popular with the school at that time, some fool had just introduced an new learning system, some sort of phonetic garbage. When asked "Why should children have to learn English twice?" They had no answer. I didn't bother with that phonetic junk, they had to get some old books out of storage for me to read. Yes a trouble maker from the start. I was only at that particular school for one year, but before I left I had read every book they had, well, all the ones that were spelled properly. This pattern continued through every school I attended, grammar school was no different, they had a huge library, which I read in less than three years. Much to the despair of my teachers reading didn't help me in my English lessons, spelling, punctuation, these things aren't important it's the story that counts. I'm sorry Miss Boll, Cider with Rosie is boring, I'm not reading it. David Eddings, now he's good. I'm making no friends amongst the English department here.

English exams were obviously interesting, mock 'O' level I scored a massive -30%. This was in the days before students got credit for just being there. The scoring system was simple, you start with 100 points, for every spelling, punctuation or grammatical error a point is deducted, it seems that in only four pages of writing I managed an impressive 130 errors. The real 'O' level was unclassified. No real surprise there. I managed to pass on the second attempt, but only by twisting the proposed essay title, and plagiarising large chunks of the sci-fi novel I was currently reading. Enough ancient history.

For those that don't know me I'm getting along in years, I'd be approaching retirement if the government didn't keep moving the goalposts. I've been writing this story for many years, but only got around to publishing it recently due to pressure from she who must be obeyed. I started this mammoth project after reading a particularly dreadful fantasy novel. I decided that even I could write something better than that. I noticed that most books of the genre were lacking in real violence and proper sex, so this series is definitely for a more adult audience. I'm hoping to have the complete set finished before the end of 2019, I have a day job that takes up a lot of my time, I also have an evening job as sound and lighting engineer for a local rock band, which eats a big chunk of my weekends, so time for writing is somewhat restricted. I'll try to get Doom finished on schedule, as there are a couple more projects in the pipe.

For me reading and writing is all about the story.

Enjoy.

Printed in Great Britain
by Amazon